IMMORTAL MASTERPIECES OF LITERATURE

SHORT STORIES

BY

GUY DE MAUPASSANT

WITH

10 FULL PAGE ILLUSTRATIONS

THE SPENCER PRESS

ILLUSTRATIONS COPYRIGHTED 1937
BY CONSOLIDATED BOOK PUBLISHERS, INC.

MANUFACTURED IN THE UNITED STATES OF AMERICA
BY THE CUNEO PRESS, INC.

THE SPENCER PRESS

The Spencer Press in presenting this new set of books to be known as the "Immortal Masterpieces of Literature" has selected volumes which have withstood the test of time, books which are even more popular, more highly regarded and more appreciated today than when they first appeared as the current sensations of a crowded publishing season.

The titles included were submitted to all the most critical literary tests by which excellence in writing may be judged. Each book is rich in certain of those enduring qualities such as truth, humbleness, grandeur, magnificence, imagination, beauty of expression, gaiety, good humor, pathos and laughter . . . the stuff of which everlasting life is carved.

Every book one reads deposits in the mind seeds of thought which grow and develop day by day until they finally help to mold the character of the reader. Through their magical power books become the mute masters of civilization.

The subject matter in this set, therefore, was our first consideration, the physical format and handsomeness of design our next concern. The books are printed from clear, newly set easy-to-read type upon fine quality opaque book papers. The illustrations appropriately adorn the text so as to enliven the reader's interest through visual portrayal of incident and character. The physical makeup of the book is such as to add to ease and comfort during the pleasant hours of reading.

The Spencer Press is dedicated to the purpose of creating books of exquisite good taste and beauty. The binding on this set was designed by that master craftsman, Mr. Leonard Mounteney, whose unimpeachable good taste and superb artistry has given us some of the world's most beautiful books.

It is with pride and great pleasure that we present this set of the "Immortal Masterpieces of Literature" confident in the knowledge that these books are worthy of the finest library. Since man owes it to himself to see that the right books are upon the bookshelves in his home, we can but hope that these volumes will find their way into your homes where they will prove a source of inspiration, pleasure and enjoyment throughout the years to come.

LEONARD S. DAVIDOW

Reading, Pa. 1937

CONTENTS

	Page
Happiness	1
A Coward	8
The Wolf	16
The Necklace	23
The Piece of String	33
La Mère Sauvage	41
Moonlight	48
The Confession	53
On the Journey	59
The Beggar	65
A Ghost	72
Little Soldier	79
The Wreck	87
One Evening	98
The Devil	111
The Drunkard	118
The Adopted Son	124
An Artifice	130

CONTENTS

	PAGE
My Uncle Sosthenes	135
Father Milon	142
Solitude	149
Yvette	154
Mademoiselle Fifi	219
Two Friends	230
A Duel	236
Miss Harriet	241
The Umbrella	259
Queen Hortense	267
At Sea	274
A Sale	279
The Return	285
The Prisoners	291
Mother and Son!	301
A Practical Joke	307

LIST OF ILLUSTRATIONS

	PAGE
"Six Francs! Six Francs!" He Shouted	Frontispiece
Then Said an Old Gentleman, "I Knew an Admirable Case of Love Which Was True"	3
The Body of the Wolf Became Lax	21
She No Longer Had the Necklace Around Her Neck!	27
He Took the Bit of Thin Cord from the Ground	35
"God Pardon Thee, My Child; Have Courage, the Moment is Now Come to Speak"	55
Carrying About His Ragged and Deformed Body from Hut to Hut on His Two Wooden Joints	67
They Always Stopped a Little While on the Bezons Bridge	81
Then He Began to Beat on the Door	123
"How Did You Receive That Wound on Your Face?"	143

HAPPINESS

It was tea-time before the appearance of the lamps. The villa commanded the sea; the sun, which had disappeared, had left the sky all rosy from his passing—rubbed, as it were, with gold-dust; and the Mediterranean, without a ripple, without a shudder, smooth, still shining under the dying day, seemed like a huge and polished metal plate.

Far off to the right the jagged mountains outlined their black profile on the paled purple of the west.

We talked of love, we discussed that old subject, we said again the things which we had said already very often. The sweet melancholy of the twilight made our words slower, caused a tenderness to waver in our souls; and that word, "love," which came back ceaselessly, now pronounced by a strong man's voice, now uttered by the frail-toned voice of a woman, seemed to fill the little *salon,* to flutter there like a bird, to hover there like a spirit.

Can one remain in love for several years in succession?

"Yes," maintained some.

"No," affirmed others.

We distinguished cases, we established limitations, we cited examples; and all, men and women, filled with rising and troubling memories, which they could not quote, and which mounted to their lips, seemed moved, and talked of that common, that sovereign thing, the tender and mysterious union of two beings, with a profound emotion and an ardent interest.

But all of a sudden some one, whose eyes had been fixed upon the distance, cried out:

"Oh! Look down there; what is it?"

On the sea, at the bottom of the horizon, loomed up a mass, gray, enormous and confused.

The women had risen from their seats, and without understanding, looked at this surprising thing which they had never seen before.

Some one said:

"It is Corsica! You see it so two or three times a year, in certain exceptional conditions of the atmosphere, when the air is perfectly clear, and it is not concealed by those mists of sea-fog which always veil the distances."

We distinguished vaguely the mountain ridges, we thought we recognized the snow of their summits. And every one remained surprised, troubled, almost terrified, by this sudden apparition of a world, by this phantom risen from the sea. Maybe that those who, like Columbus, went away across undiscovered oceans had such strange visions as this.

Then said an old gentleman who had not yet spoken:

"See here: I knew in that island which raises itself before us, as if in person to answer what we said, and to recall to me a singular memory—I knew, I say, an admirable case of love which was true, of love which, improbably enough, was happy.

"Here it is—

"Five years ago I made a journey in Corsica. That savage island is more unknown and more distant from us than America, even though you see it sometimes from the very coasts of France, as we have done to-day.

"Imagine a world which is still chaos, imagine a storm of mountains separated by narrow ravines where torrents roll; not a single plain, but immense waves of granite, and giant undulations of earth covered with brushwood or with high forests of chestnut-trees and pines. It is a virgin soil, uncultivated, desert, although you sometimes make out a village, like a heap of rocks, on the summit of a mountain. No culture, no industries, no art. One never meets here with a morsel of carved wood, or a bit of sculptured stone, never the least reminder that the ancestors of these people had any taste, whether rude or refined, for gracious and beautiful things. It is this which strikes you the most in their superb and hard country: their hereditary indifference to that search for seductive forms which is called Art.

"Italy, where every palace, full of masterpieces, is a masterpiece itself; Italy, where marble, wood, bronze, iron, metals, and precious stones attest man's genius, where the smallest old things which lie about in the ancient houses reveal that divine care for grace—Italy is for us the sacred country which we love, because she shows to us and proves to us the struggle, the grandeur, the power, and the triumph of the intelligence which creates.

Then said an old gentleman, "I knew an admirable case of love which was true."

"And, face to face with her, the savage Corsica has remained exactly as in her earliest days. A man lives there in his rude house, indifferent to everything which does not concern his own bare existence or his family feuds. And he has retained the vices and the virtues of savage races; he is violent, malignant, sanguinary without a thought of remorse, but also hospitable, generous, devoted, simple, opening his door to passers-by, and giving his faithful friendship in return for the least sign of sympathy.

"So, for a month, I had been wandering over this magnificent island with the sensation that I was at the end of the world. No more inns, no taverns, no roads. You gain by mule-paths hamlets hanging up, as it were, on a mountain-side, and commanding tortuous abysses whence of an evening you hear rising the steady sound, the dull and deep voice, of the torrent. You knock at the doors of the houses. You ask a shelter for the night and something to live on till the morrow. And you sit down at the humble board, and you sleep under the humble roof, and in the morning you press the extended hand of your host, who has guided you as far as the outskirts of the village.

"Now, one night, after ten hours' walking, I reached a little dwelling quite by itself at the bottom of a narrow valley which was about to throw itself into the sea a league farther on. The two steep slopes of the mountain, covered with brush, with fallen rocks, and with great trees, shut in this lamentably sad ravine like two sombre walls.

"Around the cottage were some vines, a little garden, and, farther off, several large chestnut-trees—enough to live on; in fact, a fortune for this poor country.

"The woman who received me was old, severe, and neat—exceptionally so. The man, seated on a straw chair, rose to salute me, then sat down again without saying a word. His companion said to me:

"'Excuse him; he is deaf now. He is eighty-two years old.'

"She spoke the French of France. I was surprised.

"I asked her:

"'You are not of Corsica?'

"She answered:

"'No; we are from the Continent. But we have lived here now fifty years.'

"A feeling of anguish and of fear seized me at the thought of those fifty years passed in this gloomy hole, so far from the cities where human beings dwell. An old shepherd returned, and we began to eat the only dish there was for dinner, a thick soup in which potatoes, lard, and cabbages had been boiled together.

"When the short repast was finished, I went and sat down before the door, my heart pinched by the melancholy of the mournful landscape, wrung by that distress which sometimes seizes travellers on certain sad evenings, in certain desolate places. It seems that everything is near its ending—existence, and the universe itself. You perceive sharply the dreadful misery of life, the isolation of every one, the nothingness of all things, and the black loneliness of the heart which nurses itself and deceives itself with dreams until the hour of death.

"The old woman rejoined me, and, tortured by that curiosity which ever lives at the bottom of the most resigned of souls:

" 'So you come from France?' said she.

" 'Yes; I'm travelling for pleasure.'

" 'You are from Paris, perhaps?'

" 'No, I am from Nancy.'

"It seemed to me that an extraordinary emotion agitated her. How I saw, or rather how I felt it, I do not know.

"She repeated, in a slow voice:

" 'You are from Nancy?'

"The man appeared in the door, impassible, like all the deaf.

"She resumed:

" 'It doesn't make any difference. He can't hear.'

"Then, at the end of several seconds:

" 'So you know people at Nancy?'

" 'Oh yes, nearly everybody.'

" 'The family of Sainte-Allaize?'

" 'Yes, very well; they were friends of my father.'

" 'What are you called?'

"I told her my name. She regarded me fixedly, then said, in that low voice which is roused by memories:

" 'Yes, yes; I remember well. And the Brisemares, what has become of them?'

" 'They are all dead.'

" 'Ah! And the Sirmonts, do you know them?'

" 'Yes, the last of the family is a general.'

"Then she said, trembling with emotion, with anguish, with I do not know what, feeling confused, powerful, and holy, with

I do not know how great a need to confess, to tell all, to talk of those things which she had hitherto kept shut in the bottom of her heart, and to speak of those people whose name distracted her soul:

"'Yes, Henri de Sirmont. I know him well. He is my brother.'

"And I lifted my eyes at her, aghast with surprise. And all of a sudden my memory of it came back.

"It had caused, once, a great scandal among the nobility of Lorraine. A young girl, beautiful and rich, Suzanne de Sirmont, had run away with an under-officer in the regiment of hussars commanded by her father.

"He was a handsome fellow, the son of a peasant, but he carried his blue dolman very well, this soldier who had captivated his colonel's daughter. She had seen him, noticed him, fallen in love with him, doubtless while watching the squadrons filing by. But how she had got speech of him, how they had managed to see one another, to hear from one another; how she had dared to let him understand she loved him—that was never known.

"Nothing was divined, nothing suspected. One night when the soldier had just finished his time of service, they disappeared together. Her people looked for them in vain. They never received tidings, and they considered her as dead.

"So I found her in this sinister valley.

"Then in my turn I took up the word:

"'Yes, I remember well. You are Mademoiselle Suzanne.'

"She made the sign 'yes,' with her head. Tears fell from her eyes. Then with a look showing me the old man motionless on the threshold of his hut, she said:

"'That is he.'

"And I understood that she loved him yet, that she still saw him with her bewitched eyes.

"I asked:

"'Have you at least been happy?'

"She answered with a voice which came from her heart:

"'Oh yes! very happy. He has made me very happy. I have never regretted.'

"I looked at her, sad, surprised, astounded by the sovereign strength of love! That rich young lady had followed this man, this peasant. She was become herself a peasant woman. She had made for herself a life without charm, without luxury, without delicacy of any kind, she had stooped to simple customs. And she loved him yet. She was become the wife of a rustic, in a cap, in a cloth skirt. Seated on a straw-bottomed chair, she ate from an earthen-ware dish, at a wooden table, a soup of potatoes and of cabbages with lard. She slept on a mattress by his side.

"She had never thought of anything but of him. She had never regretted her jewels, nor her fine dresses, nor the elegancies of life, nor the perfumed warmth of the chambers hung with tapestry, nor the softness of the down-beds where the body sinks in for repose. She had never had need of anything but him; provided he was there, she desired nothing.

"Still young, she had abandoned life and the world and those who had brought her up, and who had loved her. She had come, alone with him, into this savage valley. And he had been everything to her, all that one desires, all that one dreams of, all that one waits for without ceasing, all that one hopes for without end. He had filled her life with happiness from the one end to the other.

"She could not have been more happy.

"And all the night, listening to the hoarse breathing of the old soldier stretched on his pallet beside her who had followed him so far, I thought of this strange and simple adventure, of this happiness so complete, made of so very little.

"And I went away at sunrise, after having pressed the hands of that aged pair."

The story-teller was silent. A woman said:
"All the same, she had ideals which were too easily satisfied, needs which were too primitive, requirements which were too simple. She could only have been a fool."

Another said, in a low, slow voice, "What matter! she was happy."

And down there at the end of the horizon, Corsica was sinking into the night, returning gently into the sea, blotting out her great shadow, which had appeared as if in person to tell the story of those two humble lovers who were sheltered by her coasts.

A COWARD

In society they called him "the handsome Signoles." His name was Viscount Gontran Joseph de Signoles.

An orphan and the possessor of a sufficient fortune, as the saying goes, he cut a dash. He had a fine figure and bearing, enough conversation to make people credit him with cleverness, a certain natural grace, an air of nobility and of pride, a gallant mustache, and a gentle eye—a thing which pleases women.

In the drawing-rooms he was in great request, much sought after as a partner for the waltz; and he inspired among men that smiling hatred which they always cherish for others of an energetic figure. He passed a happy and tranquil life, in a comfort of mind which was most complete. It was known that he was a good fencer, and as a pistol-shot even better.

"I ever I fight a duel," said he, "I shall choose pistols. With that weapon I am sure of killing my man."

Now, one night, having accompanied two young ladies, his friends, escorted by their husbands, to the theatre, he invited them all after the play to take an ice at Tortoni's. They had been there for several minutes, when he perceived that a gentleman seated at a neighboring table was staring obstinately at one of his companions. She seemed put out, uneasy, lowered her head. At last she said to her husband:

"There is a man who is looking me out of countenance. I do not know him; do you?"

The husband, who had seen nothing, raised his eyes, but declared:

"No, not at all."

The young lady continued, half smiling, half vexed:

"It is very unpleasant; that man is spoiling my ice."

Her husband shrugged his shoulders:

"Bast! don't pay any attention to it. If we had to occupy ourselves about every insolent fellow that we meet we should never have done."

But the viscount had risen brusquely. He could not allow that this stranger should spoil an ice which he had offered. It was to him that this insult was addressed, because it was through him and on his account that his friends had entered this café. So the matter concerned him only.

He advanced towards the man and said to him:

"You have, sir, a manner of looking at those ladies which I cannot tolerate. I beg of you to be so kind as to cease from this insistence."

The other answered:

"You are going to mind your own business, curse you."

The viscount said, with close-pressed teeth:

"Take care, sir, you will force me to pass bounds."

The gentleman answered but one word, a foul word, which rang from one end of the café to the other, and, like a metal spring, caused every guest to execute a sudden movement. All those whose backs were turned wheeled round; all the others raised their heads; three waiters pivoted upon their heels like tops; the two ladies at the desk gave a jump, then turned round their whole bodies from the waists up, as if they had been two automata obedient to the same crank.

A great silence made itself felt. Then, on a sudden, a dry sound cracked in the air. The viscount had slapped his adversary's face. Every one rose to interfere. Cards were exchanged between the two.

When the viscount had reached home he paced his room for several minutes with great, quick strides. He was too much agitated to reflect at all. One single idea was hovering over his mind—"a duel"—without arousing in him as yet an emotion of any sort. He had done that which he ought to have done; he had shown himself to be that which he ought to be. People would talk about it, they would praise him, they would congratulate him. He repeated in a loud voice, speaking as one speaks when one's thoughts are very much troubled:

"What a brute the fellow was!"

Then he sat down and began to reflect. He must find seconds, the first thing in the morning. Whom should he choose? He thought over those men of his acquaintance who had the best positions, who were the most celebrated. He finally selected the Marquis de la Tour-Noire, and the Colonel Bourdin, a nobleman and a soldier. Very good indeed! Their names would sound well in the papers. He perceived that he was thirsty, and he drank, one after another, three glasses of water; then he began again to walk up and down the room. He felt himself full of energy. If he blustered a little, if he showed himself resolute at all points, if he demanded rigorous and dangerous conditions, if he insisted on a serious duel, very serious, terrible, his opponent would probably withdraw and make apologies.

He picked up the card which he had pulled out of his pocket and thrown on the table, and he reread it with a single glance. He had already done so at the café and in the cab, by the glimmer of every street lamp, on his way home. "George Lamil, 51 Rue Moncey." Nothing more.

He examined these assembled letters, which seemed to him mysterious, and full of a confused meaning. George Lamil? Who was this man? What had he been about? Why had he stared at that woman in such a way? Was it not revolting that a stranger, an unknown, should so come and trouble your life, all on a sudden, simply because he had been pleased to fix his eyes insolently upon a woman that you knew? And the viscount repeated yet again, in a loud voice:

"What a brute!"

Then he remained motionless, upright, thinking, his look ever planted on the card. A rage awoke in him against this piece of paper, an anger full of hate in which was mixed a strange, uneasy feeling. It was stupid, this whole affair! He took a little penknife which lay open to his hand, and pricked it into the middle of the printed name, as if he had poniarded some one.

However, they must fight! He considered himself as indeed the insulted party. And, having thus the right, should he choose the pistol or the sword? With the sword he risked less; but with the pistol he had the chance of making his adversary withdraw. It is very rare that a duel with swords proves mortal, a mutual prudence preventing the combatants from engaging near enough for the point of a rapier to enter very deep. With the pistol he risked his life seriously; but he might also come out of the affair with all the honors of the situation, and without going so far as an actual meeting.

He said:

"I must be firm. He will be afraid."

The sound of his voice made him tremble, and he looked about him. He felt himself very nervous. He drank another glass of water, then began to undress himself to go to bed.

As soon as he was in bed, he blew out the light and shut his eyes.

He thought:

"I've got all day to-morrow to attend to my affairs. I'd better sleep first so as to be calm."

He was very warm under the bedclothes, but he could not manage to doze off. He turned and twisted, remained five minutes on his back, then placed himself on his left side, then rolled over to his right.

He was still thirsty. He got up again to drink. Then an anxiety seized him:

"Shall I be afraid?"

Why did his heart fall to beating so madly at each of the well-known noises of his chamber? When the clock was about to strike, the little grinding sound of the spring which stands erect, caused him to give a start; and for several seconds after that he was obliged to open his mouth to breathe, he remained so much oppressed.

He set himself to reasoning with himself upon the possibility of this thing:

"Shall I be afraid?"

No, certainly not, he would not be afraid, because he was resolute to go to the end, because he had his will firmly fixed to fight and not to tremble. But he felt so deeply troubled that he asked himself:

"Can a man be afraid in spite of him?"

And this doubt invaded him, this uneasiness, this dread. If some force stronger than his will, if some commanding, and irresistible power should conquer him, what would happen? Yes, what could happen? He should certainly appear upon the field, since he willed to do it. But if he trembled? But if he fainted? And he thought of his situation, of his reputation, of his name.

And a curious necessity seized him on a sudden to get up again and look at himself in the mirror. He relit his candle. When he perceived his face reflected in the polished glass he hardly recognized himself, and it seemed to him that he had never seen this man before. His eyes appeared enormous; and he was pale, surely he was pale, very pale.

He remained upright before the mirror. He put out his tongue as if to test the state of his health, and all on a sudden this thought entered into him after the fashion of a bullet:

"The day after to-morrow, at this time, I shall perhaps be dead."

And his heart began again to beat furiously.

"The day after to-morrow, at this time, I shall perhaps be dead. This person before me, this 'I' which I see in this glass, will exist no longer. What! here I am, I am looking at myself, I feel myself to live, and in twenty-four hours I shall be laid to rest upon this couch, dead, my eyes shut, cold, inanimate, gone."

He turned towards his bed and he distinctly saw himself extended on the back in the same sheets which he had just left. He had the hollow face which dead men have, and that slackness to the hands which will never stir more.

So he grew afraid of his bed, and, in order not to look at it again, he passed into his smoking-room. He took a cigar mechanically, lit it, and again began to walk the room. He was cold; he went towards the bell to wake his valet; but he stopped, his hand lifted towards the bell-rope:

"That fellow will see that I am afraid."

And he did not ring, he made the fire himself. When his hands touched anything they trembled slightly, with a nervous shaking. His head wandered; his troubled thoughts became fugitive, sudden, melancholy; an intoxication seized on his spirit as if he had been drunk.

And ceaselessly he asked himself:

"What shall I do? What will become of me?"

His whole body vibrated, jerky tremblings ran over it; he got up, and approaching the window, he opened the curtains.

The day was coming, a day of summer. The rosy sky made rosy the city, the roofs, and the walls. A great fall of tenuous light, like a caress from the rising sun, enveloped the awakened world; and, with this glimmer, a hope gay, rapid, brutal, seized on the heart of the viscount! Was he mad to let himself be so struck down by fear, before anything had even been decided, before his seconds had seen those of this Georges Lamil, before he yet knew if he was going to fight at all?

He made his toilet, dressed himself, and left the house with a firm step.

He repeated to himself, while walking:

"I must be decided, very decided. I must prove that I am not afraid."

His seconds, the marquis and the colonel, put themselves at his disposition, and after having pressed his hands energetically, discussed the conditions of the meeting.

The colonel asked:

"You want a serious duel?"

The viscount answered:

"Very serious."

The marquis took up the word.

"You insist on pistols?"

"Yes."

"Do you leave us free to settle the rest?"

The viscount articulated with a dry, jerky voice:

"Twenty paces, firing at the word, lifting the arm instead of lowering it. Exchange of shots until some one is badly wounded."

The colonel declared, in a satisfied tone:

"Those are excellent conditions. You are a good shot; the chances are all in your favor."

And they separated. The viscount returned home to wait for them. His agitation, which had been temporarily calmed, was now increasing with every moment. He felt along his arms, along his legs, in his chest, a kind of quivering, a kind of continuous vibration; he could not stay in one place, neither sitting down nor standing up. He had no longer a trace of moisture in his mouth, and he made at every instant a noisy movement of the tongue as if to unglue it from his palate.

He tried to take his breakfast, but he could not eat. Then he thought of drinking in order to give himself courage, and had a decanter of rum brought him, from which he gulped down, one after the other, six little glasses.

A warmth, like a burn, seized on him. It was followed as soon by a giddiness of the soul. He thought:

"I know the way. Now it will go all right."

But at the end of an hour he had emptied the decanter, and his state of agitation was become again intolerable. He felt a wild necessity to roll upon the ground to cry, to bite. Evening fell.

The sound of the door-bell caused him such a feeling of suffocation that he had not the strength to rise to meet his seconds.

He did not even dare to talk to them any longer—to say "How

do you do?" to pronounce a single word, for fear lest they divine all from the alteration in his voice.

The colonel said:

"Everything is settled according to the conditions which you fixed. Your opponent at first insisted on the privilege of the offended party, but he yielded almost immediately, and has agreed to everything. His seconds are two officers."

The viscount said:

"Thank you."

The marquis resumed:

"Excuse us if we only just run in and out, but we've still a thousand things to do. We must have a good doctor, because the duel is not to stop till after some one is badly hit, and you know there's no trifling with bullets. A place must be appointed near some house where we can carry the wounded one of the two, if it is necessary, etc.; it will take us quite two or three hours more."

The viscount articulated a second time:

"Thank you."

The colonel asked:

"You're all right? You're calm?"

"Yes, quite calm, thanks."

The two men retired.

When he felt himself alone again, it seemed to him that he was going mad. His servant having lit the lamps, he sat down before his table to write some letters. After tracing at the top of a page, "This is my Will," he got up again and drew off, feeling incapable of putting two ideas together, of taking a single resolution, of deciding anything at all.

And so he was going to fight a duel! He could no longer escape that. What could be passing within him? He wanted to fight, he had that intention and that resolution firmly fixed; and he felt very plainly that, notwithstanding all the effort of his mind and all the tension of his will, he would not be able to retain strength enough to go as far as the place of the encounter. He tried to fancy the combat, his own attitude, and the bearing of his adversary.

From time to time, his teeth struck against one another in his mouth with a little dry noise. He tried to read, and took up de Châteauvillard's duelling code. Then he asked himself:

A Coward

"My adversary, has he frequented the shooting-galleries? Is he well known? What's his class? How can I find out?"

He remembered the book by Baron de Vaux upon pistol-shooters, and he searched through it from one end to the other. Georges Lamil was not mentioned. But, however, if the man had not been a good shot, he would not have accepted immediately that dangerous weapon and those conditions, which were mortal.

His pistol-case by Gastinne Renette lay on a little round table. As he passed he opened it and took out one of the pistols, then placed himself as if to shoot, and raised his arm; but he trembled from head to foot, and the barrel shook in all directions.

Then he said:

"It is impossible. I cannot fight like this."

At the end of the barrel he regarded that little hole, black and deep, which spits out death; he thought of dishonor, of the whispers in the clubs, of the laughter in the drawing-rooms, of the disdain of women, of the allusions in the papers, of the insults which would be thrown at him by cowards.

He went on staring at the pistol, and raising the hammer, he suddenly saw a priming glitter beneath it like a little red flame. The pistol had been left loaded, by chance, by oversight. And he experienced from that a confused inexplicable joy.

If in the presence of the other he had not the calm and noble bearing which is fit, he would be lost forever. He would be spotted, marked with a sign of infamy, hunted from society. And he should not have that calm and bold bearing; he knew it, he felt it. And yet he was really brave, because he wanted to fight! He was brave, because—. The thought which just grazed him did not even complete itself in his spirit, but, opening his mouth wide, he brusquely thrust the pistol-barrel into the very bottom of his throat and pressed upon the trigger. . . .

When his valet ran in, attracted by the report, he found him dead, on his back. A jet of blood had spattered the white paper on the table and made a great red stain below the four words:

"This is my Will."

THE WOLF

HERE is what the old Marquis d'Arville told us towards the end of St. Hubert's dinner at the house of the Baron des Ravels.

We had killed a stag that day. The marquis was the only one of the guests who had not taken any part in this chase; for he never hunted.

All through that long repast we had talked about hardly anything but the slaughter of animals. The ladies themselves were interested in tales sanguinary and often unlikely, and the orators imitated the attacks and the combats of men against beasts, raised their arms, romanced in a thundering voice.

M. d'Arville talked well, with a certain poetry of style somewhat high-sounding, but full of effect. He must have repeated this story often, for he told it fluently, not hesitating on words, choosing them with skill to produce a picture—

Gentlemen, I have never hunted, neither did my father, nor my grandfather, nor my great-grandfather. This last was the son of a man who hunted more than all of you put together. He died in 1764. I will tell you how.

His name was Jean. He was married, father of that child who became my ancestor, and he lived with his younger brother, François d'Arville, in our castle in Lorraine, in the middle of the forest.

François d'Arville had remained a bachelor for love of the chase.

They both hunted from one end of the year to the other, without repose, without stopping, without fatigue. They loved only that, understood nothing else, talked only of that, lived only for that.

They had at heart that one passion, which was terrible and inexorable. It consumed them, having entirely invaded them, leaving place for no other.

They had given orders that they should not be interrupted in

The Wolf

the chase, for any reason whatever. My great-grandfather was born while his father was following a fox, and Jean d'Arville did not stop his pursuit, but he swore: "Name of a name, that rascal there might have waited till after the view-halloo!"

His brother François showed himself still more infatuated. On rising he went to see the dogs, then the horses, then he shot little birds about the castle until the moment for departing to hunt down some great beast.

In the country-side they were called M. le Marquis and M. le Cadet, the nobles then not doing at all like the chance nobility of our time, which wishes to establish an hereditary hierarchy in titles; for the son of a marquis is no more a count, nor the son of a viscount a baron, than the son of a general is a colonel by birth. But the mean vanity of to-day finds profit in that arrangement.

I return to my ancestors.

They were, it seems, immeasurably tall, bony, hairy, violent, and vigorous. The younger, still taller than the older, had a voice so strong that, according to a legend of which he was proud, all the leaves of the forest shook when he shouted.

And when they both mounted to go off to the hunt, that must have been a superb spectacle to see those two giants straddling their huge horses.

Now towards the midwinter of that year, 1764, the frosts were excessive, and the wolves became ferocious.

They even attacked belated peasants, roamed at night about the houses, howled from sunset to sunrise, and depopulated the stables.

And soon a rumor began to circulate. People talked of a colossal wolf, with gray fur, almost white, who had eaten two children, gnawed off a woman's arm, strangled all the dogs of the *garde du pays,* and penetrated without fear into the farm-yards to come snuffling under the doors. The people in the houses affirmed that they had felt his breath, and that it made the flame of the lights flicker. And soon a panic ran through all the province. No one dared go out any more after night-fall. The shades seemed haunted by the image of the beast.

The brothers d'Arville resolved to find and kill him, and several times they assembled all the gentlemen of the country to a great hunting.

In vain. They might beat the forests and search the coverts, they never met him. They killed wolves, but not that one. And every night after a *battue,* the beast, as if to avenge himself, attacked some traveller or devoured some one's cattle, always far from the place where they had looked for him.

Finally one night he penetrated into the pig-pen of the Château d'Arville and ate the two finest pigs.

The brothers were inflamed with anger, considering this attack as a bravado of the monster, an insult direct, a defiance. They took their strong blood-hounds used to pursue formidable beasts, and they set off to hunt, their hearts swollen with fury.

From dawn until the hour when the empurpled sun descended behind the great naked trees, they beat the thickets without finding anything.

At last, furious and disconsolate, both were returning, walking their horses along an *allée* bordered with brambles, and they marvelled that their woodcraft should be crossed so by this wolf, and they were seized suddenly with a sort of mysterious fear.

The elder said:

"That beast there is not an ordinary one. You would say it thought like a man."

The younger answered:

"Perhaps we should have a bullet blessed by our cousin, the bishop, or pray some priest to pronounce the words which are needed."

Then they were silent.

Jean continued:

"Look how red the sun is. The great wolf will do some harm to-night."

He had hardly finished speaking when his horse reared; that of François began to kick. A large thicket covered with dead leaves opened before them, and a colossal beast, quite gray, sprang up and ran off across the wood.

Both uttered a kind of groan of joy, and bending over the necks of their heavy horses, they threw them forward with an impulse from all their body, hurling them on at such a pace, exciting them, hurrying them away, maddening them so with the voice, with gesture, and with spur that the strong riders seemed rather to be carrying the heavy beasts between their thighs and to bear them off as if they were flying.

Thus they went, *ventre à terre,* bursting the thickets, cleaving the beds of streams, climbing the hill-sides, descending the gorges, and blowing on the horn with full lungs to attract their people and their dogs.

And now, suddenly, in that mad race, my ancestor struck his forehead against an enormous branch which split his skull; and he fell stark dead on the ground, while his frightened horse took himself off, disappearing in the shade which enveloped the woods.

The cadet of Arville stopped short, leaped to the earth, seized his brother in his arms, and he saw that the brains ran from the wound with the blood.

Then he sat down beside the body, rested the head, disfigured and red, on his knees, and waited, contemplating that immobile face of the elder brother. Little by little a fear invaded him, a strange fear which he had never felt before, the fear of the dark, the fear of solitude, the fear of the deserted wood, and the fear also of the fantastic wolf who had just killed his brother to avenge himself upon them both.

The shadows thickened, the acute cold made the trees crack. François got up, shivering, unable to remain there longer, feeling himself almost growing faint. Nothing was to be heard, neither the voice of the dogs nor the sound of the horns—all was silent along the invisible horizon; and this mournful silence of the frozen night had something about it frightening and strange.

He seized in his colossal hands the great body of Jean, straightened it and laid it across the saddle to carry it back to the château; then he went on his way softly, his mind troubled as if he were drunken, pursued by horrible and surprising images.

And abruptly, in the path which the night was invading, a great shape passed. It was the beast. A shock of terror shook the hunter; something cold, like a drop of water, glided along his reins, and, like a monk haunted of the devil, he made a great sign of the cross, dismayed at this abrupt return of the frightful prowler. But his eyes fell back upon the inert body laid before him, and suddenly, passing abruptly from fear to anger, he shook with an inordinate rage.

Then he spurred his horse and rushed after the wolf.

He followed it by the copses, the ravines, and the tall trees, traversing woods which he no longer knew, his eyes fixed on the white speck which fled before him through the night now fallen upon the earth.

His horse also seemed animated by a force and an ardor hitherto unknown. It galloped, with out-stretched neck, straight on, hurling against the trees, against the rocks, the head and the feet of the dead man thrown across the saddle. The briers tore out the hair; the brow, beating the huge trunks, spattered them with blood; the spurs tore their ragged coats of bark. And suddenly the beast and the horseman issued from the forest and rushed into a valley, just as the moon appeared above the mountains. This valley was stony, closed by enormous rocks, without possible issue; and the wolf was cornered and turned round.

François then uttered a yell of joy which the echoes repeated like a rolling of thunder, and he leaped from his horse, his cutlass in his hand.

The beast, with bristling hair, the back arched, awaited him; its eyes glistened like two stars. But, before offering battle, the strong hunter, seizing his brother, seated him on a rock, and, supporting with stones his head, which was no more than a blot of blood, he shouted in the ears as if he was talking to a deaf man, "Look, Jean; look at this!"

Then he threw himself upon the monster. He felt himself strong enough to overturn a mountain, to bruise stones in his hands. The beast tried to bite him, seeking to strike in at his stomach; but he had seized it by the neck, without even using his weapon, and he strangled it gently, listening to the stoppage of the breathings in its throat and the beatings of its heart. And he laughed, rejoicing madly, pressing closer and closer his formidable embrace, crying in a delirium of joy, "Look, Jean, look!" All resistance ceased; the body of the wolf became lax. He was dead.

Then François, taking him up in his arms, carried him off and went and threw him at the feet of the elder brother, repeating, in a tender voice, "There, there, there, my little Jean, see him!"

Then he replaced on the saddle the two bodies one upon the other; and he went his way.

He returned to the château, laughing and crying, like Gargantua at the birth of Pantagruel, uttering shouts of triumph and stamping with joy in relating the death of the beast, and moaning and tearing his beard in telling that of his brother.

And often, later, when he talked again of that day, he said, with tears in his eyes, "If only that poor Jean could have seen me strangle the other, he would have died content, I am sure of it!"

The widow of my ancestor inspired her orphan son with that

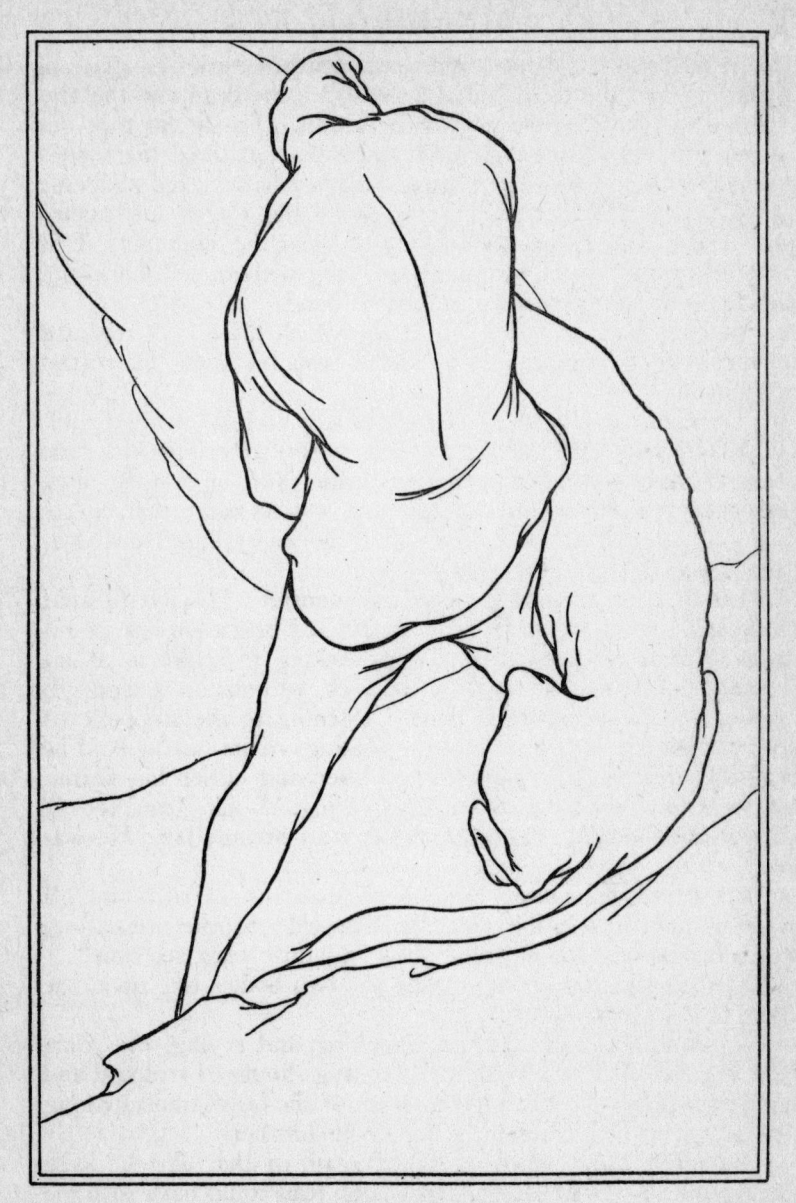

The body of the wolf became lax.

horror of the chase which has transmitted itself from father to son as far down as myself.

The Marquis d'Arville was silent. Some one asked:

"That story is a legend, isn't it?"

And the story-teller answered:

"I swear to you that it is true from one end to the other."

Then a lady declared, in a little, soft voice:

"All the same, it is fine to have passions like that."

THE NECKLACE

She was one of those pretty and charming girls who are sometimes, as if by a mistake of destiny, born in a family of clerks. She had no dowry, no expectations, no means of being known, understood, loved, wedded, by any rich and distinguished man; and she let herself be married to a little clerk at the Ministry of Public Instruction.

She dressed plainly because she could not dress well, but she was as unhappy as though she had really fallen from her proper station; since with women there is neither caste nor rank; and beauty, grace, and charm act instead of family and birth. Natural fineness, instinct for what is elegant, suppleness of wit, are the sole hierarchy, and make from women of the people the equals of the very greatest ladies.

She suffered ceaselessly, feeling herself born for all the delicacies and all the luxuries. She suffered from the poverty of her dwelling, from the wretched look of the walls, from the worn-out chairs, from the ugliness of the curtains. All those things, of which another woman of her rank would never even have been conscious, tortured her and made her angry. The sight of the little Breton peasant who did her humble house-work aroused in her regrets which were despairing, and distracted dreams. She thought of the silent antechambers hung with Oriental tapestry, lit by tall bronze candelabra, and of the two great footmen in knee-breeches who sleep in the big arm-chairs, made drowsy by the heavy warmth of the hot-air stove. She thought of the long *salons* fitted up with ancient silk, of the delicate furniture carrying priceless curiosities, and of the coquettish perfumed boudoirs made for talks at five o'clock with intimate friends, with men famous and sought after, whom all women envy and whose attention they all desire.

When she sat down to dinner, before the round table covered with a table-cloth three days old, opposite her husband, who uncovered the soup-tureen and declared with an enchanted air, "Ah, the good *pot-au-feu!* I don't know anything better than that," she thought of dainty dinners, of shining silverware, of tapestry which peopled the walls with ancient personages and with strange birds flying in the midst of a fairy forest; and she thought of delicious dishes served on marvellous plates, and of the whispered gallantries which you listen to with a sphinx-like smile, while you are eating the pink flesh of a trout or the wings of a quail.

She had no dresses, no jewels, nothing. And she loved nothing but that; she felt made for that. She would so have liked to please, to be envied, to be charming, to be sought after.

She had a friend, a former school-mate at the convent, who was rich, and whom she did not like to go and see any more, because she suffered so much when she came back.

But, one evening, her husband returned home with a triumphant air, and holding a large envelope in his hand.

"There," said he, "here is something for you."

She tore the paper sharply, and drew out a printed card which bore these words:

"The Minister of Public Instruction and Mme. Georges Ramponneau request the honor of M. and Mme. Loisel's company at the palace of the Ministry on Monday evening, January 18th."

Instead of being delighted, as her husband hoped, she threw the invitation on the table with disdain, murmuring:

"What do you want me to do with that?"

"But, my dear, I thought you would be glad. You never go out, and this is such a fine opportunity. I had awful trouble to get it. Every one wants to go; it is very select, and they are not giving many invitations to clerks. The whole official world will be there."

She looked at him with an irritated eye, and she said, impatiently:

"And what do you want me to put on my back?"

He had not thought of that; he stammered:

"Why, the dress you go to the theatre in. It looks very well,

He stopped, distracted, seeing that his wife was crying. Two great tears descended slowly from the corners of her eyes towards the corners of her mouth. He stuttered:

"What's the matter? What's the matter?"

But, by a violent effort, she had conquered her grief, and she replied, with a calm voice, while she wiped her wet cheeks:

"Nothing. Only I have no dress, and therefore I can't go to this ball. Give your card to some colleague whose wife is better equipped than I."

He was in despair. He resumed:

"Come, let us see, Mathilde. How much would it cost, a suitable dress, which you could use on other occasions, something very simple?"

She reflected several seconds, making her calculations and wondering also what sum she could ask without drawing on herself an immediate refusal and a frightened exclamation from the economical clerk.

Finally, she replied, hesitatingly:

"I don't know exactly, but I think I could manage it with four hundred francs."

He had grown a little pale, because he was laying aside just that amount to buy a gun and treat himself to a little shooting next summer on the plain of Nanterre, with several friends who went to shoot larks down there, of a Sunday.

But he said:

"All right. I will give you four hundred francs. And try to have a pretty dress."

The day of the ball drew near, and Mme. Loisel seemed sad, uneasy, anxious. Her dress was ready, however. Her husband said to her one evening:

"What is the matter? Come, you've been so queer these last three days."

And she answered:

"It annoys me not to have a single jewel, not a single stone, nothing to put on. I shall look like distress. I should almost rather not go at all."

He resumed:

"You might wear natural flowers. It's very stylish at this time of the year. For ten francs you can get two or three magnificent roses."

She was not convinced.

"No; there's nothing more humiliating than to look poor among other women who are rich."

But her husband cried:

"How stupid you are! Go look up your friend Mme. Forestier, and ask her to lend you some jewels. You're quite thick enough with her to do that."

She uttered a cry of joy:

"It's true. I never thought of it."

The next day she went to her friend and told of her distress.

Mme. Forestier went to a wardrobe with a glass door, took out a large jewel-box, brought it back, opened it, and said to Mme. Loisel:

"Choose, my dear."

She saw first of all some bracelets, then a pearl necklace, then a Venetian cross, gold and precious stones of admirable workmanship. She tried on the ornaments before the glass, hesitated, could not make up her mind to part with them, to give them back. She kept asking:

"Haven't you any more?"

"Why, yes. Look. I don't know what you like."

All of a sudden she discovered, in a black satin box, a superb necklace of diamonds; and her heart began to beat with an immoderate desire. Her hands trembled as she took it. She fastened it around her throat, outside her high-necked dress, and remained lost in ecstasy at the sight of herself.

Then she asked, hesitating, filled with anguish:

"Can you lend me that, only that?"

"Why, yes, certainly."

She sprang upon the neck of her friend, kissed her passionately, then fled with her treasure.

The day of the ball arrived. Mme. Loisel made a great success. She was prettier than them all, elegant, gracious, smiling, and crazy with joy. All the men looked at her, asked her name, endeavored to be introduced. All the attachés of the Cabinet wanted to waltz with her. She was remarked by the minister himself.

She danced with intoxication, with passion, made drunk by pleasure, forgetting all, in the triumph of her beauty, in the glory of her success, in a sort of cloud of happiness composed of all this homage, of all this admiration, of all these awakened desires, and of that sense of complete victory which is so sweet to woman's heart.

She went away about four o'clock in the morning. Her hus-

She no longer had the necklace around her neck!

band had been sleeping since midnight, in a little deserted anteroom, with three other gentlemen whose wives were having a very good time.

He threw over her shoulders the wraps which he had brought, modest wraps of common life, whose poverty contrasted with the elegance of the ball dress. She felt this and wanted to escape so as not to be remarked by the other women, who were enveloping themselves in costly furs.

Loisel held her back.

"Wait a bit. You will catch cold outside. I will go and call a cab."

But she did not listen to him, and rapidly descended the stairs. When they were in the street they did not find a carriage; and they began to look for one, shouting after the cabmen whom they saw passing by at a distance.

They went down towards the Seine, in despair, shivering with cold. At last they found on the quay one of those ancient noctambulant coupés which, exactly as if they were ashamed to show their misery during the day, are never seen round Paris until after nightfall.

It took them to their door in the Rue des Martyrs, and once more, sadly, they climbed up homeward. All was ended, for her. And as to him, he reflected that he must be at the Ministry at ten o'clock.

She removed the wraps, which covered her shoulders, before the glass, so as once more to see herself in all her glory. But suddenly she uttered a cry. She had no longer the necklace around her neck!

Her husband, already half-undressed, demanded:

"What is the matter with you?"

She turned madly towards him:

"I have—I have—I've lost Mme. Forestier's necklace."

He stood up, distracted.

"What!—how?—Impossible!"

And they looked in the folds of her dress, in the folds of her cloak, in her pockets, everywhere. They did not find it.

He asked:

"You're sure you had it on when you left the ball?"

"Yes, I felt it in the vestibule of the palace."

"But if you had lost it in the street we should have heard it fall. It must be in the cab."

"Yes. Probably. Did you take his number?"
"No. And you, didn't you notice it?"
"No."

They looked, thunderstruck, at one another. At last Loisel put on his clothes.

"I shall go back on foot," said he, "over the whole route which we have taken, to see if I can't find it."

And he went out. She sat waiting on a chair in her ball dress, without strength to go to bed, overwhelmed, without fire, without a thought.

Her husband came back about seven o'clock. He had found nothing.

He went to Police Headquarters, to the newspaper offices, to offer a reward; he went to the cab companies—everywhere, in fact, whither he was urged by the least suspicion of hope.

She waited all day, in the same condition of mad fear before this terrible calamity.

Loisel returned at night with a hollow, pale face; he had discovered nothing.

"You must write to your friend," said he, "that you have broken the clasp of her necklace and that you are having it mended. That will give us time to turn round."

She wrote at his dictation.

At the end of a week they had lost all hope.
And Loisel, who had aged five years, declared:
"We must consider how to replace that ornament."

The next day they took the box which had contained it, and they went to the jeweller whose name was found within. He consulted his books.

"It was not I, madame, who sold that necklace; I must simply have furnished the case."

Then they went from jeweller to jeweller, searching for a necklace like the other, consulting their memories, sick both of them with chagrin and with anguish.

They found, in a shop at the Palais Royal, a string of diamonds which seemed to them exactly like the one they looked for. It was forth forty thousand francs. They could have it for thirty-six.

So they begged the jeweller not to sell it for three days yet. And they made a bargain that he should buy it back for thirty-four thousand francs, in case they found the other one before the end of February.

Loisel possessed eighteen thousand francs which his father had left him. He would borrow the rest.

He did borrow, asking a thousand francs of one, five hundred of another, five louis here, three louis there. He gave notes, took up ruinous obligations, dealt with usurers, and all the race of lenders. He compromised all the rest of his life, risked his signature without even knowing if he could meet it; and, frightened by the pains yet to come, by the black misery which was about to fall upon him, by the prospect of all the physical privations and of all the moral tortures which he was to suffer, he went to get the new necklace, putting down upon the merchant's counter thirty-six thousand francs.

When Mme. Loisel took back the necklace, Mme. Forestier said to her, with a chilly manner:

"You should have returned it sooner, I might have needed it."

She did not open the case, as her friend had so much feared. If she had detected the substitution, what would she have thought, what would she have said? Would she not have taken Mme. Loisel for a thief?

Mme. Loisel now knew the horrible existence of the needy. She took her part, moreover, all on a sudden, with heroism. That dreadful debt must be paid. She would pay it. They dismissed their servant; they changed their lodgings; they rented a garret under the roof.

She came to know what heavy housework meant and the odious cares of the kitchen. She washed the dishes, using her rosy nails on the greasy pots and pans. She washed the dirty linen, the shirts, and the dish-cloths, which she dried upon a line; she carried the slops down to the street every morning, and carried up the water, stopping for breath at every landing. And, dressed like a woman of the people, she went to the fruiterer, the grocer, the butcher, her basket on her arm, bargaining, insulted, defending her miserable money sou by sou.

Each month they had to meet some notes, renew others, obtain more time.

Her husband worked in the evening making a fair copy of some tradesman's accounts, and late at night he often copied manuscript for five sous a page.

And this life lasted ten years.

The Necklace

At the end of ten years they had paid everything, everything, with the rates of usury, and the accumulations of the compound interest.

Mme. Loisel looked old now. She had become the woman of impoverished households—strong and hard and rough. With frowsy hair, skirts askew, and red hands, she talked loud while washing the floor with great swishes of water. But sometimes, when her husband was at the office, she sat down near the window, and she thought of that gay evening of long ago, of that ball where she had been so beautiful and so fêted.

What would have happened if she had not lost that necklace? Who knows? who knows? How life is strange and changeful! How little a thing is needed for us to be lost or to be saved!

But, one Sunday, having gone to take a walk in the Champs Élysées to refresh herself from the labors of the week, she suddenly perceived a woman who was leading a child. It was Mme. Forestier, still young, still beautiful, still charming.

Mme. Loisel felt moved. Was she going to speak to her? Yes, certainly. And now that she had paid, she was going to tell her all about it. Why not?

She went up.

"Good-day, Jeanne."

The other, astonished to be familiarly addressed by this plain good-wife, did not recognize her at all, and stammered:

"But—madame!—I do not know— You must have mistaken."

"No. I am Mathilde Loisel."

Her friend uttered a cry.

"Oh, my poor Mathilde! How you are changed!"

"Yes, I have had days hard enough, since I have seen you, days wretched enough—and that because of you!"

"Of me! How so?"

"Do you remember that diamond necklace which you lent me to wear at the ministerial ball?"

"Yes. Well?"

"Well, I lost it."

"What do you mean? You brought it back."

"I brought you back another just like it. And for this we have been ten years paying. You can understand that it was not easy for us, us who had nothing. At last it is ended, and I am very glad."

Mme. Forestier had stopped.

"You say that you bought a necklace of diamonds to replace mine?"

"Yes. You never noticed it, then! They were very like."

And she smiled with a joy which was proud and naive at once. Mme. Forestier, strongly moved, took her two hands.

"Oh, my poor Mathilde! Why, my necklace was paste. It was worth at most five hundred francs!"

THE PIECE OF STRING

It was market-day, and over all the roads round Goderville the peasants and their wives were coming towards the town. The men walked easily, lurching the whole body forward at every step. Their long legs were twisted and deformed by the slow, painful labors of the country:—by bending over to plough, which is what also makes their left shoulders too high and their figures crooked; and by reaping corn, which obliges them for steadiness' sake to spread their knees too wide. Their starched blue blouses, shining as though varnished, ornamented at collar and cuffs with little patterns of white stitch-work, and blown up big around their bony bodies, seemed exactly like balloons about to soar, but putting forth a head, two arms, and two feet.

Some of these fellows dragged a cow or a calf at the end of a rope. And just behind the animal, beating it over the back with a leaf-covered branch to hasten its pace, went their wives, carrying large baskets from which came forth the heads of chickens or the heads of ducks. These women walked with steps far shorter and quicker than the men; their figures, withered and upright, were adorned with scanty little shawls pinned over their flat bosoms; and they enveloped their heads each in a white cloth, close fastened round the hair and surmounted by a cap.

Now a char-à-banc passed by, drawn by a jerky-paced nag. It shook up strangely the two men on the seat. And the woman at the bottom of the cart held fast to its sides to lessen the hard joltings.

In the market-place at Goderville was a great crowd, a mingled multitude of men and beasts. The horns of cattle, the high and long-napped hats of wealthy peasants, the head-dresses of the women, came to the surface of that sea. And voices clamorous, sharp, shrill, made a continuous and savage din. Above it a huge burst of laughter from the sturdy lungs of a merry yokel would sometimes sound, and sometimes a long bellow from a cow tied fast to the wall of a house.

It all smelled of the stable, of milk, of hay, and of perspiration, giving off that half-human, half-animal odor which is peculiar to the men of the fields.

Maître Hauchecorne, of Bréauté, had just arrived at Goderville, and was taking his way towards the square, when he perceived on the ground a little piece of string. Maître Hauchecorne, economical, like all true Normans, reflected that everything was worth picking up which could be of any use; and he stooped down —but painfully, because he suffered from rheumatism. He took the bit of thin cord from the ground, and was carefully preparing to roll it up when he saw Maître Malandain, the harness-maker, on his door-step, looking at him. They had once had a quarrel about a halter, and they had remained angry, bearing malice on both sides. Maître Hauchecorne was overcome with a sort of shame at being seen by his enemy looking in the dirt so for a bit of string. He quickly hid his find beneath his blouse; then in the pocket of his breeches; then pretended to be still looking for something on the ground which he did not discover; and at last went off toward the market-place, with his head bent forward, and a body almost doubled in two by rheumatic pains.

He lost himself immediately in the crowd, which was clamorous, slow, and agitated by interminable bargains. The peasants examined the cows, went off, came back, always in great perplexity and fear of being cheated, never quite daring to decide, spying at the eye of the seller, trying ceaselessly to discover the tricks of the man and the defect in the beast.

The women, having placed their great baskets at their feet, had pulled out the poultry, which lay upon the ground, tied by the legs, with eyes scared, with combs scarlet.

They listened to propositions, maintaining their prices, with a dry manner, with an impassible face; or, suddenly, perhaps, deciding to take the lower price which was offered, they cried out to the customer, who was departing slowly:

"All right, I'll let you have them, Maît' Anthime."

Then, little by little, the square became empty, and when the *Angelus* struck mid-day those who lived at a distance poured into the inns.

At Jourdain's the great room was filled with eaters, just as the vast court was filled with vehicles of every sort—wagons, gigs,

He took the bit of thin cord from the ground.

char-à-bancs, tilburys, tilt-carts which have no name, yellow with mud, misshapen, pieced together, raising their shafts to heaven like two arms, or it may be with their nose in the dirt and their rear in the air.

Just opposite to where the diners were at table the huge fireplace, full of clear flame, threw a lively heat on the backs of those who sat along the right. Three spits were turning, loaded with chickens, with pigeons, and with joints of mutton; and a delectable odor of roast meat, and of gravy gushing over crisp brown skin, took wing from the hearth, kindled merriment, caused mouths to water.

All the aristocracy of the plough were eating there, at Maît' Jourdain's, the innkeeper's, a dealer in horses also, and a sharp fellow who had made a pretty penny in his day.

The dishes were passed round, were emptied, with jugs of yellow cider. Every one told of his affairs, of his purchases and his sales. They asked news about the crops. The weather was good for green stuffs, but a little wet for wheat.

All of a sudden the drum rolled in the court before the house. Every one, except some of the most indifferent, was on his feet at once, and ran to the door, to the windows, with his mouth still full and his napkin in his hand.

When the public crier had finished his tattoo he called forth in a jerky voice, making his pauses out of time:

"Be it known to the inhabitants of Goderville, and in general to all—persons present at the market, that there has been lost this morning, on the Beuzeville road, between—nine and ten o'clock, a pocket-book of black leather, containing five hundred francs and business papers. You are requested to return it—to the mayor's office, at once, or to Maître Fortuné Houlbrèque, of Manneville. There will be twenty francs reward."

Then the man departed. They heard once more at a distance the dull beatings on the drum and the faint voice of the crier.

Then they began to talk of this event, reckoning up the chances which Maître Houlbrèque had of finding or of not finding his pocket-book again.

And the meal went on.

They were finishing their coffee when the corporal of gendarmes appeared on the threshold.

He asked:

"Is Maître Hauchecorne, of Bréauté, here?"

The Piece of String

Maître Hauchecorne, seated at the other end of the table, answered:

"Here I am."

And the corporal resumed:

"Maître Hauchecorne, will you have the kindness to come with me to the mayor's office? M. le Maire would like to speak to you."

The peasant, surprised and uneasy, gulped down his little glass of cognac, got up, and, even worse bent over than in the morning, since the first steps after a rest were always particularly difficult, started off, repeating:

"Here I am, here I am."

And he followed the corporal.

The mayor was waiting for him, seated in an arm-chair. He was the notary of the place, a tall, grave man of pompous speech.

"Maître Hauchecorne," said he, "this morning, on the Beuzeville road, you were seen to pick up the pocket-book lost by Maître Houlbrèque, of Manneville."

The countryman, speechless, regarded the mayor, frightened already by this suspicion which rested on him he knew not why.

"I, I picked up that pocket-book?"

"Yes, you."

"I swear I didn't even know nothing about it at all."

"You were seen."

"They saw me, me? Who is that who saw me?"

"M. Malandain, the harness-maker."

Then the old man remembered, understood, and, reddening with anger:

"Ah! he saw me, did he, the rascal? He saw me picking up this string here, M'sieu' le Maire."

And, fumbling at the bottom of his pocket, he pulled out of it the little end of string.

But the mayor incredulously shook his head:

"You will not make me believe, Maître Hauchecorne, that M. Malandain, who is a man worthy of credit, has mistaken this string for a pocket-book."

The peasant, furious, raised his hand and spit as if to attest his good faith, repeating:

"For all that, it is the truth of the good God, the blessed truth, M'sieu' le Maire. There! on my soul and my salvation I repeat it."

The mayor continued:

"After having picked up the thing in question, you even looked for some time in the mud to see if a piece of money had not dropped out of it."

The good man was suffocated with indignation and with fear:

"If they can say!—if they can say .... such lies as that to slander an honest man! If they can say!—"

He might protest, he was not believed.

He was confronted with M. Malandain, who repeated and sustained his testimony. They abused one another for an hour. At his own request Maître Hauchecorne was searched. Nothing was found upon him.

At last, the mayor, much perplexed, sent him away, warning him that he would inform the public prosecutor, and ask for orders.

The news had spread. When he left the mayor's office, the old man was surrounded, interrogated with a curiosity which was serious or mocking as the case might be, but into which no indignation entered. And he began to tell the story of the string. They did not believe him. They laughed.

He passed on, button-holed by every one, himself button-holing his acquaintances, beginning over and over again his tale and his protestations, showing his pockets turned inside out to prove that he had nothing.

They said to him:

"You old rogue, *va!*"

And he grew angry, exasperated, feverish, in despair at not being believed, and always telling his story.

The night came. It was time to go home. He set out with three of his neighbors, to whom he pointed out the place where he had picked up the end of string; and all the way he talked of his adventure.

That evening he made the round in the village of Bréauté, so as to tell every one. He met only unbelievers.

He was ill of it all night long.

The next day, about one in the afternoon, Marius Paumelle, a farm hand of Maître Breton, the market-gardener at Ymauville, returned the pocket-book and its contents to Maître Houlbrèque, of Manneville.

This man said, indeed, that he had found it on the road; but not knowing how to read, he had carried it home and given it to his master.

The news spread to the environs. Maître Hauchecorne was informed. He put himself at once upon the go, and began to relate his story as completed by the *dénouement*. He triumphed.

"What grieved me," said he, "was not the thing itself, do you understand; but it was the lies. There's nothing does you so much harm as being in disgrace for lying."

All day he talked of his adventure, he told it on the roads to the people who passed; at the cabaret to the people who drank; and the next Sunday, when they came out of church. He even stopped strangers to tell them about it. He was easy, now, and yet something worried him without his knowing exactly what it was. People had a joking manner while they listened. They did not seem convinced. He seemed to feel their tittle-tattle behind his back.

On Tuesday of the next week he went to market at Goderville, prompted entirely by the need of telling his story.

Malandain, standing on his door-step, began to laugh as he saw him pass. Why?

He accosted a farmer of Criquetot, who did not let him finish, and, giving him a punch in the pit of his stomach, cried in his face: "Oh you great rogue, *va!*" Then turned his heel upon him.

Maître Hauchecorne remained speechless, and grew more and more uneasy. Why had they called him "great rogue?"

When seated at table in Jourdain's tavern he began again to explain the whole affair.

A horse-dealer of Montivilliers shouted at him:

"Get out, get out you old scamp; I know all about your string!"

Hauchecorne stammered:

"But since they found it again, the pocket-book!"

But the other continued:

"Hold your tongue, daddy; there's one who finds it and there's another who returns it. And no one the wiser."

The peasant was choked. He understood at last. They accused him of having had the pocket-book brought back by an accomplice, by a confederate.

He tried to protest. The whole table began to laugh.

He could not finish his dinner, and went away amid a chorus of jeers.

He went home, ashamed and indignant, choked with rage, with confusion, the more cast-down since from his Norman cunning, he was, perhaps, capable of having done what they accused him of, and even of boasting of it as a good trick. His innocence dimly seemed to him impossible to prove, his craftiness being so well known. And he felt himself struck to the heart by the injustice of the suspicion.

Then he began anew to tell of his adventure, lengthening his recital every day, each time adding new proofs, more energetic protestations, and more solemn oaths which he thought of, which he prepared in his hours of solitude, his mind being entirely occupied by the story of the string. The more complicated his defence, the more artful his arguments, the less he was believed.

"Those are liars' proofs," they said behind his back.

He felt this; it preyed upon his heart. He exhausted himself in useless efforts.

He was visibly wasting away.

The jokers now made him tell the story of "The Piece of String" to amuse them, just as you make a soldier who has been on a campaign tell his story of the battle. His mind, struck at the root, grew weak.

About the end of December he took to his bed.

He died early in January, and, in the delirium of the death-agony, he protested his innocence, repeating:

"A little bit of string—a little bit of string—see, here it is, M'sieu' le Maire."

LA MÈRE SAUVAGE

I HAD not been at Virelogne for fifteen years. I went back there in the autumn, to shoot with my friend Serval, who had at last rebuilt his château, which had been destroyed by the Prussians.

I loved that district very much. It is one of those corners of the world which have a sensuous charm for the eyes. You love it with a bodily love. We, whom the country seduces, we keep tender memories for certain springs, for certain woods, for certain pools, for certain hills, seen very often, and which have stirred us like joyful events. Sometimes our thoughts turn back towards a corner in a forest, or the end of a bank, or an orchard powdered with flowers, seen but a single time, on some gay day; yet remaining in our hearts like the images of certain women met in the street on a spring morning, with bright transparent dresses; and leaving in soul and body an unappeased desire which is not to be forgotten, a feeling that you have just rubbed elbows with happiness.

At Virelogne I loved the whole country-side, dotted with little woods, and crossed by brooks which flashed in the sun and looked like veins, carrying blood to the earth. You fished in them for crawfish, trout, and eels! Divine happiness! You could bathe in places, and you often found snipe among the high grass which grew along the borders of these slender watercourses.

I was walking, lightly as a goat, watching my two dogs ranging before me. Serval, a hundred metres to my right, was beating a field of lucern. I turned the thicket which forms the boundary of the wood of Sandres, and I saw a cottage in ruins.

All of a sudden, I remembered it as I had seen it the last time, in 1869, neat, covered with vines, with chickens before the door. What sadder than a dead house, with its skeleton standing upright, bare and sinister?

I also remembered that in it, one very tiring day, the good woman had given me a glass of wine to drink, and that Serval had then told me the history of its inhabitants. The father, an old poacher, had been killed by the gendarmes. The son, whom I had once seen, was a tall, dry fellow who also passed for a ferocious destroyer of game. People called them "les Sauvage."

Was that a name or a nickname?

I hailed Serval. He came up with his long strides like a crane. I asked him:

"What's become of those people?"

And he told me this story:

When war was declared, the son Sauvage, who was then thirty-three years old, enlisted, leaving his mother alone in the house. People did not pity the old woman very much, because she had money; they knew it.

But she remained quite alone in that isolated dwelling so far from the village, on the edge of the wood. She was not afraid, however, being of the same strain as her menfolk; a hardy old woman, tall and thin, who laughed seldom, and with whom one never jested. The women of the fields laugh but little in any case; that is men's business, that! But they themselves have sad and narrowed hearts, leading a melancholy, gloomy life. The peasants learn a little boisterous merriment at the tavern, but their helpmates remain grave, with countenances which are always severe. The muscles of their faces have never learned the movements of the laugh.

La Mère Sauvage continued her ordinary existence in her cottage, which was soon covered by the snows. She came to the village once a week, to get bread and a little meat; then she returned into her house. As there was talk of wolves, she went out with a gun upon her back—her son's gun, rusty, and with the butt worn by the rubbing of the hand; and she was strange to see, the tall "Sauvage," a little bent, going with slow strides over the snow, the muzzle of the piece extending beyond the black head-dress, which pressed close to her head and imprisoned her white hair, which no one had ever seen.

One day a Prussian force arrived. It was billeted upon the inhabitants, according to the property and resources of each. Four were allotted to the old woman, who was known to be rich.

They were four great boys with blond skin, with blond beards, with blue eyes, and who had remained stout notwithstanding the fatigues which they had endured already, and who also, though in a conquered country, had remained kind and gentle. Alone with this aged woman, they showed themselves full of consideration, sparing her, as much as they could, all expenses and fatigue. They would be seen, all four of them, making their toilet round the well, of a morning, in their shirt-sleeves, splashing with great swishes of water, under the crude daylight of the snowy weather, their pink-white Northman's flesh, while La Mère Sauvage went and came, making ready the soup. Then they would be seen cleaning the kitchen, rubbing the tiles, splitting wood, peeling potatoes, doing up all the house-work, like four good sons about their mother.

But the old woman thought always of her own, so tall and thin, with his hooked nose and his brown eyes and his heavy mustache which made a roll of black hairs upon his lip. She asked each day of each of the soldiers who were installed beside her hearth:

"Do you know where the French Marching Regiment No. 23 was sent? My boy is in it."

They answered, "No, not know, not know at all." And, understanding her pain and her uneasiness (they, who had mothers too, there at home), they rendered her a thousand little services. She loved them well, moreover, her four enemies, since the peasantry feels no patriotic hatred; that belongs to the upper class alone. The humble, those who pay the most, because they are poor, and because every new burden crushes them down; those who are killed in masses, who make the true cannon-fodder, because they are so many; those, in fine, who suffer most cruelly the atrocious miseries of war, because they are the feeblest, and offer least resistance—they hardly understand at all those bellicose ardors, that excitable sense of honor, or those pretended political combinations which in six months exhaust two nations, the conqueror with the conquered.

They said on the country-side, in speaking of the Germans of La Mère Sauvage:

"There are four who have found a soft place."

Now, one morning, when the old woman was alone in the house, she perceived far off on the plain a man coming towards her dwelling. Soon she recognized him; it was the postman charged to distribute the letters. He gave her a folded paper, and she drew out of her case the spectacles which she used for sewing; then she read:

"Madame Sauvage,—The present letter is to tell you sad news. Your boy Victor was killed yesterday by a shell which near cut him in two. I was just by, seeing that we stood next each other in the company, and he would talk to me about you to let you know on the same day if anything happened to him.

"I took his watch, which was in his pocket, to bring it back to you when the war is done.

"I salute you very friendly.

"Césaire Rivot,
"Soldier of the 2d class, March. Reg. No. 23."

The letter was dated three weeks back.

She did not cry at all. She remained motionless, so seized and stupefied that she did not even suffer as yet. She thought: "V'la Victor who is killed now." Then little by little the tears mounted to her eyes, and the sorrow caught her heart. The ideas came to her, one by one, dreadful, torturing. She would never kiss him again, her child, her big boy, never again! The gendarmes had killed the father, the Prussians had killed the son. He had been cut in two by a cannon-ball. She seemed to see the thing, the horrible thing: the head falling, the eyes open, while he chewed the corner of his big mustache as he always did in moments of anger.

What had they done with his body afterwards? If they had only let her have her boy back as they had given her back her husband—with the bullet in the middle of his forehead!

But she heard a noise of voices. It was the Prussians returning from the village. She hid her letter very quickly in her pocket, and she received them quietly, with her ordinary face, having had time to wipe her eyes.

They were laughing, all four, delighted, since they brought with them a fine rabbit—stolen, doubtless—and they made signs to the old woman that there was to be something good to eat.

She set herself to work at once to prepare breakfast; but when it came to killing the rabbit, her heart failed her. And yet it was not the first. One of the soldiers struck it down with a blow of his fist behind the ears.

The beast once dead, she separated the red body from the skin; but the sight of the blood which she was touching, and which covered her hands, of the warm blood which she felt cooling and coagulating, made her tremble from head to foot; and she kept seeing her big boy cut in two, and quite red also, like this still palpitating animal.

She set herself at table with the Prussians, but she could not eat, not even a mouthful. They devoured the rabbit without troubling themselves about her. She looked at them askance, without speaking, ripening a thought, and with a face so impassible that they perceived nothing.

All of a sudden, she said: "I don't even know your names, and here's a whole month that we've been together." They understood, not without difficulty, what she wanted, and told their names. That was not sufficient; she had them written for her on a paper, with the addresses of their families, and, resting her spectacles on her great nose, she considered that strange handwriting, then folded the sheet and put it in her pocket, on top of the letter which told her of the death of her son.

When the meal was ended, she said to the men:

"I am going to work for you."

And she began to carry up hay into the loft where they slept.

They were astonished at her taking all this trouble; she explained to them that thus they would not be so cold; and they helped her. They heaped the trusses of hay as high as the straw roof; and in that manner they made a sort of great chamber with four walls of fodder, warm and perfumed, where they should sleep splendidly.

At dinner, one of them was worried to see that La Mère Sauvage still ate nothing. She told him that she had the cramps. Then she kindled a good fire to warm herself up, and the four Germans mounted to their lodging-place by the ladder which served them every night for this purpose.

As soon as they closed the trap, the old woman removed the ladder, then opened the outside door noiselessly, and went back to look for more bundles of straw, with which she filled her kitchen. She went barefoot in the snow, so softly that no sound was heard. From time to time she listened to the sonorous and unequal snorings of the four soldiers who were fast asleep.

When she judged her preparations to be sufficient, she threw one of the bundles into the fireplace, and when it was alight she scattered it over all the others. Then she went outside again and looked.

In a few seconds the whole interior of the cottage was illumined with a violent brightness and became a dreadful brasier, a gigantic fiery furnace, whose brilliance spouted out of the narrow window and threw a glittering beam upon the snow.

Then a great cry issued from the summit of the house; it was a clamor of human shriekings, heart-rending calls of anguish and of fear. At last, the trap having fallen in, a whirlwind of fire shot up into the loft, pierced the straw roof, rose to the sky like the immense flame of a torch; and all the cottage flared.

Nothing more was heard therein but the crackling of the fire, the crackling sound of the walls, the falling of the rafters. All of a sudden the roof fell in, and the burning carcass of the dwelling hurled a great plume of sparks into the air, amid a cloud of smoke.

The country, all white, lit up by the fire, shone like a cloth of silver tinted with red.

A bell, far off, began to toll.

The old "Sauvage" remained standing before her ruined dwelling, armed with her gun, her son's gun, for fear lest one of those men might escape.

When she saw that it was ended, she threw her weapon into the brasier. A loud report rang back.

People were coming, the peasants, the Prussians.

They found the woman seated on the trunk of a tree, calm and satisfied.

A German officer, who spoke French like a son of France, demanded of her:

"Where are your soldiers?"

She extended her thin arm towards the red heap of fire which was gradually going out, and she answered with a strong voice:

"There!"

They crowded round her. The Prussian asked:

"How did it take fire?"

She said:

"It was I who set it on fire."

They did not believe her, they thought that the sudden disaster had made her crazy. So, while all pressed round and listened, she told the thing from one end to the other, from the arrival of the letter to the last cry of the men who were burned with her house. She did not forget a detail of all which she had felt, nor of all which she had done.

When she had finished, she drew two pieces of paper from her pocket, and, to distinguish them by the last glimmers of the

fire, she again adjusted her spectacles; then she said, showing one:
"That, that is the death of Victor." Showing the other, she added,
indicating the red ruins with a bend of the head: "That, that is
their names, so that you can write home." She calmly held the
white sheet out to the officer, who held her by the shoulders, and
she continued:

"You must write how it happened, and you must say to their
mothers that it was I who did that, Victoire Simon, la Sauvage!
Do not forget."

The officer shouted some orders in German. They seized her,
they threw her against the walls of her house, still hot. Then
twelve men drew quickly up before her, at twenty paces. She did
not move. She had understood; she waited.

An order rang out, followed instantly by a long report. A
belated shot went off by itself, after the others.

The old woman did not fall. She sank as though they had
mowed off her legs.

The Prussian officer approached. She was almost cut in two,
and in her withered hand she held her letter bathed in blood.

My friend Serval added:
"It was by way of reprisal that the Germans destroyed the
château of the district, which belonged to me."

As for me, I thought of the mothers of those four gentle
fellows burned in that house; and of the atrocious heroism of
that other mother shot against the wall.

And I picked up a little stone, still blackened by the flames.

MOONLIGHT

The Abbé Marignan, as soldier of the Church, bore his fighting title well. He was a tall, thin priest, very fanatical, of an ecstatic but upright soul. All his beliefs were fixed, without ever a wavering. He thought that he understood God thoroughly, that he penetrated His designs, His wishes, His intentions.

When he promenaded with great strides in the garden walk of his little country parsonage, sometimes a question rose in his mind: "Why did God make that?" And in fancy taking the place of God, he searched obstinately, and nearly always he found the reason. It is not he who would have murmured in a transport of pious humility, "O Lord, thy ways are past finding out!" He said to himself, "I am the servant of God; I ought to know the reason of what He does, or to divine it if I do not."

Everything in nature seemed to him created with an absolute and admirable logic. The "wherefore" and the "because" were always balanced. The dawns were made to render glad your waking, the days to ripen the harvests, the rains to water them, the evenings to prepare for sleeping, and the nights dark for sleep.

The four seasons corresponded perfectly to all the needs of agriculture; and to him the suspicion could never have come that nature has no intentions, and that all which lives has bent itself, on the contrary, to the hard conditions of different periods, of climates, and of matter.

Only he did hate women; he hated them unconscionably, and he despised them by instinct. He often repeated the words of Christ, "Woman, what have I to do with thee?" and he added, "One would almost say that God himself was ill-pleased with that particular work of his hands." Woman was indeed for him the "child twelve times unclean" of whom the poet speaks. She was the temptress who had ensnared the first man, and who still continued her work of damnation; she was the being who is feeble, dangerous, mysteriously troubling. And even more than her body of perdition, he hated her loving soul.

He had often felt women's tenderness attach itself to him, and though he knew himself to be unassailable, he grew exasperated at that need of loving which quivered always in their hearts.

God, to his mind, had only created woman to tempt man and to prove him. You should not approach her without those precautions for defence which you would take, and those fears which you would cherish, near a trap. She was, indeed, just like a trap, with her arms extended and her lips open towards a man.

He had indulgence only for nuns, rendered harmless by their vow; but he treated them harshly notwithstanding, because, ever living at the bottom of their chained-up hearts, of their chastened hearts, he perceived that eternal tenderness which constantly went out to him, although he was a priest.

He was conscious of it in their looks more moist with piety than the looks of monks, in their ecstacies, in their transports of love towards the Christ, which angered him because it was women's love; and he was also conscious of it, of that accursed tenderness, in their very docility, in the softness of their voices when they spoke to him, in their lowered eyes, and in the meekness of their tears when he reproved them roughly.

And he shook his cassock on issuing from the doors of the convent, and he went off with long strides, as though he had fled before some danger.

He had a niece who lived with her mother in a little house near by. He was bent on making her a sister of charity.

She was pretty, and hare-brained, and a great tease. When the abbé sermonized, she laughed; when he was angry at her, she kissed him vehemently, pressing him to her heart, while he would seek involuntarily to free himself from this embrace, which, notwithstanding, made him taste a certain sweet joy, awaking deep within him that sensation of fatherhood which slumbers in every man.

Often he talked to her of God, of his God, walking beside her along the foot-paths through the fields. She hardly listened, and looked at the sky, the grass, the flowers with a joy of living which could be seen in her eyes. Sometimes she rushed forward to catch some flying creature, and bringing it back, would cry, "Look, my uncle, how pretty it is; I should like to kiss it." And this necessity to "kiss flies," or lilac berries, worried, irritated, and revolted the priest, who saw, even in that, the ineradicable tenderness which ever springs at the hearts of women.

And now one day the sacristan's wife, who kept house for the Abbé Marignan, told him, very cautiously, that his niece had a lover!

He experienced a dreadful emotion, and he stood choked, with the soap all over his face, being in the act of shaving.

When he found himself able to think and speak once more, he cried: "It is not true; you are lying, Mélanie!"

But the peasant woman put her hand on her heart: "May our Lord judge me if I am lying, Monsieur le Curé. I tell you she goes to him every evening as soon as your sister is in bed. They meet each other beside the river. You have only to go there between ten o'clock and midnight, and see for yourself."

He ceased scratching his chin, and he commenced to walk the room violently, as he always did in his hours of gravest thought. When he tried to begin his shaving again, he cut himself three times from nose to ear.

All day long, he remained silent, swollen with anger and with rage. To his priestly zeal against the mighty power of love was added the moral indignation of a father, of a teacher, of a keeper of souls, who has been deceived, robbed, played with by a child. He had that egotistical choking sensation such as parents feel when their daughter announces that she has chosen a husband without them and in spite of their advice.

After his dinner, he tried to read a little, but he could not bring himself so far; and he grew angrier and angrier. When it struck ten, he took his cane, a formidable oaken club which he always carried when he had to go out at night to visit the sick. And he smilingly regarded the enormous cudgel, holding it in his solid, countryman's fist and cutting threatening circles with it in the air. Then, suddenly he raised it, and grinding his teeth, he brought it down upon a chair, the back of which, split in two, fell heavily to the ground.

He opened his door to go out; but he stopped upon the threshold, surprised by such a splendor of moonlight as you seldom see.

And since he was endowed with an exalted spirit, such a spirit as must have belonged to those dreamer-poets, the Fathers of the Church, he felt himself suddenly distracted, moved by the grand and serene beauty of the pale-faced night.

In his little garden, quite bathed with the soft brilliance, his fruit-trees, all arow, were outlining in shadow upon the walk, their slender limbs of wood scarce clothed by verdure; while the giant honeysuckle climbing on the house wall, exhaled delicious, sugared breaths, and seemed to cause to hover through the warm clear night a perfumed soul.

He began to breathe deep, drinking the air as drunkards drink their wine, and he walked slowly, being ravished, astounded, and almost oblivious of his niece.

As soon as he came into the open country he stopped to contemplate the whole plain, so inundated by this caressing radiance, so drowned in the tender and languishing charm of the serene nights. At every instant the frogs threw into space their short metallic notes, and the distant nightingales mingled with the seduction of the moonlight that fitful music of theirs which brings no thoughts but dreams, that light and vibrant melody of theirs which is composed for kisses.

The abbé continued his course, his courage failing, he knew not why. He felt, as it were, enfeebled, and suddenly exhausted; he had a great desire to sit down, to pause here, to praise God in all His works.

Down there, following the bends of the little river, wound a great line of poplars. On and about the banks, wrapping all the tortuous watercourse with a kind of light, transparent wadding, hung suspended a fine mist, a white vapor, which the moon-rays crossed, and silvered, and caused to gleam.

The priest paused yet again, penetrated to the bottom of his soul by a strong and growing emotion.

And a doubt, a vague uneasiness, seized on him; he perceived that one of those questions which he sometimes put to himself, was now being born.

Why had God done this? Since the night is destined for sleep, for unconsciousness, for repose, for forgetfulness of everything, why, then, make it more charming than the day, sweeter than the dawns and the sunsets? And this slow seductive star, more poetical than the sun, and so discreet that it seems designed to light up things too delicate, too mysterious, for the great luminary, —why was it come to brighten all the shades?

Why did not the cleverest of all songsters go to rest like the others? And why did he set himself to singing in the vaguely troubling dark?

Why this half-veil over the world? Why these quiverings of the heart, this emotion of the soul, this languor of the body?

Why this display of seductions which mankind never sees, being asleep in bed? For whom was intended this sublime spectacle, this flood of poetry poured from heaven to earth?

And the abbé did not understand at all.

But now, see, down there along the edge of the field appeared two shadows walking side by side under the arched roof of the trees all soaked in glittering mist.

The man was the taller, and had his arm about his mistress's neck, and from time to time he kissed her on the forehead. They animated suddenly the lifeless landscape, which enveloped them like a divine frame made expressly for this. They seemed, these two, like one being, the being for whom was destined this calm and silent night; and they came on towards the priest like a living answer, the answer vouchsafed by his Master to his question.

He stood stock-still, quite overwhelmed, and with a beating heart. And he thought to see here some Bible story, like the loves of Ruth and Boaz, the accomplishment of the will of the Lord in one of those great scenes talked of in the holy books. Through his head began to hum the versicles of the Song of Songs, the ardent cries, the calls of the body, all the passionate poetry of that poem which burns with tenderness and love.

And he said to himself, "God perhaps has made such nights as this to clothe with the ideal the loves of men."

He withdrew before this couple who went ever arm in arm. For all that, it was really his niece; but now he asked himself if he had not been about to disobey God. And does not God indeed permit love, since He surrounds it visibly with splendor such as this?

And he fled, in a maze, almost ashamed, as if he had penetrated into a temple where he had not the right to go.

THE CONFESSION

MARGUÉRITE DE THÉRELLES was dying. Although but fifty-six, she seemed like seventy-five at least. She panted, paler than the sheets, shaken by dreadful shiverings, her face convulsed, her eyes haggard, as if she had seen some horrible thing.

Her eldest sister, Suzanne, six years older, sobbed on her knees beside the bed. A little table drawn close to the couch of the dying woman, and covered with a napkin, bore two lighted candles, the priest being momentarily expected to give extreme unction and the communion, which should be the last.

The apartment had that sinister aspect, that air of hopeless farewells, which belongs to the chambers of the dying. Medicine bottles stood about on the furniture, linen lay in the corners, pushed aside by foot or broom. The disordered chairs themselves seemed affrighted, as if they had run, in all the senses of the word. Death, the formidable, was there, hidden, waiting.

The story of the two sisters was very touching. It was quoted far and wide; it had made many eyes to weep.

Suzanne, the elder, had once been madly in love with a young man, who had also been in love with her. They were engaged, and were only waiting the day fixed for the contract, when Henry de Lampierre suddenly died.

The despair of the young girl was dreadful, and she vowed that she would never marry. She kept her word. She put on widow's weeds, which she never took off.

Then her sister, her little sister Marguérite, who was only twelve years old, came one morning to throw herself into the arms of the elder, and said: "Big Sister, I do not want thee to be unhappy. I do not want thee to cry all thy life. I will never leave thee, never, never! I—I, too, shall never marry. I shall stay with thee always, always, always!"

Suzanne, touched by the devotion of the child, kissed her, but did not believe.

Yet the little one, also, kept her word, and despite the entreaties of her parents, despite the supplications of the elder, she never married. She was pretty, very pretty; she refused many a young man who seemed to love her truly; and she never left her sister more.

They lived together all the days of their life, without ever being separated a single time. They went side by side, inseparably united. But Marguérite seemed always sad, oppressed, more melancholy than the elder, as though perhaps her sublime sacrifice had broken her spirit. She aged more quickly, had white hair from the age of thirty, and often suffering, seemed afflicted by some secret, gnawing trouble.

Now she was to be the first to die.

Since yesterday she was no longer able to speak. She had only said, at the first glimmers of day-dawn:

"Go fetch Monsieur le Curé, the moment has come."

And she had remained since then upon her back, shaken with spasms, her lips agitated as though dreadful words were mounting from her heart without power to issue, her look mad with fear, terrible to see.

Her sister, torn by sorrow, wept wildly, her forehead resting on the edge of the bed, and kept repeating:

"Margot, my poor Margot, my little one!"

She had always called her, "Little One," just as the younger had always called her "Big Sister."

Steps were heard on the stairs. The door opened. A choirboy appeared, followed by an old priest in a surplice. As soon as she perceived him, the dying woman, with one shudder, sat up, opened her lips, stammered two or three words, and began to scratch the sheet with her nails as if she had wished to make a hole.

The Abbé Simon approached, took her hand, kissed her brow, and with a soft voice:

"God pardon thee, my child; have courage, the moment is now come, speak."

Then Marguérite, shivering from head to foot, shaking her whole couch with nervous movements, stammered:

"Sit down, Big Sister . . . listen."

The priest bent down towards Suzanne, who was still flung upon the bed's foot. He raised her, placed her in an arm-chair, and

"God pardon thee, my child; have courage, the moment is now come to speak."

taking a hand of each of the sisters in one of his own, he pronounced:

"Lord, my God! Endue them with strength, cast Thy mercy upon them."

And Marguérite began to speak. The words issued from her throat one by one, raucous, with sharp pauses, as though very feeble.

"Pardon, pardon, Big Sister; oh, forgive! If thou knewest how I have had fear of this moment all my life . . ."

Suzanne stammered through her tears:

"Forgive thee what, Little One? Thou hast given all to me, sacrificed everything; thou art an angel . . ."

But Marguérite interrupted her:

"Hush, hush! Let me speak . . . do not stop me. It is dreadful . . . let me tell all . . . to the very end, without flinching. Listen. Thou rememberest . . . thou rememberest . . . Henry . . ."

Suzanne trembled and looked at her sister. The younger continued:

"Thou must hear all, to understand. I was twelve years old, only twelve years old; thou rememberest well, is it not so? And I was spoiled, I did everything that I liked! Thou rememberest, surely, how they spoiled me? Listen. The first time that he came he had varnished boots. He got down from his horse at the great steps, and he begged pardon for his costume, but he came to bring some news to papa. Thou rememberest, is it not so? Don't speak —listen. When I saw him I was completely carried away, I found him so very beautiful; and I remained standing in a corner of the *salon* all the time that he was talking. Children are strange . . . and terrible. Oh yes . . . I have dreamed of all that.

"He came back again . . . several times . . . I looked at him with all my eyes, with all my soul . . . I was large for my age . . . and very much more knowing than any one thought. He came back often . . . I thought only of him. I said, very low:

" 'Henry . . . Henry de Lampierre!'

"Then they said that he was going to marry thee. It was a sorrow; oh, Big Sister, a sorrow . . . a sorrow! I cried for three nights without sleeping. He came back every day, in the afternoon, after his lunch . . . thou rememberest, is it not so? Say nothing . . . listen. Thou madest him cakes which he liked . . . with meal, with butter and milk. Oh, I know well how. I could make them yet if it were needed. He ate them at one mouthful, and . . . and then he drank a glass of wine, and then he said, 'It is delicious.' Thou rememberest how he would say that?

"I was jealous, jealous! The moment of thy marriage approached. There were only two weeks more. I became crazy. I said to myself: 'He shall not marry Suzanne, no, I will not have it! It is I whom he will marry when I am grown up. I shall never find any one whom I love so much.' But one night, ten days before the contract, thou tookest a walk with him in front of the château by moonlight . . . and there . . . under the fir, under the great fir . . . he kissed thee . . . kissed . . . holding thee in his two arms . . . so long. Thou rememberest, is it not so? It was probably the first time . . . yes . . . Thou wast so pale when thou camest back to the *salon*.

"I had seen you two; I was there, in the shrubbery. I was angry! If I could I should have killed you both!

"I said to myself: 'He shall not marry Suzanne, never! He shall marry no one. I should be too unhappy.' And all of a sudden I began to hate him dreadfully.

"Then, dost thou know what I did? Listen. I had seen the gardener making little balls to kill strange dogs. He pounded up a bottle with a stone and put the powdered glass in a little ball of meat.

"I took a little medicine bottle that mamma had; I broke it small with a hammer, and I hid the glass in my pocket. It was a shining powder . . . The next day, as soon as you had made the little cakes . . . I split them with a knife and I put in the glass . . . He ate three of them . . . I too, I ate one . . . I threw the other six into the pond. The two swans died three days after . . . Dost thou remember? Oh, say nothing . . . listen, listen. I, I alone did not die . . . but I have always been sick. Listen . . . He died— thou knowest well . . . listen . . . that, that is nothing. It is afterwards, later . . . always . . . the worst . . . listen.

"My life, all my life . . . what torture! I said to myself: 'I will never leave my sister. And at the hour of death I will tell her all . . .' There! And ever since, I have always thought of that moment when I should tell thee all. Now it is come. It is terrible. Oh . . . Big Sister!

"I have always thought, morning and evening, by night and by day, 'Some time I must tell her that . . .' I waited . . . What agony! . . . It is done. Say nothing. Now I am afraid . . . am afraid . . . Oh, I am afraid. If I am going to see him again, soon, when I am dead. See him again . . . think of it! The first! Before thou! I shall not dare. I must . . . I am going to die . . . I want you to forgive me. I want it . . . I cannot go off to meet him without that. Oh, tell her to forgive me, Monsieur le Curé, tell her . . . I implore you to do it. I cannot die without that . . ."

She was silent, and remained panting, always scratching the sheet with her withered nails.

Suzanne had hidden her face in her hands, and did not move. She was thinking of him whom she might have loved so long! What a good life they should have lived together! She saw him once again in that vanished by-gone time, in that old past which was put out forever. The beloved dead—how they tear your hearts! Oh, that kiss, his only kiss! She had hidden it in her soul. And after it nothing, nothing more her whole life long!

All of a sudden the priest stood straight, and, with strong vibrant voice, he cried:
"Mademoiselle Suzanne, your sister is dying!"

Then Suzanne, opening her hands, showed her face soaked with tears, and throwing herself upon her sister, she kissed her with all her might, stammering:
"I forgive thee, I forgive thee, Little One."

ON THE JOURNEY

Since leaving Cannes the carriage had been full; and being all acquainted, we conversed together. As we passed Tarascon some one said, "It is here the murders happen." And we began to talk of that mysterious assassin who has never been caught, and who from time to time during the last two years has offered up to himself some traveller's life. Every one hazarded suppositions, every one gave his opinion; the women looked shiveringly at the sombre night behind the panes, fearing to see the head of a man show suddenly in the doorway. And we began to tell dreadful stories of terrible adventures, of some tête-à-tête with a madman in an express, of hours passed opposite suspicious-looking persons, quite alone.

All the men had stories "on their honor," all had intimidated, knocked down, and choked some malefactor in surprising circumstances, and with admirable boldness and presence of mind. A physician, who passed each winter in the South, wished in his turn to tell a tale.

"I," said he, "have never had the chance to try my courage in an affair of that sort; but I knew a woman, one of my patients, who is now dead, to whom there happened the strangest thing in the world, and also the most mysterious and the most affecting.

"She was a Russian, the Countess Marie Baranow, a very great lady, of exquisite beauty. You all know how beautiful the Russian women are, or at least how beautiful they seem to us, with their fine nostrils, with their delicate mouths, with their eyes of an indefinable color—a sort of blue-gray, set close together—and with that grace of theirs which is cold and a little hard. They have about them something naughty and seductive, something haughty and gentle, something tender and severe, which is altogether charming to a Frenchman. It is perhaps, however, only the difference of race and type which makes me see so much.

"For several years her doctor had perceived that she was threatened with a malady of the chest, and had been trying to induce her to go to the South of France; but she obstinately refused to leave St. Petersburg. Finally, last autumn, the physician gave her up as lost, and so informed her husband, who at once ordered his wife to leave for Mentone.

"She took the train, alone in her carriage, her servants occupying another compartment. She leaned against the door-way, a little sad, watching the country and the passing villages, feeling herself in life so lonely, so abandoned, without children, almost without relatives, with a husband whose love was dead, and who, not coming with her, had just thrown her off to the end of the world as he would send to the hospital a valet who was sick.

"At each station her body-servant Ivan came to ask if anything was wanted by his mistress. He was an old servant, blindly devoted, ready to carry out any order which she might give.

"The night fell, the train rolled onward at full speed. She was much unstrung, she could not sleep. Suddenly she took the idea of counting the money which her husband had given her at the last moment, in French gold. She opened her little bag, and emptied the shining flood of metal upon her knees.

But all of a sudden a breath of cold air struck her in the face. She raised her head in surprise. The door had just swung open. The Countess Marie, in desperation, brusquely threw a shawl over the money which was spread upon her knees, and waited. Some seconds passed, then a man appeared, bareheaded, wounded in the hand, panting, in evening dress. He shut the door again, sat down, looked at his neighbor with glittering eyes, then wrapped a handkerchief round his wrist, from which the blood was flowing.

"The young countess felt herself grow weak with fright. This man had certainly seen her counting her gold, and he was come to murder and to rob.

"He kept staring at her, breathless, his face convulsed, ready, no doubt, to make a spring.

"He said, suddenly:

" 'Have no fear, madame!'

"She answered nothing, being unable to open her mouth, hearing her heart beat and her ears hum.

"He continued:

" 'I am not a criminal, madame.'

"She still said nothing, but, in a brusque movement which she made, her knees came close together, and her gold began to flow down upon the carpet as water flows from a gutter.

"The man, surprised, looked at this rivulet of metal, and suddenly he stooped to pick up the money.

"She rose in a mad fright, casting all her treasure to the ground, and she ran to the door to throw herself out upon the track. But he understood what she was about to do, rushed forward, caught her in his arms, made her sit down by force, and holding her wrists: 'Listen, madame, I am not a criminal, and the proof is that I am going to pick up this money and give it back to you. But I am a lost man, a dead man, unless you help me to cross the frontier. I cannot tell you more. In one hour we shall be at the last Russian station; in one hour and twenty minutes we shall pass the boundary of the empire. If you do not rescue me I am lost. And yet, madame, I have neither killed nor stolen, nor done anything against my honor. I swear it to you. I cannot tell you more.'

"And getting down on his knees, he picked up the gold, looking even for the last pieces, which had rolled far under the seats. Then, when the little leather bag was once more full, he returned it to his neighbor without adding a word, and again he went and sat in the other corner of the carriage.

"They no longer stirred, either one or the other. She remained motionless and dumb, still fainting with terror, then little by little growing more at ease. As for him, he did not make a gesture, a movement; he sat straight, his eyes fastened before him, very pale, as though he had been dead. From time to time she looked at him suddenly, and as suddenly looked away. He was a man about thirty, very handsome, with every appearance of a gentleman.

"The train ran through the darkness, cast rending cries across the night, sometimes slackened its pace, then went off again at full speed. But suddenly it slowed, whistled several times, and stopped.

"Ivan appeared at the door to get his orders.

"The Countess Marie, with a trembling voice, considered her strange companion for the last time, then said to her servant, with a brusque voice:

" 'Ivan, you are to return to the count; I have no more need of you.'

"The man, speechless, opened his enormous eyes. He stammered:

"'But—Barine!'

"She continued:

"'No, you are not to come; I have changed my mind. I desire that you remain in Russia. Here is money to return. Give me your cap and your cloak.'

"The old servant, quite bewildered, bared his head and held out his cloak. He always obeyed without reply, being well accustomed to the sudden wishes and the irresistible caprices of his masters. And he withdrew, the tears in his eyes.

"The train went on, running towards the frontier.

"Then the Countess Marie said to her neighbor:

"'These things are for you, monsieur; you are Ivan, my servant. I add only one condition to what I do: it is that you shall never speak to me, that you shall not address me a single word, either to thank me or for any purpose whatever.'

"The unknown bowed without uttering a word.

"Very soon they came to a stop once more, and officials in uniform visited the train. The countess offered them her papers, and pointing to the man seated at the back of the carriage:

"'My servant, Ivan. Here is his passport.'

"The train went on.

"During the whole night they remained in tête-à-tête, both silent.

"In the morning, when they stopped at a German station, the unknown got down; then, standing straight in the door-way:

"'Forgive my breaking my promise, madame; but I have deprived you of your servant, it is right that I should fill his place. Have you need of anything?'

"She answered, coldly:

"'Go and find my maid.'

"He went to do so, then disappeared.

"When she got out of the carriage at some restaurant or other, she perceived him from a distance looking at her. They reached Mentone."

The doctor was silent a second, then resumed:

"One day, as I was receiving my patients in my office, I saw enter a tall young fellow, who said to me:

"'Doctor, I come to ask news about the Countess Marie Baranow. I am, although she does not know me, a friend of her husband.'

"I replied:

"'She is doomed. She will never go back to Russia.'

"And the man suddenly commenced to sob, then he got up and went out, reeling like a drunkard.

"The same night I told the countess that a stranger had come to inquire from me about her health. She seemed moved, and told me all the story which I have just told you. She added:

"'That man, whom I do not know at all, now follows me like my shadow, I meet him every time I go out; he looks at me after a strange fashion, but he has never spoken.'

"She reflected, then added:

"'See, I would wager he is under my windows.'

"She left her easy-chair, went to pull back the curtains, and, sure enough, she showed me the man who had come to see me, now seated there on a bench upon the promenade, his eyes lifted towards the hotel. He perceived us, rose, and went off without once turning his head.

"And from that time forward I assisted at a surprising and sorrowful thing—at the silent love of these two beings, who did not even know one another.

"He loved her with the affection of an animal who has been saved, and who is grateful and devoted unto death. He came each day to say to me: 'How is she?' understanding that I had divined the secret. And he cried when he had seen her pass each day feebler and paler.

"She said to me:

"'I have spoken but a single time to that strange man, and it seems to me as if I had known him for twenty years.'

"And when they met, she would return his bow with a grave and charming smile. I could see that she was happy—she, the abandoned, the doomed—I could see that she was happy to be loved like this, with such respect and such constancy, with such exaggerated poetry, with this devotion which was ready for all things. And notwithstanding, faithful to her mystical resolve, she wildly refused to receive him, to know his name, to speak with him. She said: 'No, no, that would spoil for me this curious friendship. We must remain strangers one to the other.'

"As for him, he also was certainly a kind of Don Quixote, because he made no attempt to approach her. He meant to keep to the end the absurd promise of never speaking, which he had made her in the railway carriage.

"Often, during her weary hours of weakness, she rose from her long chair, and went to open the curtains a little way to see if he was there, beneath her window. And when she had seen him, always motionless upon his bench, she went back and lay down with a smile upon her lips.

"She died one day about ten o'clock. As I was leaving the hotel he came up to me with a distracted face; he had already heard the news.

"'I should like to see her, for one second, in your presence,' said he.

"I took him by the arm and went back into the house.

"When he was before the couch of the dead he seized her hand and kissed it with an endless kiss, then escaped like a madman."

The doctor again was silent; then continued:

"This is certainly the strangest railway adventure that I know. It must also be said that men take sometimes the wildest freaks."

A woman murmured, half aloud:

"Those two people were not so crazy as you think. They were—they were—"

But she could not speak further, she was crying so. As we changed the conversation to calm her, we never knew what she had wished to say.

THE BEGGAR

He had known better days, despite his wretchedness and his infirmity.

At the age of fifteen he had had both legs crushed by a carriage on the high-road of Yarville. Since then he begged, dragging himself along the roads, across the farm-yards, balanced on his crutches, which had made his shoulders mount as high as his ears, so that his head seemed sunk between two mountains.

A child found in a ditch by the curé of Les Billettes, on All Souls' Eve, and baptized, for that reason, Nicolas Toussaint, he had been brought up on charity, and had remained a stranger to all instruction. It was after the village baker had given him several glasses of brandy to drink that he had lamed his legs. And since then, a laughing-stock and a vagabond, he knew of nothing else to do but to hold out his hand and beg.

Formerly the Baroness d'Avary had allowed him to sleep in a kind of niche full of straw beside the hen-house at the farm, which was under the castle walls; and on bad days he was sure of finding a piece of bread and a glass of cider in her kitchen. He also often got a few sous thrown him by the old lady from the top of her steps or from the windows of her chamber. Now she was dead.

In the villages they hardly gave him anything: they knew him too well; this forty years they were tired of seeing him carrying about his ragged and deformed body from hut to hut on his two wooden joints. And yet he did not want to go away, because he knew of nothing else on earth but this corner of a country, these three of four hamlets in which he had dragged about his miserable life. He had set a boundary to his beggarhood, and he would never have thought of passing the limits which he was not accustomed to cross.

He did not know whether the world extended very much farther beyond the trees which had always bounded his sight. He never asked himself that. And when the peasants, tired of always meeting him on the borders of their fields or along their ditches, cried at him, "Why don't you go to the other villages instead of forever limping around here?" he made no reply, and went off seized with a vague fear of the unknown, with the fear of a poor wretch who was confusedly afraid of a thousand things—of strange faces, of insults, of the suspicious looks of people who did not know him, and of the gendarmes, who went two by two along the roads, making him dive by instinct into the thickets or behind the piles of pounded stones.

When he saw their uniforms at a distance, glittering in the sun, he suddenly discovered marvellous agility, the agility of a monster who tries to gain some hiding place. He dropped from his crutches, let himself fall as a rag falls, rolled himself into a ball, and became quite small, invisible, as close to the ground as a hare in her form, confounding his brown tatters with the earth.

He had, however, never had any trouble with the gendarmes. And yet he carried this in his blood, as though he had inherited this terror and this trick from his parents, whom he had never known.

He had no place of refuge, no roof of his own, no covering, no shelter. He slept anywhere in summer, and in winter he slipped under the barns or into the stables with remarkable address. He always stole out early in the morning before he should be perceived. He knew all the holes by which buildings could be entered. And the use of his crutches having given his arms extraordinary strength, he sometimes climbed by sheer force of his wrists up into the haylofts, where he would remain four or five days without moving, provided in going his round he had secured food enough to keep him alive.

In the midst of men, he lived like the beasts of the woods, knowing no one, loving no one, exciting only among the peasants a sort of indifferent disdain and resigned hostility. They nicknamed him "The Bell," because indeed he did swing between his two stakes of wood like a bell between its supports.

For two days he had eaten nothing. They no longer gave him anything at all. They meant to be rid of him at last. The peasant wives, on their door-steps, cried afar off, seeing him coming:

"Will you begone, you rascal! I gave you a piece of bread only three days ago!"

Carrying about his ragged and deformed body from hut to hut on his two wooden joints.

And he pivoted upon his props, and took himself off to the next house, where they received him after the same fashion.

From one door to the other the women declared:

"All very well, but we can't feed this sluggard all the year round."

And yet every day the sluggard had need to eat.

He had gone the round in Saint Hilaire, Yarville, and Les Billettes without getting a centime or an old crust. His last hope was at Tournolles; but he must go two leagues on the high-road, and he felt himself too exhausted to drag himself farther, having a stomach as empty as his pocket.

Nevertheless, he set himself to walking.

It was in December. A cold wind ran on the fields and whistled through the bare branches. And the clouds galloped across the low and sombre sky, hastening one knows not whither. The cripple went slowly, lifting his supports from their place one after the other with a painful effort, wedging himself up on his one remaining twisted leg, which was terminated by a club-foot shod with a clout.

From time to time he sat down on the edge of the ditch and rested several minutes. Hunger threw a confused and heavy distress into his soul. He had only one thought: "to eat," but how he did not know.

For three hours he toiled over the long road; then, when he perceived the trees of the village, he hastened his steps.

The first peasant whom he met, and of whom he asked alms, replied to him:

"So here you are again, you old rogue! Sha'n't we ever be rid of you?"

And "The Bell" went on. From door to door they used him roughly, they sent him away without giving him anything. He continued his round, notwithstanding, patient and obstinate. He did not receive a sou.

Then he visited the farm-houses, reeling over the ground soft with rain, so weak that he could hardly lift his sticks. Everywhere they hunted him off. It was one of those cold, sad days when hearts are shut, when minds grow angry, when the soul is sombre, when the hand does not open to succor or to give.

When he had made the tour of all the houses which he knew, he went and threw himself down in the corner of a dry ditch beside the farm-yard of Maître Chiquet. He "unhooked" himself, as people said, to express the manner in which he let himself fall from his high crutches, making them slip from under his arms. And he remained for a long time motionless, tortured by hunger, but too much of an animal to really penetrate the depths of his unfathomable misery.

He awaited, he knew not what, with that vague sense of expectation which ever persists within us. He waited in the corner of that farm-yard under the icy wind, for the mysterious help which we always hope from heaven or from men, without asking ourselves how or why, or through whom it is to come. A flock of black chickens passed by, searching their subsistence in the earth, the nourisher of all. At every instant, with one stroke of the beak, they picked up a grain or an invisible insect, then continued their slow and steady search.

"The Bell" regarded them without thinking of anything at all; then, rather in his stomach than in his brain, there came to him a feeling rather than an idea that one of these creatures broiled over a fire of dead wood would be good to eat.

The suspicion that he was about to commit a theft did not occur to him. He took a stone which lay within reach of his hand, and being adroit, he threw it and fairly killed the chicken which was nearest by. The creature fell upon its side, moving its wings. The others fled away, balanced upon their slender feet. And "The Bell," climbing his crutches once more, set off to pick up his game with movements like those of the chickens.

Just as he arrived beside the little black body stained with blood about its head, he received a terrible blow in the back which made him drop his sticks and sent him rolling ten paces before them. And Maître Chiquet, in a rage, precipitating himself upon the marauder, thrashed him soundly, pounding with fist and knee all over the body of the defenceless cripple, like a madman, or like a peasant who has been robbed.

The farm servants arrived in their turn, and, with their master, fell to beating the beggar. Then, when they were tired, they picked him up and carried him off, and shut him up in the wood-house while they went to fetch the gendarmes.

"The Bell," half-dead, bleeding, and torn with hunger, remained lying on the ground. Evening came, then night, then daybreak. All this time he had eaten nothing.

Towards mid-day the gendarmes appeared and opened the door with great precaution, expecting a resistance, since Maître Chiquet made out that he had been attacked by the beggar, and had only defended himself with the greatest difficulty.

The corporal cried:

"Come, get up!"

But "The Bell" could no longer move; he tried, indeed, to hoist himself upon his sticks, but he did not succeed. They thought it was a feint, a trick, or the ugly temper of a malefactor, and the two armed men, seizing him roughly, planted him by force upon his crutches.

Fear had taken hold of him, the fear which the game has before the hunter, which the mouse has in presence of the cat. By super-human efforts he managed to remain upright.

"Forward!" said the corporal. He walked. All the people of the farm were there to see him off. The women shook their fists; the men jeered and insulted him: he was caught at last! a good riddance.

He departed between his two guardians. He found enough energy of desperation to drag himself along till evening. He was brutalized, not even knowing what was happening to him, too much frightened to understand.

The people whom they met stopped to see him go by, and the peasants murmured:

"It is some robber!"

They arrived, towards night, at the capital of the district. He had never come as far as that. He did not even figure to himself what was going on, nor what might be about to happen. All these terrible and unexpected things, these shapes of unknown people, and these strange houses, struck him with consternation.

He did not utter a word, having nothing to say, for he no longer understood anything. Moreover, since for so many years he had conversed with no one, he had almost lost the use of his tongue; and his thoughts also were too confused to formulate themselves in speech.

They shut him up in the town jail. The gendarmes did not think of his needing food, and they left him till the next day.

But when they came to examine him, early in the morning, they found him dead, upon the ground. What a surprise!

A GHOST

We were talking of Processes of Sequestration, apropos of a recent law-case. It was towards the end of a friendly evening, in an ancient mansion in the Rue de Grenelle, and each one had his story, his story which he affirmed to be true.

Then the old Marquis de la Tour-Samuel, who was eighty-two years old, rose, and went and leaned upon the mantel-piece. He said, with a voice which shook a little:

"I too, I know a strange story, so strange that it has simply possessed my life. It is fifty-six years since that adventure happened, yet not a month passes without my seeing it all again in dreams. That day has left a mark, an imprint of fear, stamped on me, do you understand? Yes, for ten minutes I suffered such horrible terror that from that hour to this a sort of constant dread has rested on my soul. Unexpected noises make me tremble all over; objects which in the shades of evening I do not well distinguish cause me a mad desire to escape. The fact is, I am afraid of the night.

"No! I admit I should never have confessed this before arriving at my present age. But I can say what I like now. When a man is eighty-two years old it is permitted him to be afraid of imaginary dangers. And in the face of real ones I have never drawn back, *mesdames*.

"The affair so disturbed my spirit, and produced in me so profound, so mysterious, so dreadful a sense of trouble, that I have never even told it. I have kept it in the intimate recesses of my heart, in that corner where we hide our bitter and our shameful secrets, and all those unspeakable stories of weaknesses which we have committed but which we cannot confess.

"I shall tell you the tale exactly as it happened, without trying to explain it. Certainly it can be explained—unless we assume that for an hour I was mad. But no, I was not mad, and I will give you the proof of it. Imagine what you like. Here are the plain facts:

"It was in the month of July, 1827. I found myself in garrison at Rouen.

"One day, as I was taking a walk upon the quay, I met a man whom I thought I recognized, although I did not remember exactly who he might be. I instinctively made a motion to stop. The stranger noticed the gesture, looked at me, and fell into my arms.

"It was a friend of my youth whom I had once loved dearly. The five years since I had seen him seemed to have aged him fifty. His hair was quite white; and when he walked he stooped as if exhausted. He understood my surprise, and told me about his life. He had been broken by a terrible sorrow.

"He had fallen madly in love with a very young girl, and he had married her with a kind of joyful ecstasy. But after one single year of superhuman happiness, she had suddenly died of a trouble at the heart, slain, no doubt, by love itself.

"He had left his château the very day of the funeral, and had come to reside in his hôtel at Rouen. He was now living there, solitary and desperate, preyed on by anguish, and so miserable that his only thought was suicide.

"'Now that I've found you again,' said he, 'I shall ask you to do me a great service. It is to go out to the château and bring me some papers of which I stand in urgent need. They are in the secretary in my room, in *our* room. I cannot intrust this commission to an inferior, or to a man of business, because I desire impenetrable discretion and absolute silence. And as to myself, I would not go back to that house for anything in the world.

"'I will give you the key of that chamber, which I closed myself when I went away. And I will give you the key of the secretary. Besides that, you shall have a line from me to my gardener, which will make you free of the château. But come and breakfast with me to-morrow, and we can talk about all that.'

"I promised to do him this service. It was indeed a mere excursion for me, since his estate lay only about five leagues from Rouen, and I could get there on horseback in an hour.

"I was with him at ten o'clock the next morning. We breakfasted alone together; yet he did not say twenty words. He begged me to forgive him for his silence. The thought of the visit which I was about to make to that chamber where his happiness lay dead, overwhelmed him completely, said he to me. And for a fact, he did seem strangely agitated and preoccupied, as if a mysterious struggle were passing in his soul.

"Finally, however, he explained to me exactly what I must do. It was quite simple. I must secure two packages of letters and a bundle of papers which were shut up in the first drawer on the right of the desk of which I had the key. He added:

" 'I don't need to ask you not to look at them.'

"I was almost wounded by this, and I told him so a little hotly. He stammered:

" 'Forgive me, I suffer so much.'

"And he fell to weeping.

"I left him about one o'clock, to accomplish my mission.

"It was brilliant weather, and I trotted fast across the fields, listening to the songs of the larks and the regular ring of my sabre on my boot.

"Next I entered the forest and walked my horse. Branches of trees caressed my face; and sometimes I would catch a leaf in my teeth, and chew it eagerly, in one of those ecstasies at being alive which fill you, one knows not why, with a tumultuous and almost elusive happiness, with a kind of intoxication of strength.

"On approaching the château, I looked in my pocket for the note which I had for the gardener, and I found to my astonishment that it was sealed. I was so surprised and irritated that I came near returning at once, without acquitting myself of my errand. But I reflected that I should in that case display a susceptibility which would be in bad taste. And, moreover, in his trouble, my friend might have sealed the note unconsciously.

"The manor looked as though it had been deserted these twenty years. How the gate, which was open and rotten, held up, was hard to tell. Grass covered the walks. You no longer made out the borders of the lawn.

"At the noise which I made by kicking a shutter with my foot, an old man came out of a side door and seemed stupefied at the sight. I leaped to the ground and delivered my letter. He read it, read it again, turned it around, looked at me askance, put the paper in his pocket, and remarked:

" 'Well! What do you want?'

"I answered, sharply:

" 'You ought to know, since you have received the orders of your master in that letter. I want to enter the château.'

"He seemed overwhelmed. He said:

"'So, you are going into . . . into his room?'

"I began to grow impatient.

"'*Parbleu!* But do you mean to put me through an examination, my good man?'

"He stammered:

"'No . . . monsieur . . . only . . . it has not been opened since . . . since the . . . death. If you will wait five minutes, I will go . . . go and see whether . . .'

"I interrupted him, angrily:

"'Come, come! Are you playing with me? You know you can't get in. I have the key.'

"He had nothing more to say.

"'Well, monsieur, I will show you the way.'

"'Show me the staircase, and leave me alone. I shall find the room well enough without you.'

"'But . . . monsieur . . . but . . .'

"This time I went fairly into a rage:

"'Be quiet! do you hear? Or you will have to reckon with me.'

"I pushed him violently aside, and I penetrated into the house.

"First I crossed the kitchen, then two little rooms inhabited by the fellow and his wife. I next passed into a great hall, I climbed the stairs, and I recognized the door as indicated by my friend.

"I opened it without trouble, and entered.

"The room was so dark that at first I hardly made out anything. I paused, struck by that mouldy and lifeless odor so peculiar to apartments which are uninhabited and condemned, and, as you might say, dead. Then, little by little, my eyes became accustomed to the gloom, and I saw, clearly enough, a great apartment all in disorder; the bed without sheets, yet with its mattress and its pillows, one of which bore the deep impress of an elbow or a head, as if some one had just lain on it.

"The chairs seemed all in confusion. I noticed that a door (into a closet, no doubt) had remained half open.

"I went first to the window to let in some light, and I opened it; but the iron fastenings of the outside shutter were so rusty that I could not make them yield.

"I even tried to break them with my sabre, but without success. And as I was growing angry at these useless efforts, and as my eyes had at last perfectly accustomed themselves to the darkness, I gave up the hope of seeing more clearly, and I went to the desk.

"I seated myself in an arm-chair, lowered the shelf and opened the indicated drawer. It was full to the top. I needed only three packets, which I knew how to tell. And I set myself to looking.

"I was straining my eyes to decipher the inscriptions, when behind me I thought I heard a slight rustle. I paid no heed to it, thinking that a current of air had made some of the hangings stir. But, in a minute, another almost imperceptible movement caused a singular, unpleasant little shiver to pass over my skin. It was so stupid to be even in the least degree nervous that I would not turn round, being ashamed for myself in my own presence. I had then just discovered the second of the bundles which I wanted. And now, just as I lit upon the third, the breath of a great and painful sigh against my shoulder caused me to give one mad leap two yards away. In my start I had turned quite round, with my hand upon my sabre, and if I had not felt it by my side I should certainly have run like a coward.

"A tall woman dressed in white stood looking at me from behind the arm-chair in which, a second before, I had been sitting.

"Such a shudder ran through my limbs that I almost fell backward! Oh, no one who has not felt it can understand a dreadful yet foolish fear like that. The soul fairly melts away; your are conscious of a heart no longer; the whole body becomes as lax as a sponge; and you would say that everything within you was falling to pieces.

"I do not believe in ghosts at all.—Well, I tell you that at that moment I grew faint under the hideous fear of the dead. And from the irresistible anguish caused by supernatural terrors I suffered, oh, I suffered in a few seconds more than I have done all the rest of my life.

"If she had not spoken I should perhaps have died! But she did speak; she spoke in a sweet and dolorous voice which made my nerves quiver. I should not venture to say that I became master of myself and that I recovered my reason. No. I was so frightened that I no longer knew what I was doing; but a kind of personal dignity which I have in me, and also a little professional pride, enabled me to keep up an honorable countenance almost in spite of myself. I posed for my own benefit, and for hers, no doubt—for hers, woman or spectre, whatever she might be. I analyzed all this later, because, I assure you, that at the instant of the apparition I did not do much thinking. I was afraid.

"She said:

"'Oh, monsieur, you can do me a great service!'"

"I tried to answer, but it was simply impossible for me to utter a word. A vague sound issued from my throat.

"She continued:

"'Will you do it? You can save me, cure me. I suffer dreadfully. I suffer, oh, I suffer!'

"And she sat down gently in my arm-chair. She looked at me:

"'Will you do it?'

"I made the sign 'yes' with my head, for my voice was gone.

"Then she held out to me a tortoise-shell comb and she murmured:

"'Comb my hair; oh, comb my hair! That will cure me. They must comb my hair. Look at my head. How I suffer! And my hair, how it hurts me!'

"Her hair, which was loose and long and very black (as it seemed to me), hung down over the arm-chair's back and touched the ground.

"Why did I do that? Why, all shivering, did I receive the comb? And why did I take into my hands that long hair, which gave my skin a feeling of atrocious cold, as if I were touching serpents? I do not know.

"That feeling still clings about my fingers. And when I think of it I tremble.

"I combed her. I handled, I know not how, that icy hair. I twisted it. I bound it and unbound it. I plaited it as we plait a horse's mane. She sighed, bent her head, seemed happy.

"Suddenly she said to me, 'I thank you!' caught the comb out of my hands, and fled through the half-open door which I had noticed.

"For several seconds after I was left alone, I experienced that wild trouble of the soul which one feels after a nightmare from which one has just awakened. Then at last I recovered my senses; I ran to the window, and I broke the shutters open with violent blows.

"A flood of daylight entered. I rushed upon the door by which she had disappeared. I found it shut and immovable.

"Then a fever of flight seized on me, a panic, a real panic such as overcomes an army. I caught up roughly the three packets of letters from the open desk; I crossed the room at a run; I took the steps of the staircase four at a time; I found myself outside, I don't know how; and, perceiving my horse ten paces off, I mounted him with one leap and went off at full gallop.

"I did not pause till I was before the door of my lodgings in Rouen. Throwing the reins to my orderly, I escaped to my room, where I locked myself in to think.

"And then for an hour I kept anxiously asking whether I had not been the sport of some hallucination. I had certainly had one of those incomprehensible nervous shocks, one of those affections of the brain which dwarf the miracles to which the supernatural owes its power.

"And I had almost come to believe it was a delusion, an error of my senses, when I drew near the window, and my eyes lit by chance upon my breast. My dolman was covered with long woman's hairs which had rolled themselves around the buttons!

"I took them one by one and I threw them out of the window, with trembling in my fingers.

"Then I called my orderly. I felt too much moved, too much troubled, to go near my friend that day. And I wished also to ponder carefully what I should say to him about all this.

"I had the letters taken to his house. He gave the soldier a receipt. He asked many questions about me, and my soldier told him that I was unwell; that I had had a sunstroke—something. He seemed uneasy.

"I went to him the next day, early in the morning, having resolved to tell him the truth. He had gone out the evening before, and had not come back.

"I returned in the course of the day. They had seen nothing of him. I waited a week. He did not reappear. Then I informed the police. They searched for him everywhere without discovering a trace of his passing or his final retreat.

"A minute inspection of the abandoned château was instituted. Nothing suspicious was discovered.

"No sign that a woman had been hidden there revealed itself.

"The inquiry proving fruitless, the search was interrupted.

"And for fifty-six years I have learned nothing. I know nothing more."

LITTLE SOLDIER

EVERY Sunday, as soon as they were free, the two little soldiers set off.

On leaving the barracks they turned to the right; went through Courbevoie with long quick steps, as though they were on a march; then, having left the houses behind them, they followed at a calmer gait the bare and dusty high-road which leads to Bezons.

Being little and thin, they looked quite lost in their coats, which were too big and too long. The sleeves hung down over their hands, and they were much bothered by their enormous red breeches, which compelled them to walk wide. Under their stiff, high shakos their faces seemed like mere nothings—two poor, hollow Breton faces, simple in an almost animal simplicity, and with blue eyes which were gentle and calm.

During the walk they never spoke. They went straight on, each with the same idea in his head as the other. It stood them in place of conversation, for the fact is that just inside the little wood near Les Champioux they had found a place which reminded them of their own country, and it was only there that they felt happy.

When they came under the trees where the roads from Colombes and from Chatou cross, they would take off their heavy shakos and wipe their foreheads.

They always stopped a little while on the Bezons bridge to look at the Seine. They would remain there two or three minutes, bent double, leaning on the parapet. Or sometimes they would gaze out over the great basin of Argenteuil, where the skiffs might be seen scudding, with their white, slanted sails, recalling perhaps the look of the Breton water, the harbor of Vannes, near which they lived, and the fishing-boats standing out across the Morbihan to the open sea.

As soon as they had crossed the Seine they bought their provisions from the sausage merchant, the baker, and the seller of

the wine of the country. A piece of blood-pudding, four sous'
worth of bread, and a litre of "petit bleu" constituted the provisions, which they carried off in their handkerchiefs. But after
they had left this village they now went very slowly forward, and
they began to talk.

In front of them a barren plain strewn with clumps of trees
led to the wood, to the little wood which had seemed to them to
resemble the one at Kermarivan. Grain-fields and hay-fields bordered the narrow path, which lost itself in this young greenness of
the crops, and Jean Kerderen would always say to Luc le Ganidec:

"It looks like it does near Plounivon."

"Yes; exactly."

They went onward, side by side, their spirits suffused with
vague memories of their own country, filled with awakened images
—images as naïve as the pictures on the colored broadsheets which
you buy for a penny. And they kept recognizing, as it were, now
a corner of a field, a hedge, a bit of moorland, now a cross-roads,
now a granite cross.

Then, too, they would always stop beside a certain landmark,
a great stone, because it looked something like the cromlech at
Locneuven.

On arriving at the first clump of trees Luc le Ganidec every
Sunday cut a switch, a hazel switch, and began gently to peel off
the bark, thinking meanwhile of the folk there at home.

Jean Kerderen carried the provisions.

From time to time Luc mentioned a name, or recalled some
doing of their childhood in a few brief words, which caused long
thoughts. And their own country, their dear distant country,
repossessed them little by little, seized upon them, and sent to them
from afar her shapes, her sounds, her well-known prospects, her
odors—odors of the green lands where the salt sea-air was
blowing.

They were no longer conscious of the exhalations of the Parisian stables on which the earth of the *banlieue* fattens, but of the
perfume of the flowering broom, which the salt breeze of the open
sea plucks and bears away. And the sails of the boats, appearing
above the river-banks, seemed to them the sails of the coasting
vessels perceived beyond the great plain which extended from
their homes to the very margin of the waves.

They went with short steps, Luc le Ganidec and Jean Kerderen, content and sad, haunted by a sweet melancholy, by the

They always stopped a little while on the Bezons bridge.

lingering penetrating sorrow of a caged animal who remembers.

And by the time that Luc had stripped the slender wand of its bark they arrived at the corner of the wood where every Sunday they took breakfast.

They found the two bricks which they had hidden in the thicket, and they kindled a little fire of branches, over which to roast their blood-pudding at the end of a bayonet.

And when they had breakfasted, eaten their bread to the last crumb, and drunk their wine to the last drop, they remained seated side by side upon the grass, saying nothing, their eyes on the distance, their eyelids drooping, their fingers crossed as at mass, their red legs stretched out beside the poppies of the field. And the leather of their shakos and the brass of their buttons glittered in the ardent sun, and made the larks, which sang and hovered above their heads, stop short.

About mid-day they began to turn their eyes from time to time in the direction of the village of Bezons, because the girl with the cow was coming.

She passed by them every Sunday on her way to milk and change the position of her cow—the only cow of this district which ever went out of the stable to grass. It pastured in a narrow field along the edge of wood a little farther on.

They soon perceived the girl, the only human being who came walking across the land. And they felt themselves rejoiced by the brilliant reflections thrown off by her tin milk-pail under the flame of the sun. They never talked about her. They were simply glad to see her, without understanding why.

She was a great strong wench with red hair, burned by the heat of sunny days, a great sturdy wench of the environs of Paris.

Once, finding them again seated in the same place, she said:

"Good-morning. You two are always here, aren't you?"

Luc le Ganidec, the bolder, stammered:

"Yes; we come to rest."

That was all. But the next Sunday she laughed on seeing them, laughed with a protecting benevolence and a feminine keenness which knew well enough that they were bashful. And she asked:

"What are you doing there? Are you trying to see the grass grow?"

Luc was cheered up by this, and smiled likewise: "Maybe we are."

She continued: *"Hein!* That's pretty slow work."
He answered, still laughing: "Well, yes, it is."
She went on, but coming back with a milk-pail full of milk, she stopped again before them, and said:
"Would you like a drop? It will taste like home."
With her instinctive feeling that they were of the same peasant race as she, being herself also far away from home perhaps, she had divined and touched the spot.
They were both touched. Then, with some difficulty, she managed to make a little milk run into the neck of the glass bottle in which they carried their wine. And Luc drank first, with little swallows, stopping every minute to see whether he had drunk more than his half. Then he handed the bottle to Jean.
She stood upright before them, her hands on her hips, her pail on the ground at her feet, glad at the pleasure which she had given.
Then she departed, shouting: "Allons! Adieu! Till next Sunday!"
And as long as they could see her at all, they followed with their eyes her tall silhouette, which withdrew itself, growing smaller and smaller, and seeming to sink into the verdure of the fields.

When they were leaving the barracks the week after, Jean said to Luc:
"Oughtn't we to buy her something good?"
And they remained in great embarrassment before the problem of the choice of a delicacy for the girl with the cow.
Luc was of the opinion that a bit of tripe would be the best, but Jean preferred some *berlingots,* because he was fond of sweets. His choice fairly made him enthusiastic, and they bought at a grocer's two sous' worth of candies white and red.
They ate their breakfast more rapidly than usual, being nervous with expectation.
Jean saw her the first. "There she is!" said he. Luc continued: "Yes, there she is."
While yet some distance off she laughed at seeing them. She cried:
"Is everything going as you like it?"
They answered together:
"Are you getting on all right?"

Then she conversed, talked to them of simple things in which they felt an interest—of the weather, of the crops, and of her master.

They were afraid to offer her their candies, which were slowly melting away in Jean's pocket.

At last Luc grew bold, and murmured:

"We have brought you something."

She demanded, "What is it? Tell me!"

Then Jean, blushing up to his ears, managed to get at the little paper cornucopia, and held it out.

She began to eat the little pieces of sugar, rolling them from one cheek to the other. And they made lumps beneath her flesh. The two soldiers, seated before her, regarded her with emotion and delight.

Then she went to milk her cow, and once more gave them some milk on coming back.

They thought of her all the week; several times they even spoke of her. The next Sunday she sat down with them for a little longer talk; and all three, seated side by side, their eyes lost in the distance, clasping their knees with their hands, told the small doings, the minute details of their life in the villages where they had been born, while over there the cow, seeing that the milk-maid had stopped on her way, stretched out towards her its heavy head with the dripping nostrils, and gave a long low to call her back.

Soon the girl consented to eat a bit of bread with them and drink a mouthful of wine. She often brought them plums in her pocket; for the season of plums had come. Her presence sharpened the wits of the two little Breton soldiers, and they chattered like two birds.

But, one Tuesday, Luc le Ganidec asked for leave—a thing which had never happened before—and he did not return until ten o'clock at night.

Jean racked his brains uneasily for a reason for his comrade's going out in this way.

The next Thursday Luc, having borrowed ten sous from his bed-fellow, again asked and obtained permission to leave the barracks for several hours.

And when he set off with Jean on their Sunday walk his manner was very queer, quite restless and quite changed. Kerderen did not understand, but he vaguely suspected something without divining what it could be.

They did not say a word to one another until they reached their usual stopping-place, where, from their constant sitting in the same spot, the grass was quite worn away. And they ate their breakfast slowly. Neither of them felt hungry.

Before long the girl appeared. As on every Sunday, they watched her coming. When she was quite near, Luc rose and made two steps forward. She put her milk-pail on the ground, and kissed him. She kissed him passionately, throwing her arms about his neck, without noticing Jean, without remembering that he was there, without even seeing him.

And he sat there desperate, he the poor Jean, so desperate that he did not understand, his soul quite overwhelmed, his heart bursting, not yet expressing it all to himself.

Then the girl seated herself beside Luc, and they began to chatter.

Jean did not look at them: he now divined why his comrade had gone out twice during the week, and he felt within him a burning grief, a kind of a wound, that sense of rending which is caused by a treason.

Luc and the girl got up together to go and change the position of the cow.

Jean followed them with his eyes. He saw them departing side by side. The red breeches of his comrade made a bright spot on the road. It was Luc who picked up the mallet and hammered down the stake to which they tied the beast.

The girl stooped to milk her, while he stroked the cow's sharp spine with a careless hand. Then they left the milk-pail on the grass, and they went deep into the wood.

Jean saw nothing more but the wall of leaves where they had entered; and he felt himself so troubled that if he had tried to rise he would certainly have fallen.

He sat motionless, stupefied by astonishment and suffering, by a suffering which was simple but which was deep. He wanted to cry, to run away, to hide himself, never to see anybody any more.

Suddenly he saw them issuing from the thicket. They returned gently, holding each other's hands, as in the villages do those who are promised. It was Luc who carried the pail.

They kissed one another again before they separated, and the girl went off after having thrown Jean a friendly "good-evening" and a smile which was full of meaning. To-day she no longer thought of offering him any milk.

The two little soldiers sat side by side, motionless as usual, silent and calm, their placid faces betraying nothing of all which troubled their hearts. The sun fell on them. Sometimes the cow lowed, looking at them from afar.

At their usual hour they rose to go back.

Luc cut a switch. Jean carried the empty bottle. He returned it to the wine-seller at Bezons. Then they sallied out upon the bridge, and, as they did every Sunday, they stopped several minutes in the middle to watch the water flowing.

Jean leaned, leaned more and more, over the iron railing, as though he saw in the current something which attracted him. Luc said: "Are you trying to drink?" Just as he uttered the last word Jean's head over-balanced his body, his legs described a circle in the air, and the little blue and red soldier fell in a lump, entered the water, and disappeared.

Luc, his throat paralyzed with anguish, tried in vain to shout. Farther down he saw something stir; then the head of his comrade rose to the surface of the river and re-entered it as soon.

Farther still he again perceived a hand, a single hand which issued from the stream and then plunged back. That was all.

The barge-men who ran up did not find the body that day.

Luc returned alone to the barracks, running, his head filled with madness; and he told of the accident, with tears in his eyes and voice, blowing his nose again and again: "He leaned over . . . he . . . he leaned over . . . so far . . . so far that his head turned a somersault; and . . . and . . . so he fell . . . he fell. . . ."

He was strangled by emotion, he could say no more. If he had only known!

THE WRECK

It was yesterday, the 31st of December.

I had just finished breakfast with my old friend Georges Garin when the servant brought him in a letter covered with seals and foreign stamps.

Georges said:

"Will you excuse me?"

"Certainly."

And so he began to read eight pages in a large English handwriting, crossed in every direction. He read them slowly, with serious attention and the interest which we only pay to things which touch our hearts.

Then he put the letter on a corner of the mantel-piece, and he said:

"That was a curious story! I've never told you about it, I think. And yet it was a sentimental adventure, and it happened to me. Aha! That was a strange New-year's Day indeed! It must be twenty years ago, since I was then thirty, and am now fifty years old.

"I was then an inspector in the Maritime Insurance Company, of which I am now director. I had arranged to pass the fête of New-year's in Paris—since it is a convention to make that day a fête—when I received a letter from the manager, directing me to proceed at once to the island of Ré, where a three-masted vessel from Saint-Nazaire, insured by us, had just gone ashore. It was then eight o'clock in the morning. I arrived at the office at ten, to get my instructions; and the same evening I took the express, which put me down in La Rochelle the next day, December 31st.

"I had two hours to spare before going aboard the boat for Ré. So I made a tour in the town. It is certainly a fantastic city, La Rochelle, with a strong character of its own—streets tangled like a labyrinth, sidewalks running under endless arcaded galleries like those of the Rue de Rivoli, but low, mysterious, built as if to form a fit scene for conspirators, and making an ancient and striking background for those old-time wars, the savage heroic wars of religion. It is indeed the typical old Huguenot city, grave, discreet, with no fine art to show, with no wonderful monuments, such as make Rouen so grand; but it is remarkable for its severe, somewhat cunning look; it is a city of obstinate fighters, a city where fanaticisms might well blossom, where the faith of the Calvinists became exalted, and where the plot of the 'Four Sergeants' was born.

"After I had wandered for some time about these curious streets, I went aboard the black, fat-bellied little steamboat which was to take me to the island of Ré. It was called the *Jean Guiton*. It started with angry puffings, passed between the two old towers which guard the harbor, crossed the roadstead, and issued from the mole built by Richelieu, the great stones of which are visible at the water's edge, enclosing the town like an immense necklace. Then the steamboat turned off to the right.

"It was one of those sad days which oppress and crush the thoughts, tighten the heart, and extinguish in us all energy and force—a gray, icy day, salted by a heavy mist which was as wet as rain, as cold as frost, as bad to breathe as the lye of a washtub.

"Under this low ceiling of sinister fog, the shallow, yellow, sandy sea of all gradually receding coasts lay without a wrinkle, without a movement, without life, a sea of turbid water, of greasy water, of stagnant water. The *Jean Guiton* passed over it, rolling a little from habit, dividing the smooth, opaque sheet, and leaving behind a few waves, a little chopping sea, a few undulations, which were soon calm.

"I began to talk to the captain, a little man almost without feet, as round as his boat and balancing himself like it. I wanted some details about the disaster on which I was to deliver a report. A great square-rigged three-master, the *Marie Joseph,* of Saint-Nazaire, had gone ashore one night in a hurricane on the sands of the island of Ré.

"The owner wrote us that the storm had thrown the ship so far ashore that it was impossible to float her, and that they had had to remove everything which could be detached, with the utmost possible haste. Nevertheless, I was to examine the situation of the wreck, estimate what must have been her condition before the disaster, and decide whether all efforts had been used to get her afloat. I came as an agent of the company in order to bear contradictory testimony, if necessary, at the trial.

"On receipt of my report, the manager would take what measures he judged necessary to protect our interests.

"The captain of the *Jean Guiton* knew all about the affair, having been summoned with his boat to assist in the attempts at salvage.

"He told me the story of the disaster, and very simply too. The *Marie Joseph,* driven by a furious gale, lost her bearings completely in the night, and steering by chance over a heavy foaming sea—'a milk-soup sea,' said the captain—had gone ashore on those immense banks of sand which make the coasts of this region seem like limitless Saharas at hours when the tide is low.

"While talking I looked around and ahead. Between the ocean and the lowering sky lay a free space where the eye could see far. We were following a coast. I asked:

" 'Is that the island of Ré?'

" 'Yes, sir.'

"And suddenly the captain stretched his right hand out before us, pointed to something almost invisible in the middle of the sea, and said:

" 'There's your ship!'

" 'The *Marie Joseph?*'

" 'Yes.'

"I was stupefied. This black, almost imperceptible speck, which I should have taken for a rock, seemed at least three miles from land.

"I continued:

" 'But, captain, there must be a hundred fathoms of water in that place?'

"He began to laugh.

" 'A hundred fathoms, my boy! Well, I should say about two!'

"He was from Bordeaux. He continued:

" 'It's now 9.40, just high tide. Go down along the beach with your hands in your pockets after you've had your lunch at the Hôtel du Dauphin, and I'll engage that at ten minutes to three, or three o'clock, you'll reach the wreck without wetting your feet, and have from an hour and three-quarters to two hours aboard of her; but not more, or you'll be caught. The farther the sea goes out the faster it comes back. This coast is as flat as a bed-bug! But start away at ten minutes to five, as I tell you, and at half-past seven you will be aboard of the *Jean Guiton* again, which will put you down this same evening on the quay at La Rochelle.'

"I thanked the captain, and I went and sat down in the bow of the steamer to get a good look at the little city of Saint-Martin, which we were now rapidly approaching.

"It was just like all the miniature seaports which serve as the capitals of the barren islands scattered along the coast—a large fishing village, one foot on sea and one on shore, living on fish and wild-fowl, vegetables and shell-fish, radishes and mussels. The island is very low, and little cultivated, yet seems to be filled with people. However, I did not penetrate into the interior.

"After having breakfasted, I climbed across a little promontory, and then, as the tide was rapidly falling, I started out across the sands towards a kind of black rock which I could just perceive above the surface of the water, far out, far down.

I walked quickly over the yellow plain; it was elastic, like flesh, and seemed to sweat beneath my foot. The sea had been there very lately; now I perceived it at a distance, escaping out of sight, and I no longer distinguished the line which separated the sands from ocean. I felt as though I were assisting at a gigantic supernatural work of enchantment. The Atlantic had just now been before me, then it had disappeared into the strand, just as does scenery through a trap; and I now walked in the midst of a desert. Only the feeling, the breath of the salt-water, remained in me. I perceived the smell of the wrack, the smell of the wide sea, the rough good smell of sea-coasts. I walked fast; I was no longer cold; I looked at the stranded wreck, which grew in size as I approached, and came now to resemble an enormous shipwrecked whale.

"It seemed fairly to rise out of the ground, and on that great, flat, yellow stretch of sand assumed surprising proportions. After an hour's walk I reached it at last. Bulging out and crushed, it lay upon its side, which, like the flanks of an animal, displayed its broken bones, its bones of tarry wood pierced with enormous bolts. The sand had already invaded it, entered it by all the crannies, and held it, possessed it, refused to let it go. It seemed to have taken root in it. The bow had entered deep into this soft, treacherous beach; while the stern, high in air, seemed to cast at heaven, like a cry of despairing appeal, the two white words on the black planking, *Marie Joseph*.

"I scaled this carcass of a ship by the lowest side; then, having reached the deck, I went below. The daylight, which entered by the stove-in hatches and the cracks in the sides, showed sadly enough a species of long sombre cellar full of demolished woodwork. There was nothing here but the sand, which served as foot-soil in this cavern of planks.

"I began to take some notes about the condition of the ship. I was seated on a broken empty cask, writing by the light of a great crack, through which I could perceive the boundless stretch of the strand. A strange shivering of cold and loneliness ran over my skin from time to time; and I would often stop writing for a moment to listen to the vague mysterious noises in the wreck; the noise of the crabs scratching the planking with their hooked claws; the noise of a thousand little creatures of the sea already installed on this dead body; the noise, so gentle and regular, of the worms, who, with their gimlet-like, grinding sound, gnaw ceaselessly at the old timber, which they hollow out and devour.

"And, suddenly, very near me, I heard human voices; I started as though I had seen a ghost. For a second I really thought I was about to see two drowned men rise from the sinister depths of the hold, who would tell me about their death. At any rate, it did not take me long to swing myself on deck with all the strength I had in my wrists. There, below the bow, I found standing a tall gentleman with three young girls, or rather a tall Englishman with three young misses. Certainly, they were a good deal more frightened at seeing this sudden apparition on the abandoned three-master than I had been at seeing them. The youngest girl turned round and ran; the two others caught their father by the arms; as for him, he opened his mouth—that was sole sign of his emotion which he showed.

"Then, after several seconds, he spoke:

"'Aw, *môsieu,* are you the owner of this ship?'

"'I am.'

"'May I go over it?'

"'You may.'

"Then he uttered a long sentence in English, in which I only distinguished the word 'gracious,' repeated several times.

"As he was looking for a place to climb up, I showed him the best, and lent him a hand. He ascended. Then we helped up the three little girls, who were now quite reassured. They were charming, especially the oldest, a blonde of eighteen, fresh as a flower, and so dainty, so pretty! Ah yes! the pretty English-women have indeed the look of tender fruits of the sea. One would have said of this one that she had just risen from the sands and that her hair had kept their tint. They all, with their exquisite freshness, make you think of the delicate colors of pink sea-shells, and of shining pearls rare and mysterious, hidden in the unknown deeps of ocean.

"She spoke French a little better than her father, and she acted as interpreter. I must tell all about the shipwreck, to the very least details, and I romanced as though I had been present at the catastrophe. Then the whole family descended into the interior of the wreck. As soon as they had penetrated into this sombre, dim-lit gallery, they uttered cries of astonishment and admiration. And suddenly the father and his three daughters were holding sketch-books in their hands, which they had doubtless carried hidden somewhere in their heavy weather-proof clothes, and were all beginning at once to make pencil sketches of this melancholy and fantastic place.

"They had seated themselves side by side on a projecting beam, and the four sketchbooks on the eight knees were being rapidly covered with little black lines which were intended to represent the half-opened stomach of the *Marie Joseph*.

"I continued to inspect the skeleton of the ship, and the oldest girl talked to me while she worked.

"I learned that they were spending the winter at Biarritz, and that they had come to the island of Ré expressly to see the stranded three-master. They had none of the usual English arrogance; they were simple honest hearts of that class of constant wanderers with which England covers the globe. The father was long and thin, with a red face framed in white whiskers, and looking like a living sandwich, a slice of ham cut in the shape of a head, placed between two wedges of hair. The daughters, like little wading-birds in embryo, had long legs and were also thin—except the oldest. All three were pretty, especially the tallest.

"She had such a droll way of speaking, of talking, of laughing, of understanding and of not understanding, of raising her eyes to ask a question (eyes blue as deep water), of stopping her drawing a moment to make a guess at what you meant, of returning once more to work, of saying 'yes' or 'no'—that I could have listened and looked indefinitely.

"Suddenly she murmured:

"'I hear a little movement on this boat.'

"I lent an ear; and I immediately distinguished a low, steady, curious sound. What was it? I rose and looked out of the crack, and I uttered a violent cry. The sea had come back; it was about to surround us!

"We were on deck in an instant. It was too late. The water circled us about, and was running towards the coast with prodigious swiftness. No, it did not run, it slipped, it crawled, it grew longer, like a kind of great limitless blot. The water on the sands was barely a few centimetres deep; but the rising flood had gone so far that we no longer saw the flying line of its edge.

"The Englishman wanted to jump. I held him back. Flight was impossible because of the deep places which we had been obliged to go round on our way out, and into which we should certainly fall on our return.

"There was a minute of horrible anguish in our hearts. Then the little English girl began to smile, and murmured:

"'So we too are shipwrecked.'

"I tried to laugh; but fear caught me tight, a fear which was cowardly and horrid and base and mean, like the tide. All the dangers which we ran appeared to me at once. I wanted to shriek 'Help!' But to whom?

"The two younger girls were cowering against their father, who regarded, with a look of consternation, the measureless sea which hedged us round about.

"And the night fell as swiftly as the ocean rose—a lowering, wet, icy night.

"I said:

"'There's nothing to do but to stay on the ship.'

"The Englishman answered:

"'Oh yes!'

"And we waited there a quarter of an hour, half an hour, indeed I don't know how long, watching that yellow water which grew deep about us, whirled round and round, and seemed to bubble, and seemed to sport over the reconquest of the vast seastrand.

"One of the little girls was cold, and we suddenly thought of going below to shelter ourselves from the light but freezing wind which blew upon us and pricked our skins.

"I leaned over the hatchway. The ship was full of water. So we must cower against the stern planking, which shielded us a little.

"The shades were now inwrapping us, and we remained pressed close to one another, surrounded by the darkness and by the sea. I felt trembling against my shoulder the shoulder of the little English girl, whose teeth chattered from time to time. But I also felt the gentle warmth of her body through her ulster, and that warmth was as delicious to me as a kiss. We no longer spoke; we sat motionless, mute, cowering down like animals in a ditch when a hurricane is raging. And, nevertheless, despite the night, despite the terrible and increasing danger, I began to feel happy that I was there, to be glad of the cold and the peril, to rejoice in the long hours of darkness and anguish which I must pass on this plank so near this dainty and pretty little girl.

"I asked myself, 'Why this strange sensation of well-being and of joy?'

Why! Does one know? Because she was there? Who? She, a little unknown English girl? I did not love her, I did not even know her. And for all that I was touched and conquered. I should have liked to save her, to sacrifice myself for her, to commit a thousand follies! Strange thing! How does it happen that the presence of a woman overwhelms us so? Is it the power of her grace, which infolds us? Is it the seduction in her beauty and youth, which intoxicates us like wine?

"Is it not rather, as it were, the touch of Love, of Love the Mysterious, who seeks constantly to unite two beings, who tries his strength the instant he has put a man and a woman face to face, and who suffuses them with a confused, secret, profound emotion just as you water the earth to make the flowers spring?

"But the silence of the shades and of the sky became dreadful, because we could thus hear vaguely about us an infinite low roar, the dull rumor of the rising sea, and the monotonous dashing of the current against the ship.

"Suddenly I heard the sound of sobs. The youngest of the little girls was crying. Then her father tried to console her, and they began to talk in their own tongue, which I did not understand. I guessed that he was reassuring her, and that she was still afraid.

"I asked my neighbor:

" 'You are not too cold, are you, miss?'

" 'Oh yes. I am very cold.'

"I wanted to give her my cloak; she refused it. But I had taken it off, and I covered her with it against her will. In the short struggle her hand touched mine. It made a charming shiver run over my body.

"For some minutes the air had been growing brisker, the dashing of the water stronger against the flanks of the ship. I raised myself; a great gust blew in my face. The wind was rising!

"The Englishman perceived this at the same time that I did, and said, simply:

" 'That is bad for us, this—'

"Of course it was bad, it was certain death if any breakers, however feeble, should attack and shake the wreck, which was already so loose and broken that the first big sea would carry it off in a jelly.

"So our anguish increased from second to second as the squalls grew stronger and stronger. Now the sea broke a little, and I saw in the darkness white lines appearing and disappearing, which were lines of foam; while each wave struck the *Marie Joseph,* and shook her with a short quiver which rose to our hearts.

"The English girl was trembling; I felt her shiver against me. And I had a wild desire to take her in my arms.

"Down there before and behind us, to left and right, light-houses were shining along the shore—light-houses white and yellow and red, revolving like the enormous eyes of giants who were staring at us, watching us, waiting eagerly for us to disappear. One of them in especial irritated me. It went out every thirty seconds and it lit up again as soon. It was indeed an eye, that one, with its lid ceaselessly lowered over its fiery look.

"From time to time the Englishman struck a match to see the hour; then he put his watch back in his pocket. Suddenly he said to me, over the heads of his daughters, with a gravity which was supreme:

" 'I wish you a Happy New Year, *môsieu.'*

"It was midnight. I held out my hand, which he pressed. Then he said something in English, and suddenly he and his daughters began to sing 'God save the Queen,' which rose through the black and silent air and vanished into space.

"At first I felt a desire to laugh; then I was seized by a strong, fantastic emotion.

"It was something sinister and superb, this chant of the shipwrecked, the condemned, something like a prayer, and also like something grander, something comparable to the ancient sublime *'Ave Cæsar morituri te salutamus.'*

"When they had finished I asked my neighbor to sing a ballad alone, a legend, anything she liked, to make us forget our terrors. She consented, and immediately her clear young voice flew off into the night. She sang something which was doubtless sad, because the notes were long drawn out, issued slowly from her mouth, and hovered, like wounded birds, above the waves.

"The sea was rising now and beating upon our wreck. As for me, I thought only of that voice. And I thought also of the sirens. If a ship had passed near by us what would the sailors have said? My troubled spirit lost itself in the dream! A siren! Was she not really a siren, this daughter of the sea, who had kept me on this worm-eaten ship, and who was soon about to go down with me deep into the waters?

"But suddenly we were all five rolling on the deck, because the *Marie Joseph* had sunk on her right side. The English girl had fallen across me, and before I knew what I was doing, thinking that my last moment was come, I had caught her in my arms and kissed her cheek, her temple, and her hair.

"The ship did not move again, and we, we also, remained motionless.

"The father said, 'Kate!' The one whom I was holding answered, 'Yes,' and made a movement to free herself. And at that moment I should have wished the ship to split in two and let me fall with her into the sea.

"The Englishman continued:

"'A little rocking; it's nothing. I have my three daughters safe.'

"Not having seen the oldest, he had thought she was lost overboard!

"I rose slowly, and suddenly I made out a light on the sea quite near us. I shouted; they answered. It was a boat sent out in search of us by the hotel-keeper, who had guessed at our imprudence.

"We were saved. I was in despair. They picked us up off our raft, and they brought us back to Saint-Martin.

"The Englishman was now rubbing his hands and murmuring: " 'A good supper! A good supper!'

"We did sup. I was not gay. I regretted the *Marie Joseph*.

"We had to separate, the next day, after much handshaking and many promises to write. They departed for Biarritz. I was not far from following them.

"I was hard hit; I wanted to ask this little girl in marriage. If we had passed eight days together, I should have done so! How weak and incomprehensible a man sometimes is!

"Two years passed without my hearing a word from them. Then I received a letter from New York. She was married, and wrote to tell me. And since then we write to each other every year, on New-year's Day. She tells me about her life, talks of her children, her sisters, never of her husband! Why? Ah! why? . . . And as for me, I only talk of the *Marie Joseph*. That was perhaps the only woman I have ever loved. No—that I ever should have loved. . . . Ah, well! who can tell? Facts master you. . . . And then—and then—all passes. . . . She must be old now; I should not know her. . . . Ah! she of the by-gone time, she of the wreck! What a creature! . . . Divine! She writes me her hair is white. . . . That caused me terrible pain. . . . Ah! her yellow hair. . . . No, *my* English girl exists no longer. . . . They are sad, such things as that!

ONE EVENING

THE steamboat *Kleber* had stopped, and I was enraptured with the beautiful Bay of Bougie, that spread out before us. The Kabyle Mountains were covered with forests, and in the distance the yellow sands formed a beach of powdered gold, while the sun shed its fiery rays on the white houses of the town.

The warm African breeze wafted the odor of the desert, the odor of that great, mysterious continent into which men of the northern races but rarely penetrate, into my face. For three months I had been wandering on the borders of that great, unknown world, on the outskirts of that strange world of the ostrich, the camel, the gazelle, the hippopotamus, the gorilla, the lion, the tiger, and the negro. I had seen the Arab galloping in the wind, like a waving standard, and I had slept under those brown tents, the moving habitation of those white birds of the desert, and I felt, as it were, intoxicated with light, with imagination, and with space.

But now, after this final excursion, I should have to leave, to return to France and to Paris, that city of useless chatter, of commonplace cares, and of continual handshaking, and I should bid adieu to all that I had grown to love, all that was so new to me, that I had scarcely had time to see thoroughly, and that I should so much regret.

A fleet of small boats surrounded the steamer, and, jumping into one rowed by a negro lad, I soon reached the quay near the old Saracen gate, whose gray ruins at the entrance of the Kabyle town looked like an old escutcheon of nobility. While I was standing by the side of my portmanteau, looking at the great steamer lying at anchor in the roads, and filled with admiration at that unique coast and that semicircle of hills washed by the blue waves, which were more beautiful than Naples and as fine as those of Ajaccio or of Porto, in Corsica, a heavy hand was laid on my shoulder, and on turning round I saw standing beside me a tall man with a long beard. He was dressed in white flannels and wore a straw hat, and was looking at me with his blue eyes.

"Are you not an old schoolmate of mine?" he said.

"It is very possible. What is your name?"

"Trémoulin."

"By Jove! You were in the same class as I was."

"Ah! Old fellow, I recognized you immediately."

He seemed so pleased, so happy at seeing me, that, in an outburst of friendly egotism, I shook both the hands of my former schoolfellow heartily, and felt very pleased at meeting him thus.

For four years Trémoulin had been one of my best and most intimate friends, one of those whom we are too apt to forget as soon as we leave college. In those days he had been a tall, thin fellow, whose head seemed too heavy for his body; it was a large, round head, and bent his neck sometimes to the right and sometimes to the left, looking top-heavy for the narrow-chested, long-legged collegian. Trémoulin was very clever, however, with a rare suppleness and versatility of mind, and an instinctive intuition for all literary studies, and he won nearly all the prizes in our class.

We were fully convinced at school that he would turn out a celebrated man, a poet, no doubt, for he wrote verses, and was full of ingeniously sentimental ideas. His father, who kept a chemist's shop near the Pantheon, was not supposed to be very well off, and I had lost sight of him as soon as he had taken his Bachelor's degree, and now I naturally asked him what he was doing there.

"I am a planter," he replied.

"Bah! You really plant?"

"And I gather in my harvest."

"What is it?"

"Grapes, from which I make wine."

"Is your wine-growing a success?"

"A great success."

"So much the better, old fellow."

"Were you going to the hotel?"

"Of course I was."

"Well, then, you must just come home with me instead."

"But——"

"The matter is settled."

And he said to the young negro who was watching our movements: "Take that home, Ali."

The lad put my portmanteau on his shoulder and set off, raising the dust with his black feet, while Trémoulin took my arm and led me off. First of all, he asked me about my journey and what impressions it had made on me, and, seeing how enthusiastic I was about it, he seemed to like me better than ever. He lived in an old Moorish house, with an interior courtyard, without any windows looking into the street, and commanded by a terrace, which, in its turn, commanded those of the neighboring houses, as well as the bay and the forests, the hill and the open sea, and I could not help exclaiming:

"Ah! This is what I like; the whole of the Orient lays hold of me in this place. You are indeed lucky to be living here! What nights you must spend upon that terrace! Do you sleep there?"

"Yes, in the summer. We will go up to it this evening. Are you fond of fishing?"

"What kind of fishing?"

"Fishing by torchlight."

"Yes, I am particularly fond of it."

"Very well, then, we will go after dinner, and then come back and drink sherbet on my roof."

After I had had a bath, he took me to see the charming Kabyle town, a veritable cascade of white houses toppling down to the sea, and as it grew dusk we went in, and after a delicious dinner, went down to the quay. Nothing was to be seen but the lights in the streets and the stars, those large, bright, scintillating African stars. A boat was waiting for us, and as soon as we got in, a man whose face I could not distinguish began to row, while my friend was getting ready the brazier which he would light later, and he said to me: "You know I am an expert in spearing fish; no one understands it better than I."

"Allow me to compliment you on your skill." We had rowed round a kind of mole, and now we were in a small bay full of high rocks, whose shadows looked like towers built in the water, and I suddenly perceived that the sea was phosphorescent, and as the oars moved gently, they seemed to light up, a weird moving flame, that followed in our wake, and then died out. I leaned over the side of the boat and watched it, as we glided over that glimmer in the darkness.

Where were we going to? I could not see my neighbors; in

fact, I could see nothing but the luminous ripple and the sparks of water dropping from the oars; it was hot, very hot, and the darkness seemed as hot as a furnace, and this mysterious voyage with these two men in that silent boat had a peculiar effect upon me.

Suddenly the rower stopped. Where were we? I heard a slight scratching sound close to me, and saw a hand, nothing but a hand, applying a lighted match to the iron grating fastened in the bows of the boat, which was covered with wood, as if it had been a floating funeral pyre, and which soon was blazing brightly and lighting up the boat and the two men, an old, thin, pale, wrinkled sailor, with a pocket-handkerchief tied round his head, instead of a cap, and Trémoulin, whose fair beard glistened in the light.

"Go on," he said, and the other began to row again, while Trémoulin kept throwing wood on the brazier, which burned red and brightly. I leaned over the side again and could see the bottom, and a few feet below us there was that strange country of the water, which gives life to plants and animals, just as the air of heaven does. Trémoulin, who was standing in the bows with his body bent forward, and holding the sharp-pointed trident called a spearing hook in his hand, was on the lookout, with the ardent gaze of a beast of prey watching for its spoil, and, suddenly, with a swift movement, he darted his weapon into the sea so vigorously that it secured a large fish swimming near the bottom. It was a conger eel, which managed to wriggle, half dead as it was, into a puddle of the brackish water in the boat.

Trémoulin again threw his spear, and when he pulled it up, I saw a great lump of red flesh which palpitated, moved, rolled and unrolled long, strong, soft feelers round the handle of the trident. It was an octopus, and Trémoulin opened his knife, and with a swift movement plunged it between the eyes, and killed it. And so our fishing continued, until the wood began to run short. When there was not enough left to keep up the fire, Trémoulin dipped the braziers into the sea, and we were again buried in darkness.

The old sailor began to row again, slowly and regularly, though I could not tell where the land or where the port was. By and by, however, I saw lights. We were nearing the harbor.

"Are you sleepy?" my friend said to me.

"Not in the least."

"Then we will go and have a chat on the roof."

"I shall be delighted."

Just as we got on the terrace I saw the crescent moon rising behind the mountains, and around us, the white houses, with their flat roofs, descended toward the sea, while human forms were standing or lying on them, sleeping or dreaming under the stars; whole families wrapped in long flannel garments, and resting in the calm night, after the heat of the day.

It suddenly seemed to me as if the Eastern mind were taking possession of me, the poetical and legendary spirit of a simple people with poetical minds. My head was full of the Bible and of *The Arabian Nights;* I could hear the prophets proclaiming miracles and I could see the princesses in flowing silk bloomers on the terraces of the palaces, while delicate incense burned in silver dishes, the smoke as it arose taking the form of genii. I said to Trémoulin:

"You are very fortunate to live here."

"I came here quite by accident," he replied.

"By accident?"

"Yes, accident and unhappiness brought me here."

"You have been unhappy?"

"Very unhappy."

He was standing in front of me, wrapped in his burnous, and his voice had such a mournful ring that it almost made me shiver; after a moment's silence, however, he continued:

"I will tell you what my sorrow was; perhaps it will do me good to speak about it."

"Let me hear it."

"Do you really wish it?"

"Yes."

"Very well, then. You remember me at college, a sort of poet, brought up in a chemist's shop. I dreamed of writing books, and tried it, after taking my degree, but I did not succeed. I published a volume of verse, and then a novel, and neither of them sold, and then I wrote a play, which was never acted.

"Next, I lost my heart, but I will not give you an account of my passion. Next door to my father's shop there was a tailor, who had a daughter, with whom I fell in love. She was very clever, and had obtained her diplomas for higher studies, and her mind was bright and active, quite in keeping indeed with her body. She might have been taken for fifteen, although she was two-and-twenty. She was very small, with delicate features, outlines and tints, just like some beautiful water color. Her nose, her mouth, her blue eyes, her light hair, her smile, her waist, her hands, all looked as if they were fit for a stained-glass window, and not for everyday life, but she was lively, supple, and incredibly active, and I was very much in love with her. I remember two or three walks in the Luxembourg Garden, near the Médici fountain, which were certainly the happiest hours of my life. I suppose you have known that strange condition of tender madness which causes us to think of nothing but of acts of adoration! One really becomes possessed, haunted by a woman, and nothing exists for us except herself.

"We soon became engaged, and I told her my projects for the future, of which she did not approve. She did not believe that I was either a poet, a novelist, or a dramatic author, and thought a prosperous business could afford perfect happiness. So I gave up the idea of writing books, and resigned myself to selling them, and I bought a bookseller's business at Marseilles, the owner of which had just died.

"I had three very prosperous years. We had made our shop into a sort of literary drawing-room, where all the men of letters in the town used to come and chat. They came in, as if it had been a club, and exchanged ideas on books, on poets, and especially on politics. My wife, who took a very active part in the business, enjoyed quite a reputation in the town, but, as for me, while they were all talking downstairs, I was working in my studio upstairs, which communicated with the shop by a winding staircase. I could hear their voices, their laughter, and their discussions, and sometimes I left off writing in order to listen. I kept in my own room to write a novel—which I never finished.

"The most regular frequenters of the shop were Monsieur Montina, a man of good private means, a tall, handsome man, such as one meets in the south of France, with an olive skin and dark, expressive eyes; Monsieur Barbet, a magistrate; two merchants, who were partners, Messrs. Faucil and Labarrègue, and General the Marquis de la Flèche, the head of the Royalist party, the principal man in the whole district, an old fellow of sixty-six.

"My business prospered, and I was happy, very happy. One day, however, about three o'clock, when I was out on business, as I was going through the Rue Saint-Ferréol, I suddenly saw coming out of a house a woman whose figure and appearance were so much like my wife's that I should have said to myself: 'It is she!' if I had not left her in the shop half an hour before, suffering from a headache. She was walking quickly on before me, without turning round, and, in spite of myself, I followed her, as I felt surprised and uneasy. I said to myself: 'It is she; no, it is quite impossible, as she has a sick headache. And then, what could she have to do in that house?' However, as I wished to have the matter cleared up, I hurried after her. I do not know whether she felt or guessed that I was behind her, or whether she recognized my step, but she turned round suddenly. It was she! When she saw me, she grew very red and stopped, and then, with a smile, she said: 'Oh! Here you are!' I felt choking.

" 'Yes; so you have come out? And how is your headache?'

" 'It is better, and I have been out on an errand.'

" 'Where?'

" 'To Lacaussade's, in the Rue Cassinelli, to order some pencils.'

"She looked me full in the face. She was not flushed now, but rather pale, on the contrary. Her clear, limpid eyes—ah! those women's eyes!—appeared to be full of truth, but I felt vaguely and painfully that they were full of lies. I was much more confused and embarrassed than she was herself, without venturing to suspect anything, but quite convinced that she was lying, though I did not know why, and so I merely said:

" 'You were quite right to go out, if you felt better.'

" 'Oh! yes; my head is much better.'

" 'Are you going home?'

" 'Yes, of course I am.'

"I left her, and wandered about the streets by myself. What was going on? While I was talking to her I had an intuitive feeling of her falseness, but now I could not believe it, and when I returned home to dinner I was angry at having suspected her, even for a moment.

"Have you ever been jealous? It does not matter whether you have or not, but the first drop of jealousy had fallen into my heart, and that is always like a spark of fire. I did not formulate anything, and I did not believe anything, I only knew that she had lied. You must remember that every night, after the customers and clerks had left and we were alone, we would either stroll as far as the harbor when it was fine, or remain talking in my office, if the weather was bad; and I would open my heart to her without any reserve, because I loved her. She was part of my life, the greater part, and all my happiness, and in her small hands she held my trusting, faithful heart captive.

"During the first days, those days of doubt, and before my suspicions increased and assumed a shape, I felt as depressed and chilly as one does before becoming seriously ill. I was continually cold, really cold, and could neither eat nor sleep. Why had she told me a lie? What was she doing in that house? I went there, to try and find out something, but could discover nothing. The man who rented the first floor, and who was an upholsterer, had told me all about his neighbors, but without helping me the least. A midwife lived on the second floor, a dressmaker and a manicure and chiropodist on the third, and two coachmen and their families in the attics.

"Why had she told me a lie? It would have been so easy for her to have said that she had been to the dressmaker or the chiropodist. Oh, how I longed to question them also! I did not say so, for fear that she might guess my suspicions. One thing, however, was certain: she had been into that house, and had concealed the fact from me, so there was some mystery in it. But what? At one moment I thought there might be some purpose in it, some charitable deed that she wished to hide, some information which she wished to obtain, and I found fault with myself for suspecting her. Have not all of us the right to our little innocent secrets, a kind of second, interior life, for which we are not responsible to anybody? Can a man, because he has taken a girl to be his companion through life, demand that she shall neither think nor do anything without telling him in advance, or afterward? Does the word marriage mean renouncing all liberty and independence? Was it not quite possible that she was going to the dressmaker's without telling me, or that she was going to aid the family of one of the coachmen? Or she might have thought that I would criticise her visit to the house without blaming her. She knew me thoroughly, all my slightest peculiarities, and perhaps she feared a discussion, even if she did not think that I should find fault with her. She had very pretty hands, and I ended by supposing that she was having them secretly attended to by the manicure in the house which I suspected, and that she did not tell me of it, for fear that I should think her extravagant. She was very methodical and economical, and looked after all her household duties most carefully, and no doubt she thought that she should lower herself in my eyes were she to confess that slight piece of feminine extravagance. Women have so many subtleties and innate tricks in their soul!

"But none of my reasoning reassured me. I was jealous; my suspicions were affecting me terribly; I was becoming a prey to them. I cherished secret grief and anguish; a thought as yet veiled, which I dared not uncover, for beneath it I should find a terrible doubt—— A lover! Had she not a lover? It was unlikely, impossible—and yet?

"I continually saw Montina's face before my eyes. I saw the tall, silly-looking, handsome man, with his bright hair, smiling into her face, and I said to myself: 'It is he.' I concocted a story of their intrigues. They had talked a book over together, had discussed the love adventures it contained, had found something in it that resembled them, and had turned that analogy into reality. And so I watched them, a prey to the most terrible sufferings that a man can endure. I bought shoes with rubber soles, so that I might be able to move about the house noiselessly, and I spent half my time in going up and down my little spiral staircase, in the hope of surprising them, but I always found that the clerk was with them.

"I lived in a state of continual suffering. I could no longer work nor attend to my business. When I went out, as soon as I had walked a hundred yards along the street, I said to myself: 'He is there!' When I found he was not there, I went out again, but returned almost immediately, thinking: 'He is there now!' and that went on every day.

"At night it was still worse, for I felt her by my side in bed asleep, or pretending to be asleep! Was she really sleeping? No, most likely not. Was that another lie?

"I remained motionless on my back, burning from the warmth of her body, tormented, breathing hard. Oh! how intensely I longed to get up, to get a hammer and split her head open, so as to look inside it! I knew that I should see nothing but what is to be found in every head, and I should have discovered nothing, for that would be impossible. And her eyes! When she looked at me, I felt an access of fury. I looked at her—she looked at me! Her eyes were transparent, candid—and false, false! No one could tell what she was thinking of, and I felt inclined to run pins into them, and to destroy those mirrors of falsity.

"Ah! how well I understood the Inquisition! I would have applied the torture, the boot. Speak! Confess! You will not? Then wait! And I would have strangled her by degrees to make her confess and have watched her die. Or else I would have held her fingers in the fire. Oh! how I should have enjoyed doing it! Confess! Confess! You will not? I would have held them on the coals, and when the tips were burned, she would have confessed—surely she would have confessed!"

Trémoulin was sitting up, shouting, with clenched fists. Around us, on the neighboring roofs, people awoke and sat up, aroused from their sleep. As for me, I was moved and powerfully interested, and in the darkness I could see that little woman, that little, fair, lively, artful woman, as if I had known her personally. I saw her selling her books, talking with the men whom her childish ways attracted, and in her delicate, doll-like head I could see little crafty ideas, silly ideas, the dreams of a milliner perfumed with musk, who is attracted by all heroes or romantic adventurers. I suspected her just as he did, I hated and detested her, and would willingly have burned her fingers and make her confess.

Presently he continued more calmly: "I do not know why I have told you all this, for I have never mentioned it to any one, but then I have not seen anybody or spoken to anybody for two years! And it was seething in my heart like fermenting wine. I have rid myself of it, and so much the worse for you. Well, I had made a mistake, but it was worse than I thought, much worse. Just listen. I employed the means a man always employs under such circumstances, and pretended that I was going to be away from home. Whenever I did this my wife went out to luncheon. I need not tell you how I bribed a waiter in the restaurant to which they used to go, so that I might surprise them.

"He was to open the door of their private room for me, and I arrived at the appointed time, with the fixed determination of killing them both. I could imagine the whole scene, just as if it had already occurred! I could see myself going in. A small table covered with glasses, bottles and plates separated her from Montina, and they would be so surprised when they saw me that they would not even attempt to move; and, without a word, I should bring down the loaded stick which I had in my hand on the man's head. Killed by one blow, he would fall with his head face downward on the table. Then, turning toward her, I should give her time—a few moments—to understand it all and to stretch out her arms toward me, mad with terror, before dying in her turn. Oh! I was ready, strong, determined, and pleased, madly pleased at the idea. The idea of her terrified look at the sight of my raised stick, of her hands stretched out imploringly, of her strangled cry, of her face, suddenly livid and convulsed, avenged me beforehand. I would not kill her at one blow! You will think me cruel, I dare say; but you do not know what a man suffers. To think that a woman one loves, whether she be wife or sweetheart, gives herself to another, yields herself up to him as she does to you, and receives kisses from his lips as she does from yours! It is a terrible, an atrocious thing to think of. When one feels that torture, one is ready for anything. I only wonder that more women are not murdered, for every man who has been deceived longs to commit murder, has dreamed of it in the solitude of his own room or on a lonely road, and has been haunted by the one fixed idea of satisfied vengeance.

"I arrived at the restaurant, and asked whether they were there. The waiter whom I had bribed replied: 'Yes, monsieur,' and taking me upstairs, he pointed to a door, and said: 'That is the room!' I grasped my stick, as if my fingers had been made of iron, and went in. I had chosen a most appropriate moment, for they were kissing most lovingly. But it was not Montina, it was General de la Flèche, who was sixty-six years old, and I had so fully made up my mind that I should find the other one there that I was motionless from astonishment.

"And then—and then, I really do not quite know what was in my mind, no, I really do not know. If I had found myself face to face with the other, I should have been convulsed with rage; but on seeing this old man, with a prominent stomach and flabby cheeks, I was nearly choked with disgust. She, who did not look fifteen, small and slim as she was, had given herself to this big man, who was almost paralyzed, because he was a marquis and a general, the friend and representative of dethroned kings. No, I do not know what I felt, nor what I thought. I could not have lifted my hand against this old man; it would have disgraced me! And I no longer felt inclined to kill my wife, but all women who could be guilty of such things! I was no longer jealous; I was dismayed, as if I had seen the horror of horrors!

"Let people say what they like of men, they are not so vile as that! If a man is known to have given himself up to an old woman in that fashion, people point their finger at him. The husband or lover of an old woman is more despised than a thief. We men are a decent lot, as a rule, but women, many women, are absolutely bad. They will give themselves to all men, old or young, from the most contemptible and different motives, because it is their profession, their vocation, and their function. They are the eternal, conscienceless and serene prostitutes, who give up their bodies, because they are the merchandise of love, which they sell, or give, to the old man who frequents the pavements with money in his pocket, or else for glory, to a lecherous old king, or to a celebrated and disgusting old man."

He cried aloud like a prophet of old, in a tone of wrath beneath the starry sky, and with the fury of a man in despair, he told of the glorified disgrace of all the mistresses of old kings, the respectable shame of all those virgins who marry old husbands, the tolerated shame of all those young women who accept old men's kisses with a smile.

I could see them, as he evoked their memories, from the beginning of the world, surging round us in that Eastern night, girls, beautiful girls, with vile souls, who, like the lower animals who know nothing of the age of the male, are docile to senile desires. They rose up before me the handmaids of the patriarchs who are mentioned in the Bible, Hagar, Ruth, the daughters of Lot, Abigail, Abishag, the virgin of Shunam, who reanimated David with her caresses when he was dying, and the others, young, stout, white, patricians or plebeians, irresponsible females belonging to a master, and submissive slaves, whether caught by the attraction of royalty or bought as slaves!

"What did you do?" I asked.

"I went away," he replied simply. And we remained sitting side by side for a long time without speaking, only dreaming!

I have retained an impression of that evening that I can never forget. All that I saw, felt and heard, our fishing excursions, the octopus also, perhaps that harrowing story, amid those white figures on the neighboring roofs, all seemed to concur in producing a unique sensation. There is condensed in certain chance meetings, in certain inexplicable combinations of events—without its being evident on the surface—a greater amount of the secret quintessence of life than is spread over whole days of ordinary life.

THE DEVIL

The peasant and the doctor stood on opposite sides of the bed, beside the old, dying woman. She was calm and resigned and her mind quite clear as she looked at them and listened to their conversation. She was going to die, and she did not rebel at it, for her time was come, as she was ninety-two.

The July sun streamed in at the window and the open door and cast its hot flames on the uneven brown clay floor, which had been stamped down by four generations of clodhoppers. The smell of the fields came in also, driven by the sharp wind and parched by the noontide heat. The grasshoppers chirped themselves hoarse, and filled the country with their shrill noise, which was like that of the wooden toys which are sold to children at fair time.

The doctor raised his voice and said: "Honoré, you cannot leave your mother in this state; she may die at any moment." And the peasant, in great distress, replied: "But I must get in my wheat, for it has been lying on the ground a long time, and the weather is just right for it; what do you say about it, mother?" And the dying old woman, still tormented by her Norman avariciousness, replied yes with her eyes and her forehead, and thus urged her son to get in his wheat, and to leave her to die alone.

But the doctor got angry, and, stamping his foot, he said: "You are no better than a brute, do you hear, and I will not allow you to do it, do you understand? And if you must get in your wheat to-day, go and fetch Rapet's wife and make her look after your mother; I will have it, do you understand me? And if you do not obey me, I will let you die like a dog, when you are ill in your turn; do you hear?"

The peasant, a tall, thin fellow with slow movements, who was tormented by indecision, by his fear of the doctor and his fierce love of saving, hesitated, calculated, and stammered out: "How much does La Rapet charge for attending sick people?" "How should I know?" the doctor cried. "That depends upon how long she is needed. Settle it with her, by Heaven! But I want her to be here within an hour, do you hear?"

So the man decided. "I will go for her," he replied; "don't get angry, doctor." And the latter left, calling out as he went: "Be careful, be very careful, you know, for I do not joke when I am angry!" As soon as they were alone the peasant turned to his mother and said in a resigned voice: "I will go and fetch La Rapet, as the man will have it. Don't worry till I get back."

And he went out in his turn.

La Rapet, who was an old washerwoman, watched the dead and the dying of the neighborhood, and then, as soon as she had sewn her customers into that linen cloth from which they would emerge no more, she went and took up her iron to smooth out the linen of the living. Wrinkled like a last year's apple, spiteful, envious, avaricious with a phenomenal avarice, bent double, as if she had been broken in half across the loins by the constant motion of passing the iron over the linen, one might have said that she had a kind of abnormal and cynical love of a death struggle. She never spoke of anything but of the people she had seen die, of the various kinds of deaths at which she had been present, and she related with the greatest minuteness details which were always similar, just as a sportsman recounts his luck.

When Honoré Bontemps entered her cottage, he found her preparing the starch for the collars of the women villagers, and he said: "Good-evening; I hope you are pretty well, Mother Rapet?"

She turned her head round to look at him, and said: "As usual, as usual, and you?" "Oh! as for me, I am as well as I could wish, but my mother is not well." "Your mother?" "Yes, my mother!" "What is the matter with her?" "She is going to turn up her toes, that's what's the matter with her!"

The old woman took her hands out of the water and asked with sudden sympathy: "Is she as bad as all that?" "The doctor says she will not last till morning." "Then she certainly is very bad!" Honoré hesitated, for he wanted to make a few preparatory remarks before coming to his proposition; but as he could hit upon nothing, he made up his mind suddenly.

"How much will you ask to stay with her till the end? You know that I am not rich, and I cannot even afford to keep a servant girl. It is just that which has brought my poor mother to this state—too much worry and fatigue! She did the work of ten, in spite of her ninety-two years. You don't find any made of that stuff nowadays!"

La Rapet answered gravely: "There are two prices: Forty sous by day and three francs by night for the rich, and twenty sous by day and forty by night for the others. You shall pay me the twenty and forty." But the peasant reflected, for he knew his mother well. He knew how tenacious of life, how vigorous and unyielding she was, and she might last another week, in spite of the doctor's opinion; and so he said resolutely: "No, I would rather you would fix a price for the whole time until the end. I will take my chance, one way or the other. The doctor says she will die very soon. If that happens, so much the better for you, and so much the worse for her, but if she holds out till to-morrow or longer, so much the better for her and so much the worse for you!"

The nurse looked at the man in astonishment, for she had never treated a death as a speculation, and she hesitated, tempted by the idea of the possible gain, but she suspected that he wanted to play her a trick. "I can say nothing until I have seen your mother," she replied.

"Then come with me and see her."

She washed her hands, and went with him immediately.

They did not speak on the road; she walked with short, hasty steps, while he strode on with his long legs, as if he were crossing a brook at every step.

The cows lying down in the fields, overcome by the heat, raised their heads heavily and lowed feebly at the two passersby, as if to ask them for some green grass.

When they got near the house, Honoré Bontemps murmured: "Suppose it is all over?" And his unconscious wish that it might be so showed itself in the sound of his voice.

But the old woman was not dead. She was lying on her back, on her wretched bed, her hands covered with a purple cotton counterpane, horribly thin, knotty hands, like the claws of strange animals, like crabs, half closed by rheumatism, fatigue and the work of nearly a century which she had accomplished.

La Rapet went up to the bed and looked at the dying woman, felt her pulse, tapped her on the chest, listened to her breathing, and asked her questions, so as to hear her speak; and then, having looked at her for some time, she went out of the room, followed by Honoré. Her decided opinion was that the old woman would not last till night. He asked: "Well?" And the sick-nurse replied: "Well, she may last two days, perhaps three. You will have to give me six francs, everything included."

"Six francs! six francs!" he shouted. "Are you out of your mind? I tell you she cannot last more than five or six hours!" And they disputed angrily for some time, but as the nurse said she must go home, as the time was going by, and as his wheat would not come to the farmyard of its own accord, he finally agreed to her terms.

"Very well, then, that is settled; six francs, including everything, until the corpse is taken out."

And he went away, with long strides, to his wheat which was lying on the ground under the hot sun which ripens the grain, while the sick-nurse went in again to the house.

She had brought some work with her, for she worked without ceasing by the side of the dead and dying, sometimes for herself, sometimes for the family which employed her as seamstress and paid her rather more in that capacity. Suddenly she asked: "Have you received the last sacraments, Mother Bontemps?"

The old peasant woman shook her head, and La Rapet, who was very devout, got up quickly: "Good heavens, is it possible? I will go and fetch the curé"; and she rushed off to the parsonage so quickly that the urchins in the street thought some accident had happened, when they saw her running.

The priest came immediately in his surplice, preceded by a choir boy who rang a bell to announce the passage of the Host through the parched and quiet country. Some men who were working at a distance took off their large hats and remained motionless until the white vestment had disappeared behind some farm buildings; the women who were making up the sheaves stood up to make the sign of the cross; the frightened black hens ran away along the ditch until they reached a well-known hole, through which they suddenly disappeared, while a foal which was tied in a meadow took fright at the sight of the surplice and began to gallop round and round, kicking out every now and then. The acolyte, in his red cassock, walked quickly, and the priest, with his head inclined toward one shoulder and his square biretta on his head, followed him, muttering some prayers; while last of all came La Rapet, bent almost double as if she wished to prostrate herself, as she walked with folded hands as they do in church.

Honoré saw them pass in the distance, and he asked: "Where is our priest going?" His man, who was more intelligent, replied: "He is taking the sacrament to your mother, of course!"

The peasant was not surprised, and said: "That may be," and went on with his work.

Mother Bontemps confessed, received absolution and communion, and the priest took his departure, leaving the two women alone in the suffocating room, while La Rapet began to look at the dying woman, and to ask herself whether it could last much longer.

The day was on the wane, and gusts of cooler air began to blow, causing a view of Epinal, which was fastened to the wall by two pins, to flap up and down; the scanty window curtains, which had formerly been white, but were now yellow and covered with fly-specks, looked as if they were going to fly off, as if they were struggling to get away, like the old woman's soul.

Lying motionless, with her eyes open, she seemed to await with indifference that death which was so near and which yet delayed its coming. Her short breathing whistled in her constricted throat. It would stop altogether soon, and there would be one woman less in the world; no one would regret her.

At nightfall Honoré returned, and when he went up to the bed and saw that his mother was still alive, he asked: "How is she?" just as he had done formerly when she had been ailing, and then he sent La Rapet away, saying to her: "To-morrow morning at five o'clock, without fail." And she replied: "To-morrow, at five o'clock."

She came at daybreak, and found Honoré eating his soup, which he had made himself before going to work, and the sick-nurse asked him: "Well, is your mother dead?" "She is rather better, on the contrary," he replied, with a sly look out of the corner of his eyes. And he went out.

La Rapet, seized with anxiety, went up to the dying woman, who remained in the same state, lethargic and impassive, with her eyes open and her hands clutching the counterpane. The nurse perceived that this might go on thus for two days, four days, eight days, and her avaricious mind was seized with fear, while she was furious at the sly fellow who had tricked her, and at the woman who would not die.

Nevertheless, she began to work, and waited, looking intently at the wrinkled face of Mother Bontemps. When Honoré returned to breakfast he seemed quite satisfied and even in a bantering humor. He was decidedly getting in his wheat under very favorable circumstances.

La Rapet was becoming exasperated; every minute now seemed to her so much time and money stolen from her. She felt a mad inclination to take this old woman, this headstrong old fool, this obstinate old wretch, and to stop that short, rapid breath, which was robbing her of her time and money, by squeezing her throat a little. But then she reflected on the danger of doing so, and other thoughts came into her head; so she went up to the bed and said: "Have you ever seen the Devil?" Mother Bontemps murmured: "No."

Then the sick-nurse began to talk and to tell her tales which were likely to terrify the weak mind of the dying woman. Some minutes before one dies the Devil appears, she said, to all who are in the death throes. He has a broom in his hand, a saucepan on his head, and he utters loud cries. When anybody sees him, all is over, and that person has only a few moments longer to live. She then enumerated all those to whom the Devil had appeared that year: Joséphine Loisel, Eulalie Ratier, Sophie Padaknau, Séraphine Grospied.

Mother Bontemps, who had at last become disturbed in mind, moved about, wrung her hands, and tried to turn her head to look toward the end of the room. Suddenly La Rapet disappeared at the foot of the bed. She took a sheet out of the cupboard and wrapped herself up in it; she put the iron saucepan on her head, so that its three short bent feet rose up like horns, and she took a broom in her right hand and a tin pail in her left, which she threw up suddenly, so that it might fall to the ground noisily.

When it came down, it certainly made a terrible noise. Then, climbing upon a chair, the nurse lifted up the curtain which hung at the bottom of the bed, and showed herself, gesticulating and uttering shrill cries into the iron saucepan which covered her face, while she menaced the old peasant woman, who was nearly dead, with her broom.

Terrified, with an insane expression on her face, the dying woman made a superhuman effort to get up and escape; she even got her shoulders and chest out of bed; then she fell back with a deep sigh. All was over, and La Rapet calmly put everything back into its place; the broom into the corner by the cupboard, the sheet inside it, the saucepan on the hearth, the pail on the floor, and the chair against the wall. Then, with professional movements, she closed the dead woman's large eyes, put a plate on the bed and poured some holy water into it, placing in it the twig of boxwood that had been nailed to the chest of drawers, and kneeling down, she fervently repeated the prayers for the dead, which she knew by heart, as a matter of business.

And when Honoré returned in the evening he found her praying, and he calculated immediately that she had made twenty sous out of him, for she had only spent three days and one night there, which made five francs altogether, instead of the six which he owed her.

THE DRUNKARD

The north wind was blowing a hurricane, driving through the sky big, black, heavy clouds from which the rain poured down on the earth with terrific violence.

A high sea was raging and dashing its huge, slow, foamy waves along the coast with the rumbling sound of thunder. The waves followed each other close, rolling in as high as mountains, scattering the foam as they broke.

The storm engulfed itself in the little valley of Yport, whistling and moaning, tearing the shingles from the roofs, smashing the shutters, knocking down the chimneys, rushing through the narrow streets in such gusts that one could walk only by holding on to the walls, and children would have been lifted up like leaves and carried over the houses into the fields.

The fishing smacks had been hauled high up on land, because at high tide the sea would sweep the beach. Several sailors, sheltered behind the curved bottoms of their boats, were watching this battle of the sky and the sea.

Then, one by one, they went away, for night was falling on the storm, wrapping in shadows the raging ocean and all the battling elements.

Just two men remained, their hands plunged deep into their pockets, bending their backs beneath the squall, their woolen caps pulled down over their ears; two big Normandy fishermen, bearded, their skin tanned through exposure, with the piercing black eyes of the sailor who looks over the horizon like a bird of prey.

One of them was saying:

"Come on, Jérémie, let's go play dominoes. It's my treat."

The other hesitated a while, tempted on one hand by the game and the thought of brandy, knowing well that, if he went to

Paumelle's, he would return home drunk; held back, on the other hand, by the idea of his wife remaining alone in the house.

He asked:

"Any one might think that you had made a bet to get me drunk every night. Say, what good is it doing you, since it's always you that's treating?"

Nevertheless he was smiling at the idea of all this brandy drunk at the expense of another. He was smiling the contented smirk of an avaricious Norman.

Mathurin, his friend, kept pulling him by the sleeve.

"Come on, Jérémie. This isn't the kind of a night to go home without anything to warm you up. What are you afraid of? Isn't your wife going to warm your bed for you?"

Jérémie answered:

"The other night I couldn't find the door—I had to be fished out of the ditch in front of the house!"

He was still laughing at this drunkard's recollection, and he was unconsciously going toward Paumelle's Café, where a light was shining in the window; he was going, pulled by Mathurin and pushed by the wind, unable to resist these combined forces.

The low room was full of sailors, smoke and noise. All these men, clad in woolens, their elbows on the tables, were shouting to make themselves heard. The more people came in, the more one had to shout in order to overcome the noise of voices and the rattling of dominoes on the marble tables.

Jérémie and Mathurin sat down in a corner and began a game, and the glasses were emptied in rapid succession into their thirsty throats.

Then they played more games and drank more glasses. Mathurin kept pouring and winking to the saloon keeper, a big, red-faced man, who chuckled as though at the thought of some fine joke; and Jérémie kept absorbing alcohol and wagging his head, giving vent to a roar of laughter and looking at his comrade with a stupid and contented expression.

All the customers were going away. Every time that one of them would open the door to leave a gust of wind would blow into the café, making the tobacco smoke swirl around, swinging the lamps at the end of their chains and making their flames flicker, and suddenly one could hear the deep booming of a breaking wave and the moaning of the wind.

Jérémie, his collar unbuttoned, was taking drunkard's poses, one leg outstretched, one arm hanging down and in the other hand holding a domino.

They were alone now with the owner, who had come up to them, interested.

He asked:

"Well, Jérémie, how goes it inside? Feel less thirsty after wetting your throat?"

Jérémie muttered:

"The more I wet it, the drier it gets inside."

The innkeeper cast a sly glance at Mathurin. He said:

"And your brother, Mathurin, where's he now?"

The sailor laughed silently:

"Don't worry; he's warm, all right."

And both of them looked toward Jérémie, who was triumphantly putting down the double six and announcing:

"Game!"

Then the owner declared:

"Well, boys, I'm goin' to bed. I will leave you the lamp and the bottle; there's twenty cents' worth in it. Lock the door when you go, Mathurin, and slip the key under the mat the way you did the other night."

Mathurin answered:

"Don't worry; it'll be all right."

Paumelle shook hands with his two customers and slowly went up the wooden stairs. For several minutes his heavy step echoed through the little house. Then a loud creaking announced that he had got into bed.

The two men continued to play. From time to time a more violent gust of wind would shake the whole house, and the two drinkers would look up, as though some one were about to enter. Then Mathurin would take the bottle and fill Jérémie's glass. But suddenly the clock over the bar struck twelve. Its hoarse clang sounded like the rattling of saucepans. Then Mathurin got up like a sailor whose watch is over.

"Come on, Jérémie, we've got to get out."

The other man rose to his feet with difficulty, got his balance by leaning on the table, reached the door and opened it while his companion was putting out the light.

As soon as they were in the street Mathurin locked the door and then said:

"Well, so long. See you to-morrow night!"
And he disappeared in the darkness.

Jérémie took a few steps, staggered, stretched out his hands, met a wall which supported him and began to stumble along. From time to time a gust of wind would sweep through the street, pushing him forward, making him run for a few steps; then, when the wind would die down, he would stop short, having lost his impetus, and once more he would begin to stagger on his unsteady drunkard's legs.

He went instinctively toward his home, just as birds go to their nests. Finally he recognized his door, and began to feel about for the keyhole and tried to put the key in it. Not finding the hole, he began to swear. Then he began to beat on the door with his fists, calling for his wife to come and help him:

"Mélina! Oh, Mélina!"

As he leaned against the door for support, it gave way and opened, and Jérémie, losing his prop, fell inside, rolling on his face into the middle of his room, and he felt something heavy pass over him and escape in the night.

He was no longer moving, dazed by fright, bewildered, fearing the devil, ghosts, all the mysterious beings of darkness, and he waited a long time without daring to move. But when he found out that nothing else was moving, a little reason returned to him, the reason of a drunkard.

Gently he sat up. Again he waited a long time, and at last, growing bolder, he called:

"Mélina!"

His wife did not answer.

Then, suddenly, a suspicion crossed his darkened mind, an indistinct, vague suspicion. He was not moving; he was sitting there in the dark, trying to gather together his scattered wits, his mind stumbling over incomplete ideas, just as his feet stumbled along.

Once more he asked:

"Who was it, Mélina? Tell me who it was. I won't hurt you!"

He waited, no voice was raised in the darkness. He was now reasoning with himself out loud.

"I'm drunk, all right! I'm drunk! And he filled me up, the dog; he did it, to stop my goin' home. I'm drunk!"

And he would continue:

"Tell me who it was, Mélina, or somethin'll happen to you."

After having waited again, he went on with the slow and obstinate logic of a drunkard:

"He's been keeping me at that loafer Paumelle's place every night, so as to stop my going home. It's some trick. Oh, you damned carrion!"

Slowly he got on his knees. A blind fury was gaining possession of him, mingling with the fumes of alcohol.

He continued:

"Tell me who it was, Mélina, or you'll get a licking—I warn you!"

He was now standing, trembling with a wild fury, as though the alcohol had set his blood on fire. He took a step, knocked against a chair, seized it, went on, reached the bed, ran his hands over it and felt the warm body of his wife.

Then, maddened, he roared:

"So! You were there, you piece of dirt, and you wouldn't answer!"

And, lifting the chair, which he was holding in his strong sailor's grip, he swung it down before him with an exasperated fury. A cry burst from the bed, an agonizing, piercing cry. Then he began to thrash around like a thresher in a barn. And soon nothing more moved. The chair was broken to pieces, but he still held one leg and beat away with it, panting.

At last he stopped to ask:

"Well, are you ready to tell me who it was?"

Mélina did not answer.

Then, tired out, stupefied from his exertion, he stretched himself out on the ground and slept.

When day came a neighbor, seeing the door open, entered. He saw Jérémie snoring on the floor, amid the broken pieces of a chair, and on the bed a pulp of flesh and blood.

Then he began to beat on the door.

THE ADOPTED SON

The two cottages stood beside each other at the foot of a hill near a little seashore resort. The two peasants labored hard on the unproductive soil to rear their little ones, and each family had four.

Before the adjoining doors a whole troop of urchins played and tumbled about from morning till night. The two eldest were six years old, and the youngest were about fifteen months; the marriages, and afterward the births, having taken place nearly simultaneously in both families.

The two mothers could hardly distinguish their own offspring among the lot, and as for the fathers, they were altogether at sea. The eight names danced in their heads; they were always getting them mixed up; and when they wished to call one child, the men often called three names before getting the right one.

The first of the two cottages, as you came up from the bathing beach, Rolleport, was occupied by the Tuvaches, who had three girls and one boy; the other house sheltered the Vallins, who had one girl and three boys.

They all subsisted frugally on soup, potatoes and fresh air. At seven o'clock in the morning, then at noon, then at six o'clock in the evening, the housewives got their broods together to give them their food, as the gooseherds collect their charges. The children were seated, according to age, before the wooden table, varnished by fifty years of use; the mouths of the youngest hardly reaching the level of the table. Before them was placed a bowl filled with bread, soaked in the water in which the potatoes had been boiled, half a cabbage and three onions; and the whole line ate until their hunger was appeased. The mother herself fed the smallest.

A small pot roast on Sunday was a feast for all; and the father on this day sat longer over the meal, repeating: "I wish we could have this every day."

One afternoon, in the month of August, a phaeton stopped suddenly in front of the cottages, and a young woman, who was driving the horses, said to the gentleman sitting at her side:

"Oh, look at all those children, Henri! How pretty they are, tumbling about in the dust, like that!"

The man did not answer, accustomed to these outbursts of admiration, which were a pain and almost a reproach to him. The young woman continued:

"I must hug them! Oh, how I should like to have one of them —that one there—the little tiny one!"

Springing down from the carriage, she ran toward the children, took one of the two youngest—a Tuvache child—and lifting it up in her arms, she kissed him passionately on his dirty cheeks, on his tousled hair daubed with earth, and on his little hands, with which he fought vigorously, to get away from the caresses which displeased him.

Then she got into the carriage again, and drove off at a lively trot. But she returned the following week, and seating herself on the ground, took the youngster in her arms, stuffed him with cakes, gave candies to all the others, and played with them like a young girl, while the husband waited patiently in the carriage.

She returned again; made the acquaintance of the parents, and reappeared every day with her pockets full of dainties and pennies.

Her name was Madame Henri d'Hubières.

One morning, on arriving, her husband alighted with her, and without stopping to talk to the children, who now knew her well, she entered the farmer's cottage.

They were busy chopping wood for the fire. They rose to their feet in surprise, brought forward chairs, and waited expectantly. Then the woman, in a broken, trembling voice, began:

"My good people, I have come to see you, because I should like—I should like to take—your little boy with me——"

The country people, too bewildered to think, did not answer.

She recovered her breath, and continued: "We are alone, my husband and I. We would keep it. Are you willing?"

The peasant woman began to understand. She asked:

"You want to take Charlot from us? Oh, no, indeed!"

Then M. d'Hubières intervened:

"My wife has not made her meaning clear. We wish to adopt him, but he will come back to see you. If he turns out well, as there is every reason to expect, he will be our heir. If we, perchance, should have children, he will share equally with them; but if he should not reward our care, we should give him, when he comes of age, a sum of twenty thousand francs, which shall be deposited immediately in his name, with a lawyer. As we have thought also of you, we should pay you, until your death, a pension of one hundred francs a month. Do you understand me?"

The woman had arisen, furious.

"You want me to sell you Charlot? Oh, no, that's not the sort of thing to ask of a mother! Oh, no! That would be an abomination!"

The man, grave and deliberate, said nothing; but approved of what his wife said by a continued nodding of his head.

Madame d'Hubières, in dismay, began to weep; turning to her husband, with a voice full of tears, the voice of a child used to having all its wishes gratified, she stammered:

"They will not do it, Henri, they will not do it."

Then he made a last attempt: "But, my friends, think of the child's future, of his happiness, of——"

The peasant woman, however, exasperated, cut him short:

"It's all considered! It's all understood! Get out of here, and don't let me see you again—the idea of wanting to take away a child like that!"

Madame d'Hubières remembered that there were two children, quite little, and she asked, through her tears, with the tenacity of a wilful and spoiled woman:

"But is the other little one not yours?"

Father Tuvache answered: "No, it is our neighbors'. You can go to them if you wish." And he went back into his house, whence resounded the indignant voice of his wife.

The Vallins were at table, slowly eating slices of bread which they parsimoniously spread with a little rancid butter on a plate between the two.

M. d'Hubières recommenced his proposals, but with more insinuations, more oratorical precautions, more shrewdness.

The two country people shook their heads, in sign of refusal, but when they learned that they were to have a hundred francs a month, they considered the matter, consulting one another by glances, much disturbed. They kept silent for a long time, tortured, hesitating. At last the woman asked: "What do you say to it, man?" In a weighty tone he said: "I say that it's not to be despised."

Madame d'Hubières, trembling with anguish, spoke of the future of their child, of his happiness, and of the money which he could give them later.

The peasant asked: "This pension of twelve hundred francs, will it be promised before a lawyer?"

M. d'Hubières responded: "Why, certainly, beginning with to-morrow."

The woman, who was thinking it over, continued:

"A hundred francs a month is not enough to pay for depriving us of the child. That child would be working in a few years; we must have a hundred and twenty francs."

Tapping her foot with impatience, Madame d'Hubières granted it at once, and, as she wished to carry off the child with her, she gave a hundred francs extra, as a present, while her husband drew up a paper. And the young woman, radiant, carried off the howling brat, as one carries away a wished-for knick-knack from a shop.

The Tuvaches, from their door, watched her departure, silent, serious, perhaps regretting their refusal.

Nothing more was heard of little Jean Vallin. The parents went to the lawyer every month to collect their hundred and twenty francs. They had quarrelled with their neighbors, because Mother Tuvache grossly insulted them, continually, repeating from door to door that one must be unnatural to sell one's child; that it was horrible, disgusting, bribery. Sometimes she would take her Charlot in her arms, ostentatiously exclaiming, as if he understood:

"I didn't sell *you*, I didn't! I didn't sell *you*, my little one! I'm not rich, but I don't sell my children!"

The Vallins lived comfortably, thanks to the pension. That was the cause of the unappeasable fury of the Tuvaches, who had remained miserably poor. Their eldest went away to serve his time in the army; Charlot alone remained to labor with his old father, to support the mother and two younger sisters.

He had reached twenty-one years when, one morning, a brilliant carriage stopped before the two cottages. A young gentleman, with a gold watch-chain, got out, giving his hand to an aged, white-haired lady. The old lady said to him: "It is there, my child, at the second house." And he entered the house of the Vallins as though at home.

The old mother was washing her aprons; the infirm father slumbered at the chimney-corner. Both raised their heads, and the young man said:

"Good-morning, papa; good-morning, mamma!"

They both stood up, frightened! In a flutter, the peasant woman dropped her soap into the water, and stammered:

"Is it you, my child? Is it you, my child?"

He took her in his arms and hugged her, repeating: "Good-morning, mamma," while the old man, all a-tremble, said, in his calm tone which he never lost: "Here you are, back again, Jean," as if he had just seen him a month ago.

When they had got to know one another again, the parents wished to take their boy out in the neighborhood, and show him. They took him to the mayor, to the deputy, to the *curé,* and to the schoolmaster.

Charlot, standing on the threshold of his cottage, watched him pass.

In the evening, at supper, he said to the old people: "You must have been stupid to let the Vallins' boy be taken."

The mother answered, obstinately: "I wouldn't sell *my* child."

The father remained silent. The son continued:

"It is unfortunate to be sacrificed like that."

Then Father Tuvache, in an angry tone, said:

"Are you going to reproach us for having kept you?" And the young man said, brutally:

"Yes, I reproach you for having been such fools. Parents like you make the misfortune of their children. You deserve that I should leave you."

The old woman wept over her plate. She moaned, as she swallowed the spoonfuls of soup, half of which she spilled: "One may kill one's self to bring up children!"

Then the boy said, roughly: "I'd rather not have been born than be what I am. When I saw the other, my heart stood still. I said to myself: 'See what I should have been now!'" He got up: "See here, I feel that I would do better not to stay here, because I would throw it up to you from morning till night, and I would make your life miserable. I'll never forgive you for that!"

The two old people were silent, downcast, in tears.

He continued: "No, the thought of that would be too much. I'd rather look for a living somewhere else."

He opened the door. A sound of voices came in at the door. The Vallins were celebrating the return of their child.

AN ARTIFICE

The old doctor sat by the fireside, talking to his fair patient who was lying on the lounge. There was nothing much the matter with her, except that she had one of those little feminine ailments from which pretty women frequently suffer—slight anæmia, a nervous attack, etc.

"No, doctor," she said; "I shall never be able to understand a woman deceiving her husband. Even allowing that she does not love him, that she pays no heed to her vows and promises, how can she give herself to another man? How can she conceal the intrigue from other people's eyes? How can it be possible to love amid lies and treason?"

The doctor smiled, and replied: "It is perfectly easy, and I can assure you that a woman does not think of all those little subtle details when she has made up her mind to go astray.

"As for dissimulation, all women have plenty of it on hand for such occasions, and the simplest of them are wonderful, and extricate themselves from the greatest dilemmas in a remarkable manner."

The young woman, however, seemed incredulous.

"No, doctor," she said; "one never thinks until after it has happened of what one ought to have done in a critical situation, and women are certainly more liable than men to lose their head on such occasions."

The doctor raised his hands. "After it has happened, you say! Now I will tell you something that happened to one of my female patients, whom I always considered an immaculate woman.

"It happened in a provincial town, and one night when I was asleep, in that deep first sleep from which it is so difficult to rouse us, it seemed to me, in my dreams, as if the bells in the town were sounding a fire alarm, and I woke up with a start. It was my own bell, which was ringing wildly, and as my footman did not seem to be answering the door, I, in turn, pulled the bell at the head of my bed, and soon I heard a banging, and steps in the silent house, and Jean came into my room, and handed me a letter which said: 'Madame Lelièvre begs Dr. Siméon to come to her immediately.'

"I thought for a few moments, and then I said to myself: 'A nervous attack, vapors; nonsense, I am too tired.' And so I replied: 'As Dr. Siméon is not at all well, he must beg Madame Lelièvre to be kind enough to call in his colleague, Monsieur Bonnet.' I put the note into an envelope and went to sleep again, but about half an hour later the street bell rang again, and Jean came to me and said: 'There is somebody downstairs; I do not quite know whether it is a man or a woman, as the individual is so wrapped up, but they wish to speak to you immediately. They say it is a matter of life and death for two people.' Whereupon I sat up in bed and told him to show the person in.

"A kind of black phantom appeared and raised her veil as soon as Jean had left the room. It was Madame Berthe Lelièvre, quite a young woman, who had been married for three years to a large merchant in the town, who was said to have married the prettiest girl in the neighborhood.

"She was terribly pale, her face was contracted as the faces of insane people are, occasionally, and her hands trembled violently. Twice she tried to speak without being able to utter a sound, but at last she stammered out: 'Come—quick—quick, doctor. Come—my—friend has just died in my bedroom.' She stopped, half suffocated with emotion, and then went on: 'My husband will—be coming home from the club very soon.'

"I jumped out of bed without even considering that I was only in my nightshirt, and dressed myself in a few moments, and then I said: 'Did you come a short time ago?' 'No,' she said, standing like a statue petrified with horror. 'It was my servant— she knows.' And then, after a short silence, she went on: 'I was there—by his side.' And she uttered a sort of cry of horror, and after a fit of choking, which made her gasp, she wept violently, and shook with spasmodic sobs for a minute or two. Then her tears suddenly ceased, as if by an internal fire, and with an air of tragic calmness, she said: 'Let us make haste.'

"I was ready, but exclaimed: 'I quite forgot to order my carriage.' 'I have one,' she said; 'it is his, which was waiting for him!' She wrapped herself up, so as to completely conceal her face, and we started.

"When she was by my side in the carriage she suddenly seized my hand, and crushing it in her delicate fingers, she said, with a shaking voice, that proceeded from a distracted heart: 'Oh! if you only knew, if you only knew what I am suffering! I loved him, I have loved him distractedly, like a madwoman, for the last six months.' 'Is any one up in your house?' I asked. 'No, nobody except Rose, who knows everything.'

"We stopped at the door, and evidently everybody was asleep. We went in without making any noise, by means of her latch-key, and walked upstairs on tiptoe. The frightened servant was sitting on the top of the stairs with a lighted candle by her side, as she was afraid to remain with the dead man, and I went into the room, which was in great disorder. Wet towels, with which they had bathed the young man's temples, were lying on the floor, by the side of a washbasin and a glass, while a strong smell of vinegar pervaded the room.

"The dead man's body was lying at full length in the middle of the room, and I went up to it, looked at it, and touched it. I opened the eyes and felt the hands, and then, turning to the two women, who were shaking as if they were freezing, I said to them: 'Help me to lift him on to the bed.' When we had laid him gently on it, I listened to his heart and put a looking-glass to his lips, and then said: 'It is all over.' It was a terrible sight!

"I looked at the man, and said: 'You ought to arrange his hair a little.' The girl went and brought her mistress' comb and brush, but as she was trembling, and pulling out his long, matted hair in doing it, Madame Lelièvre took the comb out of her hand, and arranged his hair as if she were caressing him. She parted it, brushed his beard, rolled his mustaches gently round her fingers, then, suddenly, letting go of his hair, she took the dead man's inert head in her hands and looked for a long time in despair at the dead face, which no longer could smile at her, and then, throwing herself on him, she clasped him in her arms and kissed him ardently. Her kisses fell like blows on his closed mouth and eyes, his forehead and temples; and then, putting her lips to his ear, as if he could still hear her, and as if she were about to whisper something to him, she said several times, in a heartrending voice: 'Good-by, my darling!'

"Just then the clock struck twelve, and I started up. 'Twelve o'clock!' I exclaimed. 'That is the time when the club closes. Come, madame, we have not a moment to lose!' She started up, and I said: 'We must carry him into the drawing-room.' And when we had done this, I placed him on a sofa, and lit the chandeliers, and just then the front door was opened and shut noisily. 'Rose, bring me the basin and the towels, and make the room look tidy. Make haste, for Heaven's sake! Monsieur Lelièvre is coming in.'

"I heard his steps on the stairs, and then his hands feeling along the walls. 'Come here, my dear fellow,' I said; 'we have had an accident.'

"And the astonished husband appeared in the door with a cigar in his mouth, and said: 'What is the matter? What is the meaning of this?' 'My dear friend,' I said, going up to him, 'you find us in great embarrassment. I had remained late, chatting with your wife and our friend, who had brought me in his carriage, when he suddenly fainted, and in spite of all we have done, he has remained unconscious for two hours. I did not like to call in strangers, and if you will now help me downstairs with him, I shall be able to attend to him better at his own house.'

"The husband, who was surprised, but quite unsuspicious, took off his hat, and then he took his rival, who would be quite inoffensive for the future, under the arms. I got between his two legs, as if I had been a horse between the shafts, and we went downstairs, while his wife held a light for us. When we got outside I stood the body up, so as to deceive the coachman, and said: 'Come, my friend; it is nothing; you feel better already, I expect. Pluck up your courage, and make an effort. It will soon be over.' But as I felt that he was slipping out of my hands, I gave him a slap on the shoulder, which sent him forward and made him fall into the carriage, and then I got in after him. Monsieur Lelièvre, who was rather alarmed, said to me: 'Do you think it is anything serious?' To which I replied: 'No,' with a smile, as I looked at his wife, who had put her arm into that of her husband, and was trying to see into the carriage.

"I shook hands with them and told the coachman to start, and during the whole drive the dead man kept falling against me. When we got to his house I said that he had become unconscious on the way home, and helped to carry him upstairs, where I certified that he was dead, and acted another comedy to his distracted family, and at last I got back to bed, not without swearing at lovers."

The doctor ceased, though he was still smiling, and the young woman, who was in a very nervous state, said: "Why have you told me that terrible story?"

He gave her a gallant bow, and replied:

"So that I may offer you my services if they should be needed."

MY UNCLE SOSTHENES

Some people are Freethinkers from sheer stupidity. My Uncle Sosthenes was one of these. Some people are often religious for the same reason. The very sight of a priest threw my uncle into a violent rage. He would shake his fist and make grimaces at him, and would then touch a piece of iron when the priest's back was turned, forgetting that the latter action showed a belief after all, the belief in the evil eye. Now, when beliefs are unreasonable, one should have all or none at all. I myself am a Freethinker; I revolt at all dogmas, but feel no anger toward places of worship, be they Catholic, Apostolic, Roman, Protestant, Greek, Russian, Buddhist, Jewish, or Mohammedan.

My uncle was a Freemason, and I used to declare that they are stupider than old women devotees. That is my opinion, and I maintain it; if we must have any religion at all, the old one is good enough for me.

What is their object? Mutual help to be obtained by tickling the palms of each other's hands. I see no harm in it, for they put into practice the Christian precept: "Do unto others as ye would they should do unto you." The only difference consists in the tickling, but it does not seem worth while to make such a fuss about lending a poor devil half a crown.

To all my arguments my uncle's reply used to be:

"We are raising up a religion against a religion; Free Thought will kill clericalism. Freemasonry is the stronghold of those who are demolishing all deities."

"Very well, my dear uncle," I would reply—in my heart I felt inclined to say, "You old idiot!"—"it is just that which I am blaming you for. Instead of destroying, you are organizing competition; it is only a case of lowering prices. And then, if you admitted only Freethinkers among you, I could understand it, but you admit anybody. You have a number of Catholics among you, even the leaders of the party. Pius IX is said to have been one of you before he became pope. If you call a society with such an organization a bulwark against clericalism, I think it is an extremely weak one."

"My dear boy," my uncle would reply, with a wink, "we are most to be dreaded in politics; slowly and surely we are everywhere undermining the monarchical spirit."

Then I broke out: "Yes, you are very clever! If you tell me that Freemasonry is an election machine, I will grant it. I will never deny that it is used as a machine to control candidates of all shades; if you say that it is only used to hoodwink people, to drill them to go to the polls as soldiers are sent under fire, I agree with you; if you declare that it is indispensable to all political ambitions because it changes all its members into electoral agents, I should say to you: 'That is as clear as the sun.' But when you tell me that it serves to undermine the monarchical spirit, I can only laugh in your face.

"Just consider that gigantic and secret democratic association which had Prince Napoleon for its grand master under the Empire; which has the Crown Prince for its grand master in Germany, the Czar's brother in Russia, and to which the Prince of Wales and King Humbert, and nearly all the crowned heads of the globe belong."

"You are quite right," my uncle said; "but all these persons are serving our projects without guessing it."

I felt inclined to tell him he was talking a pack of nonsense.

It was, however, indeed a sight to see my uncle when he had a Freemason to dinner.

On meeting they shook hands in a manner that was irresistibly funny; one could see that they were going through a series of secret, mysterious signs.

Then my uncle would take his friend into a corner to tell him something important, and at dinner they had a peculiar way of looking at each other, and of drinking to each other, in a manner as if to say: "We know all about it, don't we?"

And to think that there are millions on the face of the globe who are amused at such monkey tricks! I would sooner be a Jesuit.

My Uncle Sosthenes   137

Now, in our town there really was an old Jesuit who was my uncle's detestation. Every time he met him, or if he only saw him at a distance, he used to say: "Get away, you toad." And then, taking my arm, he would whisper to me:

"See here, that fellow will play me a trick some day or other, I feel sure of it."

My uncle spoke quite truly, and this was how it happened, and through my fault.

It was close on Holy Week, and my uncle made up his mind to give a dinner on Good Friday, a real dinner, with his favorite chitterlings and black puddings. I resisted as much as I could, and said:

"I shall eat meat on that day, but at home, quite by myself. Your *manifestation,* as you call it, is an idiotic idea. Why should you manifest? What does it matter to you if people do not eat any meat?"

But my uncle would not be persuaded. He asked three of his friends to dine with him at one of the best restaurants in the town, and as he was going to pay the bill I had certainly, after all, no scruples about *manifesting.*

At four o'clock we took a conspicuous place in the most frequented restaurant in the town, and my uncle ordered dinner in a loud voice for six o'clock.

We sat down punctually, and at ten o'clock we had not yet finished. Five of us had drunk eighteen bottles of choice, still wine and four of champagne. Then my uncle proposed what he was in the habit of calling "the archbishop's circuit." Each man put six small glasses in front of him, each of them filled with a different liqueur, and they had all to be emptied at one gulp, one after another, while one of the waiters counted twenty. It was very stupid, but my uncle thought it was very suitable to the occasion.

At eleven o'clock he was as drunk as a fly. So we had to take him home in a cab and put him to bed, and one could easily foresee that his anti-clerical demonstration would end in a terrible fit of indigestion.

As I was going back to my lodgings, being rather drunk myself, with a cheerful drunkenness, a Machiavellian idea struck me which satisfied all my sceptical instincts.

I arranged my necktie, put on a look of great distress, and went and rang loudly at the old Jesuit's door. As he was deaf he made me wait a longish while, but at length appeared at his window in a cotton nightcap and asked what I wanted.

I shouted out at the top of my voice:

"Make haste, reverend sir, and open the door; a poor, despairing, sick man is in need of your spiritual ministrations."

The good, kind man put on his trousers as quickly as he could, and came down without his cassock. I told him in a breathless voice that my uncle, the Freethinker, had been taken suddenly ill, and fearing it was going to be something serious, he had been seized with a sudden dread of death, and wished to see the priest and talk to him; to have his advice and comfort, to make his peace with the Church, and to confess, so as to be able to cross the dreaded threshold at peace with himself; and I added in a mocking tone:

"At any rate, he wishes it, and if it does him no good it can do him no harm."

The old Jesuit, who was startled, delighted, and almost trembling, said to me:

"Wait a moment, my son; I will come with you." But I replied: "Pardon me, reverend father, if I do not go with you; but my convictions will not allow me to do so. I even refused to come and fetch you, so I beg you not to say that you have seen me, but to declare that you had a presentiment—a sort of revelation of his illness."

The priest consented and went off quickly, knocked at my uncle's door, and was soon let in; and I saw the black cassock disappear within that stronghold of Free Thought.

I hid under a neighboring gateway to wait results. Had he been well, my uncle would have half-murdered the Jesuit, but I knew that he would scarcely be able to move an arm, and I asked myself gleefully what sort of a scene would take place between these antagonists, what disputes, what arguments, what a hubbub, and what would be the issue of the situation, which my uncle's indignation would render still more tragic?

I laughed till my sides ached, and said half aloud: "Oh, what a joke, what a joke!"

Meanwhile it was getting very cold, and I noticed that the

Jesuit stayed a long time, and I thought: "They are having an argument, I suppose."

One, two, three hours passed, and still the reverend father did not come out. What had happened? Had my uncle died in a fit when he saw him, or had he killed the cassocked gentleman? Perhaps they had mutually devoured each other? This last supposition appeared very unlikely, for I fancied that my uncle was quite incapable of swallowing a grain more nourishment at that moment.

At last the day broke.

I was very uneasy, and, not venturing to go into the house myself, went to one of my friends who lived opposite. I woke him up, explained matters to him, much to his amusement and astonishment and took possession of his window.

At nine o'clock he relieved me, and I got a little sleep. At two o'clock I, in my turn, replaced him. We were utterly astonished.

At six o'clock the Jesuit left, with a very happy and satisfied look on his face, and we saw him go away with a quiet step.

Then, timid and ashamed, I went and knocked at the door of my uncle's house; and when the servant opened it I did not dare to ask her any questions, but went upstairs without saying a word.

My uncle was lying, pale and exhausted, with weary, sorrowful eyes and heavy arms, on his bed. A little religious picture was fastened to one of the bed curtains with a pin.

"Why, uncle," I said, "in bed still? Are you not well?"

He replied in a feeble voice:

"Oh, my dear boy, I have been very ill, nearly dead."

"How was that, uncle?"

"I don't know; it was most surprising. But what is stranger still is that the Jesuit priest who has just left—you know, that excellent man whom I have made such fun of—had a divine revelation of my state, and came to see me."

I was seized with an almost uncontrollable desire to laugh, and with difficulty said: "Oh, really!"

"Yes, he came. He heard a voice telling him to get up and come to me, because I was going to die. It was a revelation."

I pretended to sneeze, so as not to burst out laughing; I felt inclined to roll on the ground with amusement.

In about a minute I managed to say indignantly: "And you

received him, uncle? You, a Freethinker, a Freemason? You did not have him thrown out of doors?"

He seemed confused, and stammered:

"Listen a moment, it is so astonishing—so astonishing and providential! He also spoke to me about my father; it seems he knew him formerly."

"Your father, uncle? But that is no reason for receiving a Jesuit."

"I know that, but I was very ill, and he looked after me most devotedly all night long. He was perfect; no doubt he saved my life; those men all know a little of medicine."

"Oh! he looked after you all night? But you said just now that he had only been gone a very short time."

"That is quite true; I kept him to breakfast after all his kindness. He had it at a table by my bedside while I drank a cup of tea."

"And he ate meat?"

My uncle looked vexed, as if I had said something very uncalled for, and then added:

"Don't joke, Gaston; such things are out of place at times. He has shown me more devotion than many a relation would have done, and I expect to have his convictions respected."

This rather upset me, but I answered, nevertheless: "Very well, uncle; and what did you do after breakfast?"

"We played a game of bezique, and then he repeated his breviary while I read a little book which he happened to have in his pocket, and which was not by any means badly written."

"A religious book, uncle?"

"Yes, and no, or, rather—no. It is the history of their missions in Central Africa, and is rather a book of travels and adventures. What these men have done is very grand."

I began to feel that matters were going badly, so I got up. "Well, good-by, uncle," I said, "I see you are going to give up Freemasonry for religion; you are a renegade."

He was still rather confused, and stammered:

"Well, but religion is a sort of Freemasonry."

"When is your Jesuit coming back?" I asked.

"I don't—I don't know exactly; to-morrow, perhaps; but it is not certain."

I went out, altogether overwhelmed.

My joke turned out very badly for me! My uncle became

thoroughly converted, and if that had been all I should not have cared so much. Clerical or Freemason, to me it is all the same; six of one and half a dozen of the other; but the worst of it is that he has just made his will—yes, made his will—and he has disinherited me in favor of that rascally Jesuit!

FATHER MILON

For a month the hot sun has been parching the fields. Nature is expanding beneath its rays; the fields are green as far as the eye can see. The big azure dome of the sky is unclouded. The farms of Normandy, scattered over the plains and surrounded by a belt of tall beeches, look, from a distance, like little woods. On closer view, after lowering the worm-eaten wooden bars, you imagine yourself in an immense garden, for all the ancient apple trees, as gnarled as the peasants themselves, are in bloom. The sweet scent of their blossoms mingles with the heavy smell of the earth and the penetrating odor of the stables. It is noon. The family is eating under the shade of a pear tree planted in front of the door; father, mother, the four children, and the help—two women and three men—are all there. All are silent. The soup is eaten and then a dish of potatoes fried with bacon is brought on.

From time to time one of the women gets up and takes a pitcher down to the cellar to fetch more cider.

The man, a big fellow about forty years old, is watching a grape vine, still bare, which is winding and twisting like a snake along the side of the house.

At last he says: "Father's vine is budding early this year. Perhaps we may get something from it."

The woman then turns round and looks, without saying a word.

This vine is planted on the spot where their father had been shot.

It was during the war of 1870. The Prussians were occupying the whole country. General Faidherbe, with the Northern Division of the army, was opposing them.

The Prussians had established their headquarters at this farm. The old farmer to whom it belonged, Father Pierre Milon, had received and quartered them to the best of his ability.

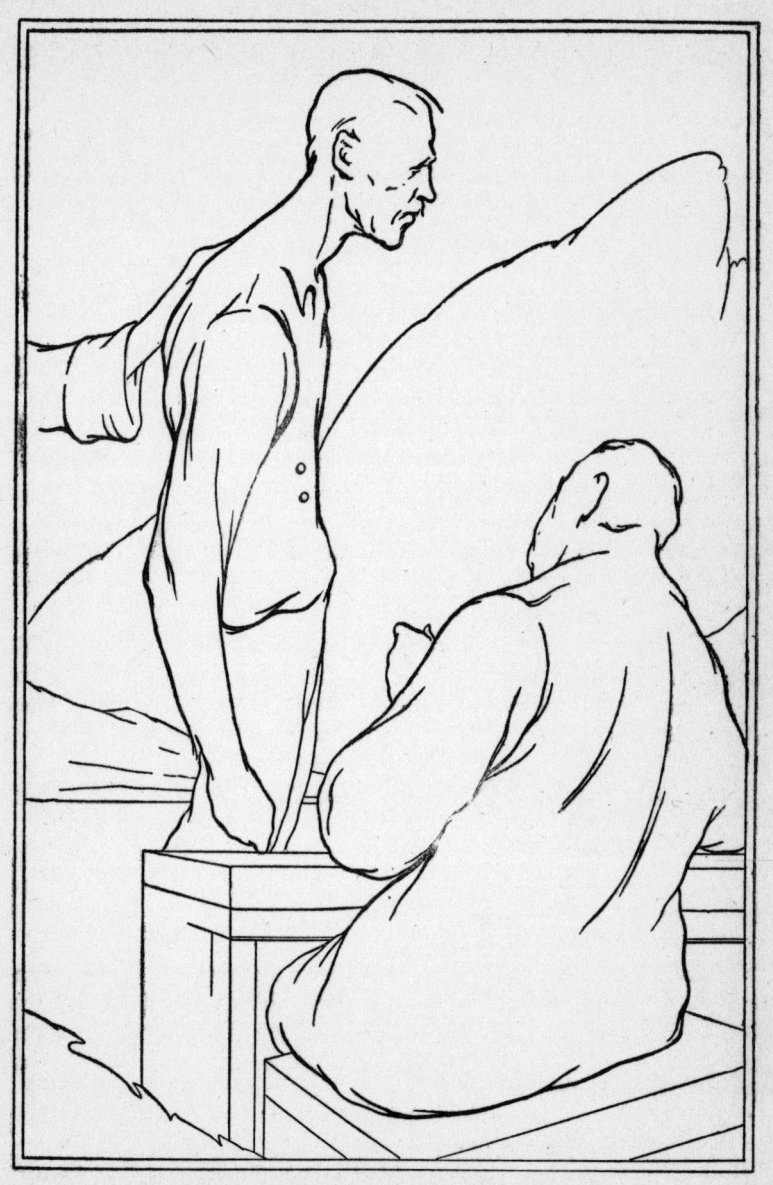

"How did you receive that wound on your face?"

For a month the German vanguard had been in this village. The French remained motionless, ten leagues away; and yet, every night, some of the Uhlans disappeared.

Of all the isolated scouts, of all those who were sent to the outposts, in groups of not more than three, not one ever returned.

They were picked up the next morning in a field or in a ditch. Even their horses were found along the roads with their throats cut.

These murders seemed to be done by the same men, who could never be found.

The country was terrorized. Farmers were shot on suspicion, women were imprisoned; children were frightened in order to try and obtain information. Nothing could be ascertained.

But, one morning, Father Milon was found stretched out in the barn, with a sword gash across his face.

Two Uhlans were found dead about a mile and a half from the farm. One of them was still holding his bloody sword in his hand. He had fought, tried to defend himself. A court-martial was immediately held in the open air, in front of the farm. The old man was brought before it.

He was sixty-eight years old, small, thin, bent, with two big hands resembling the claws of a crab. His colorless hair was sparse and thin, like the down of a young duck, allowing patches of his scalp to be seen. The brown and wrinkled skin of his neck showed big veins which disappeared behind his jaws and came out again at the temples. He had the reputation of being miserly and hard to deal with.

They stood him up between four soldiers, in front of the kitchen table, which had been dragged outside. Five officers and the colonel seated themselves opposite him.

The colonel spoke in French:

"Father Milon, since we have been here we have only had praise for you. You have always been obliging and even attentive to us. But to-day a terrible accusation is hanging over you, and you must clear the matter up. How did you receive that wound on your face?"

The peasant answered nothing.

The colonel continued:

"Your silence accuses you, Father Milon. But I want you to answer me! Do you understand? Do you know who killed the two Uhlans who were found this morning near Calvaire?"

The old man answered clearly:

"I did."

The colonel, surprised, was silent for a minute, looking straight at the prisoner. Father Milon stood impassive, with the stupid look of the peasant, his eyes lowered as though he were talking to the priest. Just one thing betrayed an uneasy mind; he was continually swallowing his saliva, with a visible effort, as though his throat were terribly contracted.

The man's family, his son Jean, his daughter-in-law and his two grandchildren were standing a few feet behind him, bewildered and affrighted.

The colonel went on:

"Do you also know who killed all the scouts who have been found dead, for a month, throughout the country, every morning?"

The old man answered with the same stupid look:

"I did."

"You killed them all?"

"Uh huh! I did."

"You alone? All alone?"

"Uh huh!"

"Tell me how you did it."

This time the man seemed moved; the necessity for talking any length of time annoyed him visibly. He stammered:

"I dunno! I simply did it."

The colonel continued:

"I warn you that you will have to tell me everything. You might as well make up your mind right away. How did you begin?"

The man cast a troubled look toward his family, standing close behind him. He hesitated a minute longer, and then suddenly made up his mind to obey the order.

"I was coming home one night at about ten o'clock, the night after you got here. You and your soldiers had taken more than fifty *écus* worth of forage from me, as well as a cow and two sheep. I said to myself: 'As much as they take from you, just so much will you make them pay back.' And then I had other things on my mind which I will tell you. Just then I noticed one of your soldiers who was smoking his pipe by the ditch behind the barn. I went and got my scythe and crept up slowly behind him, so that he couldn't hear me. And I cut his head off with one single blow, just as I would a blade of grass, before he could say 'Booh!' If you should look at the bottom of the pond, you will find him tied up in a potato-sack, with a stone fastened to it.

"I got an idea. I took all his clothes, from his boots to his cap, and hid them away in the little wood behind the yard."

The old man stopped. The officers remained speechless, looking at each other. The questioning began again, and this is what they learned.

Once this murder committed, the man had lived with this one thought: "Kill the Prussians!" He hated them with the blind, fierce hate of the greedy yet patriotic peasant. He had his idea, as he said. He waited several days.

He was allowed to go and come as he pleased, because he had shown himself so humble, submissive and obliging to the invaders. Each night he saw the outposts leave. One night he followed them, having heard the name of the village to which the men were going, and having learned the few words of German which he needed for his plan through associating with the soldiers.

He left through the back yard, slipped into the woods, found the dead man's clothes and put them on. Then he began to crawl through the fields, following along the hedges in order to keep out of sight, listening to the slightest noises, as wary as a poacher.

As soon as he thought the time ripe, he approached the road and hid behind a bush. He waited for a while. Finally, toward midnight, he heard the sound of a galloping horse. The man put his ear to the ground in order to make sure that only one horseman was approaching, then he got ready.

An Uhlan came galloping along, carrying despatches. As he went, he was all eyes and ears. When he was only a few feet away, Father Milon dragged himself across the road, moaning: *"Hilfe! Hilfe!"* (Help! Help!) The horseman stopped, and recognizing a German, he thought he was wounded and dismounted, coming nearer without any suspicion, and just as he was leaning over the unknown man, he received, in the pit of his stomach, a heavy thrust from the long curved blade of the sabre. He dropped without suffering pain, quivering only in the final throes. Then the farmer, radiant with the silent joy of an old peasant, got up again, and, for his own pleasure, cut the dead man's throat. He then dragged the body to the ditch and threw it in.

The horse quietly awaited its master. Father Milon mounted him and started galloping across the plains.

About an hour later he noticed two more Uhlans who were returning home, side by side. He rode straight for them, once more crying *"Hilfe! Hilfe!"* The Prussians, recognizing the uniform, let him approach without distrust. The old man passed between them like a cannon-ball, felling them both, one with his sabre and the other with a revolver.

Then he killed the horses, German horses! After that he quickly returned to the woods and hid one of the horses. He left his uniform there and again put on his old clothes; then going back into bed, he slept until morning.

For four days he did not go out, waiting for the inquest to be terminated; but on the fifth day he went out again and killed two more soldiers by the same stratagem. From that time on he did not stop. Each night he wandered about in search of adventure, killing Prussians, sometimes here and sometimes there, galloping through deserted fields, in the moonlight, a lost Uhlan, a hunter of men. Then, his task accomplished, leaving behind him the bodies lying along the roads, the old farmer would return and hide his horse and uniform.

He went, toward noon, to carry oats and water quietly to his mount, and he fed it well as he required from it a great amount of work.

But one of those whom he had attacked the night before, in defending himself slashed the old peasant across the face with his sabre.

However, he had killed them both. He had come back and hidden the horse and put on his ordinary clothes again; but as he reached home he began to feel faint, and had dragged himself as far as the stable, being unable to reach the house.

They had found him there, bleeding, on the straw.

When he had finished his tale, he suddenly lifted up his head and looked proudly at the Prussian officers.

The colonel, who was gnawing at his mustache, asked:
"You have nothing else to say?"
"Nothing more; I have finished my task; I killed sixteen, not one more or less."

"Do you know that you are going to die?"

"I haven't asked for mercy."

"Have you been a soldier?"

"Yes, I served my time. And then, you had killed my father, who was a soldier of the first Emperor. And last month you killed my youngest son, François, near Evreux. I owed you one for that; I paid. We are quits."

The officers were looking at each other.

The old man continued:

"Eight for my father, eight for the boy—we are quits. I didn't seek any quarrel with you. I don't know you. I don't even know where you come from. And here you are, ordering me about in my home as though it were your own. I took my revenge upon the others. I'm not sorry."

And, straightening up his bent back, the old man folded his arms in the attitude of a modest hero.

The Prussians talked in a low tone for a long time. One of them, a captain, who had also lost his son the previous month, was defending the poor wretch. Then the colonel arose and, approaching Father Milon, said in a low voice:

"Listen, old man, there is perhaps a way of saving your life, it is to——"

But the man was not listening, and, his eyes fixed on the hated officer, while the wind played with the downy hair on his head, he distorted his slashed face, giving it a truly terrible expression, and, swelling out his chest, he spat, as hard as he could, right in the Prussian's face.

The colonel, furious, raised his hand, and for the second time the man spat in his face.

All the officers had jumped up and were shrieking orders at the same time.

In less than a minute the old man, still impassive, was pushed up against the wall and shot, looking smilingly the while toward Jean, his eldest son, his daughter-in-law and his two grandchildren, who witnessed this scene in dumb terror.

SOLITUDE

Our dinner, a rollicking stag affair, was just over. One of my old friends said to me:

"Let us walk up the Champs-Elysées!"

We started off, sauntering along under the budding trees. All was quiet, except for the low, continuous rumble so characteristic of Paris. A light breeze fanned our faces, and thousands of stars dotted the dark sky like gold dust.

My companion said:

"I don't know why, but I breathe better here, at night, than in any other place. My mind seems to expand. At times, just for a second, it seems to me as though the divine secret of life were about to be discovered. Then the door is shut, and all is over!"

From time to time we could see two forms glide by alongside the trees. We were passing in front of a bench, where a couple were seated side by side, making a single dark patch.

My friend murmured:

"Poor things! It is not disgust but an immense pity which I feel for them. Of all the mysteries of human life, there is one which I have thoroughly solved: the great torture of our existence lies in the fact that we are eternally alone, and all our efforts and all our acts are only an attempt to escape this solitude. Those two lovers on the bench, in the open air, are trying, like all living creatures, to put at least a temporary stop to their loneliness; but they are, and always will be, alone, just as you and I are alone.

"Some notice it more, some less; that's all.

"For some time I have been suffering the abominable torture of having understood, of having discovered, the awful isolation in which I live, and I know that nothing can stop it—nothing, you understand!

"Whatever we attempt to do, whatever may be the impulse of

our hearts, the cry of our lips, the clasp of our arms, we are always alone!

"I dragged you out for this walk to-night so that I would not have to go home, because I am suffering terribly just now from the loneliness of my apartment. What good will it do me? I am speaking to you, you are listening to me, and we are both of us alone—side by side, but alone. Do you understand me?

" 'Blessed are the poor in spirit,' say the Scriptures. They have the illusion of happiness. They do not feel the same lonely misery that we do; they do not, as I do, wander through life without any other than superficial contact, without any other joy than the selfish satisfaction of understanding, of seeing, and of suffering endlessly from the knowledge of our eternal isolation.

"You think I am crazy, don't you?

"Listen. For a year I have felt the loneliness of my life, each day I seemed to be sinking deeper and deeper into a dark pit whose edges I cannot find, whose bottom I cannot touch. I am in there alone, with nobody near me, no living creature taking the same gloomy journey. This pit is Life. At times I seem to hear noises, voices, cries—I grope my way toward these confused sounds. But I never can tell whence they come; I never meet anyone, I never find another hand stretched out in the surrounding darkness. Do you understand?

"Some men have, at times, realized this solitude.

"Musset cried:

" 'Who comes? Who calls me? No one!
I am alone.—The hour has come.
What loneliness! What wretchedness!

"But with him it was only a passing doubt, and not a final certitude, as it is with me. He was a poet; his life was full of fancies, of dreams. He was never truly alone. I am!

"Gustave Flaubert, who was one of the great sufferers of this world, because he was one of the illuminated thinkers, wrote these hopeless words to a friend: 'We are all of us in a desert. No one understands anyone else.'

"True, no one understands anyone else, whatever he may think, say, or attempt. Does the earth know what is happening in the stars, which are scattered through space like sparks; some of them so distant that all we can do is dimly to perceive their light; others so far off that they are lost in the infinite, and yet they may be as close together as the molecules of a body?

"Well, man knows no more about his neighbor. We are as far away from one another as these stars, and more isolated, because thought is unfathomable.

"Do you know anything more terrible than constant intercourse with people whom we shall never be able to understand? We love one another as though we were chained quite near together, with arms outstretched, but unable to approach any closer. We are constantly tortured by a desire to come closer to one another, but our efforts remain unavailing, our anger vain, our confidences fruitless, our embraces without power, our caresses without hope. When we wish to mingle, our mutual efforts to do so only make us clash against each other.

"I never feel more alone than when I am opening my heart to some friend, because then I understand better the impassable barrier which exists between us. He is there, I see his eyes looking into mine, but the soul which is behind them, I cannot see. He is listening to me. What does he think? Yes, what does he think? Do you understand this torture? Perhaps he hates me or despises me; perhaps he is laughing at me. He is thinking over what I am saying, he criticises me, scoffs at me, condemns me, considers me ordinary, or else a fool. How can I find out what he thinks? How can I find out whether he loves me as I love him, and what is happening in that little round head? What a mystery this is, the unknown thoughts of a human being, the concealed individual thoughts that we can never know, guide, influence, nor conquer!

"I have tried in vain to open all the doors of my soul, to make myself understood. Yet away down in its depths there is the secret place of my *ego* which nobody can enter. Nobody can discover it or enter it, because nobody is exactly like me, because no one understands anyone else.

"Do you understand me yourself, at this moment? No, you think I am mad! You are examining me, you are wary of me! You say to yourself: 'What is the matter with him to-night? But if, some time in the future, you should manage to grasp, to guess at my horrible and subtle suffering, just come to me and say: '*I have misunderstood you!*' and you may make me happy for a second.

"It is women who best make me understand my solitude. How

they have made me suffer, because they, more than men, have given me the illusion of not being alone!

"When one is in love, one seems to expand. A superhuman happiness fills your soul! Do you know why? Do you know whence comes this feeling of great joy? It is solely because we imagine ourselves no longer alone. The isolation, the great loneliness appears to cease. What a mistake!

"Tormented even more than we are by this eternal longing for love which gnaws at our lonely hearts, woman is the great illusion of the Dream.

"You know those delightful hours spent face to face with this creature with long hair and delicate features, whose glance maddens us. What delirium seizes us—takes hold of our minds! What illusion carries us away!

"It seems as though, in a few minutes, she and I would be one! But this time never comes, and after weeks of waiting, of hoping and of deceitful joy, I suddenly find myself even more lonely than ever before. After each kiss, after each embrace, the gulf widens. It is heartrending, terrible!

"Then, farewell, all is over! You hardly recognize this woman who has been so much to you during a period of your life, and whose thoughts you have never known! At the very time when it seems that, through some mysterious accord, each had descended into the very depth of the other's soul, one little word shows us our error, shows us, like a flash of lightning in the dark night, the black abyss between us.

"And yet, perhaps, the most delightful thing in the world is to spend an evening with a beloved woman, without talking, almost perfectly happy in the very fact of her presence. Let us not ask more, for two beings never blend.

"As for me, now, I have closed my soul. I no longer tell anyone what I think, what I believe and what I love. Knowing myself condemned to this appalling loneliness, I observe things, without ever giving my opinion. What do I care for the ideas, the quarrels, the beliefs of others! Not being able to share anything with anyone, I have lost interest in everything. My hidden thoughts remain an eternal secret. I have commonplace answers for everyday questions, and a smile which says 'yes,' when I do not wish to take the trouble to answer.

"Do you understand me?"

We had gone up the long avenue to the Arc de Triomphe, and

back again to the Place de la Concorde, for he had said all this very slowly, adding many details which I cannot remember at present.

He stopped, and, suddenly stretching his arm towards the great granite obelisk, standing like a sentinel in the centre of Paris, this exiled monument, bearing on its sides the history of its country written in strange characters, he cried:

"There! We are all like that!"

Then he left me without another word.

Was he intoxicated, crazy, or very wise? I have not yet found out. At times it seems to me that he was right, and then, again, I think he must have lost his mind.

YVETTE

Chapter I

Coming out of the Café Riche, Jean de Servigny said to Léon Saval: "Shall we walk? It's too fine to drive."

"All right!" replied his friend.

Jean continued: "It's barely eleven; let's take it easy, or we shall get there long before twelve."

A busy crowd was eddying on the boulevard—such a crowd as on summer nights is always to be seen in the streets, stirring, halting, murmuring, flowing along like a river, full of placid gaiety. Here and there a café threw a brilliant shaft of light over groups on the pavement sitting round little tables covered with bottles and glasses, and so closely packed as to completely block the pathway. And in the road, cabs with red, and blue, and green eyes, shooting swiftly across the glare of the lighted front, showed for a second the lean and ambling silhouette of the horse, the profile of the driver up above, the sombre bulk of the vehicle, while the *Urbaine* cabs made pale and fleeting flashes as their yellow panels caught the light.

The two friends strolled slowly along, smoking, in evening dress, with greatcoats over their arms, flowers in their button-holes, and their hats a trifle on one side, as hats are sometimes worn, after a good dinner, when the breeze is warm.

They were old school friends, sincerely, firmly devoted to each other. Jean de Servigny, short, slight, rather bald, frail-looking, but exceedingly elegant, with curled moustache, clear eyes, and sensitive lips, was one of those night-birds who seem born and bred on the boulevards; indefatigable in spite of his look of exhaustion, vigorous in spite of his pallor, one of those wiry Parisians whom gymnastics, fencing, and Turkish baths endow with a nervous, carefully disciplined strength. He was known everywhere for his wild ways, his wit, his wealth, his amours, and for the genial amiability and worldly charm innate in certain men.

A true Parisian, light, sceptical, capricious, impulsive, energetic, irresolute; capable of everything, and yet of nothing; selfish on principle, but generous by fits and starts, getting comfortably through his income, and carefully through his constitution. Cool, yet passionate, he was continually letting himself go and continually pulling himself up, a prey to the most contrary instincts, and yielding to them all, by way of living up to his ideal of the shrewd man of the world, with weather-cock logic swinging to all the winds, and profiting by every turn, while he never stirs a finger to set it in motion.

His companion, Léon Saval, equally well off, was one of those superb giants who make women turn round and stare after them in the streets. He gave the impression of a statue come to life, a model of the human race, after the fashion of those works of Art that get sent to exhibitions. Too fine, too tall, too broad, and too strong, he sinned by the very extravagance of his good points. He had inspired innumerable passions.

"Have you informed this lady that you're bringing me?" he asked, as they passed the Vaudeville.

Servigny burst out laughing. "What! inform the Marquise Obardi? Do you inform the driver of an omnibus that you're going to get up at the next corner?"

"Why! who is she, exactly, then?" asked Saval, rather puzzled.

"A parvenue, a charming rascally adventuress," replied his friend, "from the devil knows where, who turned up one day in Bohemia, the devil knows how, and has managed to cut a dash there. What does it matter? They say her real name, I mean her maiden name—she's remained a maiden lady, except in reality of course—is Octavie Bardin; keep the first letter of the Christian, and clip the last of the surname, and you get Obardi. An attractive person; and with your physique you're bound to be her lover. Hercules isn't introduced to Messalina without something coming of it. I must say one thing, though: the entrance to the place is as free as the entrance to a shop, and you're not in the least obliged to buy what's exhibited. The stock consists of love and cards; they don't bother you to take either the one or the other. And the exit's just as free.

"It's three years since she pitched her shady tent in the Quartier de l'Etoile, and opened its doors to the cosmopolitan scum who come to exploit Paris, to exercise their dangerous talents there.

"I can't for the life of me remember how I came to know her. Suppose I must have gone, like everyone else, because there's gambling, because the women are easy-going, and the men scamps. I can't help being fond of that crowd of decorated rascals—all foreign, all noble, all titled, and all unknown at their Embassies, except, of course, the spies. There they are, trotting out their honour on every imaginable occasion, quoting their ancestors for no reason at all, telling you all about their lives—braggarts, liars and thieves, as dangerous as the cards they play; brave simply because they have to be, like robbers, who can't strip their victims without risking their own lives. In a word, the aristocracy of the hulks—yes, I'm fond of them. They're interesting to study, amusing to listen to, often witty; never commonplace, like our own blessed officials. Their womenkind, too, are always pretty, with a little flavour of foreign rascality in them, and a sense of mystery about their past lives, spent probably half the time in reformatories. They've almost always got splendid eyes and hair, the true professional physique, a sort of grace that intoxicates and seduces you into making a fool of yourself, and a charm that's altogether unholy and irresistible. They rob you in the real old highway fashion, take everything you have. Ah, yes; they're regular female birds of prey. Well, I'm fond of them too.

"The Marquise Obardi is the very type of these charming villains—full-blown, of course, but still beautiful—the sort of feline sorceress that you feel to be vicious to the very marrow. Oh! it's an amusing house. Gambling, dancing, supper—in fact, all the pleasures of this wicked world."

"Have you ever been, or are you, her lover?" asked Saval.

Servigny replied: "I haven't been, am not, and never shall be. I go there for the sake of the daughter."

"Ah! there's a daughter?"

"There is indeed! A miracle, my dear fellow. She's just at present the principal attraction of the den. A glorious creature, perfection itself, eighteen years old, as fair as her mother is dark; always in high spirits and ready for fun, always laughing and dancing like a mad thing. Who's to be the lucky man? Who *is* the lucky man? No one knows. There are ten of us waiting and hoping. A girl like that in the hands of a woman like the Marquise is a fortune. And they play such a dark game, the rogues! Can't make out what they're at—waiting for a better chance than me, I suppose. Well, I can only tell you—if the chance comes my way, I shall seize her. This girl Yvette nonplusses me completely. She's a mystery. If she isn't the most perfect monster of subtle perversity you ever saw, she's the most marvellous piece of innocence. She lives amongst all these disreputable surroundings with a quiet, triumphant unconcern that's quite amazing in its artfulness or its artlessness. There she is, an exotic offshoot of this adventuress, grown on the dunghill of Bohemia, like a magnificent plant that's nourished on manure—the child, I shouldn't wonder, of some man of rank, some great artist or great lord—a casual prince or king, perhaps—who turned in there one night. Impossible to understand what she is or what her thoughts are. But you'll see for yourself."

Saval began to laugh, and said: "You're in love with her."

"No—I'm in the running; not at all the same thing. I'm going to introduce you to my most serious rivals. But I've got a fair chance—I'm ahead even: she smiles on me."

"You're in love!" repeated Saval.

"No—o! She disturbs and allures me; she makes me uneasy, attracts, and scares me, all at the same time! I distrust her as if she were a trap, and I long for her as I long for a drink when I'm thirsty. I feel the charm of her, but I never go near her without the sort of fear one has of a pickpocket. While I'm with her I've an irrational belief in her innocence—which, mind you, is possible—and a most rational distrust of her villainy, which is just as probable. I feel I'm in contact with an abnormal being, outside the pale of natural law. Which is she, exquisite or abominable? I really can't tell you."

For the third time Saval said: "I tell you you're in love. You're talking of her with the fervour of a poet, and the sing-song of a troubadour. Come, look into yourself, sound your heart, and confess!"

Servigny took several paces without speaking, and then replied: "Well, you may be right after all. Anyway, I'm very much interested in her. Yes—perhaps I *am* in love. I think of her too much. I think of her when I'm going to sleep, and when I wake up. . . . Yes, it's pretty serious. Her image follows me, actually pursues me, it's always with me, before me, around me, in me. Can you call such a physical obsession love? Her face has gone so deep into my brain that I see her the moment I shut my eyes. My heart leaps each time I catch sight of her. I don't deny it. So be it! I love her; but in a queer sort of way. I want her frightfully, but the idea of making her my wife would seem to me mad, idiotic, monstrous. I'm a little afraid of her too, like a bird with a hawk above it. And I'm jealous, jealous of everything I don't know in that incomprehensible heart. I'm always asking myself: 'Is she simply a charming tomboy, or an abominable jade?' She says things that would make a trooper blush; but—so do parrots. She's sometimes so imprudent, or—impudent, as to make me believe in her spotless innocence, and sometimes so simple, with a kind of impossible simplicity, that it makes me doubt whether she ever was innocent. She provokes and excites me like a courtesan, and defends herself all the time like a vestal. She seems to be fond of me, yet she's always making fun of me; in public she labels herself my mistress, in private she treats me like her brother or her valet. Sometimes I fancy she has as many lovers as her mother; sometimes I think she hasn't a suspicion of what life really is like—not the smallest suspicion. Then again, she's a tremendous novel-reader—while I'm waiting like this for better days, I keep her supplied with books—she calls me her librarian. By my orders, the New Library sends her weekly every mortal thing that comes out; I believe she reads the lot pell-mell. It must make a strange salad in her head. Perhaps indeed this literary stew counts for something in her extraordinary behaviour. Anyone who looks at life through the medium of fifteen thousand novels must see it in a funny sort of light—get quaint ideas about things, eh?

"Well, I'm waiting. On the one hand, I've never had for any woman the fancy I have for this one, that's certain—as certain as that I shall never marry her. So, if she's had lovers, I shall swell the number; if not, I shall take number 1, like a tram ticket. It's a simple case. Obviously, she'll never marry. Who'd marry the daughter of the Marquise Obardi, of Octavie Bardin? No one, for a thousand reasons. Where could they find her a husband? In our class? Never. The mother's house is a place of public resort, where the daughter acts as bait. We don't marry into that sort of thing. In the middle classes? Still less. Besides, the marquise is a woman of business; she'll never give Yvette for good and all to anyone but a man of high position—and him she'll never catch. That leaves the lower classes—still less chance there. No, there's no way out of it. This young lady is not of our class, not of the middle class, not of the people; she can't marry into any of them.

She belongs, by reason of her mother, her birth, education, heredity, manners, habits, to—gilded prostitution.

"She can't escape without turning nun, which is not at all likely, considering her ways and tastes. There's only one profession possible to her: Love. She'll come to it, if she hasn't already. She can't avoid her fate. From a 'young woman' she'll simply become a 'woman,' and I should much like to be the pivot of the transformation.

"So I'm waiting—the gentlemen-in-waiting are numerous. You'll see a Frenchman, M. de Belvigne; a Russian, called Prince Kravalow; and an Italian, Chevalier Valréali; these are definite candidates, busy canvassing already. But there are a lot of unconsidered hangers-on. The marquise is watching. I think she's got views about me. She knows I'm very well off, and she's less sure of the others. Her house is really the most astonishing place that I've ever met with of its kind. You even come across very decent fellows there—we're going ourselves, you see, and we shan't be the only ones. As to the women, she's found, or rather, skimmed off the cream of all those ladies who pillage our purses. Goodness knows where she discovered them. It's apart from the regular professionals, it's not Bohemia, it's not exactly anything. She's had an inspiration of genius, too, in pitching on adventuresses with children, particularly girls. So much so that a greenhorn might fancy he was among good women!"

They had reached the Avenue of the Champs Elysées. A gentle breeze stirred softly among the leaves, touching their faces like soft sighs from a giant fan wafted to and fro somewhere in the sky. Dumb shadows wandered among the trees, or made dusky blurs on the benches. And these shadows spoke very low, as if confiding to each other weighty or shameful secrets.

Servigny resumed: "You've no idea what a collection of fancy titles we shall meet in this menagerie. Talking of that, I shall introduce you as Count Saval. An unadorned Saval would be unpopular—oh! very unpopular!"

"No! no! by Jove!" cried his friend; "I won't for a moment, even in a place like that, have them suppose me ass enough to deck myself out with a title—no, no!"

Servigny laughed. "Don't be such a duffer," said he; "they've baptized me the Duke of Servigny—I haven't the least notion how or why. And I remain the Duke of Servigny without a murmur. It really doesn't hurt, and without it I should be awfully looked down on."

But Saval was by no means open to conviction: "Ah! you've a title of your own, that's quite another thing. But as for me, for better or worse, I'll be the only commoner in the place. It'll be my distinguishing mark—my superiority."

Servigny persisted: "It can't be done, absolutely can't be done. It would seem quite monstrous. You'd be like a rag-picker in an assembly of emperors. Leave it to me; I'll present you as the Viceroy of the Upper Mississippi, nobody'll be astonished. When one's going in for titles, they can't be too big."

"No; once for all, I won't."

"Very well. I was an ass to try and persuade you, for I defy you to get in there without being decorated with a title; there are some shops, you know, where ladies can't get past the door without having a bunch of violets given them."

They turned to the right in the Rue de Berri, ascended to the first floor of a fine modern house, and gave their overcoats and sticks into the hands of four lackeys in breeches. A warm odour of festivity, suggestive of flowers, perfumes, and fair women, and a loud, sustained, confused murmur, issued from the crowded rooms.

A sort of master of the ceremonies, a tall, upright, stout, and solemn person, whose face was framed in white whiskers, came up to the newcomer, and, with a slight but haughty bow, asked:—

"What name may I announce?"

"Monsieur Saval," replied Servigny.

At which, opening the door, the man shouted into the crowd of guests:—

"M. le Duc de Servigny."

"M. le Baron Saval."

The first room was full of women, and the eye alighted at once on an array of bare necks, emerging from billows of brilliant drapery. The lady of the house, who was standing talking to three friends, turned round and majestically came forward with graceful movements, and smiling lips.

Her forehead, narrow and very low, was covered with a mass of shining black hair, thick as fleece, encroaching a little on the temples. She was tall and rather too plump and full-blown, but very beautiful, with a heavy, warm, compelling beauty. Her helmet of black hair had the power of conjuring up delightful visions, of making her mysteriously desirable; beneath it were great black eyes. The nose was rather small, the mouth large, yet infinitely seductive, eloquent of love and conquest.

But her most living charm was in her voice. It came from that mouth like water from a spring, so natural, so soft, so true in tone, so clear, that it was a physical joy to listen to it, a delight for the ear to hear the subtle words flowing out like a stream from its source, a delight for the eye to see those beautiful lips part to give them passage.

She stretched out a hand to Servigny, who kissed it, and, letting her fan drop to the full length of its thin gold chain, she gave the other to Saval, and said:—

"Welcome, Baron; any friend of the Duke is welcome here."

And she fixed her glowing eyes on the giant presented to her. There was a tiny black down on her upper lip, the suspicion of a moustache, more visible when she spoke; a delicious scent clung about her, strong and intoxicating—some American or Indian perfume. But fresh people kept arriving, marquises, counts, or princes; and saying to Servigny with motherly graciousness: "You'll find my daughter in the other room—make yourselves at home, gentlemen, the house is yours," she left them, to meet her new guests, casting at Saval that smiling, fleeting glance by which a woman shows a man that he has pleased her.

Servigny seized his friend's arm: "Come on," said he, "I'll pilot you. This room belongs to the ladies—temple of the Flesh, fresh or otherwise. Bargains as good as new, and better still, high-priced articles to be had cheap. To the left is the gambling room—temple of Gold. You know all about that. . . . In the room at the far end, they dance—temple of Innocence, the sanctuary, the maiden's market. It's there that these ladies show off their produce. Why, even real marriages would be tolerated. Yes, over there is the Future, the hope of our days and nights. And really, the most curious feature in this museum of moral maladies is the sight of these young girls, with souls as out of joint as the bodies of little clowns born of acrobats. Let's go and have a look at them."

He kept bowing courteously to right and left, distributing his compliments, and glancing rapidly with the eye of a connoisseur at every bare-necked woman that he knew.

A band at the far end of the second room was playing a waltz; and they stopped in the doorway to watch. Some fifteen couples were dancing; the men solemn, the girls with a smile fixed on their lips. Like their mothers they showed a good deal of skin, and the bodices of one or two were merely secured by a narrow ribbon over the shoulders.

Suddenly from the very end of the room darted a tall girl, rushing along past everyone, pushing the dancers aside, and holding up the outrageously long train of her dress in her left hand. She ran with quick little steps, as women do in a crowd, and cried:

"Ah! here's Muscade! How *are* you, Muscade?"

Her face was like the Spring, alight with happiness. Her warm white skin, the skin that goes with auburn hair, seemed to sparkle. And that mass of hair, twisted round her head, flame-bright, hung heavy on her forehead, and looked too weighty for her supple and still slender neck. She seemed made for motion, as her mother was made for speech, so natural, noble and simple were her gestures. To see her walk, turn, bend her head, lift her arm, was to feel a moral joy, a physical delight. She repeated:—

"Ah! here's Muscade! How *are* you, Muscade?"

Servigny shook her hand violently, as he would have shaken a man's and said:—

"Mam'zelle Yvette, this is my friend, Baron Saval."

She bowed, and staring at the stranger, said: "How do you do, Monsieur; are you always as big as that?"

In the chaffing tone that he adopted with her to hide his distrust and uncertainty, Servigny replied: "No, Mam'zelle. He's brought his largest dimensions to-night to please your mother; she's fond of the gigantic."

The young girl answered in a serio-comic voice: "All right! But when you come for me, make yourself a little smaller, please; I like moderation. Muscade, now, is just my size."

She gave the newcomer her little, wide-open hand, and said: "Are you going to dance, Muscade? Come along, do let's have a turn!"

Without answering, Servigny, with a quick, eager movement, clasped her round the waist. and they disappeared at once with the fury of a whirlwind.

They danced faster than all the others, turning and turning, flying along, whirling round and round; clasped so close that they looked like one, with bodies upright and legs almost still, as if an invisible machine hidden under their feet had made them so to twirl. They seemed tireless. The other couples stopped one by one. They alone remained, waltzing unendingly. They had a look of being far away from the dance, in ecstasy. And the band played on, their eyes fixed on this treadmill couple; every eye was fixed on them, and when they stopped at last, everyone applauded.

She was a little flushed now, with strange-looking eyes, ardent, yet timid, less frank than before; troubled, and so blue, with such black pupils, that they seemed quite unnatural.

Servigny was like a drunken man. He leaned against a door to recover himself.

"No head, my poor Muscade!" she said; "I'm tougher than you!"

He laughed nervously, devouring her with greedy longing in his eyes and in the curve of his lip; he continued to gaze at her standing before him with her bare throat heaving tumultuously.

"Sometimes," she went on, "you look just like a cat that's going to fly at someone. Come along; give me your arm, and let's go and find your friend."

Without a word he offered his arm, and they crossed the room. Saval was no longer alone. The Marquise Obardi had rejoined him. She was murmuring trivial commonplaces in that entrancing voice of hers. And looking deep into his eyes, she seemed to be meaning quite other words than those her lips pronounced. The moment she saw Servigny her face became smiling, and, turning towards him, she said: "My dear Duke, did you know that I've just taken a villa at Bougival for two months? You must come and see me, and bring your friend. Let's see, I'm going in on Monday—will you both come and dine next Saturday, and stay all Sunday?"

Servigny abruptly turned his head towards Yvette. She was smiling, tranquil and serene, and said with an assurance that left no loophole for hesitation: "Of course Muscade will come to dinner on Saturday! You needn't take the trouble to ask him. We'll have tremendous fun in the country."

He fancied he could detect the birth of a promise in her smile, some hidden intention in her voice.

The Marquise lifted her great dark eyes to Saval: "And you, Baron?" she said; and *her* smile, at any rate, was not ambiguous.

He bowed: "I shall be only too happy, Madame!"

"Ah!" said Yvette slyly, "we'll scandalise everyone down

there, won't we, Muscade? We'll make my regiment mad with rage?"

There was again that artless or artful meaning in her voice, and with a glance she pointed to a group of men, watching them from a distance.

"As much as ever you like, Mam'zelle," replied Servigny. In talking to her he never said Mademoiselle, by virtue of a sort of comradeship established between them.

"Why does Mademoiselle Yvette always call my friend Servigny 'Muscade'?" asked Saval.

The young girl put on an innocent expression: "Because he's always slipping through one's fingers, Monsieur. You think you've got hold of him, but you never have."

The Marquise, who was visibly occupied with other thoughts and had not taken her eyes off Saval, said absently: "Aren't these children funny?"

"I'm not funny," answered Yvette crossly, "I'm simply frank! I like Muscade, and he's always deserting me; it's so annoying!"

Servigny made a deep bow: "I'll never leave you again, Mam'zelle, day or night!"

She made a movement of alarm: "Ah, no! The day's all very well, but at night you'd be a mistake."

"Why, how?" he asked wickedly.

She answered with calm audacity: "Because I'm sure you can't look so nice in *déshabillé.*"

The Marquise, without appearing in the least disturbed, cried out: "Why! they're saying the most awful things! One can't be as innocent as all that."

Servigny replied chaffingly: "That's just what I think, Marquise!"

Yvette fixed her eyes on him: "You—" she said haughtily in a wounded voice; "you've made a hole in your manners: you've been doing that too often lately."

And, turning her back on him, she called out: "Chevalier, come and defend me, I'm being insulted."

There came up a lean, dark man, slow of movement, who said with a forced smile: "Which is the culprit?"

She nodded her head towards Servigny. "He!" she said; "but all the same, I like him better than the rest of you put together; he's less tiresome."

Chevalier Valréali bowed: "We do what we can," said he; "we've fewer attractions perhaps, but not less devotion."

At this moment a tall, corpulent man, with grey whiskers, approached, and said in a big voice: "Mademoiselle Yvette— your servant."

"Ah! Monsieur de Belvigne," she cried, and turning to Saval, remarked: "This is my best young man; tall, fat, rich, and stupid. That's how I like them. A real knight—of the trencher. Why! you're even taller than he! I *must* give you a nickname. Good! I shall call you 'young Mr. Rhodes,' after the Colossus—he must have been your father. But I'm certain you two have any amount of interesting things to tell each other up there over our heads— so good-night!" And off she went towards the band, to ask the musicians to play a quadrille.

Mme. Obardi, who seemed lost in reverie, turned slowly to Servigny: "You're always teasing her. You'll spoil her temper, and give her all sorts of bad habits"; but it was clearly said for the sake of talking.

"Ah! then you've not finished her education?" he retorted.

She looked as if she did not understand, and went on benignly smiling.

Just then she saw approaching a solemn personage, starred with crosses, and hastening towards him, cried: "Ah! Prince, how delightful!"

Servigny again took Saval's arm, and drew him away, "That's the latest suitor, Prince Kravalow," he said. "Well now, isn't she superb?"

Saval replied: "I call them both superb. The mother's good enough for me."

Servigny bowed: "She's quite at your service, my dear chap," he said. The dancers elbowed them, taking their places for the quadrille, couple by couple, in two opposing lines.

"Let's go and see the Greeks," said Servigny, and they made their way into the gambling room.

Round each table stood a circle of men watching, who spoke but seldom, while the chink from the gold thrown on the cloth, or sharply raked in, mingled its light, metallic murmur with the murmur of the players, as though the voice of money were making itself heard among the voices of human beings.

These men were all decorated with strange orders, and curious sorts of ribbons; and though their faces were so different, they all had the same severe expression, and were most readily distinguished one from the other by the cut of their beards. The stark American with a horseshoe round his jaw, the haughty Englishman with a hairy fan divided on his chest, the Spaniard with a fleece of black up to the eyes, the Roman with the huge moustache presented to Italy by Victor Emanuel, the Austrian with his whiskers and clean-shaven chin, a Russian general with an upper lip armed, as it were, with two lances of waxed hair, and the Frenchman with his gay moustache—revealed the fantasies of all the barbers in the world.

"Aren't you going to play?" asked Servigny.

"No, are you?"

"Never here! If you're ready, we'll be off, and come again some quieter evening. It's too crowded to-night, one can't stir."

"All right."

They disappeared through a curtained doorway which led to the vestibule.

As soon as they were in the street, Servigny said: "Well, what do you think of it?"

"Oh! interesting enough! But I prefer the women's quarters to the men's."

"Rather! Those women are our very finest specimens. One scents love in them as one scents perfumes at a hairdresser's. This is really the only kind of house where you get your money's worth. Ah! and what craftswomen, my dear chap! What artists! . . . Have you ever eaten tarts at a baker's? They look good, but they're good-for-nothing. The man who made them is a fellow who only knows how to make bread. Well, the love of an ordinary woman of the world always seems to me like baker's pastry. Whereas, the love that one gets at these Marquise Obardis, well —it's the real thing. Ah! they know how to make cakes, those little confectioners! One pays 2½d. for what costs a penny anywhere else, that's all!"

"Who's the lord of the manor just now?" asked Saval.

Servigny shrugged his shoulders. "I know nothing about it," said he; "the last I heard of was an English peer, who departed three months ago. Just now she must be living on the community, perhaps on the gambling, for she's capricious. But we've settled to dine with her at Bougival next Saturday, haven't we? In the country one has more opportunity; I shall find out at last what Yvette has in that head of hers!"

"There's nothing I should like better. I've no engagements that day," replied Saval.

Returning through the Champs Elysées, under the fiery field of the stars, they disturbed a couple on a bench, and Servigny muttered: "Love! How idiotic, and yet how tremendous it is! How commonplace, and yet how amusing! It's always the same, and always different. And the ragamuffin who pays that girl a franc asks of her the very same thing for which I should pay ten thousand to some Obardi, no younger or less stupid perhaps than that drab. What folly!"

He said nothing for some minutes, then began again: "It would be rare luck all the same to be Yvette's first lover. Ah! for that I'd give—I'd give——"

He did not discover what he would give. And Saval wished him good-night at the corner of the Rue Royale.

Chapter II

The dinner table had been laid on the verandah overlooking the river. The Villa Printemps, taken by the Marquise Obardi, was placed half-way up the slope, just where, below the garden wall, the Seine made a curve in the direction of Marly.

Opposite the house loomed the island of Croissy, a mass of great trees and foliage, and a long reach of the broad river was visible, stretching as far as the floating café of *La Grenouillière*, hidden amongst the green.

The evening was falling, a calm, river-side evening, full of sweetness and colour, one of those quiet evenings that bring with them a sense of happiness. Not a breath stirred the leaves, no puff of wind ruffled the smooth, pale surface of the Seine. It was not too hot; just pleasantly warm—good to be alive. The benign sweetness of the river banks mounted towards the quiet sky.

The sun was going down behind the trees, on its way to other lands, and one seemed to inhale the peace of the sleeping earth, inhale the unheeding breath of life itself, in that calm, broad space.

When the party came out from the drawing-room to sit down to dinner, they were all in ecstasies. A tender gaiety invaded their hearts; it seemed so delicious to be dining out there in the open, breathing the clear sweet-scented air, with the great river and the sunset for background.

The Marquise had taken Saval's arm, and Yvette Servigny's. There were only the four of them. The two women seemed quite unlike what they had been in Paris, particularly Yvette; she hardly spoke, and appeared languid and grave.

Saval had difficulty in recognizing her: "What's the matter, Mademoiselle?" he asked; "you're utterly changed since the other day. You've become quite a reasonable being!"

"It's the country," she replied; "I *am* changed. I feel quite strange. But then, you know, I never do feel the same for two days running. One day I'm full of mischief and the next I'm like a funeral. I change like the weather, I can't think why. You see, I have all sorts of moods. Some days I could really kill people—not animals, I could never kill an animal—but people I could, and at other times I could cry for nothing at all. I get so many different ideas into my head. It depends a good deal on how you get up in the morning. When I wake, I could tell you what I'm going to be like all day. Perhaps it's one's dreams that make one like that; or perhaps the book one's just been reading has something to do with it."

She had on a dress of white flannel, falling about her in soft, delicate folds. The loose bodice, with big pleats, set off, without too much defining, her firm, free, well-formed figure. Her slender throat rose out of a foam of heavy lace, and, whiter than her dress, curved softly, a miracle of beauty, beneath the heavy burden of her red-gold hair.

Servigny looked at her fixedly. "Yes," he said, "you're adorable this evening, Mam'zelle. I should like to see you always like this."

With a touch of her usual michief she answered: "Don't offer me your heart, Muscade; I might take it seriously to-day, and that would cost you dear!"

The Marquise looked supremely happy. She was dressed in a dignified and simple robe of black, which showed the statuesque lines of her fine figure; there was a touch of red in the bodice, a garland of red carnations falling from the waist like a chain, looped up on the hip, and a red rose in her dark hair. In that simple toilette with the sanguine flowers, in those eyes with their compelling gaze, in that slow speech and infrequent gesture, her whole personality gave the idea of hidden flame.

Saval, too, seemed serious and absorbed. He now and then caressed his brown beard—pointed *à la Henri III.*—with a gesture habitual to him, and appeared to be lost in thought. For several minutes no one spoke.

Then, while some trout were being served, Servigny remarked: "Silence is a fine thing sometimes. It can often make a closer link between two people than speech—don't you think so, Marquise?"

Turning a little towards him, she replied: "You are right. It's so beautiful to be thinking at the same moment about the same delightful things."

She rested her ardent glance on Saval; and for some seconds they remained so, gazing into each other's eyes. A tiny movement, almost imperceptible, occurred beneath the table.

Servigny began again: "Mam'zelle Yvette, you'll make me think you're in love if you keep on being as good as this. Now, with whom could you be in love? Let's see; shall we run through them together? I'll leave out the rank and file, and only take the chiefs. Is it Prince Kravalow?"

At this name Yvette roused herself. "My poor Muscade, what are you thinking of? Why, the prince looks like a waxwork Russian who's taken a prize in a hairdresser's competition."

"Good! Off with the prince! Then you must have favoured the Vicomte Pierre de Belvigne?"

This time she burst out laughing: "Ha, ha, ha! Can't you see me hanging round Raisiné's neck" (she called him indifferently Raisiné, Malvoisie, Argenteuil, for she nick-named everyone), "murmuring in his ear: 'Dear little Pierre, my divine Pedro, my adored Pietri, my darling little Pierrot, put down your dear, fat, ducky head for your own little wife to kiss'?"

Servigny proclaimed: "Off with those two! That leaves the marquise's favourite—Chevalier Valréali!"

Yvette recovered all her gaiety: "Watery eyes? I'm sure he's a professional weeper at the Madeleine, hired out for first-class funeral processions. I always fancy I'm dead every time he looks at me."

"Three gone! Well, then, you're smitten with the Baron Saval, here present?"

"With young Mr. Rhodes? No, there's too much of him. I should feel as if I were in love with the Arc de Triomphe!"

"Then, Mam'zelle, you must be in love with me—I'm the only one of your adorers we haven't mentioned. I kept myself in the background in my modesty and prudence. It only remains for me to thank you."

In an ecstasy of mirth she replied: "You, Muscade? No-o. I like you very much—but I don't love you. Wait a moment, though —I don't want to discourage you. I don't love you—yet. You've got a chance—perhaps. Persevere, Muscade; be devoted, eager, humble, full of attentions and forethought, submissive to my smallest caprice, ready to do everything to please me—and, we'll see—later on."

"But, Mam'zelle, I'd rather exhibit all those qualities after, than before, if you don't mind."

She asked with a soubrette-like air of innocence: "After what, Muscade?"

"Why! after you've shown that you love me!"

"Well, *pretend* that I love you; believe it if you like——!"

"But——"

"Be quiet, Muscade, that's enough."

He gave her a military salute and held his tongue.

The sun had hidden itself behind the island, but the whole sky remained flaming like a brazier, and the still water of the river seemed turned to blood. Houses, things, people, all were reddened by the glow of the sunset. The crimson rose in the marquise's hair looked like a drop of carmine fallen from the clouds on to her head.

Choosing a moment when Yvette's eyes were far away, her mother, as though by accident, laid her hand upon Saval's. The young girl stirred, and the marquise's hand flew lightly back to adjust something in the folds of her bodice.

Servigny, who was watching them, said: "Shall we take a turn on the island after dinner, Mam'zelle?"

She was charmed with this idea: "Yes, yes! That will be lovely; we'll go all alone, won't we, Muscade?"

"Yes, all alone, Mam'zelle."

And silence fell on them again.

The broad stillness of the horizon, the sleepy quiet of the evening stole over their hearts, and bodies, and voices. There are tranquil, precious hours, when it is well-nigh impossible to speak. Noiselessly the lackeys served the dinner. The blaze in the sky died down, and the slow-falling night marshalled its shadows over the earth.

"Are you going to make a long stay?" asked Saval.

"Yes," replied the marquise, dwelling on each word; "just so long as I am happy here."

When the light failed, lamps were brought, and cast on the table a weird, pale light amid the vast, indefinite darkness; and instantly a rain of flies began falling on the cloth—tiny flies, which burnt themselves passing over the lamp chimneys, and with scorched legs and wings powdered the damask, the plates, the glasses, with a sort of grey, dancing dust. The diners swallowed them in their wine, ate them in the sauces, saw them struggling about the bread, and all the time their faces and hands were tickled by this countless flying swarm of tiny beasts.

The wine had constantly to be thrown away, the plates covered, the courses eaten furtively, with infinite precautions. This game amused Yvette, Servigny taking care to shelter all she put to her lips, to guard her wine-glass, and hold over her head, like a roof, his outspread napkin. But the marquise, a little nauseated, began to show signs of upset nerves, and the dinner came quickly to an end.

Yvette had by no means forgotten Servigny's proposition: "Now we're going to the island, aren't we?" she said to him.

"Be sure not to stay long," advised her mother languidly. "We are going with you as far as the ferry."

They started along the towing-path, two by two, the young girl and her friend in front. Behind they could hear the Marquise and Saval talking very low and very quick. All was black, velvet black, as black as ink; but the sky, swarming with grains of fire, seemed to be sowing them in the river, for the dark water was powdered with stars. The frogs were croaking now, raising all along the banks their rolling, monotonous chant; and innumerable nightingales flung their soft song into the calm air.

All of a sudden Yvette said: "Why! they're not following! Where are they?" And she called out: "Mother!"

No voice replied. The young girl continued: "They can't be far off, at any rate; I heard them just now."

"They may have turned back," murmured Servigny. "Perhaps your mother was cold." He drew her along.

In front of them glowed a light. It came from the inn of Martinet, fisherman and vendor of refreshments. At the call of the strollers a man came out of the house; they embarked in a broad punt moored in the middle of the reeds at the water's edge. The ferryman took his oars, and the advance of the heavy boat awoke the stars sleeping on the water, making them dance a frenzied dance, which little by little came to rest again behind them.

They touched the other bank, and stepped out under the great trees. The freshness of damp earth floated there, below those high, clustering branches, which seemed to harbour as many nightingales as leaves. A distant piano began playing a popular waltz.

Servigny had taken Yvette's arm, and very quietly he slipped his hand round her waist and pressed it gently. "What are you thinking of?" he said.

"Nothing! I'm just happy."

"So you don't care for me at all, then?"

"Of course I care for you, Muscade; I care a great deal; but do drop all that now! It's too beautiful here to listen to your nonsense!"

He pressed her against him, for all she tried with little jerks to get free, and through the soft texture of her flannel dress he could feel the warmth of her body.

"Yvette!" he stammered.

"Well, what?"

"*I* care for *you.*"

"You're not in earnest, Muscade?"

"I am; I've cared for you a long time."

She was trying all the time to get away from him, trying to pull away her arm, crushed between them. And they walked with difficulty, hindered by this link and by their struggles, zigzagging like a couple of drunkards.

He knew not what to say to her next, feeling it was impossible to speak to a young girl as he would have spoken to a woman; in his perplexity he kept seeking for the right thing to do, wondering whether she consented or simply did not understand—ransacking his brain for just the right, tender, irrevocable words.

He kept on saying: "Yvette! No—but—Yvette!"

Then, suddenly, he hazarded a flying kiss upon her cheek.

She swerved a little, and said in a vexed voice: "Oh! how silly you are! Why can't you leave me alone?"

The tone of her voice told nothing of what she was feeling or wishing; but, judging that she was not so very angry, he put his lips to the nape of her neck, close to the lowest-growing golden down of her hair, that fascinating spot he had coveted so long.

Then she struggled hard to escape, with jerks and starts. But he held her tight, and throwing his other hand upon her shoulder, forced her face round to his own, and stole from her lips a maddening, long kiss.

She slipped down through his arms with a quick undulation of her whole body, dived, and freeing herself swiftly from his embrace, disappeared in the darkness with a great rustling of skirts, like the noise of a bird taking flight.

He stood for a moment quite still, astounded by her suppleness and her disappearance, but, hearing no further sound, he called softly: "Yvette!" There was no answer. He started walking, probing the darkness with his gaze, searching the bushes for the white blur that her dress must surely make. It was all dark. Again he cried, and louder: "Mam'zelle Yvette!"

The nightingales stopped singing.

He hastened on, vaguely alarmed, calling louder and louder: "Mam'zelle Yvette! Mam'zelle Yvette!"

Nothing! He stopped and listened. The whole island was still—scarcely a shiver among the leaves above his head. Alone, the frogs continued their sonorous croaking on the banks.

Then he proceeded to range from copse to copse, descending to the steep, bushy bank of the main stream, and returning to the bare, flat bank of the backwater. He went on till he found himself opposite Bougival, came back to *La Grenouillière,* searched in all the thickets, crying continually: "Mam'zelle Yvette! Where are you? Do answer! It was only a joke! I say, do answer! Don't keep me hunting for you like this!"

A distant clock began to strike. He counted the strokes: Midnight! He had been patrolling the island for two hours. Then he thought that perhaps she had gone home, and he returned also, very uneasy, making the round by the bridge.

A servant, asleep in an armchair, was waiting up in the hall. Servigny woke him and asked: "Has Mlle. Yvette been in long? I was obliged to leave her over there, to pay a call."

The man replied: "Oh yes, M. le Duc, Mlle. came in before ten o'clock."

He reached his room and went to bed, but his eyes remained wide open, he was unable to sleep. That stolen kiss had disturbed him, and he mused: What was she meaning? What was she thinking? What did she know? How pretty she was, how maddening!

His senses, jaded by the life he led, by all the women he had known, all the loves he had exploited, awoke before this strange child, so fresh, so exciting, so inexplicable.

He heard the clock strike one, then two. Assuredly he would never get to sleep! He was hot, perspiring, the blood pulsing hard in his temples; he got up and opened the window.

A puff of fresh air came in, and he drew in a long, deep breath of it. The night was silent, densely dark, unmoving. But suddenly he perceived before him, in the depths of the garden, a glowing speck, like a little live coal. "Hallo!" he thought; "a cigar! That must be Saval"; and he called out softly: "Léon!"

A voice replied: "Is that you, Jean?"

"Yes; wait for me, I'm coming down."

He dressed, went out, and joined his friend, who was smoking, astride of an iron garden-chair.

"What are you up to at this time of night?"

"I? Resting!" replied Saval with a laugh.

Servigny pressed his hand: "My compliments, my dear fellow. And I—am not."

"That's to say?"

"That's to say that Yvette and her mother are not alike."

"What's happened? Tell me!"

Servigny recounted his efforts, and their failure. "This child beats me altogether," he went on; "just think—I haven't been able to get to sleep. What an odd thing a young girl is! She looks simplicity itself, but one really knows nothing about her. A woman who has lived, and loved, and knows what life is, one sees into at once. When it's a question of a young girl, on the contrary, one can't deduce anything at all. At the bottom of my heart, I begin to think she's making a fool of me."

Saval tilted his chair, and said very slowly: "Take care, my dear fellow, she's leading you towards marriage. Remember all the illustrious examples. By that same process Mlle. de Montijo, who was at any rate well-born became an empress. Don't play at being Napoleon!"

"Don't be afraid of that!" murmured Servigny; "I'm neither a fool nor an emperor, and you must be one or the other to do anything so mad. But, I say, are you sleepy?"

"No, not a bit!"

"Then let's go for a stroll along the river!"

"All right!"

They opened the gate, and started along the river-side towards Marly. It was the chill hour that precedes the dawn, the hour of deepest sleep, of deepest rest, of profound quiet. Even the vague noises of the night were hushed. Nightingales no longer sang; frogs had ceased their uproar; alone, some unknown creature, a bird, perhaps, was making somewhere a sound as of a grating saw, feeble, monotonous, and regular, like something mechanical at work.

Servigny, who had his moments of poetry as well as of philosophy, said all of a sudden: "Look here! This girl is too much for me. In arithmetic, one and one make two. In love, one and one ought to make one, but they make two for all that. Have you ever felt this longing to absorb a woman into yourself, or to be absorbed in her? Im not speaking of the animal instinct, but of that moral, mental torment to be at one with her, to open all one's heart and soul to her, to penetrate to the very depths of her thought. And yet one never really knows her, never fathoms all the ups and downs of her will, her wishes, her opinions; never unravels even a little the mystery of that soul so near you, the soul behind those eyes that look at you, as clear as water, as transparent as if there were nothing hidden behind; the soul speaking to you through lips you love so that they seem to be your very own; the soul which utters its thoughts to you, one by one in words, and yet remains further from you than those stars are from each other, and more inscrutable. Odd, isn't it?"

Saval replied: "I don't ask so much from them. I don't look past their eyes. I don't bother myself much about the inside, but a good deal about the out."

"The fact is," murmured Servigny, "that Yvette is abnormal. I wonder how she'll greet me this morning!"

Just as they reached Marly they noticed that the sky was growing lighter; cocks were beginning to crow in the poultry-houses, and the sound came to them deadened by the thickness of the walls. A bird chirped in an enclosure on the left, repeating ceaselessly a simple, comic little flourish.

"It's about time we went home," remarked Saval.

They returned. And Servigny, entering his room, noticed the horizon all rosy through the still open window. He closed the shutter, drew and pulled together the thick curtains, went to bed, and at last fell asleep. He dreamed of Yvette all through his slumbers. A singular noise awoke him. He sat up in bed, listened, and heard nothing. Then suddenly, against his shutters came a curious crackling like falling hail.

He jumped out of bed, ran to the window, threw it open and saw Yvette standing in the garden path, flinging great handfuls of gravel up into his face.

She was dressed in pink, with a large, broad-brimmed straw hat trimmed with one cavalier plume, and laughing a sly, malicious laugh, she cried: "Well, Muscade! are you still asleep? What *can* you have been doing last night to wake up so late? Did you meet with an adventure, my poor Muscade?"

He was dazzled by the brilliant daylight suddenly striking on eyes still heavy with fatigue, and surprised at the young girl's mocking serenity.

"Coming, coming, Mam'zelle!" he called back; "just a second to dip my head in water, and I'll be down."

"Well, be quick," she cried; "it's ten o'clock. And I've a splendid plan to tell you about; a conspiracy we're going to carry out. Breakfast's at eleven, you know."

He found her sitting on a bench, with a book on her knees. She took his arm with a friendly familiarity, as frank and gay as if nothing had happened the night before, and drawing him away to the end of the garden, said: "Now, this is my plan. We're just going to disobey mother, and you're going to take me to *La Grenouillière*. I want to see it. Mother says that decent women can't go there. But I don't care whether they can or can't. You will take me, won't you, Muscade? We'll have such fun with all those boating people!"

There was a sweet scent about her, and he could not determine what that vague and delicate aroma was. It was not one of her mother's heavy perfumes, but a subtle fragrance in which he seemed to catch a suspicion of iris powder, and possible a touch of verbena.

Whence came that indefinable scent? From her dress, her hair, her skin? He wondered, and as she spoke quite close to him, her fresh breath came full in his face, and that too seemed delicious to inhale. Then he fancied that this fleeting perfume, so impossible to put a name to, was perhaps conjured up by his fascinated senses—nothing but a sort of delusive emanation of her young, seductive grace.

"That's settled, then, Muscade?" she said. "It will be very hot after breakfast, and mother's sure not to wish to go out. She's always so limp when it's hot. We'll leave her with your friend, and you shall take me. We shall be supposed to be going into the wood. Oh, if you only knew how much I want to see *La Grenouillière!*"

They came to the gate opposite the river. A ray of sunlight fell on the slumberous, glistening stream. A light heat mist was rising, the fume of evaporated water, which lay on the surface of the river in a thin, shining vapour. Now and then a boat would pass, a rapid yawl, or clumsy wherry, and they heard in the distance short or prolonged whistles, of trains pouring the Sunday crowd from Paris into the surrounding country, and of steamboats giving warning of their approach to the lock at Marly.

But a little bell rang, announcing breakfast, and they went in. The meal was a silent one, almost. A heavy July noon crushed the Earth, weighed down all her creatures. The heat seemed nearly solid, paralyzing to body and spirit. Torpid words refused to leave the lips, and movement was laborious, as if the air had acquired the power of resistance, and become a difficult medium. Yvette alone, though silent, seemed brisk and nervously impatient. When dessert was over she said: "Now, shall we go for a walk in the wood? It would be so jolly under the trees!"

The marquise, who seemed quite done up, murmured: "Are you mad? As if one could go out in such a heat!"

Delighted, the young girl went on: "All right, then! We'll leave the baron to keep you company. Muscade and I are going to climb the hill and sit on the grass and read!"

She turned towards Servigny: "Well, is that settled?" she said.

"At your service, Mam'zelle," he replied.

She flew off to get her hat.

The marquise shrugged her shoulders: "She's mad really," she sighed. Then, with languid fatigue in the slow, amorous gesture, she stretched her fine, white hand to the baron, who kissed it solemnly.

Yvette and Servigny started. Following the river at first, they crossed the bridge, went on to the island, and sat themselves down on the bank of the main stream under the willows, for it was still too early to go to *Grenouillière*.

The young girl at once drew a book from her pocket and said with a laugh: "Now, Muscade, you're going to read to me!"

She held the book out to him.

He made a gesture towards flight. "I, Mam'zelle? But I don't know how to read!"

She went on gravely: "Come, now, no excuses, no explanations! There you are again, you see—a fine sort of suitor! 'Everything for nothing,' that's your motto, isn't it?"

He took the book, opened it, and was amazed. It was a treatise on entomology—a history of the ant, by an English writer. And he remained silent under the impression that she was chaffing, till at last she grew impatient, and said: "Come, begin!"

"Is this for a bet, or is it simply a whim?"

"No, my dear sir, I saw that book at a book-shop. They told me it was the best thing written on ants; I thought it would be amusing to learn about the life of the little beasts, and watch them running about in the grass at the same time; so now, begin!"

She stretched herself out on her face, her eyes fixed on the grass, and he began reading: "Without doubt the anthropoid apes are, of all animals, those which most nearly approach to man in their anatomical structure; but if we consider the habits of the ants, their organization into societies, their immense communities, their dwellings, the roads they construct, their custom of keeping domestic animals, and sometimes even of having slaves, we are forced to admit that they have the right to claim a place near to man on the ladder of intelligence. . . ." And he went on in a monotonous voice, stopping now and then to ask: "Isn't that enough?"

She shook her head, and having caught a wandering ant on the point of a blade of grass she had plucked, was amusing herself by making it run from end to end of the stalk, which she turned the moment the creature had reached one extremity. She listened with a quiet, concentrated attention to all the surprising details in the life of these frail creatures, their subterranean works, their habit of rearing, stabling, and feeding greenfly, so as to obtain the sugary liquor secreted by them, just as we ourselves keep cows in stables; their customs of domesticating little blind insects to keep their establishments clean, and of going to war and bringing back slaves to take such care of the conquerors that the latter even lose the habit of feeding themselves.

And gradually, as though a motherly tenderness had awakened in her heart for this beastie, so minute and so intelligent, Yvette made the ant climb up her finger, and looked at it with soft eyes, quite longing to kiss it. And as Servigny read of how they live in a commonwealth, how they have sports and friendly trials of strength and skill, the young girl in her enthusiasm actually attempted to kiss the insect, which escaped from her finger and ran about her face. Whereupon she gave as piercing a scream as if she had been threatened by some terrible danger, and, with the wildest gestures, brushed at her cheek to get rid of the creature. Servigny, in fits of laughter, caught it on her forehead, and planted a long kiss on the spot he had taken it from, without her turning away her face.

Then, rising, she declared: "I like that better than a novel. Now let's go to *La Grenouillière*."

They came to a part of the island planted like a park with huge, shady trees. Along the river, where boats kept gliding by, some couples were strolling under the branches; work-girls and their lovers, who slouched along in their shirt-sleeves, with a dissipated, jaded air, tall hats on the back of their heads, and coats over their arms; citizens, too, and their families, the women in their Sunday clothes, the children trotting around their parents like broods of chickens.

A distant, continuous hubbub of human voices, a dull and muttering clamour, proclaimed the favourite spot of the river crowd. They came in sight of it all of a sudden—a huge barge crowned with a roof, moored to the bank, and crowded with males and females, some seated drinking at little tables, others on their feet, shouting, singing, howling, dancing, capering, to the sound of a wheezy piano all out of tune and as vibrant as an old kettle.

Great red-haired girls, displaying all the curves of their opulent figures, were promenading around, three parts drunk, with provocation in their eyes and obscenities on their crimson lips. Others danced wildly in front of young men dressed in rowing shorts, cotton vests, and jockey caps. And the whole place exhaled an odour of heat and violet powder, of perfumery and perspiration.

Those seated at the tables were gulping down white, and red, and yellow, and green drinks; shouting and yelling all the time, yielding apparently to a violent longing to make a noise, an animal desire to fill their ears and brains with uproar.

Every minute or so, a swimmer, standing erect on the roof, would spring into the water, showering splashes on those at the nearest tables, who yelled at him like savages.

On the river a fleet of boats kept passing. Long slender, gliding skiffs, lifted along by the strokes of oarsmen with bare arms, whose muscles rolled under the burnt skin. Their dames, in red or blue flannel, with blue or red sunshades open, dazzling in the brilliant sunlight, lolled on the rudder seats, and seemed to float along the water in their slumberous immobility. A tipsy student, bent on showing off, was rowing a kind of windmill stroke, and knocking up against all the boats, whose occupants greeted him with howls. He just missed drowning two swimmers, then disappeared aghast—followed by the jeers of the crowd packed on the floating café.

In the midst of this raffish medley Yvette strolled, all radiant, on Servigny's arm; she seemed quite content to be jostled by these dubious people, and stared undisturbed with her friendly eyes at the women.

"Look at that one, Muscade!" she said; "what pretty hair! They *do* look as if they were enjoying themselves!"

The pianist, an oarsman in red, hatted with a sort of enormous parasol of straw, dashed into a waltz; Yvette, seizing her companion round the waist, carried him off with the fury she always threw into her dancing. They went on so long and so frenziedly that everyone looked at them. Some mounted the tables and beat a kind of measure with their feet; others clinked their glasses. The musician seemed suddenly to go mad, and, throwing his hands about, banged the keys with wild contortions of his whole body, nodding his head passionately under its vast cover. All at once he stopped, and, sliding to the floor, flattened himself out at full length, enshrouded under his headgear, as if he had perished of fatigue.

A roar of laughter burst out all over the café, and everyone applauded. Four friends hastened forward as if there had been an accident, and picking up their comrade, carried him off by his four limbs, after carefully depositing on his stomach the sort of roof he had worn on his head.

A joker, following them, intoned the *De Profundis;* and a procession was formed behind the counterfeit corpse, winding along the paths of the island, and gathering in its wake topers, and strollers, and everyone it met.

Yvette flew along delighted, laughing heartily, chatting with any and everyone, half wild with the noise and excitement. Young men looked right into her eyes and pushed against her; their glances were full of meaning and Servigny began to fear the adventure might turn out ill.

The procession, however, continued its course, faster and faster, for the four bearers had begun to race, followed by the yelling crowd.

But suddenly they made for the bank, stopped dead at the edge, swung their comrade for a second, and, letting go all together, shot him into the river.

An immense shout of delight burst from every mouth, while the bewildered pianist shivered, swore, coughed, spat out the water, and, sticking in the mud, strove to remount the bank. His hat, floating down stream, was brought back by a boat.

Yvette, hopping with joy and clapping her hands, kept crying, "Oh! Muscade! oh! Muscade! What fun!"

But Servigny, who had recovered his seriousness, was watching her uneasily, annoyed to see her so thoroughly at home in these dubious surroundings. He instinctively revolted; for there was in him the natural aversion to vulgarity of every well-bred man, who, even in letting himself go, avoids familiarities too vile, contacts too soiling.

"Great Scot!" he thought, marvelling: "you must have some nice blood in you, my dear!" He felt inclined to use out loud the familiarity that already he applied to her in thought; the familiarity men use to women who are common property, the first time they set eyes on them.

In his thoughts he hardly distinguished her now from the auburn-haired creatures who brushed against them, bawling coarse words in their raucous voices. The air was full of those words—gross, short, and sounding—that seemed to hover over their heads, born of the crowd as flies are of a dunghill. They appeared to surprise and shock no one, and to pass unnoticed by Yvette.

"Muscade, I want to bathe," she said; "we'll go right out into mid-stream."

"Very well," he replied; and they went off to the office for bathing-dresses. She was ready first, and waited for him, standing on the bank, and smiling, under the eyes of all. They started side by side into the sun-warmed water.

Her swimming was full of a sort of ecstatic delight; and lapped by the ripples, shivering with a sensuous joy, she rose with every stroke as if she would spring out of the river. He followed with difficulty, panting, and by no means pleased to find himself so second-rate a performer. Then, slackening speed, she turned over abruptly and floated with her arms crossed and her eyes lost in the blue of the sky. He gazed at her stretched thus on the surface of the water, at the curving lines of her body, her bosom firm and round under the stuff of the clinging gown, her half-submerged limbs, her bare calves gleaming through the water, her little feet peeping out.

There she was from head to foot, as if thus displayed on purpose to tempt, and once more to fool him. His nerves were all on edge with the intensity of his exasperated longing. Suddenly she turned over again, and said laughingly:—

"Oh, you do look funny!"

Piqued by her raillery, and possessed by the spiteful rage of a baffled lover, he gave way suddenly to a subtle desire for reprisals, a longing to avenge himself and wound her.

"So that sort of life would suit you?" he said.

"What life?" she asked, with her most innocent air.

"Don't play the fool with me! You know very well what I mean!"

"No, honour bright."

"Now, let's have done with this nonsense. Will you, or won't you?"

"I don't in the least understand."

"You're not so stupid as that. Besides, I told you last night."

"What? I forget."

"That I love you."

"You?"

"I."

"Rubbish!"

"I swear it."

"Very well, then; prove it."

"That's just what I want."

"How do you mean, what you want——?"

"To prove."

"Very well, do."

"You didn't say that last night."

"You didn't propose anything."

"This is absurd!"

"Besides, it's not to me you ought to speak."

"You're very kind. To whom then?"

"Why, to mother, of course!"

He gave a shout of laughter.

"To your mother? Oh no! That's a little too much."

She had suddenly become very serious, and looking straight into his eyes, said: "Listen, Muscade, if you really love me enough to marry me, speak to mother first; I'll give you my answer afterwards."

He still thought she was chaffing him, and losing his temper completely cried, "Mam'zelle, what do you take me for?"

She still gazed at him with her soft, clear eyes; and hesitating, said, "I still don't understand you, really!"

Then, with something harsh and stinging in his voice, he exclaimed, "Now then, Yvette, once for all let's have done with this absurd farce; it's been going on too long. You're playing the little simpleton; believe me, it's a rôle that doesn't suit you. You know well enough it can't be a question of marriage between us—but of love. I told you I loved you—it's the truth, and I say it again, I love you. Don't pretend not to understand me any longer, and don't treat me as if I were an idiot."

They were face to face in the water, keeping themselves up simply by little movements of their hands. She remained quite still for some seconds, as if she could not decide to take in the sense of his words, then suddenly blushed to the roots of her hair. The whole of her face was flooded with crimson from her throat to her ears, which grew almost purple, and, without answering a word, she fled towards the bank, swimming with all her strength. He could not catch up with her, and gasped with the effort of following. He saw her leave the water, snatch up her cloak and gain her cabin, without once turning her head. He was a long time dressing, completely puzzled as to what to do next, racking his brains for what to say to her, and asking himself whether he ought to apologize or to persevere. When he was ready, she was gone, alone. He walked home slowly, anxious and perturbed.

The Marquise, on Saval's arm, was strolling round the path encircling the lawn.

On seeing Servigny she said with the air of serene indolence she had worn since the night before: "What did I tell you about going out in such a heat? There's Yvette with a sort of sunstroke. She's gone to lie down. The poor child was as red as a poppy, and has got a frightful headache. You must have been walking in the hot sun; you know you've been up to some nonsense—you're just as crazy as she!"

The young girl did not come down to dinner. When asked what she would have, she replied, without opening the door, that she was not hungry—she had locked herself in—and begged only to be left alone. The two young men departed by the ten o'clock train, promising to come again on the following Thursday; and the Marquise sat down to dream happily at her open window, while in the distance the orchestra at *La Grenouillière* flung its flighty music into the solemn silence of the night.

There were times when a passion for love would sweep over her, as a passion for riding or rowing will seize on a man; a mood of sudden tenderness would take possession of her like an illness. These passions pounced on her, invaded her body and soul, maddened, enervated, or overwhelmed her, according as they were of an inspiring, violent, dramatic, or sentimental nature.

She was one of those women born to love and to be loved. From a very low beginning she had climbed by means of that love, of which she had made a profession almost without knowing. Behaving intuitively with innate ability, she accepted money and kisses without distinction, employing her wonderful instinct in the natural, unreasoning way that animals, made sagacious by their daily needs, have. She had had many lovers for whom she had felt no tenderness, yet at whose embraces she had known no disgust. She endured all their caresses with a quiet indifference, just as, when travelling, a man eats all sorts of foods to keep himself alive. But, now and then, her heart or her flesh took fire, and she gave way to a real passion, which lasted weeks or even months, according to the physical or moral qualities of her lover. These were the perfect moments of her life. She loved with all her soul, with all her body, with enthusiasm, with ecstasy. She cast herself into that love as one flings oneself into a river to drown; and she let herself be swept away, ready to die, if so she must, intoxicated, maddened, yet infinitely happy. Each time she imagined that never before had she felt anything so wonderful; and she would have been vastly astonished if you had recalled to her all the different men over whom she had dreamed passionately, the whole night long, gazing at the stars.

Saval had captured her, body and soul. Under the spell of his image she mused over precious memories, deep in the supreme calm of fulfilled happiness, of present and certain joy.

A sound from behind made her turn. Yvette had just come in, dressed as she had been all day, but pale now, with the brilliant eyes that great fatigue will cause.

She leaned against the side of the window, opposite her mother.

"I've something to tell you," she said.

The Marquise looked at her in surprise. She was fond of her daughter in a selfish sort of fashion, proud of her beauty as one might be of great wealth; she was herself still too handsome to be jealous, and too lazy to make the plans that others

credited her with; at the same time she was too subtle not to be
aware of the girl's value.

"I'm listening, child," she said; "what is it?"

Yvette gazed at her as if she would read the depths of her
soul, as if she meant to grasp all the shades of expression that her
coming words might awaken.

"It's—— Something extraordinary happened to-day!"

"What?"

"M. de Servigny told me he loved me."

The Marquise waited uneasily, but as Yvette said nothing,
she asked: "How did he tell you that? Let me hear!"

Yvette nestled down in her favourite attitude at her mother's
feet, and squeezing her hands, said: "He asked me to marry him."

Mme. Obardi made an abrupt movement of stupefaction, and
cried out: "Servigny! You must be mad."

Yvette had not taken her eyes off her mother's face, searching
for the true meaning of her astonishment.

In a grave voice she asked: "Why mad? Why shouldn't
M. de Servigny want to marry me?"

The Marquise stammered in embarrassment: "You've made
a mistake—it's out of the question. You couldn't have heard—
you misunderstood. M. de Servigny is too rich for you, and too—
too—Parisian ever to marry."

Yvette got up slowly. "But if he loves me, mother, as he
says he does?" she asked.

Her mother went on with a certain impatience: "I thought
you were big enough and knew enough about things not to have
any such ideas as that. Servigny is a selfish man of the world.
He'll only marry a woman of his own rank and fortune. If he
did ask you to marry him, he simply meant——"

The Marquise, unable to speak out her suspicions, was silent
for a moment, then went on: "There, don't bother me; go
to bed."

And the young girl, as if she now knew all she wanted, replied
obediently: "Yes, mother."

Just as she was going out of the door, however, the Marquise
called: "And what about your sunstroke?"

"I never had one. It was all this other affair."

"We'll talk about that again," added the Marquise; "but take
care not to be alone with him after this; you may be quite sure
he doesn't mean to marry you, only to—to— compromise you."

She could find no better words to express her thought. Yvette went back to her room.

Mme. Obardi set to work to reflect.

Living for years in the serene atmosphere of gilded love, she had carefully guarded her mind from every thought that could preoccupy, trouble or sadden it. Never once had she allowed herself to face the question of what would become of Yvette; it would be time enough to think about that when the difficulty arose. Her courtesan's instinct told her that her daughter could never marry a rich and well-born man save by some quite improbable chance, one of those surprises of love that have placed adventuresses upon thrones.

She was not counting on any such thing, moreover, being too self-centred to make any plans not directly concerned with her own affairs.

Yvette would live for love, as her mother had done, no doubt. But the Marquise had never dared to ask herself when or how it would come about. And now here was her daughter, suddenly, without preparation, demanding of her an answer to one of those questions to which no answer could be given, forcing her to take up a definite attitude in an affair so difficult, so delicate, so dangerous in every way, so disturbing to her conscience, the conscience a mother is bound to have towards her child, in matters such as these. She had too much natural acumen, slumbering, it is true, but never quite asleep, to be deceived for a moment as to Servigny's intentions, for she had acquired a wide knowledge of men, and particularly of men of his kind. So, at the first words Yvette had spoken, she had been unable to help that exclamation: "Servigny marry you! you must be mad!"

Why had he made use of such a stale trick? He, that shrewd man of the world, that pleasure-loving rake? What would he do now? And how should she warn the child more plainly, how defend her? Obviously she was capable of making a complete fool of herself. Who would have believed that that great girl had remained so simple, so ignorant, so artless?

And the Marquise, puzzled, and already fatigued with too much thinking, racked her brains for what to do now, without finding any way out of so truly embarrassing a situation.

Tired of this bother she suddenly decided: "Ah, well! I'll watch them carefully, and act according to circumstances; if necessary, I'll speak to Servigny; he's sharp enough to understand a hint."

She did not ask herself what she would say to him, nor what he might reply, nor what sort of arrangement could be arrived at between them, but happy at having smoothed out this troublesome matter without having had to make any decision, she went back to dreams of her Saval. With eyes lost in the night, turned towards the glowing haze that hung over Paris, she wafted kisses towards the great city, flinging them with both hands into the darkness, one after another, kisses without number; and in a low voice, as though still speaking to him, she murmured: "I love you! I love you!"

Chapter III

YVETTE, too, did not sleep. Like her mother, she leaned on her elbows at the open window, and tears, the first tears of real sadness, filled her eyes.

Till now she had grown up in the heedless, confident serenity of a joyous youth. What was there indeed to make her brood, reflect, or wonder? What to make her different from other young girls? Why should doubt, or fear, or painful suspicions visit her? She had seemed knowing because she had seemed to talk knowingly, having, naturally, caught up the tone, the manner, the risky sayings of the people round about her. But in reality she knew little more of life than a child brought up in a convent; her audacious speeches were like a parrot's, and came rather from her feminine faculty for assimilation and mimicry, than from any daring depth of knowledge.

She talked of love as the son of a painter or musician will talk of painting or music at the age of ten or twelve. She knew —or rather suspected—what sort of mystery lay behind that word; too many jokes had been whispered in her hearing for her innocence to have remained entirely unenlightened. But was that a reason for concluding that other families were not like her own?

Everyone kissed her mother's hand with ostentatious respect; their friends were all titled, and all were, or appeared to be, rich; all talked familiarly of royal personages. Two princes of the blood had actually come to some of her mother's evenings. How was she to know? Then, too, she was by nature simple, and far from inquisitive; she had none of her mother's intuitive perception. Her mind was undisturbed, she was too much in love with life to worry over things which might have seemed suspicious to a quieter, more thoughtful, more reserved nature—to one less open-hearted, less exultant.

And now, in a moment, Servigny, with a few words, whose

brutality she had felt rather than comprehended, had roused in her a sudden and at first unreasoning disquiet, which had gradually become a galling dread. She had fled home like a wounded creature, pierced to the heart by those words which she kept repeating over and over again, in the effort to sound all their meaning, and grasp their true import: "You know well enough it can't be a question of marriage between us—only of love!"

What had he meant by that? And why had he insulted her? There was clearly something that she did not know, something secret or shameful! No doubt she was the only one in ignorance. But what was it? She felt scared, overwhelmed, as if she had discovered some hidden infamy, treachery in some beloved friend —one of those disasters that wring the heart.

And she went on brooding, reflecting, searching, weeping, consumed by her doubts and fears.

But at last her young, buoyant nature reasserted itself. She began constructing a story, an abnormal and dramatic situation woven out of many memories of the many romantic novels she had read. She recalled startling turns of fortune, sombre, heartbreaking plots, and out of the jumble made up a life-story of herself, to adorn this half-hidden mystery surrounding her life.

She was already a little less miserable, and, wrapped in reverie, began lifting mysterious veils, imagining impossible complications, a thousand curious and terrible events, whose very strangeness had a fascination.

Could she, by any chance, be the natural child of some prince? Her poor mother, seduced and abandoned, created Marquise by the King, Victor Emanuel himself perhaps, and obliged to fly from the wrath of the family? Or was she not more likely the off-shoot of a guilty passion, abandoned by very illustrious parents, and rescued by the Marquise, who had adopted her and brought her up?

And fresh ideas kept coming into her head, which she accepted or rejected according to her fancy. She began to have a sort of tender pity for herself, happy and sad, too, in the depths of her heart, yet on the whole content to find herself a heroine of romance, who would have to show herself capable of playing a dignified and noble part.

And she thought over the rôle she would assume, according to these various sets of circumstances. She pictured it vaguely, this rôle, like a character of M. Scribe's or Mme. Sand's. It should be made up of devotion, nobility, self-sacrifice, greatness of soul, tenderness, and beautiful speeches. Her flexible nature almost rejoiced in this new prospect.

So she stayed until the evening, thinking what she was going to do, and how best she should set to work to drag the truth out of the Marquise. And when night was come, the hour of tragic situations, she had at last devised this simple but subtle trick to obtain what she wanted:—

To tell her mother suddenly that Servigny had asked her to marry him.

At the news Mme. Obardi, in her surprise, would certainly let fall some word, some ejaculation that would throw light into her daughter's soul.

And Yvette had forthwith carried out her plan.

She had expected an outburst of astonishment, an outpouring of love, some disclosure full of caresses and tears.

And behold! Her mother, neither astounded nor distressed, had only seemed annoyed; and from the embarrassed, displeased, troubled tone of her reply, the young girl, in whom had suddenly awakened all a woman's shrewd subtlety and dissimulation, understood that she must not insist, that the mystery was of some other kind, more painful to learn, probably, and that she would have to guess it for herself. She had gone back to her room with a heavy heart, in dire distress, crushed now by the sense of a real misfortune, without knowing exactly whence or wherefore came this new feeling. Leaning on her elbows at the window, she wept.

She sobbed a long time, without thinking at all now, or trying to make any more discoveries; then little by little fatigue overcame her, and her eyes closed. She fell for a few minutes into that unrefreshing slumber of people too exhausted to make the effort of undressing and getting to bed—a heavy sleep, broken by sudden starts, as her head kept slipping between her hands. She did not go to bed till the first gleam of dawn, when the penetrating chill of the early morning forced her to leave the window.

The next day, and the day after, she maintained a reserved and melancholy demeanour.

A ceaseless ferment of thought was going on within her; she was learning to watch, and deduce, and reflect. A new and lurid light seemed cast on everyone and everything around; she was beginning to look with suspicion on all she had once believed in, even on her mother. During those two days all kinds of surmises flitted through her brain, and, facing each possible contingency, she flung herself, with all the abruptness of her headlong, unbalanced nature, from one extreme decision to another.

On Wednesday she fixed on a plan which embodied a complete scheme of conduct, and a system of espionage. She got up on Thursday morning with the resolve to outvie the subtlety of a detective, to be armed for battle against all the world. She even resolved to take for her motto the two words, "Myself alone!" and considered for over an hour how they would make the best effect engraved round the monogram on her writing paper.

Saval and Servigny arrived at ten o'clock. The young girl held out her hand to them quite simply, but coolly, saying in a friendly, rather grave voice: "How do you do, Muscade?"

"Thank you, Mam'zelle, pretty well—and you?"

He watched her. "What game is she up to now?" he asked himself.

The Marquise had taken Saval's arm, and he gave his own to Yvette; they all sauntered round the lawn, winding in and out of the clumps of bushes and trees. Yvette moved along reflectively, her eyes fixed on the gravel path; she hardly seemed to listen to her companion, hardly answered him. All at once she asked: "Are you really my friend, Muscade?"

"I am, Mam'zelle."

"Really, really and truly?"

"Absolutely your friend, Mam'zelle, body and soul."

"Friend enough not to tell me a fib for once, just for this once?"

"Even for twice, if necessary."

"Friend enough to tell me the whole truth, the whole horrid truth?"

"Yes, Mam'zelle."

"All right then: what do you really, *really* think of Prince Kravalow?"

"Phe-e-ew!"

"There, you see, you're getting ready to tell me a fib directly."

"Not at all, I'm merely choosing the exact words. Well, then, Prince Kravalow is a Russian—a Russian of the Russians, speaks Russian, was born in Russia, who quite possibly had a passport for France, and has nothing false about him but his name and his title."

She looked straight into his eyes: "You mean that he's——"

After a moment's hesitation he replied: "An adventurer, Mam'zelle."

"Thank you. And the Chevalier Valréali is no better, I suppose?"

"Just so."

"And M. de Belvigne?"

"Ah! he's different. He's a gentleman—provincial, of course; honourable—up to a certain point—but a little burnt about the wings, from having flown too fast——"

"And you?"

He answered without hesitation: "I? Oh, I'm what you call a 'gay bird'—of good enough family, who once had brains, and has hashed them up making jokes; who once had a constitution, and has run through it playing the fool; who once had a certain value perhaps, and has squandered it doing nothing. To sum up, I've got money, and experience of life, a complete absence of prejudice, a pretty fair contempt for men, including women, profound consciousness of my own futility, and vast toleration of riff-raff in general. However, I've still got my moments of frankness, you see, and I'm even capable of affection, as you *might* see—if you liked. With these defects and qualities, I put myself, morally and physically, at your service, to dispose of as you please. There!"

She did not laugh; but seemed, as she listened, to be weighing the meaning of his words.

She began again: "What do you think of the Comtesse de Lammy?"

He said very quickly: "Ah! Allow me to give no opinion on women."

"On none?"

"None."

"Then, it's because you think very badly of them all. Come, now, can't you think of a single exception?"

His insolent smile that was half a sneer reappeared, and with the cynical audacity he used like a weapon, both for attack and defence, said: "Present company always excepted."

She flushed a little, but asked quite calmly: "Well, what do you think of *me*?"

"You *will* have it? Very well. I think that you're a person of excellent practical sense, or, if you like it better, of excellent common sense, understanding perfectly how to mask your game, amuse yourself at other people's expense, hide your plans, throw out your nets, and wait calmly—for the result."

"Is that all?"

"That's all.

"I shall make you change that opinion, Muscade," she said very gravely; and joined her mother, who was strolling languidly along with her head bent, like a woman talking of tender, intimate things, and tracing as she went patterns, or perhaps letters, on the gravel path with the point of her sunshade. She was not looking at Saval, but speaking on and on in a slow voice, leaning on his arm, and pressing against him. Yvette suddenly fixed her eyes upon her; a suspicion, so vague that she could not seize it, a sensation rather than a doubt, flitted through her brain, like the shadow of a wind-chased cloud passing over the earth.

The bell sounded for breakfast.

It was a silent, almost mournful meal.

There was the feeling of storm in the air. Great motionless clouds seemed ambushed on the far horizon, dumb, weighty, loaded with tempest. They had just taken coffee on the terrace, when the Marquise said: "Well, darling, are you going for a walk to-day with M. de Servigny? It's just the weather for strolling under the trees!"

Yvette gave her a rapid glance, quickly averted: "No, mother, I'm not going out to-day."

The Marquise seemed annoyed: "Oh! go and take a turn, my child," she persisted; "it's so good for you."

"No, mother," repeated Yvette brusquely, "I mean to stay at home to-day, and you know quite well why, I told you the other evening."

Mme. Obardi, absorbed in the desire to be alone with Saval, had forgotten. She reddened, grew confused; and, uneasy on her own account, wondering how on earth she would get an hour or so free, she stammered: "Of course, that never occurred to me; you're quite right. I don't know what I was thinking about."

Taking up a piece of embroidery which she had nicknamed the "public welfare," and on which she employed her fingers when in the doldrums—perhaps five or six times in the year— Yvette sat down in a low chair near her mother, while the two young men, astride of their seats, smoked their cigars.

So the hours passed, in languid talk that was continually

dying away. The Marquise, her nerves on edge, and casting despairing glances at Saval, was seeking some pretext for getting rid of her daughter. She realized at last that she would never succeed, and at her wit's end said to Servigny: "You know, my dear Duke, I mean to keep you both here to-night. To-morrow we'll go and breakfast at the Restaurant Fournaise, at Chatou."

He understood at once, smiled, and replied with a bow: "We are entirely at your disposal, Marquise."

The day slipped slowly and sadly away, under the menace of the storm. At last the dinner-hour came. The lowering sky kept filling with slow, heavy clouds. There was not a breath of air.

The evening meal was silent too. A feeling of discomfort and constraint, a sort of vague fear, seemed to hold the two men and the two women dumb.

When the table was cleared they stayed on the terrace, speaking only now and then. The night fell, a stifling night. All at once, the horizon was torn by a great hook of fire, which, with a blinding, wan flame, illumined the four faces shrouded in the gloom. And a distant sound, a dull, faint noise, like the rolling of a carriage over a bridge, travelled along the earth, and the heat of the atmosphere seemed to increase, to become suddenly more overwhelming, the silence of the evening more profound.

Yvette got up. "I'm going to bed," she said; "the storm makes me feel so queer."

She bent her forehead to the Marquise, gave her hand to the two young men, and disappeared.

Her room was just over the terrace, and the leaves of a great chestnut-tree planted opposite the front door were presently lit up with a greenish light; Servigny kept his eyes fixed on that pale glow among the foliage, across which he fancied he could now and then see a shadow pass. But suddenly the light went out. Mme. Obardi drew a long, deep breath. "My daughter's in bed," she said.

Servigny got up: "I think I'll follow her example, Marquise, if you'll excuse me."

He kissed the hand she gave him, and disappeared.

She remained alone with Saval in the darkness, and the next moment she was in his arms, clasping him to her. Then, though he tried to prevent it, she knelt before him, murmuring: "I must look at you by the blaze of the lightning."

But Yvette, having blown out her candle, had come back to

her balcony, stealing barefoot like a shadow; she listened, consumed by painful and confused suspicions.

She could not see, being exactly above them, on the roof of the verandah itself.

She heard nothing but a murmur of voices, and her heart beat so fast that it filled her ears with its noise. A window was suddenly shut above her head. So Servigny had gone up to his room! Her mother was alone with the other. A second flash cleft the sky in two, and for a second made the whole well-known landscape start forth with a violent, sinister clearness; and she saw the great river, the colour of molten lead, like a river in the fantastic land of dreams. And at that moment a voice beneath her said: "I love you!"

She heard no more. A strange shiver passed through her whole body, and her brain wandered in the whirl of a frightful emotion. A heavy, unending silence, that seemed the very silence eternal, brooded over the world. She could no longer breathe, her heart weighed down by something unknown and horrible. Once more a flash kindled the sky, and illumined the horizon, another followed, and yet others.

And the voice that she had already heard repeated in a louder tone: "Ah! how I love you! how I love you!"

Yvette knew that voice too well—the voice of her mother.

A large drop of lukewarm water fell on her forehead, and a tiny tremor, barely perceptible, ran through the leaves, the shiver of the rain just beginning.

Then a clamour came hurrying from afar, a confused clamour, like wind among branches; the heavy shower beating in a sheet upon the earth, the river, the trees. Quickly the water streamed all round her, splashing, covering, soaking her like a bath. She did not stir, thinking only of what they were doing on the terrace. She heard them get up, and mount the stairs to their rooms; the noise of doors shutting in the house. And, obeying an irresistible longing to know, that tortured and maddened her, the young girl flew down the stairs, gently opened the outer door, and crossing the lawn under the furious beat of the rain, ran and hid herself in the bushes, to watch the windows.

Her mother's alone was lighted. And suddenly two shadows appeared, framed in the bright square, side by side. Then, drawing closer, they made but one; and by the lightning which again flung a vivid blinding jet of fire on the face of the house, she saw them embracing, their arms clasped around each other's necks.

Wildly, without thinking or knowing what she did, she cried with all her strength, in a piercing voice: "Mother!" as one cries out to warn another of some deadly danger.

Her despairing appeal was smothered in the splashing of the rain, but the embracing couple started uneasily apart, and one of the shadows vanished, while the other sought to distinguish something among the dark shadows of the garden.

Then, fearing to be discovered, to meet her mother at such a moment, Yvette fled towards the house, flew up the stairs, leaving behind her a trail of water that dripped from step to step, and shut herself in her room, resolved to open her door to no one.

Without taking off the streaming dress that clung to her skin, she fell on her knees, and clasping her hands, implored in her distress, divine protection, that mysterious help from heaven, that unknown aid we pray for in hours of agony and despair.

Every minute great flashes kept throwing their livid light into the room, and suddenly she saw her reflection in the glass of her wardrobe, with hair unbound and dripping, so strange that she failed to recognize herself.

She remained there a long time, so long that the storm had passed over without her being conscious of it. The rain ceased falling, light came into the sky, though it was still dark with clouds, and a warm, sweet, fragrant freshness, the freshness of wet grass and leaves, drifted in at the open window.

Yvette rose, mechanically took off her limp, cold clothes, and went to bed. There she remained, with eyes fixed on the dawn.

She wept again, then again she began thinking.

Her mother with a lover! The shame of it! But she had read so many books where women, mothers even, abandoned themselves like that, to rise again to honour at the end of the story, that she was not beyond measure amazed to find herself thus entangled in a drama so like all the dramas she had read of.

Her grief, the cruel bewilderment of the shock, were already losing a little of their violence in the confused memory of similar situations. Her thoughts had roved among such tragic adventures, so romantically introduced by novelists, that the horrible discovery began little by little to seem like the natural continuation of a story commenced yesterday.

"I will save my mother," she said to herself. And, almost

tranquillized by this heroic resolve, she felt strong, great, ready all at once for her devoted struggle. She thought over the means she would employ. One only commended itself to her romantic nature. And as an actor prepares the scene he is about to play, so she began to prepare the interview she would have with the Marquise.

The sun had risen. The servants were busy about the house, and the maid came with her chocolate. Yvette told her to put the tray down on the table, and said: "Go and tell my mother that I'm not well to-day, that I'm going to stay in bed till those gentlemen are gone. I haven't been able to sleep all night, and I don't wish to be disturbed; I'm going to try and rest now."

The maid looked in surprise at the wet dress, lying like a rag on the carpet: "Why, Mademoiselle, you've been out!" she said.

"Yes, I went for a walk in the rain to freshen myself up."

The girl picked up the petticoats, stockings, and muddy shoes, and went off, carrying them over one arm, with disdainful precautions; they were soaked for all the world like the clothes of a drowned woman. Yvette waited, knowing that her mother would come. The Marquise entered, having jumped out of bed at the first words of the maid, for a doubt had remained in her mind ever since that cry of "Mother!" heard out of the darkness.

"What's the matter with you?" she asked.

Yvette looked at her, and faltered: "I— I've——" Then, overcome by a sudden and terrible emotion, she began to choke with sobs.

The Marquise, in astonishment, asked again: "What *is* the matter with you?"

Forgetting all her plans and prepared phrases, the young girl hid her face in her two hands and sobbed out: "Oh! mother, oh! mother!"

Mme. Obardi remained standing by the bedside, too disturbed to altogether understand, but guessing nearly all, with that subtle instinct wherein lay her strength.

And since Yvette, choked by her sobs, could not speak, her mother, at last quite unstrung, and feeling the approach of some formidable explanation, abruptly asked: "Come, will you tell me what's taken possession of you?"

Yvette could scarcely articulate the words: "Last night—I saw —your window!"

Very pale, the Marquise exclaimed: "Well, what then?"

Her daughter continued to sob: "Oh! mother, oh! mother!"

Mme. Obardi, whose dread and embarrassment were quickly changing into anger, shrugged her shoulders, and turned to go away: "I really think you're mad," she said; "when this is over, perhaps you'll let me know."

But the young girl suddenly took her hands from her face, which was streaming with tears. "No! listen! I *must* speak—listen! Promise me!—we'll go away together, ever so far, into the country, and live like peasants; and no one will know what has become of us! Oh! mother, will you? I beg, I implore—will you?"

The Marquise, dumbfounded, remained in the middle of the room. She had the irascible blood of the "people" in her veins. Then, a feeling of shame, the shame of a mother, began to mingle with the vague alarm and exasperation of a passionate woman whose love is menaced; she was shivering, ready either to ask pardon or fling herself into a fury. "I don't understand you," she said.

Yvette went on: "I saw you! Oh! mother—last night. It must never—if you only knew! Let's go away together—I'll love you so, that you'll forget——"

In a trembling voice Mme. Obardi began: "Listen, my child; there are things that you don't yet understand. Well—don't forget—never forget, that I forbid you—ever to speak to me—of—of those things."

But Yvette, suddenly assuming the rôle of saviour she had marked out for herself, declared: "No, mother, I'm no longer a child; I've a right to know. Well, I *do* know that we receive all sorts of people, adventurers—and that we're not respected, because of that; and I know something else too. It mustn't be, can't you understand? I can't bear it; we'll work if we must, and live like honest women, somewhere, far away. And if I should happen to marry, so much the better."

Her mother looked at her with her black, angry eyes, and answered: "You're mad. You'll do me the favour of getting up, and coming down to lunch with us all."

"No, mother. There's someone I won't see again; you know what I mean. He must leave this house, or I will. You must choose between us."

She was sitting up in bed, and she raised her voice, speaking as people speak on the stage, entering fully at last into the drama of which she had dreamed, and almost forgetting her grief in the absorption of her mission.

The Marquise, finding nothing else to say, repeated the words: "You must be mad——"

Yvette continued with theatrical energy: "No, mother, that man must leave the house, or I will myself—I shan't flinch."

"And where will you go? What will you do?"

"I don't know; I don't care. Only let us be honest women!"

The recurrence of this expression, "honest women," aroused the fury of a street girl in the Marquise, and she shouted: "Hold your tongue! I won't allow you to speak to me like that! I'm as good as anyone else, d'you hear? I'm a courtesan! and I'm proud of it! I'm worth a dozen of your 'honest women'!"

Yvette gazed at her aghast, stammering: "Oh, mother!"

But the Marquise, more and more excited, cried: "Well, I *am* a courtesan; what then? If I were not a courtesan, you'd be a kitchen-maid, as I was once; and you'd earn thirty sous a day, and wash up plates and dishes, and your mistress would send you on errands to the butcher's—do you hear? and she'd turn you out of doors if you idled; whereas you idle and amuse yourself all day long, just because I *am* a courtesan. So there! When you're only a servant, a poor girl with fifty francs of savings, you've got to find a way out of it; if you don't mean to die in the workhouse; yes, and there are no two ways for us women, d'you hear, no two ways, when you're a servant! Women can't make their fortunes by jobbery and swindling. We've nothing but our bodies—nothing but our bodies!"

She beat her breast like a penitent confessing, and all flushed and excited, came towards the bed, crying: "So much the worse for a girl that's handsome, she must live on her looks, or grind along in poverty all her life—all her life! There's no choice!"

Then, reverting to her original idea: "And do *they* starve themselves, your good women? Not they! It's *they* who are the drabs, d'you hear?—because they're not obliged to. They have money, plenty to live on, plenty to amuse them—and yet they have their lovers! That's vice! It's *they* who are the drabs!"

She stood close to the bed, where Yvette, distraught, ready to shout for help, ready to rush away, was crying loudly like a child that is being beaten.

The Marquise stopped, and seeing her daughter in such a desperate state, was herself seized with grief, remorse, tenderness, pity; falling on the bed with outstretched arms, she too began to sob, murmuring: "My child, my poor child; if you only knew how you hurt me!"

And so they wept together, for a long time.

Then the Marquise, with whom grief never lasted, gently raised herself, and said very gently: "Come, darling, things *are* like that, you know! We can't alter them now. We must take life as it comes!"

But Yvette continued to weep. The blow had been too heavy and unexpected for her to collect and control herself.

Her mother went on: "Come, get up, and come to lunch, so that nobody will notice anything."

The young girl shook her head, unable to speak; at last she said in a halting voice, strangled with sobs: "No, mother, you know what I told you; I can't change. I will not come out of my room until they're gone. I don't want to see any more of men of that kind—never—never. If they come back I— I— you'll never see me again."

The Marquise had dried her eyes, and tired by her emotion, murmured: "Come, think; be reasonable!" Then, after a minute of silence, she added: "Well, perhaps it *is* better for you to rest this morning. I'll come and see you in the afternoon."

And, already quite calm again, she kissed her daughter on the forehead, and left the room to finish dressing.

As soon as her mother had disappeared, Yvette sprang up to bolt the door, so that she might be quite alone, and set to work to think.

Towards eleven o'clock the maid knocked and asked through the door: "Mme. la Marquise wishes to know if Mademoiselle wants anything, and what she would like for breakfast?"

"I'm not hungry," replied Yvette; "I only want to be left alone."

And she remained in bed, as though she had been seriously ill.

Towards three o'clock there came another knock. "Who's there?" she asked.

Her mother's voice replied: "It's I, darling; I've come to see how you are——"

She hesitated what to do, then unfastened the door, and went back to bed.

The Marquise came up to her, and speaking in a hushed voice, as though to a convalescent, asked: "Well, do you feel better? Couldn't you eat an egg?"

"No, thank you, nothing."

Mme. Obardi sat down beside the bed, and they stayed without speaking; then, at last, as her daughter remained motionless, with hands resting inertly on the sheets, she asked: "Aren't you going to get up?"

"Presently," replied Yvette.

Then in a grave and slow voice, she added: "Mother, I've been thinking a great deal; and this is what I've decided. The past is the past; we won't talk about it again. But the future must be different—or else—or else, I know what's left for me to do. Now, we won't talk about it any more."

The Marquise, who had believed the explanation over, felt her impatience rising again. It was really too much. This great goose of a girl ought to have understood long ago! But she made no answer, and only repeated: "Are you going to get up?"

"Yes, I'm ready now."

Her mother acted as lady's-maid, fetching her stockings, corset, and petticoats; then, kissing her, said: "Shall we go for a stroll before dinner?"

"Yes, mother."

They went for a walk along the river-side, talking chiefly of the most trivial things.

Chapter IV

Next morning Yvette went off alone, and seated herself at the spot where Servigny had read to her the history of the ant. "I won't stir from here until I've made up my mind," she said to herself.

The swift current of the main stream flowed by just at her feet; it was full of eddies and great bubbles that passed in a silent flight of little swirling pools. Already she had stared at every side of the problem, at every possible way of solution.

What would she do if her mother failed to scrupulously preserve the condition she had imposed, failed to renounce her life, her friends, everything, to go and hide with her in some far distant place?

She might run away—go alone. But where—and how? And what was she to live on?

By working! But at what? To whom would she go to find work? And then the mournful, humble existence of a poor workgirl seemed to her a little ignominious, not quite worthy of her. She thought of becoming a governess, like the young persons in novels, and of being loved and wedded by the son of the house. But for *that,* high birth was a *sine quâ non,* so that when the angry father reproached her for stealing his son's love, she might be able to reply proudly: "My name is Yvette Obardi!"

And this she could not do. Besides, it was a commonplace, stale idea.

The convent was hardly better. She felt no vocation for the religious life, having but fitful, intermittent moments of piety. No one would step in and marry a girl with her antecedents. No help from any *man* was to be thought of for an instant. There was no possible way out, nothing definite that she could have recourse to. And then, it must be some forceful issue, something really great and strong, that would serve as an example; and she resolved on death. She decided on it all at once, quietly, as if it were a question of taking a journey; without reflecting or realizing the nature of death, without seeing that it is the end without possibility of recommencement, the departure without return, the eternal farewell to this earth, to life.

She felt at once well-disposed towards this great resolution, with all the irresponsibility of a young, romantic spirit.

She mused over the means she might employ; but all seemed so painful and hazardous in the doing, and demanded, too, an act of violence, which was repugnant to her.

She very quickly abandoned the idea of dagger or pistol, which may merely wound, cripple, or disfigure, and require, too, a steady, practised hand; rejected hanging as too common, a ridiculous and ugly method only fit for paupers; and drowning, because she could swim. So there only remained poison; but which? Nearly all caused suffering and provoked violent sickness. She wished neither to suffer, nor to be sick. At last she thought of chloroform, having read in some paper how a young woman had set to work to suffocate herself by this method.

And she felt at once a kind of joy in her resolve, a certain private pride, a sense of self-esteem. They should see what she was made of, what she was worth!

Returning to Bougival, she went into a chemist's, and asked him for a little chloroform for an aching tooth. The man, who knew her, gave her a very small phial of the narcotic.

Then she started off on foot to Croissy, where she procured another little bottle of the poison. She obtained a third at Chatou, and a fourth at Reuil, and got home late for lunch. Being very hungry after this round, she ate a hearty meal, thoroughly famished after so much exercise.

Her mother, delighted to see her with such an appetite, and feeling herself safe at last, said, as they rose from table: "All our friends are coming to spend Sunday with us. I've invited the prince, the chevalier, and M. de Belvigne."

Yvette turned rather white, but made no reply.

She went out almost at once, and making for the station took a ticket for Paris.

During the whole afternoon, she went from chemist to chemist, buying from each a few drops of chloroform.

She returned in the evening with her pockets full of little bottles. This campaign she renewed on the morrow, and going by chance into a druggist's, succeeded at one stroke in buying about half a pint. On Saturday she did not go out; it was a close, overcast day, and she spent the whole of it on the terrace, lounging in a long cane chair. She hardly thought about anything at all, but felt very resolute and calm.

The next day, wishing to look her best, she put on a blue dress that suited her extremely well, and, gazing at herself in the glass, thought suddenly: "To-morrow I shall be dead!" A strange shiver passed through her from head to foot.

"Dead! Never to speak, never to think; no one to see me any more. And I—I shall never see all this again."

She scrutinized her face as if she had never seen it before, and especially her eyes—discovering a thousand new traits, a hidden character in that face that she had been quite unaware of; and she was astonished at the look of herself, as if she had in front of her some strange person, some new friend. She thought: "It's I, yes! it's I, in that glass. How weird it is to look at oneself! And yet, without mirrors we should never know our faces. Everyone else would know what we were like, but *we* should never know." She took her thick, plaited tresses of hair, and brought them over on to her bosom, following each gesture and attitude with attentive eyes. "How pretty I am!" she thought. "To-morrow I shall be dead; dead, over there, on my bed."

She looked at her bed, and seemed to see herself stretched upon it, white, like the sheets.

Dead! in a week that face, those eyes and cheeks would be nothing but a black horror, in a box, deep down in the earth! And a terrible anguish wrung her heart.

The clear sunlight fell in flecks on all the country round, and in at the window came the sweet morning air. She sat down, still thinking: "Dead!" It seemed as if the world must be coming to an end before her eyes; and yet, it was not that! For nothing in the world would be changed, not even her room. No, her room would be there just the same, with the same bed and chairs and mirror, but *she* would be gone for ever and ever, and no one would be grieved, except perhaps her mother.

People would say: "Little Yvette! How pretty she was!" and that would be all. And as she looked at her hand resting on the arm of the chair, she mused again over that decay, that black nauseous mass that would be her body. And once more a great shiver of horror ran over her whole frame. She could not comprehend how it was that she could disappear without the whole world coming to naught, so deeply did she feel that she was a part of everything, of the earth, the air, the sun, and of life.

There was a burst of laughter from the garden, a hubbub of voices and cries, the noisy merriment of a country-house party just assembled; she recognized the sonorous organ of M. de Belvigne, singing:—

> "Je suis sous ta fenêtre,
> Ah! daigne enfin paraître!"

She got up without thinking, and looked out. They all applauded. The whole five of them were there, as well as two other men whom she did not know.

She started back, torn by the thought that these men had come to amuse themselves at the house of her mother, the courtesan.

The lunch-bell rang.

"I will show them how to die," she said to herself.

And she walked firmly downstairs, with something of the resolution of the Christian martyrs entering the arena where the lions awaited them.

She shook hands with the guests, smiling rather superciliously.

"Are you less grumpy to-day, Mam'zelle?" asked Servigny.

In a grave and curious tone of voice she answered: "To-day I'm going to run wild. I'm in my Paris mood; take care!"

Then, turning towards M. de Belvigne, she added: "You shall be my pet to-day, my little Malvoisie. I'm going to take you all to Marly fair, after lunch." Marly fair was, in fact, going on.

The two newcomers were presented to her as Count Tamine and the Marquis de Briquetot. During the meal she hardly spoke, setting her mind hard on being gay all the afternoon, so that no one might guess anything, but be all the more astonished, and say: "Who could have thought it? She seemed so happy and contented! What enigmas they are—people like that!"

She forced herself not to think at all about the evening, for that was the time she had chosen, when they would all be on the terrace.

She drank as much wine as she could, to raise her spirits, and two liqueur glasses of brandy; she rose from the table flushed and a little giddy, hot all over her body, hot, as it seemed to her, to the very soul; but reckless and ready for anything.

"Come along!" she cried.

Taking M. de Belvigne's arm, she issued her marching orders to the others: "Now, battalion, form up! Servigny, you're to be sergeant; take the outside, on the right, and make the two Exotics, the foreign legion, march in front—the prince and the chevalier, of course; in the rear, the two recruits, who are under arms for the first time. March!"

They started. Servigny began to imitate the bugle, while the two newcomers made believe to play the drum. M. de Belvigne, a little embarrassed, said in a whisper: "Do be reasonable, Mlle. Yvette; you'll compromise yourself, you know!"

"It's you I'm compromising, Raisiné," she replied; "as to myself, I don't care a rap. It'll be all the same to-morrow! So much the worse for you; you shouldn't go about with a girl like me!"

They passed through Bougival, to the amazement of the folk in the streets, who all turned to stare at them. People came out on their doorsteps; travellers by the little railway from Reuil to Marly hooted at them, and men standing on the platform of the cars, shouted: "Give 'em a ducking!"

Yvette marched with a military step, holding M. de Belvigne by the arm as if he were a prisoner. She was far from laughing, but had a frozen, sinister expression on her pale, grave face.

Every now and then Servigny would stop bugling and shout commands. The prince and the chevalier were vastly amused, finding it all extremely droll and *chic;* the two young men continued to play the drum without ceasing.

On arriving at the fair they made quite a sensation. Girls clapped their hands; young men sniggered; a fat gentleman with his wife on his arm said in an envious tone: "Well, *they're* not bored!" She caught sight of a merry-go-round, and made Belvigne get up alongside her, while her squadron scrambled up behind them on to the wooden horses. And when that turn was over, she refused to dismount, compelling her escort to take five journeys running on their ridiculous nags, to the immense joy of the public, who kept up a fire of jokes. M. de Belvigne returned to earth livid and giddy.

Then she began wandering through the booths, and caused all her companions to be weighed in the midst of a ring of spectators. She insisted on their buying absurd toys and carrying them in their arms. The prince and the chevalier began to find the joke a little overdone; Servigny and the two drummers alone maintained their spirits.

At last they arrived at the far end, and she gazed at her followers with eyes full of subtle malevolence, full of a weird fancy that had come into her head. Ranging them on the right bank overlooking the river, she called out: "Let him who cares for me most throw himself into the water!"

No one stirred. A regular mob had formed behind them. Some women in white aprons watched them open-mouthed, and two troopers, in red trousers, laughed a stupid laugh.

"So," she began again, "not one of you will throw himself into the water when I ask you!"

Servigny muttered: "H'm! Needs must when the——!" and leaped upright into the river.

His plunge flung drops to Yvette's very feet. A murmur of astonishment and glee arose from the crowd.

The young girl picked up a little piece of wood from the ground and threw it out into the stream. "Fetch it, then!" she cried.

The young man started swimming, and seizing the floating stick in his mouth like a dog, brought it back, and climbing the bank, dropped on one knee to present it to her.

"Good dog!" she said, taking it and giving him a friendly pat on the head.

A stout lady exclaimed in great indignation: "Is it possible!"

"Pretty way of amusing yourself!" said another.

"Wouldn't catch me taking a bath for the sake of a wench!" remarked a man.

She took Belvigne's arm once more with the cutting remark: "*You're* a slacker, my friend; you don't know what you've missed!"

And now they started for home. She flung angry looks to right and left at the passers-by. "How silly all these people look!" she said; and, raising her eyes to her companion's face, added: "And you too!"

M. de Belvigne bowed. Turning round, she perceived that the prince and the chevalier had disappeared. Servigny, mournful and dripping, no longer played the bugle, but walked with a melancholy air alongside the two weary young men who no longer played the drum. She laughed dryly. "You seem to have had enough of it! And yet you call this amusing yourselves, don't you? That's what you came for; well, I've given you your money's worth!"

She walked on without another word; and all of a sudden Belvigne saw that she was crying: "What's the matter?" he asked in amazement.

"Let me alone," she murmured, "it's nothing to do with you."

But like an idiot he insisted: "Come, Mademoiselle; what *is* the matter? Has anyone annoyed you?"

"Do be quiet!" she repeated impatiently.

And suddenly, no longer able to withstand the despairing sadness that flooded her heart, she began to sob so violently that she could not go on.

Covering her face with her two hands, she stood gasping for breath, strangled, stifled by the violence of her grief.

Belvigne remained standing by her side, quite distracted, saying over and over again: "I can't understand it!"

But Servigny came hastily forward: "Let's get home, Mam'zelle; don't let people see you crying in the streets! Why do you do these mad things; they only upset you!" And, taking her by the elbow, he hurried her along. But as soon as they had reached the villa gate, she broke away, darted across the garden, rushed upstairs, and shut herself in her room. She did not reappear till dinner-time, and then was very pale and grave. All the rest, however, were in excellent spirits. Servigny had bought a suit of workman's clothes at a neighboring shop, corduroy trousers, flowered shirt, vest, and overall, and had assumed the accent of the working man.

Yvette longed for the end of dinner. She felt her courage failing, and as soon as coffee had been served, she again went up to her room.

Under her window she could hear their festive voices. The chevalier was indulging in risky jokes—clumsy, foreign witticisms. She listened despairingly. Servigny, a little tipsy, began imitating a drunken workman, calling the Marquise "Missis!" Suddenly he turned to Saval, and said, "Hallo, Master!"

There was a general laugh.

At this Yvette hesitated no longer. She first took a sheet of her writing-paper, and wrote:

"BOUGIVAL,
"*Sunday,* 9 *p. m.*

"I am dying, to keep myself an honest girl.
"YVETTE."

Then a postscript

"Good-bye, dear mother; forgive me!"

She addressed the envelope "Mme. la Marquise Obardi," and sealed it; then wheeled her sofa up to the window, drew a little table within reach of her hand, and placed on it the large bottle of chloroform beside a handful of cotton-wool.

An immense rose-tree covered with flowers, which grew from the terrace close to her window, gave out into the night air a faint, sweet perfume, drifting up in soft breaths, and for some minutes she sat drinking it in. The moon in its first quarter floated in the dark sky, nibbled, as it were, on the left-hand edge, and veiled at times by little clouds.

"I am going to die!" thought Yvette; "to die!" And sobs welled up in her heart, that seemed to be breaking, to be suffocating her. She felt a longing to ask for mercy, to be rescued, to be loved.

Then she heard Servigny's voice telling an improper story, interrupted every moment by peals of laughter. The Marquise was more amused than all the rest, and kept repeating: "Nobody can tell a story like him! Ha! ha! ha!"

Yvette took up the bottle, uncorked it, and poured a little of the liquid on the cotton-wool. A powerful, sweet, strange odour was diffused, and putting the lump of wadding to her lips she inhaled the strong, irritating essence till it made her cough. Then, shutting her mouth, she began to breathe it steadily in. She took long draughts of the deadly vapour, closing her eyes, and striving to quench all thought within her, to deaden all reflection and consciousness.

Her first feeling was of a certain expansion and broadening of the chest, and it seemed to her that her soul, a moment before so heavy, so weighed down with grief, was growing light, as if the burden which had crushed her had been lifted, and eased, that it had finally taken wing.

A sensation both keen and pleasant penetrated her in every

limb, to the very tips of her toes and fingers, permeated her whole body with a sort of vague intoxication and gentle fever.

She perceived that the cotton-wool was dry, and was surprised to find that she was not yet dead. She felt instead that her senses were sharpened, more subtle and alert.

She could now hear every single word spoken on the terrace. Prince Kravalow was relating how he had killed an Austrian general in a duel. And, far away in the country, she heard the noises of the night, the casual barking of a dog, the short croak of a toad, the lightest fluttering of the leaves.

She took up the bottle, again soaked the lump of cotton-wool, and again began to breathe it in. For some instants she felt nothing at all; then that slow, delightful sense of well-being which had already invaded her began again.

Twice she poured chloroform on the cotton-wool, greedy now for this strange mental and physical sensation, this dreamy torpor in which her soul was wandering. She felt as if she had no longer bones and flesh, legs and arms; all seemed to have gently vanished without her noticing. The chloroform had spirited away her body, leaving her brain more alert, alive, spacious, and free than it had ever felt before. She remembered a thousand things she had forgotten, details of her childhood, trifles that had pleased her. Her spirit, gifted suddenly with incredible activity, leaped far and wide from one strange notion to another, rambled through a thousand adventures, roamed in the past, strayed among happy plans for the future. And her busy, careless thoughts gave her a sensuous delight; she felt a divine joy in dreaming like that.

All the time she could hear those voices, but no longer distinguished words, which seemed indeed to have taken new meanings. She had wandered deep into a sort of weird and ever-changing fairy land. She was on a great boat, passing through beautiful country all covered with flowers. She saw people on the bank who were talking loudly, and she found herself on shore without knowing or caring how she had come there. Servigny, dressed as a prince, had come to take her to a bull-fight.

The streets were full of passers-by, all talking, and she listened to their conversation without surprise—they seemed all to be acquaintances, for throughout her dreamy intoxication she could hear her mother's friends laughing and talking on the terrace. Then everything became vague.

She awoke, deliciously numb, and had some difficulty in recalling herself to consciousness. So she was not dead yet; but she felt so rested, so full of physical well-being and mental peace, that she was in no hurry to bring it to an end. She longed for that state of exquisite assuagement to last for ever. Softly breathing, she gazed at the moon in front of her above the trees. Something in her soul was changed. She no longer thought as she had thought just now. The chloroform had enervated her, body and soul, smoothed away her grief, lulled to sleep her resolve to die.

Why should she not live, and be loved? Why not be happy? All things seemed possible now, and easy, and certain. Everything in life was sweet and good and lovely. But as it was needful to keep on dreaming for evermore, she poured more of this dream-water on to the wadding, and began again to breathe it in, removing the poison now and then from her nostrils, so as not to absorb too much, and die.

She gazed at the moon, and saw a face in it, a woman's face, and began again her flight among the dizzy pictures of her opium-dream. That face was wavering in the middle of the sky, and started singing, in a voice she knew well, the "Alleluia of Love." It was the Marquise who had just gone indoors, and seated herself at the piano.

Yvette had wings now. She flew through the night, the sweet, clear night, over the woods and streams. She flew with delight, opening her wings, fluttering her wings, wafted on the wind as though by caresses. She whirled through the air, it kissed her skin, and she glided along so quick, so quick, that she had no time to see what was below, and she found herself down on the bank of a pond—a line in her hand; she was fishing.

Something dragged at the line, and she pulled it out of the water, bringing up a splendid pearl necklace which she had set her heart on having, some time ago. She was not in the least surprised at this haul, and looked at Servigny, who was seated by her side, without her knowing how he had come there; he, too, was fishing, and had just caught a wooden horse. Then, again, she had the sensation that she was waking, and heard them calling her from below.

Her mother had said, "Blow out your candle!"

Then the voice of Servigny, clear and whimsical, "Blow out your candle, Mam'zelle Yvette!"

And they all took up the chorus, "Blow out your candle, Mam'zelle Yvette!"

She poured more chloroform over the wadding, but now, wishing not to die, held it just far enough from her face to breathe the fresh air, yet to fill the room with the suffocating scent of the narcotic, for she realized that some one would come up. Lying back, as though dead, she waited.

"I'm a little uneasy!" said the Marquise; "that thoughtless child has gone to sleep and left her candle alight on the table. I'll send Clémence to put it out, and shut her balcony window—it's wide open."

Presently the maid knocked at the door and called, "Mademoiselle, Mademoiselle!"

She paused, and began again—"Mademoiselle! Mme. la Marquise wishes you to put out your candle and shut your window."

Again Clémence waited a little, then knocked louder, and cried, "Mademoiselle! Mademoiselle!"

But as Yvette did not reply she went downstairs, and said to the Marquise, "Mademoiselle must have gone to sleep; she's bolted her door, and I can't wake her."

"But she mustn't stay like that," murmured Mme. Obardi.

At Servigny's suggestion they all stood together close under the young girl's window, and shouted in chorus, "Hip—hip—hurrah! Mam'zelle Yvette!"

Their loud cry rose in the quiet night, took its flight under the moon, through the clear air, away over the sleeping country, and they heard it dying in the distance, like the echo of a receding train. But there was no reply from Yvette, and the Marquise said, "I hope there is nothing wrong with her, I'm beginning to be frightened."

Thereupon Servigny, plucking crimson flowers and buds from the great rose-tree growing on the wall, began throwing them up through the window into the room.

At the first that struck her, Yvette started and nearly cried out. Some dropped on her dress, some in her hair, others, flying over her head, fell right on the bed, and covered it with a rain of flowers.

Once more the Marquise called out, in a choking voice, "Come, Yvette—do answer!"

Servigny, remarked: "Really, it's not natural; I'm going to climb the balcony."

But the chevalier demurred. "Allow me," he said; "that's

much too great a favour—I protest; both time and place are quite too perfect, for obtaining a rendezvous."

The others, too, feeling sure the young girl was playing some joke on them, cried out: "We protest. It's a trick! He shan't go!" But the Marquise repeated uneasily: "Someone *must* go and see!" With a dramatic gesture the prince declared: "She favours the Duke; we are betrayed!"

"Let's toss who shall go!" cried the chevalier. And he drew a gold five-louis piece from his pocket.

He began with the prince.

"Tails!" said he.

It came down heads.

The prince spun the coin in turn, saying to Saval: "Your cry, sir!"

"Heads!" said Saval.

It came down tails.

Thereupon, the prince put the same question to all the others. They all lost.

"By Jove! He's cheating!" declared Servigny, with his insolent smile. He was the only one left.

The Russian placed his hand on his heart, and handed the gold piece to his rival, saying: "Do the tossing yourself, then, my dear duke!"

Servigny took the coin and spun it, crying: "Heads!"

It came down tails.

He bowed, and waving his hand towards the pillar of the balcony, said: "Climb away, prince!"

But the prince looked round about him uneasily.

"What are you looking for?" asked the chevalier.

"Well—er—I should like—a—a ladder!"

There was a general laugh, and Saval, coming forward, said: "We will help you!"

"Catch hold of the balcony!" he said, and raised the prince in his Herculean arms.

The prince at once caught hold, but Saval, letting go, left him suspended, waving his legs in space. Whereupon Servigny, seizing the limbs that were so frenziedly hunting for a resting-place, pulled at them with all his strength; the hands gave way, and the prince fell in a lump on to the stomach of M. de Belvigne, who was advancing to his assistance.

"Whose turn now?" asked Servigny.

But no one came forward.

"Come, Belvigne, a little pluck!"

"No, thank you, my dear fellow; I prefer my bones whole!"

"Now, chevalier, *you* ought to know how to scale a fortress!"

"I resign the post to you, my dear Duke."

"Hey—hey—I don't know that I'm so keen about it as all that!" And with a calculating eye Servigny sidled round the pillar. Then, springing, he caught hold of the balcony, raised himself by his wrists, and with a gymnastic manœuvre, surmounted the balustrade.

With noses in the air, the spectators all applauded.

He reappeared at once, crying: "Quick! quick! Yvette's unconscious!"

The Marquise screamed loudly, and flew towards the staircase. The young girl, with closed eyes, lay like one dead. In a frenzy of terror her mother came rushing in, and threw herself down close to her. "What is it? What is it?" she kept saying.

Servigny picked up the bottle of chloroform which had fallen on the floor. "She's suffocated herself," he said. Putting his ear down to her heart, he added: "But she is not dead yet; we shall pull her round. Have you any ammonia?"

The maid repeated distractedly: "Any what, sir? What?"

"Sal volatile."

"Yes, sir."

Fetch it at once, and leave the door open, to make a draught."

The Marquise, now on her knees, sobbed: "Yvette! Yvette, my child, my little one, my child! Listen, answer me! Yvette, my child! Oh! my God! my God! What *is* the matter with her?"

The frightened men moved to and fro, some bringing water, towels, glasses and vinegar, some doing nothing.

Some one said: "She ought to be undressed!"

Half out of her senses, the Marquise tried to unfasten her daughter's clothes, but she no longer knew what she was doing—her hands trembled, all muddled and useless, and she groaned: "I —I can't, I can't!"

The maid had returned with a medicine bottle, which Servigny uncorked and half emptied over a handkerchief. He put it close under Yvette's nose, who began to choke.

"Good! She's breathing!" he said. "It'll soon be all right!" He bathed her temples, cheeks, and throat with the sharp-scented liquid; then signed to the maid to unlace her, and when there was nothing but a petticoat left over the chemise, took her up in his arms and carried her to the bed. He quivered all over, disturbed by the contact of the half-clothed body in his embrace. When he had placed her on the bed he raised himself, very pale.

"She'll come round," he said; "it's all right!" for he had heard her steady, even breathing. But, perceiving all those men with their eyes fixed on Yvette lying on her bed, he felt a sudden spasm of jealous anger shaking him. Going up to them, he said: "Gentlemen, we're far too many in this room; kindly leave M. Saval and myself alone here, with the Marquise!"

He spoke in a dry, authoritative tone, and the others at once withdrew.

Mme. Obardi had thrown her arms around her lover, and with her face raised to his, was crying: "Save her—oh! save her!"

Meanwhile Servigny, turning round, caught sight of a letter on the table. With a quick movement he picked it up, and read the address. He understood at once, and reflected: "Perhaps the Marquise had better not know about this!" And tearing open the envelope, he ran his eyes over the two lines which it contained:

"I am dying, to keep myself an honest girl.
"YVETTE."
"Good-bye, dear mother, forgive me."

"The devil!" he thought, "this needs thinking over," and he slipped the letter into his pocket. Coming back to the bedside, he at once realized that the young girl had regained consciousness, but from embarrassment and fear of being questioned, was ashamed to show it.

The Marquise had fallen on her knees, and was weeping, her head bowed at the foot of the bed. Suddenly, she cried: "A doctor! we must send for a doctor!"

But Servigny, who had been whispering to Saval, said: "No! it's all right. Now, just go away for a minute, only one minute, and I promise you she shall give you a kiss when you come back!"

The baron, supporting Mme. Obardi by the arm, hurried her away.

Then Servigny, sitting down by the bedside, took Yvette's hand, and said: "Mam'zelle, listen to me!"

She did not answer. She felt so happy, so sweetly, warmly nested, that she wished never to stir or speak again, but to stay like that for ever. An infinite well-being had come upon her, the like of which she had never felt before.

Light breaths of the mild night air, soft as velvet, kept floating in and, faintly, exquisitely, touching her face. It was a caress, like a kiss of the wind, like the slow, refreshing whiffs from a fan made of all the leaves of the woods, and all the shadows of the night, of the river haze, and of every flower; for the roses thrown from below into her room and on to her bed, and the roses climbing up the balcony, all mingled their languorous perfume with the sane savour of the night breeze.

She drank in that sweet air, her eyes closed, her heart at rest in the still unspent dreaminess of the narcotic; she had no longer the faintest desire to die, but instead, a great, imperious longing to live, to be happy, no matter how—to be loved, ah!— loved!

"Mam'zelle Yvette," repeated Servigny, "listen to me!"

She made up her mind to open her eyes. Seeing her thus reviving, he went on: "Come, come! What does all this mean?"

"I was so miserable, my poor Muscade," she murmured.

He gave her hand a fatherly squeeze. "Well, that was a fine way out of it, wasn't it?" he said. "Come, "you're going to promise me never to do it again?"

She gave no answer but a little sign with her head, and a smile that he felt rather than saw.

Taking from his pocket the letter he had found on the table, he asked: "Are we to show this to your mother?"

She frowned a "No."

And now he was at a loss what to say, for there seemed no way out of the situation. "My dear little soul," he murmured, "one has to put up with many very sad things. I understand your grief, and I promise you——"

"Ah! you are good——" she stammered.

They were silent. He looked at her. There was a kind of swooning tenderness in her eyes; all at once she held out her arms, as if to draw him to her. He bent over, feeling that her heart had spoken; and their lips met.

So for a long time they stayed, their eyes closed. Then, feeling that he was losing his head, he raised himself. She smiled at him now, a real smile of tenderness; and held him, with both hands on his shoulders.

"I must fetch your mother," he said.

"Wait one second, I'm so happy!" Then, after a pause, she said quite low, so low that he could hardly hear: "You *will* love me, won't you?"

He knelt by the bed, and kissed the wrist she let him hold. "I worship you," he said.

There were footsteps near the door, and he sprang up, calling out in his usual voice, with its habitual touch of irony: "You can come in. It's all over now!"

The Marquise flew to her daughter with open arms, and embraced her frantically, covering her face with tears; while Servigny, radiant and quivering, went out on the balcony, to take deep breaths of the pure night air, humming:—

> "Souvent femme varie
> Bien fol est qui s'y fie!"

MADEMOISELLE FIFI

MAJOR COUNT FARLSBERG, the Prussian Commandant, was just finishing the contents of his post-bag. His back was screwed deep into a big tapestry armchair, and his booted feet rested on the elegant marble mantelpiece, where his spurs, during a three months' occupation of the chateau d'Uville, had made two deep ruts, growing a little deeper every day.

A cup of coffee was steaming on a little marqueterie table, spotted with the cigar-burns, liqueur-stains, and pen-knife cuts left by this conquering hero, who, following the dictates of idle fancy, would sometimes stop sharpening a pencil to cut-in a quaint design or perhaps a row of figures on the rich wood.

When he had finished his letters and gone through the German newspapers that his orderly had just brought in, he got up, threw on the fire some three or four immense green logs—for these gentlemen were gradually cutting down the park for their firewood—and went towards the window.

It was pouring with rain, that Normandy rain which always seems as if hurled down by a furious hand, a slanting rain, thick as a curtain, or a diagonally striped wall; a lashing, splashing rain, drowning everything, a regular rain of Rouen, that wash-pot of all France.

The commandant looked long at the sopping lawns, then at the swollen Andelle, overflowing its banks down there below them; and while he gazed he drummed a Rhineland waltz on the window-pane. Turning, at a sound behind him, he saw his second in command, Baron Kelweingstein, now holding the rank of captain.

The major was a broad-shouldered giant, beautified by a long beard that spread fan-shaped on his chest; the whole of his tall person made one think of a peacock, a military peacock, carrying his tail unfurled from his chin. His eyes were blue, cold, and mild; and one cheek had been slashed across by a sabre in the war with Austria. He had the reputation of being a good sort and a brave soldier.

The captain, a little rubicund fellow with a big, tight-belted stomach, was not too clean-shaven, and the traces of his fiery beard and moustache, under certain conditions of light, made his face look as if it had been rubbed with phosphorus. Two teeth, lost one festive night (he never quite remembered how), made his speech thick and queer, so that he was not always to be understood. He was bald on the top of the head only, tonsured like a priest, with a crop of short, reddish, glistening hair round that circle of bare skull.

The commandant shook hands with him, and, swallowing at a gulp his sixth cup of coffee since the morning, listened to his junior's report of the day. Then they both went back to the window, with the remark that "things were not too lively." The major, a quiet man with a wife at home, put up with the situation well enough; but the captain, a regular rake, frequenter of night clubs and of women, raged continually at being shut up for months together in the celibacy of this desolate outpost.

At a knock on the door the commandant cried, "Come in!" and a drilled puppet of a soldier appeared in the gap, announcing by his mere presence that lunch was served.

In the dining-room they found their three junior officers, Lieutenant Otto von Grössling, Second Lieutenants Fritz Scheunaburg, and the Marquis Wilhelm von Eyrik, a little blond cock-sparrow, haughty and harsh of manner, merciless towards the conquered, and as explosive as a pistol.

Since their arrival in France his comrades never called him anything but Mademoiselle Fifi, a nickname suggested by his smart appearance, his slender figure which looked as if he wore corsets, his pale face where the budding moustache hardly showed at all, and also by reason of his new habit of continually using the French phrase, "Fi, fi donc!" pronounced with a slight hiss, to express his sovereign contempt for things and people.

The dining-room in the chateau d'Uville was a long, majestic apartment, whose mirrors of old crystal, now starred by pistol-shots, and high-hung Flemish tapestries, slashed by sabre-cuts till they drooped here and there, bore witness to the prowess of Mlle. Fifi in his hours of ease.

On the walls three family portraits—a warrior in armour, a cardinal, and a president—had long porcelain-bowled pipes thrust into their mouths, while in her ancient, faded-gold frame a noble dame, very tight-laced, sported with an air of arrogance a huge pair of blacked-on moustaches.

In this mutilated room, darkened by the storm outside, with its mournful look of defeat, and its old oak parquet floor hard now as that of a tavern, the officers lunched almost in silence.

Not till they had finished eating, and had come to spirits and tobacco, did they begin their daily lamentation on their boredom. Passing the liqueurs from hand to hand, they leaned back and sipped away, without removing from the corners of their mouths those long curved pipe-stems, with egg-shaped china bowls daubed with little pictures in a style that could appeal only to a Hottentot.

As soon as a glass was empty it was wearily refilled. But Mlle. Fifi made a point of breaking his each time, and an orderly would at once bring him another.

Enveloped in a fog of pungent smoke, they seemed to be steeping themselves in a dreary, drowsy drunkenness, the gloomy soaking of men with nothing else to do.

But suddenly the baron, in a spasm of revolt, pulled himself together and ejaculated: "By gad! we simply can't go on like this. We must damn well invent something!"

Lieutenant Otto and Second Lieutenant Fritz, both types of the stodgy, solemn-faced young German, answered as one man: "Yes; only—what?"

The baron reflected a moment: "Well, we must get up a spree, if the colonel will let us."

The major took his pipe out of his mouth: "How do you mean—a spree?"

The baron came across to him: "You leave it all to me, sir. I'll send Old Automaton to Rouen to bring some girls out here. I know where they're to be found. We'll give 'em a supper; we can do it in great style, and we'll have a jolly good evening, for once."

Count Farlsberg smiled, and said, with a shrug of his shoulders: "You're cracked, my dear fellow."

But all the young men had got up, and came crowding round the commandant, adding their entreaties. "Oh, do let him, sir! It's so infernally dull here."

"All right!" said the major, giving in at last. And at once the baron sent for Old Automaton—a veteran who had never been seen to smile, but who could be relied on to carry out fanatically any order given by his officers. This veritable ramrod of a man received the baron's instructions without moving a muscle of his face, and left the room. Five minutes later a military waggon, with a hooped canvas cover, went rattling off through the furious rain behind four horses at full gallop.

And at once a thrill of reviving animation went stealing through their spirits; they lounged no more, their faces brightened, and conversation flowed.

Although the rain continued to come down with unabated fury, the major swore that the clouds were not so heavy, and Lieutenant Otto affirmed that it was certainly going to clear. As for Mlle. Fifi, he simply could not keep still, fidgeting up and down, and searching with his clear hard eyes for something to break. They lighted suddenly on the moustachioed lady. Drawing out his revolver, the blond young beast remarked: *"You're not going to look on, though!"* and, without getting up, he fired, putting out the portrait's eyes with two consecutive shots.

Then he called out: "Let's play the mine game!" And instantly all conversation ceased, under the spell of this new and powerful attraction. The mine game was entirely Mlle. Fifi's invention, his pet amusement for gratifying his genius for destruction.

The owner of the chateau, Count Fernand d'Amoys d'Uville, had left in too great haste to be able to take away or hide anything except the silver, which had been stowed away in a hole in the wall. The great salon, opening into the dining-room, of this very rich and lordly person, had, up to the moment of his precipitate flight, presented the appearance of a museum gallery.

The walls of the vast room were garnished with pictures, drawings, and valuable water-colours. On the tables, shelves, and in elegant cabinets a thousand knicknacks were arranged—Chinese vases, statuettes, Dresden shepherds, oriental monsters, old ivories, and Venetian glass—a perfect medley of rare and precious stuff.

There was little left of it all by now. Not that there had been any looting. Major Count Farlsberg would by no means have permitted that, but from time to time Mlle. Fifi played the mine game, and on such occasions at any rate all the officers were thoroughly amused for full five minutes.

The little marquis went off to the salon for what he needed, and came back with a very charming little porcelain teapot, Famille Rose. Filling it with gunpowder, he delicately inserted down the spout a long piece of tinder, lighted it, and ran back with his infernal machine into the next room.

He returned with remarkable celerity, and shut the door. And all the Germans waited, stiff with expectation and curious child-like smiles. The moment the explosion came off, shaking the whole chateau, they all darted together into the salon.

Mlle. Fifi, the first in, was clapping his hands ecstatically before a terra-cotta Venus, whose head had been blown off at last. They all proceeded to pick up fragments of porcelain, admiring the strange lacework of the splinters, examining the latest havoc, and disclaiming for to-day certain ravages undoubtedly done in the previous explosion; while the major, with a fatherly air, contemplated the splendid room thus spiflicated by that Neronic bomb, and sanded with the smithereens of Art. He was the first to retire, remarking genially: "It was a great success, this time!"

But such a smother of smoke had got into the dining-room, mingling with the tobacco fumes, that it was impossible to breathe. The commandant opened the window, and all the officers, who had returned for a last liqueur of brandy, gathered round it.

The damp air drew in, with its scent of flooded country; a powdering of rain pearled their beards. They could see the great trees bending under the storm, the broad valley half hidden beneath a mist of dark, low-hanging clouds, and in the far distance the belfry of the church, a grey point piercing the downpour.

Since their coming its bell had never rung. This was the sole resistance the invaders had met with in those parts—this of the church bell. The priest had not refused to billet Prussian soldiers, had even accepted invitations to drink beer or wine with the hostile commandant, who often made use of him as a friendly intermediary; but it was no good asking him to have the church bell rung; he would sooner have let himself be shot. It was his way of protesting against the invasion, a peaceful, silent protest, the only one that in his view befitted a priest, a man of peace, not war; and everybody, for ten miles round, lauded the steady heroism of the Abbé Chantavoine, who dared thus to proclaim the national grief by the stubborn muteness of his church bell. The whole village, fired by this resistance, were ready to back up their pastor through thick and thin, to face anything, considering that by this tacit protest they held the national honour safe. It seemed to the peasants that they had deserved better of their country than Belfort or Strasbourg, that they had shown as fine an example, that the name of their hamlet was earning immortality. Apart from this, they refused nothing to their Prussian conquerors.

The commandant and his junior officers had many a laugh over this harmless courage, and since the whole countryside showed itself obliging and submissive, they tolerated that mute exhibition of patriotism quite cheerfully.

The little Marquis Wilhelm, alone, wanted badly to make the church bell ring. The politic condescension of his chief towards the priest enraged him, and every day he besought the commandant to let him make "Ding-don-don" just once, only once, just for a joke. And he would put a feline grace into his begging, and use the dulcet tones of some wheedling minx crazy for the gratification of her whim. But Count Farlsberg was adamant, and Mlle. Fifi had to console himself by playing the mine game in the Chateau d'Uville.

The five men stayed some minutes at the window, inhaling the damp air, till Lieutenant Fritz said, with a thick laugh: "These young ladies haven't much of a day for their outing."

On that they separated, going to their various duties, the captain having a lot to do in preparation for the dinner.

When they met again at dusk they all burst out laughing, so smart and glossy were they all, so perfumed and pomaded, as if just starting off to a review. The commandant's hair seemed less grey than in the morning; the captain had shaved, keeping only his moustache—a veritable flame beneath his nose.

In spite of the rain they left the window open, and every now and then one of them would go and listen. At ten minutes past six the baron announced a distant rumbling; they all rushed to the door. Very soon the waggon came dashing up, with its four horses still at a gallop, muddied up to their eyes, blown, and steaming.

Five ladies alighted at the front-door, five good-looking damsels, carefully picked out by a friend of the captain, to whom Old Automaton had taken a private note from the baron.

Not that the ladies had made any bones about it, sure of good terms, and having three months' experience now of the Prussians. They had to take men and things as they found them. "It's all in the day's work," they said to each other during the drive, by way of stilling any remaining pricks of conscience.

They all went at once into the dining-room. Lighted up it

looked more lugubrious than ever in its pitiful dilapidation, and the table, loaded with viands and the fine dinner service, as well as the silver rescued from that wall where the owner had hidden it, made one think of a brigand's supper, set after a successful raid. The captain, in his element, took charge of the ladies, past master of the art as he was, scrutinizing and appraising their charms; and when the three younger men showed signs of pairing off, he jumped on them at once, undertaking the work of partition himself, so that the strict demands of hierarchy might be properly fulfilled.

In order to avoid all discussion, dispute, suspicion of partiality, he lined the ladies up according to their height, and, addressing the tallest in the tone of a colonel on parade, asked: "Your name?"

"Pamela," she answered, making her voice as manly as she could.

"No. 1, name of Pamela, allotted to the commandant."

Having kissed Blondine, the second, in token of proprietorship, he assigned the chubby Amanda to Lieutenant Otto, the auburn-haired Eva to Second Lieutenant Fritz, and the shortest of all, Rachel, a dark and very young Jewess with eyes as black as ink (whose upturned nose proved the rule, among her race, of turned-down noses), he gave to the youngest officer, the little Marquis Wilhelm von Eyrik.

All, moreover, were plump and pretty, though without much distinction of feature, being reduced to somewhat the same pattern in style and complexion by the conditions of their life.

The three young men were for taking their ladies to have a wash and brush-up, but the captain, in his wisdom, was against that. They did not need it, in his opinion, and it would certainly lead to confusion. His ruling as a man of great experience was adopted. So there was only a certain amount of osculation.

All of a sudden Rachel began choking, and coughing till the tears came into her eyes, and the smoke out of her nostrils. The marquis, under pretext of a kiss, had puffed tobacco-smoke into her mouth. She showed no temper, and did not say a word, but she fixed her dark eyes on that young man; in the depths of them anger had begun to glow.

They sat down to dinner. Even the commandant appeared enraptured; he had on his right Pamela, and on his left Blondine. As he unfolded his napkin, he remarked: "Really a splendid idea of yours, captain!"

Lieutenants Otto and Fritz, as polite as if to women of their own class, were a little alarming to their neighbours; but Baron Kelweingstein, at the top of his form, was positively sparkling and bubbling with jokes, while his red head seemed to be in flames. He made himself extremely gallant in French as spoken on the Rhine, and his coarse compliments, hurled through the gap left by the departure of those two teeth, reached the ladies amid volleys of saliva. They were far from understanding a word of what he said, and only became animated as his talk became more gross, full of allusions, murdered by his vile accent. Then, indeed, they went into fits of laughter, leaning across their neighbours and repeating to each other lubricities that the baron now purposely mispronounced for the pleasure of hearing them respoken. The wine had not been long in going to the girls' heads, and they were soon behaving after their kind, playing with the moustaches to right and left, squeezing the men's arms, drinking out of everyone's glass, singing French ditties and tags of German songs learned in their daily encounters with the enemy.

Soon the men, too, began to play the fool, shouting and smashing the crockery, while the soldier servants behind their backs, perfectly impassive, went on serving.

The commandant alone maintained a certain dignity.

Mlle. Fifi had taken Rachel on his knee, and with a sort of cold fury began to kiss the little dark hairs curling on her neck, and to breathe her in luxuriously. Then he would pinch her through her thin dress hard enough to make her cry out; for he was perpetually driven by a longing to hurt something. Once in the middle of a long kiss he suddenly bit her lip so severely that blood trickled down her chin on to her bodice.

Again she looked at him fixedly, and murmured, as she dabbed the wound: "You'll have to pay for that!"

"All right," he said, with a harsh laugh, "I'll pay!"

They were at dessert by now, and champagne was being served. The commandant rose, and in a tone he might have used for proposing the health of the Empress Augusta, called out: "I give you—the health of the ladies!"

After that came a stream of tipsy toasts, jocular and gross, and all the worse for the bad French in which they were proposed. One after another the young men got up, trying to be funny; while the ladies, very far gone by now, with vacant eyes and loosened mouths, applauded wildly. Then the captain, in a supreme effort to be gallant, raised his glass once more, and said: "To our conquests of the fair!"

At that Lieutenant Otto, a regular Black Forest bear, drew himself up, and in a sudden heat of tipsy patriotism, cried: "To our conquest of France!"

Intoxicated though they were, the girls were suddenly silent; but Rachel, turning to him, stammered out in her rage: "You—you—I know some Frenchmen you wouldn't dare say that to!"

The little marquis, who still held her on his knee, began to laugh. "Ha! ha! I've never seen a Frenchman. As soon as we show ourselves they cut and run!"

"You beast! You liar!" the infuriated girl shouted in his face.

He looked at her for a second much as he had looked at the portraits before putting their eyes out with his bullets, then said mockingly: "Well, that's a brilliant thing to say! Should we be here if they were any good?" And with sudden exultation he shouted out: "We're their masters. France is ours!"

She jerked herself off his knee back on to her own chair. And he got up, stretching out his wineglass over the table, and shouted again: "France is ours, and the French; and the woods, and the fields, and the homes of France!"

And all the others, in a burst of drunken brutal ardour, lifted their glasses, and shouting, "Prussia for ever!" emptied them at a gulp.

Dumbed with a sudden fear the girls made no protest; even Rachel was silent.

The little marquis filled up his glass, and placing it on her dark head, went on: "And ours, too, every woman of France!"

She started up; the glass, tilting over, baptized her black hair with its golden wine, and broke on the floor. Her lips trembled, her eyes defied his mocking eyes, and in a voice choking with rage she stammered out: "That's—that's not true! You'll never have the women of France!"

He laughed so that he fell back into his chair. And aping as best he could the true Parisian accent, he said: "She's killing, she really is! What have you come here for, then, my dear?"

She was silent a moment, too wildly upset to take in these last words. Then, suddenly catching on to his meaning, she flung out furiously: "I! I! I'm not a woman, I'm only a—a—slut! That's good enough for a Prussian!"

Before she had finished he caught her a swinging box on the ear; but just as he was raising his hand again, blind with rage, she seized a little silver dessert-knife from the table, and, so quickly that no one saw it done, drove the point right into his throat just where it joined the chest.

The word he was saying was cut in half within his windpipe; his mouth fell open, his eyes gave one horrified look.

In confusion every one jumped up, shouting; but, hurling her chair at the legs of Lieutenant Otto, who fell over it full-length, she flew to the window, threw it open, and, before anyone could reach her, vanished into the darkness and the rain that was still falling.

In two minutes Mlle. Fifi was dead. Fritz and Otto drew their swords and were for massacring the women, who were clinging round their knees. With difficulty the major prevented this butchery, and getting the four terrified girls into another room, put a guard of two soldiers over them. Then, as if marshalling his forces for a battle, he organized the pursuit of the fugitive, quite certain of recapturing her.

Fifty men, spurred on by threats, were set to scour the park, two hundred more to search the woods and every house in the valley.

The table, cleared in a second, was now serving for a deathbed, and the four officers, stern and sobered, with the rigid faces of soldiers on duty, posted themselves at the windows, and peered forth into the night.

Torrents of rain were still coming down. An unending clamour filled the darkness, the whispering hiss of falling water and flowing water, of water trickling down, and water splashing up from the ground.

Suddenly a shot rang out, then another, very distant; and from time to time, for full four hours, they kept hearing shots, now near, now far, and voices hailing, and calling out queer guttural words.

At dawn the soldiers came back. Two had been killed, three others wounded by their comrades in the ardour of the chase and the scared confusion of that night pursuit. But they had not caught Rachel.

From that time on the inhabitants were terrorized, their

houses turned upside down, the whole valley quartered, and searched again and again. The Jewess seemed to have left not a trace of her flight.

The general, who had to be told, ordered the whole affair to be hushed up, so as not to set a bad example to the army, and he severely dropped on the commandant, who in turn took it out of his juniors. "We don't make war," the general had said, "for the pleasure of kissing courtesans." And Count Farlsberg, in exasperation, resolved to avenge himself upon the countryside.

Thinking out a plausible pretext for severity, he sent for the priest, and ordered him to toll the church bell for the funeral of the Marquis von Eyrik.

Contrary to all expectation, the priest promised, with the utmost docility, to comply. And when the body of Mlle. Fifi, carried by soldiers, preceded, surrounded, and followed by soldiers with loaded rifles, set out from the Chateau d'Uville, on its way to the cemetery, the bell at last regained its voice, tolling out a funeral knell, but with a certain mirth, as if some loving hand were stroking it.

It rang again in the evening, and the next day, and every day; it chimed as often as heart could wish. Sometimes even during the night it began of itself just shaking out into the darkness two or three silvery gay notes inexplicably. The peasants of the neighbourhood declared it was bewitched, and none but the priest and the sacristan would now go near the belfry.

In truth, a poor girl was living up there, lonely and anxious, secretly looked after by those two men.

So she stayed, till the German troops departed. Then one evening, the priest, having borrowed the baker's char-à-banc, himself drove his prisoner to the gate of Rouen. When he had embraced her, she jumped out and made her way quickly to the house she belonged to, where they had long given her up for dead.

Some time afterwards a patriot, who had no prejudices, took her away from there; he loved her first for her fine deed, but later for herself. And marrying her, he made of her a Lady as good as many another.

TWO FRIENDS

PARIS was blockaded, famished, at the last gasp. Sparrows were scarce on the roofs, and the sewers depleted of their rats. Every mortal thing was being eaten.

Strolling sadly along the outer boulevard on a fine January morning, with his hands in the pockets of his military trousers, and his stomach empty, M. Morissot, a watchmaker by profession, and a man of his ease when he had the chance, caught sight of a friend, and stopped. This was M. Sauvage, an acquaintance he had made out fishing.

For before the war Morissot had been in the habit of starting out at dawn every Sunday, rod in hand, and a tin box on his back. He would take the train to Argenteuil, get out at Colombes, then go on foot as far as the Island of Marante. The moment he reached this Elysium of his dreams he would begin to fish, and fish till night. Every Sunday he met there a little round and jovial man, this M. Sauvage, a haberdasher of Rue Notre Dame de Lorette, also a perfect fanatic at fishing. They would often pass half the day side by side, rod in hand, feet dangling above the stream, and in this manner had become fast friends. Some days they did not talk, other days they did. But they understood each other admirably without words, for their tastes and feelings were identical.

On spring mornings, about ten o'clock, when the young sun was raising a faint mist above the quiet-flowing river, and blessing the backs of those two passionate fishermen with a pleasant warmth, Morissot would murmur to his neighbour: "I say, isn't it heavenly?" and M. Sauvage would reply: "Couldn't be jollier!" It was quite enough to make them understand and like each other.

Or in autumn, towards sunset, when the blood-red sky and crimson clouds were reflected in the water, the whole river stained with colour, the horizon flaming, when our two friends looked as red as fire, and the trees, already russet and shivering at the touch of winter, were turned to gold, M. Sauvage would look smilingly at Morissot, and remark: "What a sight!" and Morissot, not taking his eyes off his float, would reply ecstatically: "Bit better than it is in town, eh?"

* * * * *

Having made sure of each other, they shook hands heartily, quite moved at meeting again in such different circumstances. M. Sauvage, heaving a sigh, murmured: "Nice state of things!" Morissot, very gloomy, quavered out: "And what weather! To-day's the first fine day this year!"

The sky was indeed quite blue and full of light.

They moved on, side by side, ruminative, sad. Morissot pursued his thought: "And fishing, eh? What jolly times we used to have!"

"Ah!" muttered M. Sauvage. "When shall we go fishing again?"

They entered a little café, took an absinthe together, and started off once more, strolling along the pavement.

Suddenly Morissot halted: "Another nip?" he said.

"Right-o!" responded M. Sauvage. And in they went to another wine-shop. They came out rather light-headed, affected by so much alcohol on their starving stomachs. The day was mild, and a soft breeze caressed their faces.

M. Sauvage, to whose light-headedness this warmth was putting the finishing touch, stopped short: "I say—suppose we go!"

"What d'you mean?"

"Fishing!"

"Where?"

"Why, at our island. The French outposts are close to Colombes. I know Colonel Dumoulin; he'll be sure to let us pass."

Morissot answered, quivering with eagerness: "All right; I'm on!" And they parted, to get their fishing gear.

An hour later they were marching along the highroad. They came presently to the villa occupied by the Colonel, who, much amused by their whim, gave them leave. And furnished with his permit, they set off again.

They soon passed the outposts, and, traversing the abandoned village of Colombes, found themselves at the edge of the little vineyard fields that run down to the Seine. It was about eleven o'clock.

The village of Argenteuil, opposite, seemed quite deserted.

The heights of Orgemont and Sannois commanded the whole countryside; the great plain stretching to Nanterre was empty, utterly empty of all but its naked cherry-trees and its grey earth.

M. Sauvage jerking his thumb towards the heights, muttered: "The Prussians are up there!" And disquietude stole into the hearts of the two friends, looking at that deserted land. The Prussians! They had never seen any, but they had felt them there for months, all round Paris, bringing ruin to France, bringing famine; pillaging, massacring; invisible, yet invincible. And a sort of superstitious terror went surging through their hatred for this unknown and victorious race.

Morissot stammered: "I say—suppose we were to meet some?"

With that Parisian jocularity which nothing can repress M. Sauvage replied: "We'd give 'em some fried fish."

None the less, daunted by the silence all round, they hesitated to go further.

At last M. Sauvage took the plunge. "Come on! But we must keep our eyes skinned!"

They got down into a vineyard, where they crept along, all eyes and ears, bent double, taking cover behind every bush.

There was still a strip of open ground to cross before they could get to the riverside; they took it at the double, and the moment they reached the bank plumped down amongst some osiers.

Morissot glued his ear to the ground for any sound of footsteps. Nothing! They were alone, utterly alone.

They plucked up spirit again, and began to fish.

In front of them the Island of Marante, uninhabited, hid them from the far bank. The little island restaurant was closed, and looked as if it had been abandoned for years.

M. Sauvage caught the first gudgeon, Morissot the second, and every minute they kept pulling in their lines with a little silvery creature wriggling at the end. Truly a miraculous draught of fishes!

They placed their spoil carefully in a very fine-meshed net suspended in the water at their feet, and were filled by the delicious joy that visits those who know once more a pleasure of which they have been deprived too long.

The good sun warmed their shoulders; they heard nothing, thought of nothing, were lost to the world. They fished.

But suddenly a dull boom, which seemed to come from underground, made the earth tremble. The bombardment had begun again.

Morissot turned his head. Away above the bank he could see on the left the great silhouette of Mont Valerien, showing a white plume high up—an ashy puff just belched forth. Then a second spurt of smoke shot up from the fort's summit, and some seconds afterwards was heard the roar of the gun.

Then more and more. Every minute the hill shot forth its deadly breath, sighed out milky vapours that rose slowly to the calm heaven, and made a crown of cloud.

M. Sauvage shrugged his shoulders. "At it again!" he said.

Morissot, who was anxiously watching the bobbing of his float, was seized with the sudden fury of a man of peace against these maniacs battering at each other, and he growled out: "Idiots I call them, killing each other like that!"

"Worse than the beasts!" said M. Sauvage.

And Morissot, busy with a fish, added: "It'll always be like that, in my opinion, so long as we have governments."

M. Sauvage cut him short. "The Republic would never have declared war——"

Morissot broke in: "Under a monarchy you get war against your neighbours; under a republic—war amongst yourselves."

And they began tranquilly discussing and unravelling momentous political problems with the common sense of two gentle, narrow creatures, who agreed at any rate on this one point, that Man would never be free.

And Mont Valerien thundered without ceasing, shattering with its shells the homes of France, pounding out life, crushing human beings, putting an end to many a dream, to many a longed-for joy, to many a hoped-for happiness; opening everywhere, too, in the hearts of wives, of girls, of mothers, wounds that would never heal.

"That's life!" declared M. Sauvage.

"I should call it death," said Morissot, and laughed.

They both gave a sudden start; there was surely someone coming up behind them. Turning their eyes they saw, standing close to their very elbows, four men, four big bearded men, dressed in a sort of servant's livery, with flat caps on their heads, pointing rifles at them.

The rods fell from their hands and floated off down-stream.

In a few seconds they were seized, bound, thrown into a boat, and taken over to the island.

Behind the house that they had thought deserted they perceived some twenty German soldiers.

A sort of hairy giant, smoking a great porcelain pipe, and sitting astride of a chair, said in excellent French: "Well, gentlemen, what luck fishing?"

Whereupon a soldier laid at his officer's feet the net full of fish, which he had carefully brought along.

The Prussian smiled. "I see—not bad. But we've other fish to fry. Now listen to me, and keep cool. I regard you two as spies sent to watch me. I take you, and I shoot you. You were pretending to fish, the better to disguise your plans. You've fallen into my hands; so much the worse for you. That's war. But, seeing that you passed through your outposts, you must assuredly have been given the password to get back again. Give it me, and I'll let you go."

Livid, side by side, the two friends were silent, but their hands kept jerking with little nervous movements.

The officer continued: "No one will ever know; it will be all right; you can go home quite easy in your minds. If you refuse, it's death—instant death. Choose."

They remained motionless, without a word.

The Prussian, calm as ever, stretched out his hand towards the water, and said: "Think! In five minutes you'll be at the bottom of that river. In five minutes. You've got families, I suppose?"

Mont Valerien went on thundering. The two fishermen stood there silent.

The German gave an order in his own language. Then he moved his chair so as not to be too near his prisoners. Twelve men came forward, took their stand twenty paces away, and grounded arms.

The officer said: "I give you one minute; not a second more."

And, getting up abruptly, he approached the two Frenchmen, took Morissot by the arm, and, drawing him aside, whispered: "Quick, that password. Your friend need never know. It will only look as if I'd relented." Morissot made no answer.

Then the Prussian took M. Sauvage apart, and asked him the same question.

M. Sauvage did not reply.

Once again they were side by side. The officer gave a word of command. The soldiers raised their rifles.

At that moment Morissot's glance lighted on the net full of gudgeons lying on the grass a few paces from him. The sunshine was falling on that glittering heap of fishes, still full of life. His spirit sank. In spite of all effort his eyes filled with tears.

"Adieu, M. Sauvage!" he stammered out.

M. Sauvage answered: "Adieu, M. Morissot."

They grasped each other's hands, shaken from head to foot by a trembling that they could not control.

"Fire!" cried the officer.

Twelve shots rang out as one.

M. Sauvage fell forward like a log. Morissot, the taller, wavered, spun round, and came down across his comrade, his face upturned to the sky; blood spurted from his tunic, torn across the chest.

The German gave another order. His men dispersed. They came back with ropes and stones, which they fastened to the feet of the two dead friends, whom they carried to the river bank. And Mont Valerien never ceased rumbling, crowned now with piled-up clouds of smoke.

Two of the soldiers took Morissot by the head and heels, two others laid hold of M. Sauvage. The bodies, swung violently to and fro, were hurled forward, described a curve, then plunged upright into the river, where the stones dragged them down feet first.

The water splashed up, bubbled, wrinkled, then fell calm again, and tiny waves rippled out towards the banks.

A few bloodstains floated away out there.

The officer, calm as ever, said quietly: "It's the fish who've got the luck now!" and went back towards the house.

But suddenly catching sight of the net full of gudgeons on the grass, he took it up, looked it over, smiled, and called out: "Wilhelm!"

A soldier in a white apron came running up. The Prussian threw him the spoil of the two dead fishermen.

"Get these little affairs fried at once while they're still alive. First-rate like that!"

And he went back to his pipe.

A DUEL

The war was over; the Germans occupied all France; the country was gasping like a defeated wrestler beneath the victor's knee.

Out from starving, terrified, despairing Paris the first trains had begun to run again, towards new frontiers, slowly traversing the country and wayside towns. The first passengers were gazing out at the devastated plains and the burnt villages. In front of the doors of such houses as still stood, Prussian soldiers with copper-spiked black helmets sat straddling across chairs, smoking their pipes. Others were working or chatting, as if they were in the bosoms of their families. Whole regiments could be seen manœuvring on the open spaces of such towns as were passed, and now and then, above the rattling of the train, raucous voices could be heard shouting out words of command.

M. Dubuis, who had served in the Garde Nationale throughout the siege of Paris, was on his way to Switzerland, to rejoin his wife and daughter, whom he had prudently sent abroad before the invasion.

Famine and fatigue had failed to reduce the bulk of this rich and peaceable merchant. He had lived through terrible things with a sort of broken-hearted resignation and many a bitter comment on the savagery of Man. Now that the war was at an end and he was about to cross the frontier, he was seeing the Prussians for the first time, although he had taken duty on the ramparts and mounted guard many a cold night.

He looked with timid anger at these bearded and armed men, installed on the soil of France as if it were their home; he felt within his soul a fever of impotent patriotism, struggling with an insistent need for prudence—that new instinct, as it were, which has never left us since.

In his compartment two Englishmen, come over to have a look at things, were gazing out with eyes of placid curiosity.

They, too, were stout, both of them, and talked together in their own tongue, sometimes quoting paragraphs out loud from their guide-book, in their endeavours to identify the places spoken of therein.

The train having stopped at the station of a little town, a Prussian officer suddenly got in, his sword clattering after him on the carriage steps. He was tall, buttoned tight in his uniform, and bearded up to the eyes. His red hair seemed to blaze, and his long moustaches, of a paler hue, swept out to either side, cutting his face in twain.

The Englishmen set to work at once to gaze at him, with smiles of gratified curiosity, while M. Dubuis pretended to read his newspaper, tucked away in his corner like a thief in presence of a policeman.

The train went on again. The Englishmen continued to talk, and hunt out the exact sites of battlefields. Suddenly, as one of them was pointing to a village on the horizon, the Prussian officer, stretching out his long legs and lounging back in his seat, remarked in his peculiar French:

"I killed twelve Frenchmen in that village. I took more than a hundred prisoners."

The Englishmen, thoroughly interested, asked at once:

"Ah! What's it called—that village?"

"Pharsbourg," replied the Prussian; and he went on: "I caught 'em by the ears, those rascally Frenchmen."

Then, looking at M. Dubuis, he laughed provocatively. The train rolled on and on, through villages full of the enemy. There were German soldiers on the roads, in the fields, standing at the level crossings, or chatting in front of cafés. They covered the earth like a swarm of African locusts.

The officer waved his hand.

"If I'd been in command I'd have taken Paris and burnt it down, and killed the lot of 'em. No more France!"

Out of politeness, the Englishmen replied:

"Er—ye-es!"

"In twenty years' time," continued the Prussian, "the whole of Europe will belong to us—the whole. Prussia is the greatest Power in the world."

The Englishmen, somewhat uneasy, did not answer. Their faces, inscrutable now, seemed made of wax, between their long whiskers. The Prussian officer laughed. Still lounging back in his seat, he began to boast. He boasted of the crushing of France, insulting the fallen enemy; jeering at Austria's recent defeat, jeering at the desperate, futile defence made by the French provinces, jeering at the *garde mobile,* at the useless artillery. He announced that Bismarck was going to build a town of iron with the guns taken. And suddenly he put his boots against the thigh of M. Dubuis, who, reddening to the ears, turned his eyes away.

The Englishmen seemed to have become totally oblivious, as if they were once more back in their own island, shut away from the sounds of this world.

The officer took out his pipe, and, looking hard at the Frenchman, said:

"Have you got some tobacco about you?"

M. Dubuis replied:

"No, monsieur."

The German went on:

"I beg you will go and buy me some when the train stops." And laughing again, he added: "I'll give you something for yourself."

The train whistled, slackened, passed the burnt-out buildings of a station, and stopped.

The German opened the carriage door, and, taking M. Dubuis by the arm, said:

"Go, and do what I tell you! Hurry up!"

A guard of Prussian soldiers occupied the station. Others stood looking on behind the wooden railings. Just as the engine was whistling for departure, M. Dubuis shot out on to the platform, and, in spite of the gesticulations of the station-master, dashed into another compartment.

* * * * *

He was alone there! He mopped his forehead, and opened his waistcoat, for his heart was beating hard, and he was out of breath. The train stopped again at a station. The officer appeared suddenly at the carriage door and got in, followed almost at once by the two Englishmen, spurred on by their curiosity. The German seated himself opposite the Frenchman, and said with his laugh:

"So you didn't want to do my commission?"

M. Dubuis replied:

"No, monsieur."

The train had just started again.

"Well," said the officer, "I'll just cut off your moustache to fill my pipe."

And he put out his hand towards his neighbour's face. The Englishmen, unmoved as ever, stared with round eyes. The German had already taken hold of some hairs and was pulling at them, when M. Dubuis, with a backhander, knocked up his arm, and, seizing him by the collar, flung him down on the seat. Then, mad with rage, the veins in his temples swollen, and his eyes bloodshot, he squeezed the German's throat steadily with one hand, while, with the other, clenched, he smote him in the face. The Prussian struggled, tried to draw his sword, to catch hold of his adversary, recumbent upon him. But M. Dubuis kept him down with the weight of his vast body, and smote, smote without ceasing, without taking breath, without knowing where his blows were falling. Blood flowed; the throttled German gasped, spat out teeth, and went on trying, but vainly, to throw off this huge infuriated man who was beating him to death.

The Englishmen had risen from their seats and closed in to get a better view; and there they stood, full of delighted curiosity, ready to make any sort of bet on the event.

But suddenly M. Dubuis, exhausted by that terrific effort, raised himself and sat down without a word.

The Prussian was too bewildered, too paralyzed with astonishment and pain, to hurl himself on his opponent. But the moment he had recovered his breath, he said:

"If you don't give me satisfaction in a duel, I'll kill you."

"When you like," replied M. Dubuis; "I ask nothing better."

The German continued:

"Here's Strasbourg; I'll find two officers for seconds; I've just time before the train goes on."

M. Dubuis, who was puffing almost as much as the locomotive, said to the Englishmen:

"Will you be my seconds?"

They replied, as one man:

"Oh, yes!"

And the train stopped.

In a minute the Prussian had found two comrades, who provided the pistols, and a start was made for the ramparts.

The Englishmen were continually looking at their watches, hurrying on, and urging forward the preliminaries, very anxious not to miss their train.

M. Dubuis had never handled a pistol in his life. They placed him twenty paces from his opponent, and asked him:

"Are you ready?"

As he replied "Yes," he noticed that one of the Englishmen had opened his umbrella to protect himself against the sun.

"A voice said: "Fire!"

And M. Dubuis fired, anyhow, immediately, and with stupefaction saw the Prussian opposite him stagger, raise his arms, and fall like a log. He had killed him.

One of the Englishmen cried, "Ha!" in a voice vibrating with joy, sated curiosity, and a kind of happy impatience. The other one, who still had his watch in his hand, seized hold of M. Dubuis' arm, and dragged him off at a rattling pace towards the station.

His friend counted time as he ran, with fists doubled and elbows well in to his sides: "One, two; one, two!"

And, three abreast, they bowled along in spite of their bulk, looking like any three grotesques in a comic paper.

The train was on the point of moving out as they leaped into their compartment. Then the Englishmen, taking off their travelling caps, swung them round their heads, and shouted: "Hip, hip, hip, hurrah!" After which each gravely extended his right hand to M. Dubuis. And at once, returning to their corner, they sat down side by side.

MISS HARRIET

We were a party of seven in the wagonette, four ladies and three men, one on the box beside the coachman; and our horses were slowly mounting the road that wound up the steep hillside. We had started from Étretat at daybreak, to visit the ruins of Tancarville, and, bemused by the sharpness of the morning air, were still half asleep. The ladies especially, little accustomed to these early hours, kept continually closing their eyes, nodding their fields, yellow with the stubble of oats or wheat, covering the soil the dawn.

It was autumn, and on both sides of the road stretched bare fields, yellow with the stubble of oats or wheat, covering the soil like a badly shaven beard. The mist rose like smoke from the earth. Larks were singing in the sky, and many birds piping in the bushes. The sun rose at last before our eyes, all red on the edge of the horizon; and, as he climbed, brighter and brighter each minute, the country seemed to awake, to smile, and stir itself, throwing off, like a girl rising from bed, its white, misty garment.

The Comte d'Etrailles, on the box seat, suddenly cried: "Mark hare!" and pointed to a patch of clover on the left. There was the creature, slipping away, nearly hidden by the crop, and showing only his great ears; he doubled across a ploughed field, stopped, and set off again wildly; changed his mind and stopped again, uneasy, scenting danger near, undecided as to his route; then off he went, with great leaps and bounds of the hind-quarters, and disappeared in a broad square of beetroot. The men all woke up to watch the creature's flight.

"We don't seem to be making ourselves over-agreeable this morning," said René Lemanoir; and looking at his neighbour, the little Baroness Serennes, who was struggling to keep awake, he said in a low voice: "Thinking of your husband, Baroness? Don't worry! he won't be back till Saturday. You've still got four days."

"How silly you are!" she answered, with a sleepy smile; then shaking off her torpor, added: "Come now, tell us something to make us laugh. Monsieur Chenal, you've the reputation of having had more love affairs than the Duc de Richelieu, now do tell us a love story of your own, whichever one you like."

Léon Chenal, an old painter, who in his prime had been a very handsome, powerfully built man, proud of his physique, and a great favourite with women, ran his hand through his long white beard and smiled; after a few minutes' thought, he suddenly became grave.

"This won't be amusing, ladies; I'm going to tell you the most tragic love affair of my life—I hope no friend of mine may ever inspire a love like that:—

I

"I was five-and-twenty at the time, and scouring the country all along the Normandy coast. 'Scouring the country,' as I call it, is to idle along with a knapsack from inn to inn, on the pretext of making landscape studies from Nature. I know nothing pleasanter than that wandering, heedless life. You are perfectly free, without ties or cares or plans of any sort, without even a thought of the morrow. You go tramping along the pleasantest-looking road, just as the fancy takes you, with no object but to satisfy the eye. You stop here because a stream fascinates you, there because you catch an appetizing whiff of fried potatoes at the door of some hostelry. Or, it's a scent of clematis that brings you to a standstill, or perhaps a naïve challenge from the eyes of some country wench in an inn. Never despise those simple hearts! Girls like that have plenty of soul and passion too, their cheeks are firm, and their lips are sweet, their kisses are full and hearty, as delicious as wild raspberries. Love has always a value, no matter where it springs from. A heart that beats when you come near, eyes that weep when you go away, are things so rare and sweet and precious, that they should never be despised. I can remember meetings in ditches full of primroses, behind stables where the cows were asleep, on the straw in granaries still warm from the day's sun. I have memories of coarse homespun, and strong, supple bodies, and, I can tell you, they were good, those naïve, free kisses; more delicate in their frank animality than all the subtle caresses you get from charming and distinguished ladies.

"But the real heart of this happy-go-lucky wandering is the country itself, the woods, the sunrise, the dusk, the moonlight. For us painters they are regular honeymoon journeys with Nature. You are alone and quite close to her in those long, tranquil meetings. Stretched out in some meadow amongst daisies and poppies, you fix your eyes, under the clear fall of the sunlight, on a little village in the distance with a pointed church steeple, whose clock is striking noon. Or perhaps by some spring bubbling up at the foot of an oak tree, in the midst of a tangle of tall, frail grasses, glistening with life, you kneel and lean over to drink the cold, clear water that wets your nose and moustache; you drink with sheer physical delight, as if you were kissing the very lips of the spring. Sometimes in the course of these narrow streamlets, you come across a pool and plunge in, naked, and you feel on your skin from head to foot the quiver of the rapid nimble current, just like a delicious icy caress.

"You are gay up on the hills; melancholy down beside the ponds; and when the sun drowns himself in an ocean of crimson clouds and throws a ruddy glare on the river, your spirit goes soaring. Then again in the evening, under a moon sailing across the furthest heights of the sky, you muse over a thousand strange things that would never come into your head in the full blaze of daylight.

"Well, as I was wandering like this through the very country we're in now, I arrived one evening at the little village of Bénouville, on the cliffs between Yport and Étretat—I had come from Fécamp along the coast, which, about there, is as high and straight as a wall, with jutting chalky rocks that fall perpendicularly into the sea. I had walked the whole day on that short turf, as fine and yielding as a carpet, which springs up all along the edge of the cliff under the salt sea-wind.

"Striding along, singing at the top of my voice, looking up at the slow circling flight of a sea-gull, with its curved wings against the blue sky, or down at the brown sail of a fishing boat on the green sea, I had spent as happy and careless and free a day as anyone could wish. Somebody pointed out to me a little farm where they put up travellers, a sort of inn kept by a peasant woman, in the middle of the usual Normandy yard, surrounded by a double row of beeches.

"So leaving the cliff, I dropped down to this little homestead shut in by its big trees, and presented myself to Mme. Lecacheur.

"She was a wrinkled, stern-looking old country-woman, who seemed to be in the habit of receiving her customers with obvious reluctance, not to say distrust. It was May, and the apple-trees in full blossom spanned the yard with a roof of fragrant flowers showering down a never-ceasing rain of slow-falling pink petals on people's shoulders, and on the grass.

" 'Well, Mme. Lecacheur,' I began, 'have you got a room for me?'

" 'That's as may be,' she replied, astonished at my knowing her name; 'everything's let; but we might see what we can do, perhaps.'

"In five minutes we had come to terms, and I had deposited my knapsack on the bare earth floor of a rural apartment furnished with a bed, two chairs, a table, and a washstand. It looked into the great smoke-dried kitchen, where the guests took their meals in company with the farm hands and the hostess, who was a widow.

"I washed my hands and went out again. The old lady had set about fricasseeing me a chicken for dinner at the huge fireplace wherein hung a smoke-blackened jack.

" 'So you've got some visitors just now?' said I.

" 'There's one lady,' she replied in her discontented way, 'an Englishwoman, middlin' old. She's got the other room.'

"By paying an extra twopence ha'penny a day I secured the right to have my meals in the yard when it was fine; so they set my table in front of the door, and I proceeded to devour the lean, tough joints of a Normandy fowl, drinking pale cider the while, and munching at a huge white loaf, four days old, but exceedingly good for all that.

"All at once the wooden gate into the road was thrown open, and a strange person came towards the house. She was very thin, very tall, and so wrapped up in a plaid shawl with red checks, that one would certainly have thought she had no arms, if a long hand had not emerged at the level of her hips, holding the white umbrella sacred to tourists. Her mummy-like face, framed in tight-rolled curls of grey hair, bobbing up and down at every step, made me think, heaven knows why, of a red herring in curl papers. She passed me quickly, with lowered eyes, and plunged into the cottage.

"I was greatly diverted by this singular apparition, who was doubtless my neighbour, the 'middlin' old' Englishwoman of whom my hostess had spoken.

"I did not see her again that day; but the following day, after I had settled myself down to paint in the depths of that charming valley which comes out at Étretat—you know the one I mean— happening to raise my eyes suddenly, I saw something peculiar reared up on the crest of the hill, something like a hop-pole, draped. It was she. On seeing me she vanished.

"I went in at midday for lunch and took my place at the public table, for the express purpose of making the acquaintance of this original old party. But she by no means responded to my politeness, remaining insensible even to such little attentions as pouring out water for her assiduously, and diligently passing her the dishes. A slight movement of the head, almost imperceptible, and an English word mumbled so that I could not hear what it was, were the only thanks I got.

"I ceased trying to make myself agreeable, but she still continued to occupy my thoughts.

"At the end of three days I knew all that Mme. Lecacheur knew about her.

"Her name was Miss Harriet. In searching apparently for some quiet village wherein to spend the summer, she had lighted on Bénouville six weeks ago, and seemed by no means inclined to leave it. She never spoke at table, and ate quickly, reading away all the time at some pious little book of the strongest Protestant tendency. She distributed these tracts to everybody. The parish priest himself had received four, brought by one of the village urchins who had been given a penny for the errand. Sometimes without anything having led up to it, she would suddenly say to our hostess:—

" 'Je aimé le Seigneur plus que tout; je le admiré dans toute son création, je le adoré dans toute son nature; je le pôrté toujours dans mon cœur.'* And she would instantly hand the amazed

*Miss Harriet's French, too precious to be lost, is given in the original. Its probable meaning is appended in footnotes.
"I love the Lord more than anything; I admire Him in the whole of His creation; I adore Him in all His nature; I carry Him always in my heart."

peasant woman one of her tracts for the conversion of the universe.

"She was not liked in the village. The schoolmaster had said that she was an atheist, and a sort of cloud rested upon her. The parson on being consulted by Mme. Lecacheur had replied: 'Yes, she's a heretic, but God graciously spares the life of the sinner, and I believe her to be a person of irreproachable morals.'

"These words, 'Atheist—Heretic,' of which the meanings were not precisely understood, threw a doubt into every mind. It was supposed that the Englishwoman was rich and had spent her life travelling all over the world, because her family had driven her from home. Why had her family driven her from home? Well, naturally, because of her impiety.

"She was, in truth, one of those highly principled, enthusiastic, headstrong Puritans, whom England produces in shoals; one of those excellent and unendurable old maids who haunt every *table d'hôte* in Europe, spoil Italy, poison Switzerland, render the charming towns along the Mediterranean quite uninhabitable, carrying about with them everywhere their bizarre hobbies, the manners of petrified vestals, indescribable toilettes, and a certain smell of indiarubber, which fosters the theory that at night they must be slipped into 'hold-alls.'

"Whenever I used to see one in a hotel, I would take flight like a bird that sights a scarecrow in a field.

"This one, however, seemed so extremely peculiar that she was really far from displeasing to me.

"Mme. Lecacheur, instinctively hostile to all that was not of her own class, felt a sort of hatred in her narrow soul for the old maid's mystic transports. She had found a word to describe her, a decidedly contumelious word, that sounded very odd on her lips, whereto it must have come after God knows what mysterious spiritual labour.

"'She's a demoniac,' she said. And this word, applied to that austere and sentimental being, struck me as so irresistibly comic, that I myself took to calling her 'the demoniac,' experiencing a quaint pleasure in pronouncing the word out loud whenever I caught sight of her.

"I would ask Mme. Lecacheur: 'Well, what's our "demoniac" doing to-day?'

"And the good lady would reply with a scandalized air:—

"'Would you believe it, sir, she's picked up a toad, whose leg's got crushed somehow, and she's taken it to her room, and she's put it in the wash-basin, and she's puttin' on a dressin' like yo' might on a man. If that ain't profanity!'

"Another time, during a walk at the foot of the cliff, she had bought a big fish, that had just been caught, for no other purpose than to throw it back into the sea. And the fisherman, though handsomely paid, had begun abusing her profusely, more really exasperated than if she had stolen money out of his pocket. For a month afterwards he could not speak of the affair without getting into a rage and swearing horribly.

"'Oh yes! Miss Harriet was assuredly a "demoniac"!'

"Mme. Lecacheur had had an inspiration of genius in so baptizing her.

"The stable-man, who was called Sapeur, because in his youth he had served in Africa, was of quite a different opinion:—

"'The old un's been a rare rip in her time!' he said slyly.

"Ah! if the poor old maid had only known!

"The servant girl, Céleste, never took to the idea of waiting on her, nor could I understand why. Perhaps only because she was a foreigner, of a different race, tongue, religion. In short, she was a 'demoniac!'

"She spent her time wandering about the country, seeking and adoring her God as manifested in Nature. I found her, one evening, on her knees in a thicket. Catching sight of something red among the leaves, I thrust aside the branches, and there was Miss Harriet, who scrambled up in confusion at being seen like that, and fastened on me a pair of eyes as wild-looking as the eyes of a night-jar surprised by daylight.

"Sometimes when I was working down among the rocks, I would suddenly catch sight of her on the top of the cliff, looking like a semaphore. She would be gazing passionately at the vast sea, all golden in the sun, and the wide expanse of sky deep-coloured with the heat. Sometimes I would make her out in the depths of a valley, walking quickly, with her springy English step; and I would go to meet her, attracted, heaven knows why!—solely to see her ecstatic face, that dry ineffable visage, lit up with a deep, inward joy. Often, too, I would come on her in some nook down by a farm, seated on the grass, under the shade of an apple-tree, with her little pious book open on her knees, and her gaze wandering far away.

"For I too stayed on and on, bound to this peaceful countryside by a thousand ties of love for its broad, gentle landscapes—I felt so happy down in this obscure farm, far from the world, and close to the earth, the good, sane, beautiful green earth that we ourselves shall help to nourish with our bodies some day. And perhaps I ought to admit, too, that a spark of curiosity had a little to do with keeping me at Mme. Lecacheur's. I wanted to get to know something of that queer Miss Harriet, to know something of what goes on in the lonely souls of these wandering old maids of England.

II

"We struck up an acquaintance at last in rather an odd way.

"I had just finished a study which seemed to me first-rate; and so it was. It sold for four hundred pounds fifteen years later. It was as simple as 'two and two make four,' but clean away from the academic. The whole right side of my canvas represented a rock, an enormous rugged rock covered with seaweed, brown and yellow and red, over which the sunshine streamed like oil.

"The light from the sun, invisible behind me, fell on the stone, turning it to fiery gold. That was the whole thing. A foreground dazzlingly bright, and flaming, and superb. On the left the sea, not the blue, nor the slate-coloured sea, but of jade-green, milky and hard under the deep blue of the sky.

"I was so pleased with my work that I danced along, taking it back to the inn. I should have liked the whole word to see it at that moment—I remember I showed it to a cow close by the path, and shouted to her:—

" 'Look at that, old girl! You won't see a thing like that every day!'

"Arrived at the house, I called to Mme. Lecacheur at the top of my voice:—

" 'Hi! Missis! hi! Come out and look at this!'

"The good lady appeared, and ruminated over my sketch with her stupid unseeing eyes that obviously made out nothing, not even whether the thing was meant for an ox or a house.

"Miss Harriet was on her way in, and passed behind me just as I was holding my canvas at arm's length to show it to Mme. Lecacheur. The 'demoniac' could not help seeing, for I took care to turn the canvas so that it should not escape her glance. She stopped short, in petrified amazement. It was her own rock, it appeared, the one she was wont to climb, that she might indulge in reveries at her ease.

"She murmured so marked and flattering a British 'Aoh!' that I turned towards her smiling:—

"'This is my latest study, Mademoiselle,' I said.

"She muttered in an ecstasy both comic and touching:—

"'Oh! Monsieur, vô comprené le nature d'une fâçon palpitante!'*

"I blushed, yes, I blushed, more moved by that compliment than if I had received one from a queen. I was seduced, vanquished, overcome. I give you my word, I could have kissed her. I sat down to table beside her, as usual. For the first time she spoke, following up her thoughts out loud:—

"'Oh! j'aimé tant le nature!'†

"I passed her the bread, the water, the wine. She accepted them now with a little mummy-like smile; and I began to talk 'landscape' to her. After the meal, we rose at the same moment, and going out, strolled about the yard; then, attracted doubtless by the wonderful blaze the sunset was lighting up over the sea, I opened the gate, and off we went towards the cliffs side by side, as happy as two people who have just come to understand, and see into, each other's minds.

"It was a warm, soft evening, one of those happy evenings when body and soul feel at rest. All is beauty and charm. The warm, fragrant air is full of the scent of grasses and sea-weeds, and comes sane and fresh to the nostril; it caresses the palate with the savour of the sea, and soothes the soul with its penetrating sweetness. We were walking now on the edge of the cliff above the vast ocean, with its little waves rolling in, a hundred yards below. And taking deep breaths through our open lips, we drank in the fresh breeze, which had come so far across the sea, and, salt from the long kiss of the waves, slid lingering over our faces. Swathed in her plaid shawl, with an inspired face, and with teeth bared to the wind, the Englishwoman gazed at the great sun as it sank toward the sea. Before us, far below, and far away as the eye could distinguish, a three-masted ship with all sail set showed her silhouette against the flaming sky; closer in, a steamer passed, unfurling a scroll of smoke, that left behind an endless streak of cloud across the whole horizon.

"Slowly, slowly, the red orb went down. Soon it touched the water, just behind the quiet sailing-ship, which appeared as in a

---

*"Oh! sir, you've got the breath of life into it!"
†"Oh! I do so love Nature!"

frame of fire, in the centre of the blazing globe. Little by little, conquered by the ocean, the sun sank. We saw it merge, lessen, disappear. It was all over. Alone, the little vessel still showed its clear-cut profile against the golden background of the farthest sky.

"With passionate eyes Miss Harriet gazed at the flaming end of the day. I felt certain she was possessed by an intense longing to embrace the sky, the sea, the whole horizon.

"She murmured: 'Aoh! j'aimé, j'aimé, j'aimé!'

"I saw the tears standing in her eyes. She went on:—

"'Je vôdré étre une petite oiseau pour m'envolé dans le firmament!'*

"She remained standing, as I had often seen her, bolt upright on the edge of the cliff, with a face as glowing as her crimson shawl. I longed to put her in my sketch-book—title: 'Caricature of Ecstasy'; and I turned away to hide a smile.

"Then I began talking to her about painting, as I might have talked to a chum, discussing tone, and values, and strengths, in fact, all the technical terms. She listened attentively and intelligently, trying to penetrate my thoughts and divine the obscurer meaning behind my words; from time to time she exclaimed:—

"'Oh! je comprené, je comprené. C'été très palpitante!'†

We went indoors.

"The next day she came up the moment she saw me, and held out her hand. We were friends from that minute. She was a good creature, whose soul was, as it were, on springs, leaping with startling suddenness into enthusiasms. She lacked balance, like nearly all women who reach the age of fifty without marrying. She seemed as though preserved in a sort of innocence gone sour; but in her heart she had kept something of youth, of extreme youth, and that was always taking fire. She loved nature and animals with a feverish love, fermented like liquor kept too long, with the sensual love that she had never given to man.

"I am certain that the sight of a mother dog suckling her puppies, or a mare running in a meadow with her foal at heel, or a bird's nest full of enormous-headed naked-bodied little squeakers, made her quiver all over with a passion of feeling. Poor solitary souls, sad wanderers of the *table d'hôte,* poor, lamentable, ridiculous beings—since knowing her, I have loved you all.

* "Oh! how I love it! I wish I were a little bird, and could fly away into that sky!"
† "Oh! I understand, I understand. It's got the breath of life!"

"I soon perceived that she had something to say to me, but dared not say it, and I was amused at her timidity.

"When I set off in the morning with my painting-gear on my back, she would go with me as far as the end of the village, silent, visibly troubled, trying to find words to begin. Then, all at once, she would leave me, and march briskly off with her skipping step.

"At last one day she plucked up courage:—

"'Je vôdré voir vô comment vô faites le peinture? Volé vô? J'été très curieux.'* And she blushed as if she had said something extremely bold.

"I took her off to the bottom of the Petit-Val, where I was beginning a large study.

"She stood just behind me, following all my movements with the strictest attention.

"Then suddenly, afraid perhaps that she might be bothering me, she said:—

"'Thank you!' and went away.

"But after a little she became more at ease, and used to come with me every day with obvious pleasure. She would take her camp-stool under her arm, never allowing me to carry it for her, and sit down at my side; she would stay there for hours, motionless and silent, following with her eyes every movement of my brush. When with a blot of colour stuck roughly on with the knife I succeeded in producing some true and unforeseen effect, she would utter, in spite of herself, a little 'Aoh!' of astonishment, joy, and admiration. She had a feeling of tender respect for my canvases, of almost religious reverence for the reproduction by human means of a part of the Divine work. My studies evidently were to her in a way sacred pictures; and she would sometimes talk to me of God, and try to convert me. Ah! he was a queer sort of person, that God of hers, a kind of village philosopher, without much ability or power, for she always imagined him heart-broken at the injustice that went on under his eyes—as if he had not been able to prevent it.

"She was, moreover, on excellent terms with him, and seemed to be the confidante of all his secrets and dislikes. She would say, 'God wishes,' or 'God doesn't wish,' like a sergeant who tells a recruit that the colonel 'has given orders.' From the bottom of her heart she lamented my ignorance of the Divine will, which she so eagerly sought to reveal to me; and every day I found in

* "I should like to watch you paint. May I? I'm so interested!"

my pockets, in my hat when I dropped it on the ground, in my colour-box, in the fresh-cleaned shoes standing outside my door in the morning, those little pious tracts which she doubtless received direct from heaven.

"I treated her with frank cordiality, like an old friend. I soon began to perceive, however, that her behaviour had altered a little, though I had not noticed how it came about.

"When I was at work, either down in the valley or in some deep lane, I would see her suddenly appear, coming on at a rapid, rhythmical walk. She would sit down abruptly, breathing quickly as if she had been running, or some deep emotion were at work within her. Her face, too, would be red all over, that peculiar English red that no other nation possesses. Then, without any cause, she would turn pale, a sort of earthy colour, and seem about to faint. Gradually she would recover her ordinary looks and begin to talk.

"But suddenly she would leave off in the middle of a sentence, get up, and make off at such a pace and in such a strangely abrupt way, that I used to rack my brains to see if I had done anything to displease or wound her.

"At last I decided that this must be her usual method of behaving, which had been a little modified no doubt for my sake during the first moments of our acquaintanceship. When she came back to the farm after hours of walking along the coast, battling with the wind, her long corkscrew ringlets were often out of curl, and hung as if their springs had broken. Formerly she had never bothered about them, and used to come into dinner unceremoniously, all ruffled by that sister of hers, the breeze. But now she would go up to her room to adjust what I called her lamp-chimneys; and when, with one of those chaffing compliments that always scandalized her so, I said gallantly, 'Why, you're as beautiful as a star to-day, Miss Harriet!' a little blush would cover her face, like the blush of a girl of fifteen.

"Presently she reverted entirely to the wild state, and ceased coming to see me paint. 'It's a mood,' thought I, 'that will pass off.' But it did not. If I spoke to her now, she either replied with affected indifference or glum exasperation. And she had fits of abruptness, impatience, and nerves. I only saw her now at meals, and we scarcely spoke at all. I thought I really must have annoyed her in some way, and one evening I asked her:—

"'Miss Harriet, why aren't you the same to me as you used

to be? What have I done to offend you? You're making me quite unhappy!'

"She answered angrily in the queerest tone of voice:—

" 'J'été toujours avec vô le mème qu'autre fois! Ce n'été pas vrai, pas vrai!'* and she ran off and shut herself up in her own room.

"Sometimes she would look at me very strangely. I have often thought since, that prisoners condemned to death must look like that when they are called on the morning of their execution. There was a sort of madness in her eye, a mystic, violent madness; and something besides, a fever, an overstrained longing, chafing at the impossibility of its fulfilment or realization. And it seemed to me as if there were a fight raging within her, and her heart were struggling with some unknown force which she was trying to subdue. Ah! yes, and something else too . . . how can I express it?

III

"The revelation was strange to a degree.

"For some time I had been working every day, from dawn on, at a picture which had the following for its subject:—

"A deep sheltered ravine, overtopped by two slopes covered with trees and brambles, stretching away from the eye till it was lost in a bath of the milky vaporous mist that floats over valleys at sunrise. And coming towards you from far away through the heavy transparent haze, you saw, or rather divined, two human forms, youth and maiden, linked in a close embrace, her face raised to his, his bent to hers, their lips meeting.

"A first ray of sunlight, gliding through the branches, shot across this daybreak mist, and, turning it to a shaft of rose colour behind these simple lovers, made their dim shapes move as it were through silver light. It was good, I can *tell* you; really good!

"I was working on the slope leading to the little Étretat valley, and was lucky enough that particular morning to have just the sort of floating wrack I wanted. Suddenly something rose up in front of me like a ghost; it was Miss Harriet. Catching sight of me she was on the point of running off, but I called out to her:—

" 'Ah! do come here, Mademoiselle; I've got a little picture to show you.'

*"I am just the same to you as I always was. It's not true, it's not true."

"She came, reluctantly enough as it seemed, and I held out my sketch. She said nothing, but remained looking at it a long time motionless; then suddenly—she began to cry. She wept with the spasmodic sobbing of one who has long fought against her tears, and worn out, abandons herself, still protesting.

"I started up, myself moved by this grief that I could not understand; and with the instinct of a true Frenchman, who acts before he thinks, I gave her hands a quick affectionate grasp. She left them in mine for some seconds, and I felt them tremble as if all her nerves were writhing. Then suddenly she drew, or rather tore them away. But I had recognized that shiver. I had felt it before—there's no mistaking it. Ah! that quiver of a woman's love, whether she's fifteen or fifty, gentle or simple, goes straight to your heart, you can't mistake it. All her poor being was vibrating, responding, swooning; and I knew it. Before I could say a word, she was gone, leaving me as amazed as though I had seen a miracle, as unhappy as if I had committed a crime.

"I did not go in for lunch, but took a stroll along the cliff, feeling as much like crying as laughing; the affair was so comic, yet so lamentable; my position was so ridiculous, and hers miserable enough to drive her mad.

"I asked myself what on earth I ought to do.

"I felt there was nothing for it but to go away, and made up my mind to do so. After wandering about sad and thoughtful till dinner time, I went in as the soup appeared.

"We sat down to table as usual. Miss Harriet was there, eating solemnly, and neither speaking nor raising her eyes. In other respects she looked and behaved as usual. I waited for the end of the meal, then turned to our hostess and said:—

"'Well, Mme. Lecacheur, I shall have to be off in a day or two!'

"The good woman, surprised and vexed, instantly droned out:—

"'What's that you say, sir? Going to leave us? Why, we we've got so used to havin' you!'

"I was looking at Miss Harriet out of the corner of my eye; her face did not change. But Céleste, the little maid, looked up at me. She was a big, ruddy, fresh-looking girl of eighteen, as strong as a horse, and, strange to say, very clean. I used to kiss her sometimes in the corner, just to keep myself in practice, nothing more. Dinner came to an end.

"I went out to smoke my pipe under the apple trees, walking backwards and forwards from one end of the yard to the other. All the reflections I had made during the day, the morning's weird discovery of that grotesque passionate love which had fixed on me, and all sorts of sweet and disturbing reminiscences that followed in the train of that discovery, perhaps even the look the servant girl had given me when I spoke of departure, all these joined in putting me into a wanton mood. My lips began tingling as if they had been kissed, and the blood ran madly in my veins.

"Night came, throwing dark shadows under the trees; I caught sight of Céleste going to shut the fowl-house at the far side of the enclosure. I ran forward on tiptoe, so that she heard nothing, and just as she was raising herself, after having lowered the little trapdoor where the fowls go in and out, I seized her in my arms, and covered her moon face with a shower of kisses. She struggled with me, but, laughing all the time, pretty well used, no doubt, to that sort of thing. Something made me leave hold of her suddenly and fly around. I felt somehow there was someone behind us!

"It was Miss Harriet on her way indoors; she had seen us, and stood petrified, as if she had seen a ghost. Then she disappeared in the darkness.

"I went back to the house ashamed and disturbed, more miserable at being caught by her doing such a thing than if she had found me committing a criminal act.

"My nerves were all unstrung, and I slept badly, haunted by dismal thoughts. I seemed to hear someone crying. No doubt I was mistaken; several times I thought I heard footsteps about the house, and someone opening the outer door. Towards morning fatigue overwhelmed me, and I slept at last. I woke late, and only made my appearance at lunch time, still upset, and without having made up my mind what line to take.

"No one had seen Miss Harriet. We waited for her; she did not appear. Mme. Lecacheur went into her room. The Englishwoman was not there. She must have gone out at daybreak, as she often did, to see the sun rise. No one expressed surprise, and we began the meal in silence.

"It was extremely hot, one of those burning, heavy days, when not a leaf is stirring. The table had been dragged out of doors, under an apple tree, and from time to time Sapeur went to the cellar to fill the cider jug; everyone was so thirsty. Céleste brought the dishes from the kitchen, a ragoût of mutton with potatoes, a fried rabbit, and a salad. Then she placed before us a dish of cherries, the first of the season.

"Thinking they would be more delicious if they were freshened up, I begged the little maid to draw me a bucket of cold water from the well.

"She came back in five minutes saying there was something wrong with it. She had let the rope out to the full, and the bucket had touched the bottom, but had come up again empty. Mme. Lecacheur wished to see for herself, and went off to peer into the depths. She came back saying that she could see something in her well that oughtn't to be there. A neighbour must have thrown in some bundles of straw out of spite. I also went to have a look, hoping to be better able to make out this object, whatever it was. I leaned over the edge, and saw something that seemed white. But what? It then occurred to me to let down a lantern on the end of a rope. The yellow glare danced about on the stone sides, sinking deeper and deeper. Sapeur and Céleste had joined us, and we were all four leaning over the opening. The lantern stopped above an indistinct mass of black and white, of a strange, puzzling appearance.

"'It's an 'orse,' cried out Sapeur. 'I can see the 'oof. For sure 'e got out of the medder last night and fell in!'

"But suddenly a shiver went through me to the very marrow. I had just distinguished a foot and then a leg straight upon end; the whole body and the other leg were hidden under the water.

"Trembling so violently that the lantern danced wildly above that shoe, I stammered out in an almost inaudible voice:—

"'It's a woman down there . . . it's—it's—Miss Harriet!'

"Sapeur was the only one who did not move a muscle. He had seen all sorts of things in Africa!

"Mme. Lecacheur and Céleste, uttering piercing shrieks, fled from the spot.

"The body had to be recovered, so I tied the rope firmly round the man's waist, and let him down very slowly by means of the pulley, watching him as he sank into the shadow. He had the lantern and another rope in his hands. Presently his voice, which seemed to come from the middle of the earth, cried, 'Stop!' and I saw him fishing something up from the water; it was the other leg; then he tied the heels together with the spare rope, and cried again, 'Haul away!'

"I pulled him up, but I felt my arms cracking, and the muscles going slack. I was terrified I should leave go of the rope and let him fall.

" 'Well?' I exclaimed, as his head appeared above the curb, as if I had expected him to give me tidings of her who was lying there at the bottom.

"We both got on to the stone ledge, and, face to face, bending over the orifice, began to hoist the body.

"Mme. Lecacheur and Céleste watched us from a distance, hiding behind the house wall. When they perceived the black shoes and white stockings of the drowned woman appearing, they vanished.

"Sapeur seized the ankles, and in this attitude the poor modest old maid was dragged out. The head was in a frightful state, black with mud and wounds; her long grey hair, quite loose, and out of curl for all time, hung dripping and slimy. Sapeur said scornfully:

" 'Oh! lor! ain't she lean?'

"We carried her to her room, and as the two women did not appear, the stableman and I laid out the body. I washed the sad, distorted face. Under my touch one eye opened a little and gazed at me with the pale, cold, terrible gaze of a corpse, the gaze that seems to come from so far beyond all life. I did the best I could with the scattered hair, and, with my clumsy hands, arranged it on her forehead in a new and odd-looking fashion. Then bashfully, as though committing a sacrilege, I took off her soaked garments, exposing her shoulders, her chest, and her long arms that were as thin as sticks.

"Then I went out to look for flowers—poppies, cornflowers, marguerites, and fresh sweet-scented grasses—and with these I covered her death-bed.

"Being the only friend near her, I had to fulfil the usual formalities. A letter found in her pocket, written at the last moment, asked that she might be buried in the village where her last days had been spent. A terrible thought wrung my heart. Was it because of me that she wished to be laid to her rest here?

"Towards evening all the gossips and neighbours came to have a look at the body, but I kept them out; I intended to be alone with her, and to watch there all night. I gazed at her by the light of the candles, poor unhappy woman, dying, an utter stranger, so pitifully, so far from home. Somewhere perhaps she had friends and relatives; and I wondered what her childhood and her life had been like! From whence had she come, wandering, all by herself, like a lost dog driven from home? What secret of suffering and despair lay hidden in that poor body, the awkward body she had carried about with her throughout life, like some shameful burden; the ridiculous exterior which had driven far away from her all affection and love?

"How many unhappy creatures there are in this world! Upon this poor human being I felt the eternal injustice of implacable Nature had been laid! All was over for her, and perhaps she had never felt the one thing that sustains the greatest outcast, that hope of being loved some day! Else why did she hide herself like this, why shun people so? Why love so passionately, so tenderly, every living thing and creature that was not man? And I began to understand that here was one who really believed in God, believed that hereafter her sufferings would be made up to her. And now she was going to become one with the earth, to return to life as a plant, to blossom in the sun, yield grass for the cattle, grain for the birds, and so through the flesh of animals once more become the flesh of human beings. But that which we call her soul was quenched for ever at the bottom of that dark well. She would never suffer again. She had exchanged that life of hers for those other lives that would be born again of her.

"Hours passed in our sinister, silent communion. A pale glimmer heralded the dawn; there came a rosy beam gliding to the bed, laying a bar of light across the sheets and on the hands. It was the hour she loved so much. The awakening birds began singing in the trees.

"I threw the window wide open, flung back the curtains that the whole sky might see us, and bending over the icy body, I took her poor bruised head between my hands, and slowly, without any feeling of terror or disgust, I gave those lips a long kiss—the first they had ever known. . . ."

Léon Chenal ceased speaking. The women were all in tears. The Comte d'Etrailles could be heard using his handkerchief vigorously on the box. The coachman, alone unmoved, had fallen into a doze; and his horses, no longer feeling the touch of the whip, had slackened their pace to a lazy walk. The wagonette seemed hardly to move; it had suddenly grown heavy, as though laden with grief.

THE UMBRELLA

Mme. Oreille was thrifty. She knew the exact value of a halfpenny, and possessed a perfect arsenal of hard and fast maxims upon the multiplication of money. Her servant certainly had bitter work to secure any perquisites, and M. Oreille found it extremely difficult to get his pocket money. They were comfortably off, however, having children; but Mme. Oreille suffered real physical pain when she had to let the good silver coins slip out of her grasp—it was like a rent in her heart; and whenever she was compelled to make an outlay of any importance she always slept badly the night after. Oreille was continually saying:—

"You really might be more open-handed; we don't live up to our income."

"You never can tell what might happen," she would reply; "better to have too much than too little."

She was a woman of forty, short, bustling, wrinkled, clean, and frequently out of temper.

Her husband was continually groaning over the privations she made him suffer; some of them he felt to be particularly painful, for they wounded his vanity.

He was one of the head clerks at the War Office, and had remained there solely at his wife's command, to augment an income already more than sufficient.

Well, it so happened that for two whole years he had been going to business with a certain patched umbrella which was a standing joke to his colleagues. Tired of their chaff, he insisted, at last on Mme. Oreille buying him a new one. She bought one for six-and-eightpence, a speciality at one of the big shops. His fellow-clerks, who recognized in this object an article to be seen in thousands all over Paris, began of course to chaff him afresh, and Oreille suffered tortures. The umbrella turned out good for nothing. In three months it was done for, and the whole War Office resounded with jokes. They even made a song on the subject, which was to be heard from morning till night, from top to bottom of the huge building.

Thereupon, Oreille, in his exasperation, ordered his wife to choose him a new gamp, of good silk, at not less than sixteen shillings, and to bring him the receipt as a guarantee that she had paid that price. She bought one for fourteen-and-sevenpence-farthing, and, reddening with anger as she handed it to her husband, announced:

"There, that'll have to do for at least five years."

Oreille was triumphant; he had a real success at the office. When he returned that evening, his wife said to him, with an uneasy glance at the umbrella:

"You oughtn't to keep the elastic done up like that, it's the very way to cut the silk. You'll have to look after *this* one carefully, for I shan't buy you another in a hurry."

She caught hold of it, unfastened it, and shook out the folds. But she stood transfixed with horror. A round hole, as big as a farthing, was to be seen in the middle of the umbrella. It was a cigar-burn!

"What's this?" she stammered.

All unconscious, her husband blandly replied:

"Eh, what? What do you say?"

She choked so dreadfully with rage that she could not get her words out:

"You—you—you've burnt—your umbrella. You—you're mad! Do you want to ruin us?"

He turned round, feeling himself grow pale.

"What did you say?"

"I say that you've burnt your umbrella. Look here!"

And rushing up as though about to beat him, she thrust the little round burn under his very nose.

He was aghast at the sight of the rent, and babbled:

"*That*—that—why, what is it? I—I don't know. I've done nothing to it, nothing. I swear. *I* don't know what's the matter with the umbrella!"

"I'll wager you've been playing the fool with it at the office, you've been peacocking about, showing it off to everyone."

He replied:

"Well, I opened it just once to show what a beauty it was. That's all, I swear."

But she was trembling with rage, and began treating him to

one of those conjugal scenes that make the family hearth, to a peaceful man, more formidable than a bullet-raked battle-field.

She made a patch with a piece cut from the old umbrella, which was of a different colour; and the next day Oreille went off with his mended weapon. He put it in his locker, and thought no more about it, except as a vague unpleasant memory.

But, hardly had he got indoors that evening before his wife seized the umbrella from him, opened it to take note of its condition, and was struck dumb before an irreparable disaster. It was riddled with little holes, evidently burns, as if someone had emptied the contents of a lighted pipe over it. The thing was ruined, ruined beyond recall.

She gazed at it without saying a word, her rage was such that no sound would come out of her throat. Her husband also contemplated the wreck, and stood there in a stupor of horrid consternation.

Then they looked at each other; presently he dropped his eyes, and next moment had the ruined object hurled at his face. Recovering her voice, she shouted in a transport of fury:

"Ah! You scoundrel! You utter scoundrel! You've done it on purpose! But I'll pay you out! You'll get no other——"

The conjugal scene was played over again. After an hour of storm, he was at last able to get in a remark. He swore that he knew nothing about it, and that it could only have been done out of spite or revenge.

He was delivered by the ringing of the door bell, and the entrance of a friend who had come to dine with them.

Mme. Oreille laid the case before him. As to buying another umbrella, it was out of the question.

"In that case," argued the friend with some reason, "his clothes, which are worth more than the umbrella, will certainly get spoilt."

Still in a rage, the little woman replied:

"Well, then, he'll have to take the marketing umbrella. I will *not* get him a new silk."

At this proposition, Oreille rebelled:

"Then I shall hand in my resignation," he said: "I will *not* go to the War Office with a marketing gamp."

The friend went on:

"Why not get this one recovered; it won't cost so very much!"

Mme. Oreille stammered angrily:

"It'll cost at least six-and-sixpence to have it recovered. Six-and-six added to fourteen-and-sevenpence makes one pound one and a penny. Twenty-one shillings for an umbrella; why, it's madness, imbecility!"

The friend, a person of very moderate means, here had an inspiration:

"Make your Insurance Company pay for it. They pay for anything that's burnt, so long as the damage is done in your own house."

On receiving this piece of advice the little woman at once calmed down, and after a moment's reflection said to her husband:

"To-morrow before going to the War Office you'll just go to the office of the 'Maternelle,' show the state of your umbrella, and claim the damage."

M. Oreille gave a start.

"I wouldn't dare to do such a thing!" he said; "it's just a loss of fourteen-and-sixpence, and there's an end of it. We shan't die of that."

And he went out next day with a stick. It was luckily fine. Left alone, at home, Mme. Oreille could not forget the loss of her fourteen-and-sevenpence. She put the umbrella on the dining-table and moved round it, unable to make up her mind.

The thought of the fire insurance company haunted her incessantly, but she dared not face the supercilious glances of the men to whom she would have to speak; she was a timid woman in public, a mere trifle made her blush, and she was always embarrassed when she had to talk to strangers.

And yet her regrets over that fourteen-and-sevenpence gave her actual bodily suffering. She tried not to think about it, but the grievous memory of the loss continued without ceasing to torment her. What was to be done? Time passed, and she could not decide. Then all at once, with the desperate valour that cowards suddenly develop, she made up her mind.

"I'll go; we shall just see!"

But it was first necessary to prepare the umbrella, so that the damage should be unmistakable, and the cause thereof easily proved. She took a match from the mantelpiece and made a big burn, the size of her hand, between the ribs; then she daintily rolled up what was left of the silk, fixed the elastic band round it, put on her hat and coat, and walked quickly towards the Rue de Rivoli, where the insurance office was situated.

She looked at the numbers on the houses. There were still twenty-eight to come. All the better! She would be able to think the thing over a little. She advanced more and more slowly. Suddenly she gave a start. There was the door, on which was emblazoned in gold letters: "'La Maternelle'—Insurance against fire." Already! She stood still for a second, bashful and uneasy, then walked past, came back, passed the door again, and once more came back.

At last she said to herself:

"I've got to go in, so, the sooner the better."

But as she entered the building, she felt her heart beating fast. She went into a huge apartment, with wickets all round; and behind every wicket could be seen the head of a man, whose body was hidden by the wire screen.

A gentleman appeared, with papers in his hand.

She stopped him, and said in a small, timid voice:

"Excuse me, sir, but could you tell me where I ought to go to make a claim for damage to burnt property?"

He replied in a sonorous voice:

"First floor, to the left. The Serious Disaster department."

These words increased her nervousness; she longed to creep silently away and sacrifice her fourteen-and-sevenpence. But at the thought of that sum, a little of her courage returned, and she went upstairs, breathless, and pausing at every step.

On the first floor she saw a door, and knocked. A high-pitched voice cried out:

"Come in."

She entered, and found herself in a large apartment where three gentlemen, all adorned with the ribbon of the legion of honour, stood solemnly talking.

"What may your pleasure be, madame?" asked one of them.

She could hardly find the words, and stuttered out:

"I have come—I have come—here—about—an accident."

The polite gentleman handed her a chair.

"Kindly take a seat; I shall be at your service in one minute."

And, turning again to the other two, he resumed his conversation:

"The Company, gentlemen, does not admit its responsibility towards you to any greater extent than sixteen thousand pounds. We cannot entertain your claim for the four thousand beyond that. Besides, the estimate——"

One of the two here interrupted:

"Very well, sir, the Court will decide the matter. There is nothing left for us but to take our leave."

And bowing ceremoniously, they went out of the room. Oh! if she had only dared to go out with them, she would have fled and abandoned everything! But how could she? The gentleman returned, and making her a bow, said:

"Now, madame, of what use can I be to you?"

With great difficulty she got out the words:

"I have come—for this——"

The director lowered his eyes, in frank astonishment, towards the object she held out to him.

She tried, with a trembling hand, to undo the elastic. After several efforts she succeeded, and opened the ragged skeleton with a jerk.

The man said in a compassionate voice:

"It *does* appear to be in a bad way."

She declared hesitatingly:

"It cost me sixteen shillings."

He was surprised.

"Really! So much?"

"Yes, it was a thoroughly good one. I wished you to see the state of it."

"Quite so; I do see. Quite so. But I do *not* see in what way this concerns me."

An uneasy thought assailed her. Perhaps this company did not refund small losses, and she said:

"But—it's *burnt*."

The gentleman did not deny it.

"I quite see it is."

Her jaw dropped; she was at a loss what to say. Then, suddenly realizing what she had neglected to explain, she went on hurriedly:

"I am Mme. Oreille. We are insured in the 'Maternelle,' and I have come to make a claim for this damage." Fearing a positive refusal she hastened to add:

"I only ask that you should see to the recovering of it."

"But—madame——" said the embarrassed director, "we're not an umbrella shop. We really cannot undertake repairs of this kind."

The little woman felt her self-possession returning. There

was to be a fight—well, she would fight! She was no longer frightened.

"Oh!" she said. "I am only asking you to refund me the price of the repairs. I can easily get it done myself."

The gentleman seemed confused.

"Really, madame, it's so very trivial. We are never asked for damages in cases of accident of such a minute nature. You must see that we positively cannot refund for handkerchiefs, gloves, brooms, old slippers, all the little things daily exposed to risk of damage by fire."

She reddened, feeling her temper rising.

"Well, sir," she said, "we had a chimney on fire last December, which meant a loss of at least twenty pounds, and M. Oreille never claimed anything from the Company then; so it's certainly only fair that they should pay for my umbrella now!"

The director, who scented an untruth, said with a smile:

"You will admit, madame, that it is rather remarkable that M. Oreille, after claiming nothing over a loss of twenty pounds, should want us to get an umbrella repaired, a matter of four or five shillings."

In no way disconcerted by this, she replied:

"Pardon me, sir, the twenty pounds damage was entirely M. Oreille's affair, whereas this loss of fourteen-and-sixpence is entirely Mme. Oreille's, which is not at all the same thing."

He began to see that he would never get rid of her, and was only wasting his time, so he said resignedly:

"Be so kind as to tell me how the accident occurred."

She felt that victory was hers, and began her story:

"This is how it was, sir. I have in my hall a sort of bronze receptacle, for sticks and umbrellas. The other day, on coming home, I placed this umbrella there. I must tell you, that just over this receptacle there is a little shelf where candles and matches are kept. I reached up for the matches, you see. I was obliged to strike four; the first one missed fire, the second lighted and went out, and the same with the third."

The director interrupted her to launch a witticism:

"Ah! they must have been Government matches!"

She completely failed to see the joke, and went on:

"Very likely. Anyway, the fourth burned properly, and I lighted my candle; then I went to my room, and went to bed. After about a quarter of an hour, I thought I smelt something burning. I am always terrified of fire. Oh! if ever we have a real disaster you may be sure it won't be my fault. Particularly since that chimney on fire of which I told you; since then I'm really frightened to death. So up I got, and went about hunting and sniffing like a pointer, and at last I discovered that my umbrella was on fire. It was, no doubt, one of those matches dropped into it. You see the state it's in now!"

The director had made up his mind:

"At what do you estimate the damage?" he asked.

She remained speechless, not daring to fix on any sum. Then, wishing to appear generous, she said:

"I will leave it to you to get it repaired. I have every confidence in you."

He shook his head.

"No, madame, that I cannot do. Tell me how much you want."

"Well—I think I ought to—now—I don't want to take advantage of you—we might manage it this way. I will take my umbrella to a shop, and have it covered with good silk, good durable silk, and I'll bring you the bill. Will that suit you?"

"Perfectly, madame; that is understood then. Here is the order for the cashier, who will refund you whatever you spend."

And he held out a card to Mme. Oreille, who seized it, and, expressing her thanks, rose and left the room, in a hurry to get out of doors, for fear he should change his mind.

This time she marched gaily down the street, looking for a fashionable umbrella shop. When she discovered one that had an extremely superior appearance, she went in and said in a confident voice:

"This umbrella is to be covered with silk, really good silk. Use the very best you have. I am not particular as to price."

QUEEN HORTENSE

In Argenteuil she was called Queen Hortense; no one ever knew why. Possibly because she spoke in the tone of an officer giving orders, or because she was tall and bony and imperious, or perhaps because she ruled over a community of those domestic creatures dear to the hearts of old maids: fowls and dogs and cats, canaries and parrots. But she never spoiled her pets, never babbled those tender endearments that seem to pour so naturally from women's lips over the velvet fur of their purring cats; no, she ruled her creatures autocratically—she reigned.

She was a regular old maid; one of those old maids whose voices are harsh and gestures spare, whose very soul seems to have hardened. She brooked neither contradiction nor reply, neither hesitation, carelessness, sloth nor fatigue. No one had ever heard her complain, express regret, or envy of anybody whatsoever. "Everyone has his lot in life," she used to say, with the conviction of a fatalist. She never went to church, disliked parsons, believed but little in God, and called all things connected with religion, "pap for cry-babies."

During the thirty years she had occupied her tiny house with its little front-garden bordering the street, she had never changed her mode of life, but her maids she changed pitilessly, as soon as they reached the age of twenty-one.

Without ever a sigh or tear she replaced her dogs and cats and birds when they died of old age or accident, interring the departed animals in a certain garden-bed by means of a small spade, then treading down the earth unconcernedly on top of them.

She had various acquaintances in the town among the families of business men who went to their office work in Paris every day. From time to time she was asked in to take a cup of tea with them in the evenings. She invariably fell asleep at these gatherings, and had to be awakened when it was time to go home. She never allowed anyone to escort her, for she was not afraid of anything either by day or by night. She seemed to have no liking for children.

She occupied herself with countless masculine labours, with carpentering and gardening, with the sawing and chopping of wood, and the repairing of her old house, even doing the mason's work herself, when necessary.

She had some relations who came to see her twice a year, the Cimmes and the Colombels; her two sisters had married, one a herbalist, the other a man of small independent means. The Cimmes had no descendants, the Colombels possessed three: Henry, Pauline and Joseph. Henry was twenty, Pauline seventeen, and Joseph, who had arrived on the scene when it seemed impossible that madame should again become a mother, was only three. There was no particular bond of affection between the old maid and her relatives.

In the spring of 1882 Queen Hortense fell suddenly ill. The neighbours went for a doctor, but she would have none of him; and on a priest presenting himself, she got out of bed half dressed to turn him out of her house.

The little maid, dissolving into tears, made gruel for her. After three days in bed, things began to look so grave that her next-door neighbour, the cooper, on the advice of the doctor, who had insisted on re-entering the house, took upon himself to send for the two sets of relatives.

They came by the same train about ten in the morning, the Colombels bringing with them their little boy Joseph.

On arriving at the garden gate, the first thing they saw was the little maid sitting on a chair against the wall, weeping. The dog was lying asleep on the door-mat in the blazing sun, and two cats were stretched out like dead things on the sills of the two windows, with closed eyes, and paws and tails extended.

A huge clucking hen was marshalling across the garden her squad of chicks clothed with yellow, fluffy down, and a large cage hanging on the wall, well supplied with chickweed, held a colony of birds twittering themselves hoarse in the sunshine of the warm spring morning. In another little cage, chalet-shaped, two lovebirds sat side by side on their perch.

M. Cimme, a very stout, puffy person, who always got in first everywhere by pushing everybody, even women, out of his way, proceeded to ask:—

"Well, Céleste, so things aren't going on well, eh?"

The little maid quavered out through her tears:—

"She doesn't even know me now. The doctor says it's the end."

They all looked at each other. Mme. Cimme and Mme. Colombel instantly embraced without a word. They were extremely alike, having worn their hair in smooth bands all their lives, together with red shawls of French cashmere that blazed like furnaces.

Cimme turned to his brother-in-law, a pale, thin, sallow man, who was a martyr to dyspepsia and had a frightful limp, and said in a serious voice:—

"By Jove! We're only just in time!"

But nobody volunteered to enter the dying woman's bedroom on the ground floor. Even Cimme hung back. It was Colombel who first plucked up courage and went in, swaying this way and that like a ship's mast, with the ferrule of his stick resounding on the flagstones.

The two women ventured next, and M. Cimme brought up the rear. Little Joseph had remained outside, fascinated by the sight of the dog.

A ray of sunlight fell across the middle of the bed, shining with peculiar brightness on the hands, which, nervously agitated, were opening and shutting unceasingly. The fingers worked as though possessed by thoughts, as if their movements had a definite significance, conveyed a meaning, obeyed a directing spirit. The rest of the body was motionless beneath the sheet. Not a quiver passed over the angular face. The eyes remained closed.

The dying woman's relations, spreading in a semicircle, proceeded to gaze silently at the spasmodic heaving of her labouring chest. The little maid had followed them in, crying all the time.

At last Cimme asked:—

"Now, tell us what the doctor says exactly?"

The servant faltered:—

"He says she's to be left in peace, and there's nothing more to be done."

But suddenly the old maid's lips began to move. She seemed to be giving utterance to silent words, words hidden within her dying brain, and more and more rapid grew those strange movements of the hands.

All at once she began speaking in a little, thin voice, quite unlike her own—a voice that seemed to come from a great distance, from the depths of that heart which had never perhaps been opened till now.

Cimme made for the door on tiptoe, finding the scene too painful for him. Colombel, whose crippled leg was getting tired, sat down.

The two women remained standing.

Queen Hortense was babbling very fast now; no one was able to understand a word. She kept pronouncing names, many names, appealing tenderly to imaginary persons.

"Philip, come here, my boy; kiss mother! You love mother, don't you, my mannie? Rose, look after your little sister while I'm out! Don't leave her alone on any account, do your hear? And, mind, I forbid you to touch the matches!"

For some seconds she was silent, then, in a louder voice, as if calling to someone: "Henriette!" She waited a little, then went on: "Tell your father I want to speak to him before he goes to the office." Then quickly: "I'm not very well to-day, darling; promise me not to be late home. You can tell your chief that I'm ill. You know how dangerous it is to leave the children alone when I'm in bed. I'm going to give you a rice pudding for dinner. The children are so fond of it. Won't Clare be delighted, eh?"

She began laughing, a young, boisterous laugh utterly unlike her own. "Just look at Jean; what a face! He's messed it up with jam, the grubby little rascal. Oh! do look, darling; isn't he funny?"

Continually fidgeting his leg, which was tired from the journey, Colombel muttered:—

"She's dreaming that she's got a husband and children—it's the beginning of the end."

Stolid and amazed, the two sisters never stirred.

"Perhaps you'd like to take off your bonnets and shawls," said the little maid; "please to walk into the sitting-room."

They went out of the room without having said a single word. Colombel followed them limping, and the dying woman was left quite alone again.

When they had taken off their outdoor things, the two women at last sat down. Whereupon, one of the cats got up from the window, stretched itself, sprang into the room, and then on to the knees of Mme. Cimme, who began stroking it.

They could hear the dying woman's voice close by, living in her last minutes an existence that she had no doubt been awaiting all her life long, emptying her heart even of her dreams at this moment when everything for her was coming to an end.

Cimme, in the garden, was playing with little Joseph and the dog, enjoying himself thoroughly, as a stout man out for a day in the country will do, with never a thought of the dying woman within.

But all of a sudden he came indoors, and said to the maid:—

"Look here, my girl, can't you see about our lunch? Ladies, what would you like to eat?"

They agreed on a savoury omelette, a piece of fillet of beef with some new potatoes, then cheese, and a cup of coffee.

And as Mme. Colombel was feeling in her pocket for her purse, Cimme stopped her, and turning to the maid, said:—

"I dare say you've got some money in hand?"

"Yes, sir," she replied.

"How much?"

"Fifteen francs."

"That's enough. Make haste, my good girl, I'm beginning to feel hungry."

Mme. Cimme, looking out of the window at the climbing plants all bathed in sunshine, and at two amorous pigeons on the roof opposite, said in a heart-broken voice:—

"It's a pity to have had to come on such a sad errand; it should be *so* lovely in the country to-day."

Her sister sighed without answering, and Colombel, uneasy at the very idea of a walk, murmured:—

"My leg's worrying me confoundedly."

Little Joseph and the dog were making a terrible noise, one shrieking with joy and the other barking desperately. They were playing at hide-and-seek round the three garden beds, and racing one after the other like two mad things.

The dying woman continued to call to her children, talking to each in turn, in imagination dressing them, kissing them, teaching them to read:—

"Come now, Simon, say, A, B, C, D. No, that's not right. See, now! D, D, D, D, don't you hear? Now, again. . . ."

"It's curious what people say at such times," pronounced Cimme.

Whereupon Mme. Colombel asked:

"Oughtn't we to go back to her?"

But Cimme at once dissuaded her:—

"What's the good? You can't do anything to help. We might just as well stay here."

Nobody insisted, and Mme. Cimme, turning her attention to the pair of green love-birds (so-called), began to hold forth in praise of their singular fidelity, and inveigh against men for not following the example of these devoted creatures.

Cimme began to laugh, glanced at his wife, and hummed mockingly:—

"Tra, la, la; Tra, la, la, la,"

as if he wished a good deal to be understood on the subject of *his* fidelity.

Colombel, taken all at once with cramp in the stomach, began striking the ground with his stick.

The other cat now entered, its tail in the air.

It was one o'clock by the time they sat down to table.

Directly he had tasted the wine, Colombel, who had been recommended to drink nothing but superior Bordeaux, called the maid back:—

"I say, child, isn't there anything better than this in the cellar?"

"Yes, sir; there's the best wine, that you always used to have when you came."

"Well, go and fetch us three bottles of it."

This wine was tasted and found excellent; not that it was anything remarkable in the way of vintage, but it had been in the cellar fifteen years.

"It's a perfect wine for an invalid," declared Cimme.

Colombel, seized by a violent longing to possess this Bordeaux, put another question to the maid:—

"How much is there left, my girl?"

"Oh! Nearly the whole lot, sir! Mam'zelle never drank it. It's the bottom bin."

Then turning to his brother-in-law, Colombel said:—

"Cimme, I'll take over this wine, if you like, against anything you may fancy. It suits me down to the ground."

The hen had now come in with her brood of chickens, and the two women amused themselves throwing her crumbs.

Little Joseph and the dog, having had enough to eat, were sent back to play in the garden.

Queen Hortense still went on talking, but in a low voice now, so that the words were no longer distinguishable.

When they had finished their coffee, everyone went to see how the sick woman was going on. She seemed to be calm.

They went out again, and sat down in a circle in the garden, to digest their lunch.

All of a sudden the dog began flying round and round the chairs as hard as he could go, holding something in his mouth. The child pursued him desperately; then both disappeared indoors.

Cimme fell asleep with the sun full upon his stomach.

The dying woman again began talking aloud. Then, suddenly she cried out.

The two ladies and Colombel hastened indoors to see what was the matter. Cimme, though he woke up, did not stir; he could not bear that sort of thing.

Queen Hortense was sitting up, her eyes haggard. Her dog, to escape little Joseph, had leaped on to the bed, bounded across the dying woman, and, entrenched behind her pillow, was glaring at his playfellow with glittering eyes, ready to dash out again and begin the game afresh. He held in his teeth one of his mistress's slippers, all torn during the hour or more he had been playing with it.

The child, frightened by this woman suddenly rising up in front of him, stood motionless opposite the bed.

The hen now came in; alarmed by the noise, she flew on to a seat, and in heartrending clucks called to her chicks, who were chirping in a scared cluster round the four legs of the chair.

Queen Hortense cried out in a lamentable voice:—

"No, no. I don't want to die, I don't want to die! I won't. Who will bring up my children? Who will take care of them, and love them? No, no, I won't die. I won't——"

She sank back again suddenly. It was all over.

The dog, in great excitement, began rushing round and round the room.

Colombel ran to the window, and called out to his brother-in-law:—

"Quick, quick. I fancy she's just passed away."

Then Cimme got up, and, making up his mind, entered the room, stammering:—

"It's taken less time than I should have thought."

AT SEA

The following paragraph appeared recently in the newspapers:—

"From our Boulogne Correspondent,
"*January 22nd.*

"A terrible disaster has just spread consternation among our fisher-folk, so severely tried during the last two years. The fishing-boat belonging to Captain Javel, on its way into port, was driven to the west of the harbour mouth, and dashed to pieces on the rocks forming the breakwater of the jetty.

"In spite of the efforts of the life-boat and the rocket-apparatus, four men and the boy were lost. The bad weather still continues, and further accidents are to be feared."

I wonder who this skipper Javel is? Is he the brother of the man who had lost an arm?

If this poor fellow, carried off by the seas, and dying, entangled perhaps in the wreckage of his own boat, is the man I am thinking of, he took part eighteen years ago in another drama, terrible and simple as are all these formidable dramas of the sea.

This Javel, the elder of two brothers, was then skipper of a trawler. Of all fishing-boats the trawler is the most staunch. Strong enough to stand any kind of weather, round-flanked, tumbling about perpetually like a cork on the waves, lashed by the harsh, salt winds of the Channel, it toils upon the sea, with a bellying sail, untiring, dragging on its beam a great net that, scraping in the bed of the ocean, sweeps up and gathers in all the creatures that sleep among the rocks, flat fish sticking to the sand, heavy crabs with crooked claws, and lobsters with pointed whiskers.

When the breeze is fresh, with a short sea running, the boat starts work. The net of the trawl is fixed the whole length of a great wooden beam, banded with iron, which is let down by means of two ropes running over rollers at either end of the vessel.

At Sea

And the boat, drifting broadside to wind and tide, drags with it this contrivance for the spoiling and devastation of the ocean plains.

Javel had with him on board his younger brother, four men, and a boy. He had left Boulogne in fine weather to start trawling. But the wind soon rose, and a gale coming on, the trawler was forced to run before it.

They made for the English coast, but a heavy sea was beating against the cliffs, and hurling itself on shore with such baffled fury that it was impossible to attempt the entrance to any port. The little boat stood out again and made for the French coast. But the heavy weather still made it dangerous to go near the jetties, enveloping all approaches to the sheltering harbours with foam, uproar, and peril.

The trawler had to stand off again, riding over the waves, tossed and shaken and streaming, struck by great lumps of water, but behaving well in spite of all, quite used to rough weather that often kept her out five or six days at a time, stretching back and forth between the two neighbouring coasts, unable to land on either.

At last, while they were far from land, the storm abated, and though the seas still ran high, the skipper ordered the trawl to be got overboard.

The huge fishing machine was accordingly put over the side, and two men at bow and two at stern began to pay out the ropes of it. Suddenly it touched bottom, but a big sea making the boat roll, Javel the younger, who was in the bow tending the fore-warp of the trawl, stumbled, and got his arm caught between the momentarily eased rope and the roller over which it was passing. He made a desperate effort to lift the rope with his other hand, but the trawl was dragging already, and the taut warp could not be moved.

Writhing with pain, the man called for help. Everyone came running to him. His brother left the tiller. They threw themselves all together on the rope, trying to free the limb that was being crushed by it. It was no use.

"Must be cut!" said one of the "hands," pulling out of his pocket a huge knife, which was capable in a stroke or two of saving young Javel's arm.

But to cut the warp meant losing the net, and the net meant money, a great deal of money, fifteen hundred francs, and it was the property of the elder Javel, who could not bear to lose it. With anguish in his heart, he called out, "No, don't cut—wait! I'll luff up!" and rushing to the tiller he put it hard down. But the boat would not answer, her way deadened by the net which hampered her steering, and she swept on with the wind and the drift she already had on her.

Javel the younger had dropped on to his knees, with clenched teeth and haggard eyes. He did not utter a word. In continual dread of the knife being used, his brother came back again, "Hold on, hold on, don't cut; we'll let go the anchor."

The anchor was let go, the whole long chain running out; then they began heaving in at the capstan, to ease the trawl ropes, which slackened at last, and the inert limb was disengaged, in its blood-stained woollen sleeve.

Javel the younger seemed to have become imbecile. His pea-jacket was removed, revealing a horrible sight, a shapeless pulp of flesh which spurted blood in jets as if forced from a pump. Then the man gazed at his arm, and muttered, "It's done for!" And, as the blood was making a pool on the deck one of the men exclaimed, "He'll bleed to death; we must tie the veins." Then they took a line, a coarse, brown, tarry yarn, and, twisting it round the limb above the wound, drew it taut with all their strength. The jets of blood grew gradually less, and at last ceased entirely.

Javel the younger got up, his arm dangling at his side. He took hold of it with the other hand, lifted it, turned it about, shook it. Everything was broken, the bones smashed; this fragment of his body hung by the muscles alone. He contemplated it with gloomy, thoughtful eyes. Then he sat down on a spare sail, and his mates advised him to keep the wound continually wet, to keep mortification from setting in.

They put a bucket near him, and every few minutes he dipped a glass into it and bathed the horrible place, letting a thin stream of clear water trickle over it.

"You'd be better down below," said his brother. He went below, but came up again in about an hour's time, not liking to be alone; he had need of the fresh air too. So he sat down again on his sail and recommenced bathing his arm.

They had a good catch. Great white-bellied fish lay alongside of him, tossing about in their death-throes; he gazed at them without ever stopping the bathing of his mutilated flesh.

Just as they were nearing Boulogne a fresh gale sprang up; the little boat started off again on her senseless cruise, plunging and dipping, knocking the poor sad-faced wretch about.

Night came on. The bad weather continued till dawn. At daybreak they were again in sight of the English coast, but as the sea was going down, they started once more for France, tacking.

Towards evening Javel the younger called his mates to look at some black marks, an ugly appearance of decay in that part of the limb which could hardly be said to be his any longer. The "hands" gazed at it, and gave their opinions.

"It's the black rot, sure enough," thought one.

"Better pour salt water over it," declared another.

Some sea water was brought and poured on to the wound. The sick man turned livid, ground his teeth, writhed a little, but did not cry out.

Then, when the burning pain had abated, he said to his brother, "Give me your knife."

The brother held out his knife.

"Hold up my arm, straight out; hang on to it tight."

What he asked was done.

Then he himself began to cut. He cut quietly and thoughtfully, severing the last sinews with that blade, which had an edge as keen as a razor's; and at last there was only the stump left. He heaved a deep sigh, and declared: "It had to be done! 'Twould ha' been all up with me!"

He seemed relieved, and kept taking deep breaths. He began again to pour water over the stump.

It was another rough night, and they were unable to get in.

When day dawned, Javel the younger picked up his severed arm and examined it minutely. Decomposition had set in. His messmates also came and examined it, passing it from hand to hand, tapping it, turning it over, sniffing at it.

His brother said: "It's about time to throw that into the sea."

But Javel the younger was annoyed. "Not if I know it! Not if I know it!" said he. "It belongs to me, I suppose, seeing it's my own arm."

He took hold of it again, and placed it between his knees.

" 'T'll go bad all the same," said the elder. Then an idea seemed to strike the maimed man. When the boats are kept out a long time, the catch of fish is packed in barrels of salt to keep it fresh.

He asked: "Couldn't I put it in the brine?"

"Yes, you could do that," declared the others.

Whereupon they emptied one of the barrels already full of fish from the catch of the last few days, and right at the bottom they laid down the arm. A layer of salt was put over it; then, one by one, the fish were replaced.

One of the "hands" made the following joke: "Let's hope it won't get sold in the auction!"

At which everyone laughed except the two Javels.

The wind had not abated. They tacked about in sight of Boulogne till ten o'clock on the following morning. And the injured man continued without ceasing to pour water over his stump. Now and then he would get up and pace the deck from end to end. His brother, at the tiller, gazed after him, shaking his head.

At last they entered the harbour.

The doctor examined the wound, and pronounced it to be going on as well as possible. He dressed it thoroughly, and prescribed rest for the patient. But Javel would not go to bed without having regained possession of his arm, and returned at once to the harbour to find the barrel, which he had chalked with a cross.

It was emptied in his presence, and he snatched up his arm, which, thoroughly pickled by the brine, was shrivelled, but quite fresh. He wrapped it in a cloth he had brought for the purpose, and went back home.

For a long time his wife and children examined this fragment of the father, touching the fingers, brushing away the grains of salt that had got under the nails. Then the carpenter was sent for, to take measurements for a little coffin.

Next day the whole of the trawler's crew followed the funeral of the severed arm. The two brothers, side by side, were chief mourners.

The sexton of the parish carried the corpse under his arm.

Javel the younger gave up the sea. He obtained some light employment at the harbour, and later on, when talking about his accident, he would whisper confidentially in his listener's ear: "If my brother would only have cut the rope, I should have had my arm now, right enough. But he was thinking of his pocket."

A SALE

The parties, Brument (Cæsar Isidor) and Cornu (Prosper Napoleon), were appearing before the Lower Seine Assize Court on a charge of attempting to murder the woman Brument, lawful wife of the first named, by drowning.

The two accused are seated side by side on the time-honoured bench. They are both peasants. The first is little and fat, with short arms, short legs, and a round, red, pimply head planted direct upon the trunk, which is also round and short, and devoid of any appearance of neck.

He is a pig-breeder, living at Cacheville-la-Goupil, in the district of Criquetot.

Cornu (Prosper Napoleon) is thin, of medium height, with enormously long arms. His head is askew, his jaw twisted, and he has a squint. A blue blouse as long as a shirt falls to his knees, and his thin, yellow hair, plastered down on his skull, gives his face a worn-out, dirty, fallen-in kind of look, that is really frightful. He bears the nickname of "the parson," because he can imitate Church chanting to perfection, and even the tones of the serpent.* He is an innkeeper at Criquetot, and this talent of his attracts to the inn plenty of customers who prefer "mass a la Cornu" to mass proper. Mme. Brument, seated in the witness-box, is a thin country-woman who looks half asleep throughout the proceedings. She sits motionless, her hands crossed on her knees, with a fixed stare and stolid expression.

The magistrate continues his inquiry. "So, Mme. Brument, they came into your house and threw you into a barrel full of water. Now, tell us the facts in detail. Stand up."

She stands up, looking as tall as a ship's mast, her cap topping her head with white. She makes her statement in a droning voice:

"I was shellin' beans. They comes in. I says to myself:

*An out-of-date musical instrument, used in church.

'What's the matter with 'em? They look funny; they're up to something.' They kept watchin' me sideways, like this— 'specially Cornu, 'cos, you see, he squints. I never likes to see them two together; they're never up to any good when they're together. I says to 'em: 'What d'you want with me?' They didn't give no answer, and I felt sort o' frightened like. . . ."

The prisoner Brument here suddenly interrupts the statement by exclaiming:

"I was tight."

Whereupon Cornu, turning to his accomplice, pronounced, in a voice as deep as the bass note of an organ:

"If ye said we were both tight, ye wouldn't be far wrong."

The magistrate (severely): "You mean to say that you were drunk?"

Brument: "That's about it."

Cornu: " 'T might happen to anyone."

The magistrate (to the victim): "Go on with your statement, Mme. Brument."

"Well," she resumed, "Brument, he says to me, 'Would ye like to earn a crown?'

" 'Yes,' says I, 'seein' ye don't pick a crown-piece off the road every day.'

" 'Well, look sharp, then,' he says to me, 'and do what I tell ye'; and off he goes to fetch the big open barrel that's underneath the gutter in the corner. Then he turns 'er over, then he gets 'er into my kitchen, and he stands 'er up on end in the middle o' the room, and he says to me, 'You go an' fetch water,' he says, 'an' keep on pourin' it in till she's full.'

"So off I goes to the pond with two buckets, and I keeps on fetchin' water, an' more water, an' more water, for a good hour. That old barrel's as big as a vat, savin' your worship's presence.

"All that time Brument and Cornu they was havin' drinks, first one, and then another, and then another. They was just gettin' their back teeth under, both of 'em, and I says to 'em: 'It's you that's full up, that's what you are—fuller than that there barrel.'

"So Brument he gives it me back: 'Don't you worry yourself,' says he; 'go on wi' your work, your time's comin'—everyone mind his own business.' But I didn't take no notice, he bein' tight.

"When the barrel was full to the brim, I says: 'There you

are.' And Cornu he gives me a crown-piece. 'Twasn't Brument, 'twas Cornu that giv' it to me.

"And Brument he says to me: 'D'ye want to earn another?'

"'Yes,' says I, 'seein' I'm not used to gettin' presents so easy.'

"'Well,' he says, 'undress yourself!'

"'Undress!' says I.

"'Yes,' says he. 'If ye feel it awkwardlike,' he says, 'ye can keep yer shift on,' he says; 'we don't mind that.'

"A crown's a crown, so I undresses; but it was clean against the grain, you understand, doin' it before them two good-for-nothin's. I takes off my cap, and then my bodice, an' then my skirt, and then my shoes.

"'Brument,' he says, 'you can keep yer stockin's on too; we're a good sort, we are.'

"An' Cornu, he says: 'Yes! we're a good sort, we are.'

"So there I was, pretty near like our Mother Eve. Then up they get, an' they could hardly stand, they was that tight, savin' your worship's presence.

"I says to myself: 'Now, whatever are they up to?'

"And Brument he says: 'Are ye ready?'

"And Cornu he says: 'Ready! aye, ready!'

"An' if they didn't catch hold o' me, Brument by the head and Cornu by the heels, like a bundle o' linen for the wash, as ye might say. And didn't I just scream! An' Brument he says: 'Hold your noise, ye cat!'

"An' they hoists me up over their heads and pops me into that there barrel full o' water, an' it just turned my blood cold, and froze the marrow in my bones.

"An' Brument says, 'Will that do?'

"An' Cornu says, 'Aye! That'll do.'

"An' Brument says, 'The head an't in. That counts!'

"An' Cornu says, 'In wi' the head.'

"Then Brument he pushes my head right under, just as if he meant drownin' me, and the water runs up me nose, and I begins to see Paradise, an' then he gives me another shove, an' down I goes.

"Well, then, he must ha' got scared. He pulls me out, and says, 'Take an' dry yourself quick, ye scarecrow!'

"An' off I makes as hard as I can run to the parson, and he lends me a skirt belonging to his servant, seein' I was pretty nigh naked, an' he goes an' fetches M. Chicot the keeper; an' he goes off to Criquetot to fetch the police, and they all come to my house with me.

"And there we find Brument an' Cornu goin' for each other like two rams.

"Brument, he shouts, 'It's a lie, I tell ye, there's a cubic metre, for sure. That's not the way to measure.'

"Cornu, he howls, 'Four bucketsful, 'tisn't hardly *half* a cubic metre. Hold your tongue, I say it's all right.'

"The brigadier claps his hands on 'em. That's all."

She sits down. There was some laughter in court. The jurymen looked at one another in astonishment. The magistrate pronounced, "Prisoner Cornu, you seem to have been the instigator of this infamous plot. What have you to say?"

Cornu gets up in his turn.

"Your worship, we were tight."

The magistrate replied gravely, "That I know. Go on."

"I *am* going on. Well, Brument comes to my place about nine o'clock an' calls for two drinks, an' says to me, 'There's one for you, Cornu.' So I sit down opposite him, and I take my drink, an' out o' politeness, I stand him one in return. Then he stands me one again, and I stand him another, and so we go on nippin' and nippin' till, about midday, we were properly fuddled.

"Then Brument he begins to cry, and that touches my heart, that does, an' I ask him what's the matter.

"He says to me, 'I must have forty pound by Thursday.' But that chills me off at once, ye understand. And then he proposes to me, point blank, 'I'll sell ye my wife.'

"I was tight, and I'm a widower. It stirred up my feelin's, I can tell ye. I didn't know her at all, his wife, but a woman's a woman, anyhow, an't she? So I ask him, 'How much d'ye want for her?'

"He thought a bit, or he pretended to. When ye're tight ye're not so very clear in the head, and then he answers, 'I'll sell her to ye by the cubic metre.'

"Well, that didn't surprise me, for I was as tight as he was, and as for the cubic metre, I knew all about that in my trade. It means a thousand litres, and it just suited me properly.

"Only there was still the price to settle. *That* all depends on the quality. I said to him, 'How much the cubic metre?'

" 'Eighty pound,' he says.

"That made me jump like a rabbit, but then it struck me that a woman couldn't be equal to more than three hundred litres. All the same I said, 'It's too dear!'

"'Can't do it under,' says he. 'I should lose by it.'

"You an't a pig-dealer for nothing, you understand—he knows his trade. But if he's a bit sharp at selling lumps o' fat, I'm a bit sharper at selling drops o' liquor. Ha! ha! ha! So I said to him, 'If she was new goods, I don't say, but ye've had your wear and tear, she's second-hand. I'll give ye sixty pound the cubic metre, not a ha'penny more. Is it a deal?' 'Right,' he says, 'done with ye.'

"I said, 'Done,' too, and off we go, arm in arm. Must help each other along, y' know, in this life.

"But it came into my head uneasy-like, 'However are ye goin' to measure her without makin' her into liquid?'

"Then he explains me his notion, and 'twasn't so easy for him, seeing he was tight. 'I take a barrel,' he says to me, 'I fill it to the brim with water; I put her in, and I measure all the water that runs over; that'll do the trick.'

"I said to him, 'That's all very well, that is, but the water that runs over 'll run away. How are ye going to get it up?'

"And then he laughed at me for a softy, an' explained how there was nothing to do but to fill up the barrel again, once his wife was out of it. As much water as ye put in again is the measure of what's to pay. Suppose there's ten bucketsful, that'll be one cubic metre. He an't so stupid after all when he *is* tight, the varmint!

"To cut it short, we got to his place, and I had a look at the female party. As far as beauty goes, she an't no beauty, ye can see that for yourselves, for there she sits. I said to myself, 'Never mind, 't all counts; I'm getting a new start in life, and good-looking or plain, they all answer the same purpose, eh, your worship?' An' then I noticed she was as thin as a lath, and I said to myself, 'Why, she won't make four hundred litres!' I know something about it, being in the liquor trade.

"As to the doing, she's told ye about that. I even let her keep her shift and her stockin's on, which was all to the bad for me.

"When it was done, if she didn't fly out of the place. 'Look out, Brument,' I says, 'she's off!'

"'Don't ye worry yourself,' he says, '*we* shall get her back all right. She'll have to come home to sleep. Let's measure what ye've got to pay me.'

"I measured. Not four bucketsful! Ha! ah! ah! ah!"

The prisoner gives way to such persistent laughter that a gendarme is obliged to slap him on the back. Regaining his composure, he goes on: "To cut it short, Brument he declares, 'The bargain's off; it an't enough!' I bawl at him, he bawls at me, I bawl louder, he dots me one, I give 'im one better. It looked like lasting till the day o' judgment, seeing we were both tight.

"In comes the gendarmes, and begin swearing at us, an' they put *handcuffs* on us and take us off to prison. I ask for damages."

He sits down.

Brument declares his accomplice's confession to be true in every detail. The astounded jury retire to consider their verdict.

They came back in an hour's time, and acquitted the prisoners, but added a severe rider, pointing out the sanctity of marriage, and laying down the exact limits proper to commercial transactions.

Brument set out for the conjugal abode in company with his wife.

Cornu returned to his business.

THE RETURN

THE surf lashes the shore with quick, monotonous beats. White clouds, chased by the wind, speed across the vast blue dome of the sky, like flights of great birds, and the village, which lies in the lap of the valley, is warm in the sunshine. The house at the entrance to the village, standing alone by the roadside, is that of Martin-Levesque. It is a little fishing hut with mud walls, and a thatched roof on which the iris is growing, crowning the whole with its tall plumes. There is a garden before the door, not much larger than a handkerchief, where some onions, cabbage and parsley are growing. A hedge closes it in along the road.

The man is away fishing on the sea; the wife is before the house mending the meshes of a large, brown seine stretched along the wall like an immense spider web. A young girl of fourteen years, seated at the entrance to the garden, on a straw-bottomed chair tipped back against the wall, is mending the family linen, linen already poor, patched and repatched. Another girl, about a year younger, is rocking a very young baby in her arms, while two little things, from two to three years old, sitting in the dirt, are digging into the soil with their hands and throwing dust into each other's faces.

Nobody is talking; only the baby whom the girl is trying to put to sleep keeps whining continuously in a feeble, wailing voice. A cat is sleeping on the window sill and some gilliflowers in full bloom at the foot of the wall make a pretty cushion of white blossoms on which a swarm of flies is buzzing.

The girl who sits at the garden entrance calls out suddenly —"Mamma!"

The mother answers—"What is it?"

"There he is!"

They have been worried all the morning because a man is prowling around the house—an old man who looks like a pauper. They saw him first when they accompanied the father to his boat in the morning. He was sitting on the edge of the ditch, opposite the door of their house. When they came back from the beach they found him there still, looking at the house.

He seemed sick and miserable. He had not moved for more than an hour, then seeing that they were looking at him as if he might be a convict, he had risen and gone away, dragging his lame leg. But they saw him return pretty soon with slow and wearied step. He seated himself again, but this time a little farther off as if to watch them.

The mother and her girls were afraid. The mother was especially worried, because she was timid by nature and because Levesque, her husband, was not to return until nightfall.

Her husband was called Levesque, she was called Martin, and so they were known as the Martin-Levesque. This is the reason: She had married for her first husband a sailor named Martin, who used to go every summer to Newfoundland, cod fishing. After two years of married life she had a little girl and was about to become a mother again when the ship on which Martin had sailed, the "Two Sisters," a three-masted bark of Dieppe, disappeared.

She was never heard from and none of the sailors who had shipped with her ever came back. She was considered as lost—vessel and cargo.

Madame Martin waited ten years for her husband's return, raising her two girls with great difficulty. Then as she was a brave and honest woman, a fisherman of the neighborhood, Levesque, a widower with a son, asked her hand in marriage. She married him and had two children by him in three years.

They lived in the hardest way, painfully and laboriously. Bread was dear and meat almost unknown in the hovel. Sometimes in the bad winter weather they got in debt to the baker. The children kept well though. The neighbors used to say: "These Martin-Levesques are worthy people. Martin is used to suffering and Levesque hasn't his equal as a fisherman."

The girl seated on the straw-bottomed chair resumed by saying: "It would appear that he knows us. It may be he is one of the poor people from Epreville or Augebosc."

But the mother was not so easily deceived. No, no, it was not anybody belonging to these parts, that was sure.

As the man was as immovable as a post, and as he kept his eyes fixed with a curious obstinacy on the house, Madame Martin became furious, and her very fear making her brave, she seized a spade and went outside before the gate.

"What are you doing there?" she cried, addressing the vagabond.

He answered in a rasping voice: "I'm resting a bit. Does it worry you?"

Then she asked again, "Why are you spying about my house?"

The man answered doggedly—"I'm not hurting anybody. Mayn't I sit alongside the road?"

Having nothing to offer in rebuttal of this argument, the woman re-entered the house. The day wore slowly away.

Towards noon the man disappeared, but he passed along again about five o'clock. He was not seen again during the evening.

Levesque came home after dark. They told him what had happened. He concluded, "It is either a half-witted fellow, or a foot-pad," and went to bed without thinking more about it, while his wife lay awake haunted by the eyes of the wanderer who had looked at her so strangely.

When the morning came the wind was blowing hard and the fisherman, seeing that he could not go out on the water that day, set to work to help his wife mend the nets. Towards nine o'clock the older girl, a Martin, who had gone for bread, came running back with a scared face exclaiming—

"Oh! Mamma, there he is."

The mother was much moved and turning very pale, said to her husband: "Go and talk to him, Levesque, and tell him not to watch us like that. Such things give me a turn." Levesque, who was a tall man with a brick-colored complexion, a thick, close-set red beard, blue eyes with black pupils, and a strong, thick neck, who was always dressed in woolens for fear of the wind and rain, rose peacefully and went to meet the stranger. Then they began to talk. The mother and children watched them from a distance. All at once the unknown arose, and with Levesque came towards the house. The woman, alarmed, started back. Her husband said to her—"Give him a piece of bread and a glass of cider. He has not eaten anything since day before yesterday;" and both men entered the house, followed by the woman and children. The vagabond sat down and began to eat, bowing his head under the looks of the woman and her children. The woman, standing before him, stared at him; the two big girls, the Martins, their backs to the door, the one carrying the baby, devoured him with their eager eyes, and the two children who were seated in the ashes of the fireplace stopped playing with the frying-pan long enough to gaze also at this stranger.

Levesque, having taken a chair, asked: "Well, have you come a long way?"

"I come from Cette."

"Afoot?"

"Yes, afoot. When one has no money he has to travel that way."

"Where are you going?"

"I was coming here."

"Do you know anybody here?"

"Maybe I do."

Then both men ceased talking. The vagabond ate slowly, although he was famished, and drank a swallow of cider with each mouthful of bread. His face was faded, wrinkled and hollowed everywhere. He looked as if he had suffered a great deal. Suddenly Levesque asked:

"What is your name?"

He answered without lifting his nose from his plate: "I am called Martin."

The mother felt a strange, shivering sensation. She took a step nearer the man and stood looking at him, her arms hanging idly at her sides, her mouth open. Nobody said anything for a moment. Then Levesque resumed: "Do you belong here?" The other answered: "Yes, I belong here." When at last he lifted his head the eyes of the woman encountered his and they stared at each other as if fascinated. She spoke then in a changed voice, low and trembling: "Is it indeed thee, my husband?"

The man answered simply:

"Yes, it is I."

The second husband then asked: "Where have you come from then?"

The other answered: "From the coast of Africa. We were stranded on a bar. Three of us were saved, Picard, Vatinal and I. Then we were captured by savages and kept in slavery twelve years. Picard and Vatinal are dead. An English traveler passing through the country, took me and brought me to Cette, and here I am."

The woman began to sob, her face buried in her apron. Levesque next spoke: "What are you going to do now?" In reply Martin asked: "Aren't you her husband?" Levesque answered: "Yes, I'm her husband." They looked at each other and said nothing.

Then Martin, looking at the children who stood around him, nodded toward the two older girls and said: "Are those mine?" Levesque answered: "Yes, they are yours."

Martin did not rise; he did not embrace them; he was content to say simply: "Good God! how they have grown."

Levesque inquired: "What are we going to do about it?" Martin, in his perplexity, knew not what to say. At last he decided: "I will do what you desire. I do not wish to do you a wrong. It is vexatious, all the same, considering the house. I have two children; you have three. Let each take his own. The mother, is she yours or is she mine? I am willing to consent to what will please you; but the house is mine, seeing that my father left it to me. I was born here, the papers are at the notary's."

The woman was crying all this time, her sobs partly concealed in her blue apron. The two larger girls had come nearer and were gazing at their father with anxious faces. He had finished eating, and said in his turn: "What are we going to do?"

Levesque had an idea: "We must go to the curé, he will decide."

Martin rose and as he advanced toward his wife she threw herself upon his breast sobbing: "My husband! My poor Martin!" And she held him in a tight embrace, and through her mind passed memories of her youth, when at twenty years of age, she had received the caresses of this man, then her lover and affianced husband.

Martin, himself much moved, kissed her under her bonnet.

The two children sitting in the fireplace began to howl in unison, on hearing their mother cry, and the baby in the arms of the second of the Martin girls yelled with a voice which sounded like a fife out of tune.

Levesque, still standing, was waiting. "Come," said he, "this matter will have to be regulated."

Martin released his wife, and as he kept looking at his two daughters, the mother said to them:

"Kiss your father at least."

Then they came forward together with dry eyes, very much astonished, and a little afraid. He kissed them one after the other, pecking them on the cheeks in true peasant style. When the baby saw this stranger coming so close it began to scream as if it would go into convulsions.

Then the two men left the house together. As they were passing the Café Commerce, Levesque said: "Let us take a drop together."

"I am very willing," declared Martin.

They entered and seated themselves in an unoccupied room.

"Ah, Chicot," said Levesque, "let us have two glasses of your best cider. This is Martin, who has returned, he who used to be the husband of my wife. You know, Martin of the 'Two Sisters,' who was lost."

And the master of the cabaret, three glasses in one hand and a pitcher in the other, fat, red-faced and greasy, said tranquilly: "Hello! you here, Martin?"

And Martin responded: "I'm here."

THE PRISONERS

There was no sound in the forest except the slight rustle of the snow as it fell upon the trees. It had been falling, small and fine, since midday; it powdered the branches with a frosty moss, cast a silver veil over the dead leaves in the hollow, and spread upon the pathways a great, soft, white carpet that thickened the immeasurable silence amid this ocean of trees.

Before the door of the keeper's lodge stood a bare-armed young woman, chopping wood with an ax upon a stone. She was tall, thin and strong—a child of the forest, a daughter and wife of gamekeepers.

A voice called from within the house: "Come in, Berthine; we are alone to-night, and it is getting dark. There may be Prussians or wolves about."

She who was chopping wood replied by splitting another block; her bosom rose and fell with the heavy blows, each time she lifted her arm.

"I have finished, mother. I'm here. There's nothing to be frightened at; it isn't dark yet."

Then she brought in her fagots and her logs, and piled them up at the chimney-side, went out again to close the shutters—enormous shutters of solid oak—and then, when she again came in, pushed the heavy bolts of the door.

Her mother was spinning by the fire, a wrinkled old woman who had grown timorous with age.

"I don't like father to be out," said she. "Two women have no strength."

The younger answered: "Oh, I could very well kill a wolf or a Prussian, I can tell you." And she turned her eyes to a large revolver hanging over the fireplace. Her husband had been put into the army at the beginning of the Prussian invasion, and the two women had remained alone with her father, the old gamekeeper, Nicholas Pichou, who had obstinately refused to leave his home and go into the town.

The nearest town was Rethel, an old fortress perched on a rock. It was a patriotic place, and the townspeople had resolved to resist the invaders, to close their gates and stand a siege, according to the traditions of the city. Twice before, under Henry IV and under Louis XIV, the inhabitants of Rethel had won fame by heroic defenses. They would do the same this time; by Heaven, they would, or they would be burned within their walls.

So they had bought cannons and rifles, and equipped a force, and formed battalions and companies, and they drilled all day long in the Place d'Armes. All of them—bakers, grocers, butchers, notaries, attorneys, carpenters, booksellers, even the chemists—went through their manœuvres in due rotation at regular hours, under the orders of M. Lavigne, who had once been a non-commissioned officer in the dragoons, and now was a draper, having married the daughter and inherited the shop of old M. Ravaudan.

He had taken the rank of major in command of the place, and all the young men having gone to join the army, he enrolled all the others who were eager for resistance. The stout men now walked the streets at the pace of professional pedestrians, in order to bring down their fat, and to lengthen their breath; the weak ones carried burdens, in order to strengthen their muscles.

The Prussians were expected. But the Prussians did not appear. Yet they were not far off, for their scouts had already twice pushed across the forest as far as Nicholas Pichou's lodge.

The old keeper, who could run like a fox, had gone to warn the town. The guns had been pointed, but the enemy had not shown.

The keeper's lodge served as a kind of outpost in the forest of Aveline. Twice a week the man went for provisions, and carried to the citizens news from the outlying country.

He had gone that day to announce that a small detachment of German infantry had stopped at his house, the day before, about two in the afternoon, and had gone away again almost directly. The subaltern in command spoke French.

When the old man went on such errands he took with him his two dogs—two great beasts with the jaws of lions—because of the wolves who were beginning to get fierce; and he left his two women, advising them to lock themselves into the house as soon as night began to fall.

The young one was afraid of nothing, but the old one kept on trembling and repeating:

"It will turn out badly, all this sort of thing. You'll see, it will turn out badly."

This evening she was more anxious even than usual.

"Do you know what time your father will come back?" said she.

"Oh, not before eleven for certain. When he dines with the Major he is always late."

She was hanging her saucepan over the fire to make the soup, when she stopped short, listened to a vague sound which had reached her by way of the chimney, and murmured:

"There's some one walking in the wood—seven or eight men at least."

Her mother, alarmed, stopped her wheel and muttered: "Oh, good Lord! And father not here!"

She had not finished speaking when violent blows shook the door.

The women made no answer, and a loud guttural voice called out: "Open the door."

Then, after a pause, the same voice repeated: "Open the door, or I'll break it in."

Then Berthine slipped into her pocket the big revolver from over the mantelpiece, and, having put her ear to the crack of the door, asked: "Who are you?"

The voice answered: "I am the detachment that came the other day."

The woman asked again: "What do you want?"

"I have lost my way, ever since the morning, in the forest, with my detachment. Open the door, or I will break it in."

The keeper's wife had no choice; she promptly drew the great bolt, and pulling back the door she beheld six men in the pale snow-shadows—six Prussian men, the same who had come the day before. She said in a firm tone: "What do you want here at this time of night?"

The officer answered: "I had lost my way, lost it completely; I recognized the house. I have had nothing to eat since the morning, nor my men either."

Berthine replied: "But I am all alone with mother, this evening."

The soldier, who seemed a good sort of fellow, answered: "That makes no difference. I shall not do any harm; but you must give us something to eat. We are faint and tired to death."

The keeper's wife stepped back.

"Come in," said she.

They came in, powdered with snow and with a sort of mossy cream on their helmets that made them look like meringues. They seemed tired, worn out.

The young woman pointed to the wooden benches on each side of the big table.

"Sit down," said she, "and I'll make you some soup. You do look quite knocked up."

Then she bolted the door again.

She poured some more water into her saucepan, threw in more butter and potatoes; then, unhooking a piece of bacon that hung in the chimney, she cut off half, and added that also to the stew. The eyes of the six men followed her every movement with an air of awakened hunger. They had set their guns and helmets in a corner, and sat waiting on their benches, like well-behaved school children. The mother had begun to spin again, but she threw terrified glances at the invading soldiers. There was no sound except the slight purring of the wheel, the crackle of the fire, and the bubbling of the water as it grew hot.

But all at once a strange noise made them all start—something like a horse breathing at the door, the breathing of an animal, deep and snorting.

One of the Germans had sprung toward the guns. The woman with a movement and a smile stopped him.

"It is the wolves," said she. "They are like you; they are wandering about, hungry."

The man would hardly believe, he wanted to see for himself; and as soon as the door was opened, he perceived two great gray beasts making off at a quick, long trot.

He came back to his seat, murmuring: "I should not have believed it."

And he sat waiting for his meal.

They ate voraciously; their mouths opened from ear to ear to take the largest of gulps; their round eyes opened sympathetically with their jaws, and their swallowing was like the gurgle of rain in a water-pipe.

The two silent women watched the rapid movements of the great red beards; the potatoes seemed to melt away into these moving fleeces.

Then, as they were thirsty, the keeper's wife went down into the cellar to draw cider for them. She was a long time gone; it was a little vaulted cellar, said to have served both as prison and hiding-place in the days of the Revolution. The way down was by a narrow winding stair, shut in by a trap-door at the end of the kitchen.

When Berthine came back, she was laughing, laughing slyly to herself. She gave the Germans her pitcher of drink. Then she, too, had her supper, with her mother, at the other end of the kitchen.

The soldiers had finished eating and were falling asleep, all six, around the table. From time to time, a head would fall heavily on the board, then the man, starting awake, would sit up.

Berthine said to the officer: "You may just as well lie down here before the fire. There's plenty of room for six. I'm going up to my room with my mother."

The two women went to the upper floor. They were heard to lock their door and to walk about for a little while, then they made no further sound.

The Prussians stretched themselves on the stone floor, their feet to the fire, their heads on their rolled-up cloaks, and soon all six were snoring on six different notes, sharp or deep, but all sustained and alarming.

They had certainly been asleep for a considerable time when a shot sounded, and so loud that it seemed to be fired close against the walls of the house. The soldiers sat up instantly. There were two more shots, and then three more.

The door of the staircase opened hastily, and the keeper's wife appeared, barefooted, a short petticoat over her night-dress, a candle in her hand, and a face of terror. She whispered: "Here are the French—two hundred of them at least. If they find you here, they will burn the house. Go down, quick, into the cellar, and don't make a noise. If you make a noise, we are lost." The officer, scared, murmured: "I will, I will. Which way do we go down?"

The young woman hurriedly raised the narrow square trap-door, and the men disappeared by the winding stair, one after another going underground, backward, so as to feel the steps with their feet. But when the point of the last helmet had disappeared, Berthine, shutting down the heavy oaken plank, thick as a wall, and hard as steel, kept in place by clamps and a padlock, turned the key twice, slowly, and then began to laugh with a laugh of silent rapture, and with a wild desire to dance over the heads of her prisoners.

They made no noise, shut in as if they were in a stone box, only getting air through a grating.

Berthine at once relighted her fire, put on her saucepan once more, and made more soup, murmuring: "Father will be tired to-night."

Then she sat down and waited. Nothing but the deep-toned pendulum of the clock went to and fro with its regular tick in the silence. From time to time, the young woman cast a look at the dial—an impatient look, which seemed to say: "How slowly it goes!"

Presently she thought she heard a murmur under her feet; low, confused words reached her through the vaulted masonry of the cellar. The Prussians were beginning to guess her trick, and soon the officer came up the little stair, and thumped the trap-door with his fist. Once more he cried: "Open the door."

She rose, drew near, and imitating his accent, asked: "What do you want?"

"Open the door!"

"I shall not open it."

The man grew angry.

"Open the door, or I'll break it in."

She began to laugh.

"Break away, my man; break away."

Then he began to beat, with the butt end of his gun, upon the oaken trap-door closed over his head; but it would have resisted a battering-ram.

The keeper's wife heard him go down again. Then, one after another, the soldiers came up to try their strength and inspect the fastenings. But, concluding no doubt that their efforts were in vain, they all went back into the cellar and began to talk again.

The young woman listened to them; then she went to open the outer door, and stood straining her ears for a sound.

A distant barking reached her. She began to whistle like a huntsman, and almost immediately two immense dogs loomed through the shadows and jumped upon her with signs of joy. She held them by the neck, to keep them from running away, and called with all her might: "Halloa, father!"

A voice, still very distant, answered: "Halloa, Berthine!"

The Prisoners

She waited some moments, then called again: "Halloa, father!"

The voice repeated, nearer: "Halloa, Berthine!"

The keeper's wife returned: "Don't pass in front of the grating. There are Prussians in the cellar."

All at once the black outline of the man showed on the left, where he had paused between two tree-trunks. He asked, uneasily: "Prussians in the cellar! What are they doing there?"

The young woman began to laugh.

"It is those that came yesterday. They got lost in the forest ever since the morning; I put them in the cellar to keep cool."

And she related the whole adventure; how she had frightened them with shots of the revolver, and shut them up in the cellar.

The old man, still grave, asked: "What do you expect me to do with them at this time of night?"

She answered: "Go and fetch M. Lavigne and his men. He'll take them prisoners; and won't he be pleased!"

Then Father Pichou smiled: "Yes; he will be pleased."

His daughter resumed: "Here's some soup for you; eat it quickly and go off again."

The old keeper sat down and began to eat his soup, after having put down two plates full for his dogs.

The Prussians, hearing voices, had become silent.

A quarter of an hour later, Pichou started again. Berthine, with her head in her hands, waited.

The prisoners were moving about again. They shouted and called, and beat continually with their guns on the immovable trap-door of the cellar.

Then they began to fire their guns through the grating, hoping, no doubt, to be heard if any German detachment were passing in the neighborhood.

The keeper's wife did not stir; but all this noise tried her nerves, and irritated her. An evil anger awoke in her; she would have liked to kill them, the wretches, to keep them quiet.

Then, as her impatience increased, she began to look at the clock and count the minutes.

At last the hands marked the time which she had fixed for their coming.

She opened the door once more to listen for them. She perceived a shadow moving cautiously. She was frightened and screamed.

It was her father.

He said: "They sent me to see if there's any change."

"No, nothing."

Then he in his turn gave a long, strident whistle into the darkness. And soon, something brown was seen coming slowly through the trees—the advance guard composed of ten men.

The old man kept repeating: "Don't pass before the grating."

And the first comers pointed out the formidable grating to those who followed.

Finally, the main body appeared, two hundred men in all, each with two hundred cartridges.

M. Lavigne, trembling with excitement, posted them so as to surround the house on all sides, leaving, however, a wide, free space round the little black hole, level with the earth, which admitted air to the cellar.

Then he entered the dwelling and inquired into the strength and position of the enemies, now so silent that it might be thought they had disappeared, flown away, or evaporated through the grating. M. Lavigne stamped his foot on the trap-door and called: "Mr. Prussian officer!"

The German did not reply.

The Major repeated: "Mr. Prussian officer!"

It was in vain. For a whole twenty minutes he summoned this silent officer to capitulate with arms and baggage, promising him life and military honors for himself and his soldiers. But he obtained no sign of consent or of hostility. The situation was becoming difficult.

The soldier-citizens were stamping their feet and striking wide-armed blows upon their chests, as coachmen do for warmth, and they were looking at the grating with an ever-growing childish desire to pass in front of it. At last one of them risked it, a very nimble fellow called Potdevin. He took a start and ran past like a stag. The attempt succeeded. The prisoners seemed dead.

A voice called out: "There's nobody there."

Another soldier crossed the space before the dangerous opening. Then it became a game. Every minute, a man ran out, passing from one troop to the other as children at play do, and raising showers of snow behind him with the quick movement of his feet. They had lighted fires of dead branches to keep themselves warm, and the flying profile of each Garde-National showed in a bright illumination as he passed over to the camp on the left.

"Some one called out: "Your turn, Maloison."

Maloison was a big baker whom his comrades laughed at, because he was so fat.

He hesitated. They teased him. Then, making up his mind, he started at a regular breathless trot which shook his stout person. All the detachment laughed till they cried. They called out: "Bravo, Maloison!" to encourage him.

He had gone about two-thirds of the distance when a long flame, rapid and red, leaped from the grating. A report followed, and the big baker fell upon his nose with a frightful shriek.

No one ran to help him. Then they saw him drag himself on all fours across the snow, moaning, and when he was beyond that terrible passage he fainted. He had a bullet high up in the flesh of the thigh.

After the first surprise and alarm there was more laughter.

Major Lavigne appeared upon the threshold of the keeper's lodge. He had just framed his plan of attack, and gave his word of command in a ringing voice: "Plumber Planchet and his men!"

Three men drew near.

"Unfasten the gutters of the house."

In a quarter of an hour some twenty yards of leaden gutter-pipe were brought to the Major.

Then, with innumerable prudent precautions, he had a little round hole bored in the edge of the trap-door, and having laid out an aqueduct from the pump to this opening, announced with an air of satisfaction: "We are going to give these German gentlemen something to drink." A wild cheer of admiration burst forth, followed by shouts of delight and roars of laughter. The Major organized gangs of workers, who were to be employed in relays of five minutes. Then he commanded: "Pump!"

And the iron handle having been put in motion, a little sound rustled along the pipes and slipped into the cellar, falling from step to step with the tinkle of a waterfall, suggestive of rocks and little red fishes.

They waited.

An hour passed; then two, then three.

The Major walked about the kitchen in a fever, putting his ear to the floor from time to time, trying to guess what the enemies were doing and whether they would soon capitulate.

The enemy was moving now. Sounds of rattling, of speaking, of splashing, could be heard. Then toward eight in the morning a voice issued from the grating: "I want to speak to the French officer."

Lavigne answered from the window, without putting out his head too far: "Do you surrender?"

"I surrender."

"Then pass out your guns."

A weapon was immediately seen to appear out of the hole and fall into the snow; then a second, a third—all; and the same voice declared: "I have no more. Make haste. I am drowned."

The Major commanded: "Stop."

And the handle of the pump fell motionless.

Then, having filled the kitchen with soldiers, all standing armed, he slowly lifted the trap-door.

Six drenched heads appeared, six fair heads with long light hair, and the six Germans were seen issuing forth one by one, shivering, dripping, scared.

They were seized and bound. Then, as a surprise was apprehended, the troops set out in two parties, one in charge of the prisoners, the other in charge of Maloison, on a mattress, carried on poles.

Rethel was entered in triumph.

M. Lavigne received a decoration for having taken prisoner a Prussian advance-guard; and the fat baker had the military medal for wounds received in face of the enemy.

MOTHER AND SON!

We were chatting in the smoking-room after a dinner, and the talk was about unexpected legacies, strange inheritances. Then M. le Brument, who was sometimes called "the illustrious master" and at other times the "illustrious advocate," came and stood with his back to the fire.

"I have," he said, "just now to search for an heir who disappeared under very strange circumstances. It is one of those simple dramas of ordinary life, a thing which possibly happens every day, and which is nevertheless one of the most dreadful things I know. Here are the facts:

"About six months ago I got a message to come to the side of a dying woman. She said to me:

"'Monsieur, I want to intrust to you the most delicate, the most difficult, and the most wearisome mission that can be conceived. Be good enough to take cognizance of my will, which is there on the table. A sum of five thousand francs is left to you as a fee if you do not succeed and of a hundred thousand francs if you do succeed. I want to have my son found after my death.'

"She asked me to assist her to sit up in the bed, in order that she might be able to speak with greater ease, for her voice, broken and gasping, was gurgling in her throat.

"I saw that I was in the house of a very rich person. The luxurious apartment was upholstered with materials solid as the walls, and their soft surfaces imparted a caressing sensation, so that every word uttered seemed to penetrate their silent depths and to disappear there.

"The dying woman went on:

"'You are the first to hear my horrible story. I will try to have strength enough to go on to the end of it. You must know everything so that you, whom I know to be a kind-hearted man, should have a sincere desire to aid me with all your power.

"'Listen to me.

"'Before my marriage, I loved a young man, whose suit was rejected by my family because he was not rich enough. Not long afterward, I married a man of great wealth. I married him through ignorance, through obedience, through indifference, as young girls do marry.

"'I had a boy child. My husband died in the course of a few years.

"'He whom I had loved had got married, in his turn. When he saw that I was a widow, he was crushed by horrible grief at knowing that he was not free. He came to see me; he wept and sobbed so bitterly before my eyes that it was enough to break my heart. He at first came to see me as a friend. Perhaps I ought not to have seen him. What could I do? I was alone, so sad, so solitary, so hopeless! And I loved him still. What sufferings we women have sometimes to endure!

"'I had only him in the world, my parents also being dead. He came frequently; he spent whole evenings with me. I should not have let him come so often, seeing that he was married. But I had not enough will-power to prevent him from coming.

"'How am I to tell you what next happened? He became my lover. How did this come about? Can I explain it? Can anyone explain such things? Do you think it could be otherwise when two human beings are drawn toward each other by the irresistible force of a passion by which each of them is possessed? Do you believe, Monsieur, that it is always in our power to resist, that we can keep up the struggle forever, and refuse to yield to the prayers, the supplications, the tears, the frenzied words, the appeals on bended knees, the transports of passion, with which we are pursued by the man we adore, whom we want to gratify in his slightest wishes, whom we desire to crowd with every possible happiness, and whom, if we are to be guided by a worldly code of honor, we must drive to despair. What strength would it not require? What a renunciation of happiness? what self-denial? and even what virtuous selfishness?

"'Monsieur, I was his mistress; and I was happy. For twelve years, I was happy. I became—and this was my greatest weakness and my greatest piece of cowardice—I became his wife's friend.

"'We brought up my son together; we made a man of him, a thorough man, intelligent, full of sense and resolution, of large and generous ideas. The boy reached the age of seventeen.

"'He, the young man, was fond of my—my lover, almost as

fond of him as I was myself, for he had been equally cherished and cared for by both of us. He used to call him his "dear friend" and respected him immensely, having never received from him anything but wise counsels and a good example of rectitude, honor, and probity. He looked upon him as an old, loyal, and devoted comrade of his mother, as a sort of moral father, tutor, protector—how am I to describe it?

" 'Perhaps the reason why he never asked any questions was that he had been accustomed from his earliest years to see this man in the house, by his side, and by my side, always concerned about us both.

" 'One evening the three of us were to dine together (these were my principal festive occasions), and I waited for the two of them, asking myself which of them would be the first to arrive. The door opened; it was my old friend. I went toward him with outstretched arms; and he drew his lips toward mine in a long, delicious kiss.

" 'All of a sudden, a sound, a rustling which was barely audible, that mysterious sensation which indicated the presence of another person, made us start and turn round with a quick movement. Jean, my son, stood there, livid, staring at us.

" 'There was a moment of atrocious confusion. I drew back holding out my hands toward my son as if in supplication; but I could see him no longer. He had gone.

" 'We remained facing each other—my lover and I—crushed, unable to utter a word. I sank down on an armchair, and I felt a desire, a vague desire to fly, to go out into the night and to disappear forever. Then, convulsive sobs rose up in my throat, and I wept, shaken with spasms, with my heart torn asunder, all my nerves writhing with the horrible sensation of an irremediable misfortune, and with that dreadful sense of shame which, in such moments as this, falls on a mother's heart.

" 'He looked at me in a scared fashion, not venturing to approach me or to speak to me or to touch me, for fear of the boy's return. At last he said:

" ' "I am going to follow him—to talk to him—to explain matters to him. In short, I must see him and let him know—"

" 'And he hurried away.

" 'I waited in a distracted frame of mind, trembling at the least sound, convulsed with terror, and filled with some unutterably strange and intolerable emotion by every slight crackling of the fire in the grate.

"'I waited for an hour, for two hours, feeling my heart swell with a dread I had never before experienced, with such an anguish as I would not wish the greatest of criminals to experience. Where was my son? What was he doing?

"'About midnight, a messenger brought me a note from my lover. I still know its contents by heart:

"'"Has your son returned? I did not find him. I am down here. I do not want to go up at this hour."

"'I wrote in pencil on the same slip of paper:

"'"Jean has not returned. You must go and find him."

"'And I remained all night in the armchair, waiting for him.

"'I felt as if I were going mad. I longed to run wildly about, to roll myself on the floor. And yet I did not even stir, but kept waiting hour after hour. What was going to happen? I tried to imagine, to guess. But I could form no conception, in spite of my efforts, in spite of the tortures of my soul!

"'And now my apprehension was lest they might meet. What would they do in that case? What would my son do? My mind was lacerated by fearful doubts, by terrible suppositions.

"'You understand what I mean, do you not, Monsieur?

"'My maid, who knew nothing, who understood nothing, was coming in every moment, believing, naturally that I had lost my reason. I had sent her away with a word or a movement of the hand. She went for the doctor, who found me in the throes of a nervous fit.

"'I was put to bed. Then came an attack of brain-fever. When I regained consciousness, after a long illness, I saw beside my bed my—lover—alone. I exclaimed:

"'"My son? Where is my son?"

"'He replied:

"'"I assure you every effort has been made by me to find him, but I have failed!"

"'Then, becoming suddenly exasperated and even indignant,— for women are subject to such outbursts of unaccountable and unreasoning anger,—I said:

" ' "I forbid you to come near me or to see me again unless you find him. Go away!"

" 'He did go away.

" 'I have never seen one or the other of them since, Monsieur, and thus I have lived for the last twenty years.

" 'Can you imagine what all this meant to me? Can you understand this monstrous punishment, this slow, constant laceration of a mother's heart, this abominable, endless waiting? Endless, did I say? No: it is about to end, for I am dying. I am dying without ever again seeing either of them—either one or the other!

" 'He—the man I loved—has written to me every day for the last twenty years; and I—I have never consented to see him, even for one second; for I had a strange feeling that if he came back here, it would be at that very moment my son would again make his appearance! Ah! my son! my son! Is he dead? Is he living? Where is he hiding? Over there perhaps, at the other side of the ocean, in some country so far away that even its very name is unknown to me! Does he ever think of me? Ah! if he only knew! How cruel children are! Did he understand to what frightful suffering he condemned me, into what depths of despair, into what tortures, he cast me while I was still in the prime of life, leaving me to suffer like this even to this moment when I am going to die—me, his mother, who loved him with all the violence of a mother's love! Oh! isn't it cruel, cruel?

" 'You will tell him all this, Monsieur—will you not? You will repeat for him my last words:

" ' "My child, my dear, dear child, be less harsh toward poor women! Life is already brutal and savage enough in its dealing with them. My dear son, think of what the existence of your poor mother has been ever since the day when you left her. My dear child, forgive her, and love her, now that she is dead, for she has had to endure the most frightful penance ever inflicted on a woman."

"She gasped for breath shuddering, as if she had addressed her last words to her son and as if he stood by her bedside.

"Then she added:

" 'You will tell him also, Monsieur, that I never again saw—the other.'

"Once more she ceased speaking, then, in a broken voice she said:

" 'Leave me now, I beg of you. I want to die all alone, since they are not with me.' "

Maître le Brument added:
"I left the house, Messieurs, crying like a fool, so vehemently, indeed, that my coachman turned round to stare at me.

"And to think that every day heaps of dramas like this are being enacted all around us!

"I have not found the son—that son—well, say what you like about him, but I call him that criminal son!"

A PRACTICAL JOKE

Some of the jokes that are played nowadays are somewhat dismal. Not like the inoffensive, laughable jokes of our forefathers; still, there is nothing more amusing than to play a good joke on some people; to force them to laugh at their own foolishness and if they get angry, to punish them by playing a new joke on them.

Many a joke have I played in my lifetime and some have been played on me; some very good ones, too. I have played some very laughable ones and some terrible ones. One of my victims died of the consequences; but it was no loss to anyone. Some day I will tell about it, but it will not be an easy task, as the joke was not at all a nice one. It happened in the suburbs of Paris and those who witnessed it are laughing yet at the recollection of it; though the victim died of it. May he rest in peace!

I will tell of two to-day. One in which I was the victim and another of which I was the instigator. I will begin with the former, as I do not find it so amusing, being the victim myself.

I had been invited by some friends in Picardie to come and spend a few weeks. They were fond of a joke like myself (I would not have known them had they been otherwise).

They gave me a rousing reception on my arrival, and made such a fuss over me that I became suspicious.

"Be careful, old fox," I said to myself, "there is something up."

During dinner they all laughed immoderately. I thought to myself, they are certainly projecting some good joke and intend to play it on me, for they laugh at nothing apparently. So I was on my guard all evening and looked at everybody with suspicion, even the servants.

When bedtime came, all escorted me to my room to bid me good night. I wondered why, and after shutting my door, I stood in the middle of the room with the candle in my hand, listening to their whispers and laughter; they were watching me no doubt. Looking at the walls, inspecting the furniture, the ceiling, the floor, I found nothing suspicious. I heard footsteps close to my door; surely they were looking through the keyhole. Then it struck me that perhaps my light would go out suddenly, so I lighted all the candles and looked around once more; but I discovered nothing. After having inspected the windows and the shutters, I closed the latter with care, then I drew the curtains and placed a chair against them. If some one should try to come in that way, I would be sure to hear him. Then I sat down cautiously. I thought the chair might give way beneath me, but it was solid. I was afraid to go to bed, although it was getting late. If they were watching me, they certainly must laugh heartily at my uneasiness, so I resolved to go to bed. Having made up my mind, I approached the alcove. The bed looked particularly suspicious to me and I drew the heavy curtains back, pulled on them, but they held fast. Perhaps a bucket of water is hidden on the top all ready to fall on me, or else the bed may fall apart. I searched my brain to try and remember different jokes I had played on others, so as to guess what might be in store for me; I was not going to be caught.

Suddenly, an idea struck me which I thought capital. I pulled the mattress off the bed, along with the sheets and blankets. I dragged them in the middle of the room, near the door, and made my bed up again the best way I could, put out all the lights, and felt my way into bed. I lay awake at least another hour, starting at every little sound, but everything seemed quiet, so I at last went to sleep.

I must have slept soundly for some time, when suddenly I woke up with a start. Something heavy had fallen on me and at the same time, a hot liquid streamed all over my neck and chest, which made me scream with pain. A terrible noise filled my ears; as if a whole sideboard full of dishes had fallen. I was suffocating under the weight, so I reached out my hand to feel the object and I felt a face, a nose, and whiskers. I gave that face a terrible blow with my fist; but instantaneously, I received a shower of blows which drove me out of bed in a hurry and out into the hall.

To my amazement, I found it was broad daylight and everybody coming up the stairs to find out the cause of the noise. What we found was the valet, sprawled out on the bed, struggling among the broken dishes and tray. He had brought me some breakfast and having encountered my improvised couch, had very unwillingly dropped the breakfast as well as himself on my face!

The precautions I had taken to close the shutters and curtains and to sleep in the middle of the room had been my undoing. The very thing I had so carefully avoided had happened.

They certainly had a good laugh on me that day!

The other joke I speak of dates back to my boyhood days. I was spending my vacation at home as usual, in the old castle in Picardie.

I had just finished my second term at college and had been particularly interested in chemistry and especially in a compound called *phosphure de calcium* which, when thrown in water, would catch fire, explode, followed by fumes of an offensive odor. I had brought a few handfuls of this compound with me, so as to have fun with it during my vacation.

An old lady named Mme. Dufour often visited us. She was a cranky, vindictive, horrid old thing. I do not know why, but somehow she hated me. She misconstrued everything I did or said and she never missed a chance to tattle about me, the old hag! She wore a wig of beautiful brown hair, although she was more than sixty, and the most ridiculous little caps adorned with pink ribbons. She was well thought of because she was rich, but I hated her to the bottom of my heart, and I resolved to revenge myself by playing a joke on her.

A cousin of mine, who was of the same age as I, was visiting us and I communicated my plan to him; but my audacity frightened him.

One night, when everybody was downstairs, I sneaked into Mme. Dufour's room, secured a receptacle into which I deposited a handful of the calcium phosphate, having assured myself beforehand that it was perfectly dry, and ran to the garret to await developments.

Soon I heard everybody coming upstairs to bed. I waited until everything was still, then I came downstairs barefooted, holding my breath, until I came to Mme. Dufour's door and looked at my enemy through the keyhole.

She was putting her things away, and having taken her dress off, she donned a white wrapper. She then filled a glass with water and putting her whole hand in her mouth as if she were trying to tear her tongue out, she pulled out something pink and white which she deposited in the glass. I was terribly frightened, but soon found it was only her false teeth she had taken out. She then took off her wig and I could see a few straggling white hairs on the top of her head. They looked so comical that I almost burst out laughing. She kneeled down to say her prayers, got up and approached my instrument of vengeance. I waited awhile, my heart beating with expectation.

Suddenly, I heard a slight sound; then several explosions. I looked at Mme. Dufour; her face was a study. She opened her eyes wide, then shut them, then opened them again and looked. The white substance was crackling and exploding at the same time, and a thick, white smoke curled up toward the ceiling.

The poor woman probably thought it was some satanic fireworks, or perhaps that she had been suddenly afflicted with some horrible disease; at all events, she stood there speechless with fright, her gaze riveted on the supernatural phenomenon. Suddenly, she screamed and fell fainting to the floor. I ran to my room, jumped into bed, and closed my eyes trying to convince myself that I had not left my room and had seen nothing.

"She is dead," I said to myself; "I have killed her," and I listened anxiously to the sound of footsteps. I heard voices and laughter and the next thing I knew my father was soundly boxing my ears.

Mme. Dufour was very pale when she came down the next day and she drank glass after glass of water. Perhaps she was trying to extinguish the fire which she imagined was in her, although the doctor had assured her that there was no danger. Since then, when anyone speaks of disease in front of her, she sighs and says:

"Oh, if you only knew! There are such strange diseases."